W9-BEL-136

3

Isabel's Daughter

A Novel

JUDITH RYAN HENDRICKS

HARPER

NEW YORK · LONDON · TORONTO · SYDNEY

Axel Schonfeld

About the Author

JUDITH RYAN HENDRICKS is the author of *Bread Alone* and

The Baker's Apprentice. She lives in Santa Fe, New Mexico.

www.judihendricks.com

LITTLE FREE LIBRARY:
ALWAYS A GIFT,
NEVER FOR SALE!

Isabel's Daughter

LITTLE FREE LIBRARY
ALWAYS A GIFT.
NEVER FOR SALE!

Also by the Author

Bread Alone
The Baker's Apprentice

HARPER

A hardcover edition of this book was published in 2003 by William Morrow,
an imprint of HarperCollins Publishers.

ISABEL'S DAUGHTER. Copyright © 2003 by Judith Ryan Hendricks. All rights
reserved. Printed in the United States of America. No part of this book may be used
or reproduced in any manner whatsoever without written permission except in the case
of brief quotations embodied in critical articles and reviews. For information address
HarperCollins Publishers Inc., 10 East 53rd Street, New York, NY 10022.

HarperCollins books may be purchased for educational, business,
or sales promotional use. For information please write: Special Markets Department,
HarperCollins Publishers Inc., 10 East 53rd Street, New York, NY 10022.

First Perennial edition published 2004.
First Harper paperback published 2006.

Designed by Claire Naylon Vaccaro

The Library of Congress has catalogued the hardcover edition as follows:

Hendricks, Judith Ryan.
Isabel's daughter: a novel / Judith Ryan Hendricks.—1st ed.
p. cm.
ISBN 0-06-050346-7
1. Mothers and daughters—Fiction. 2. Abandoned children—Fiction.
3. Foster home care—Fiction. 4. Birthmothers—Fiction.
5. New Mexico—Fiction. I. Title.

PS3608.E53I83 2003
813'.6—dc21   2003041207

ISBN 0-06-050347-5 (pbk.)

09   ❖/RRD   10 9 8 7 6 5 4

For my parents,

Ruth Adrian Huggins

and

Jerald Douglas Huggins

Your absence has gone through me like thread through a needle.

Everything I do is stitched with its color.

—W.S. MERWIN

LITTLE FREE LIBRARY:
ALWAYS A GIFT,
NEVER FOR SALE!

PART ONE

santa fe

April 2000

**LITTLE FREE LIBRARY:
ALWAYS A GIFT,
NEVER FOR SALE!**

one

The first time I saw my mother was the night she died. The second time was at a party in Santa Fe.

Once in history class I made a time line. It was a thick, straight black line, intersected by crosshatches representing dates and events. The teacher claimed that you could tell by studying it how events were related to each other, the causes and effects.

The problem is, time isn't a straight line. I think of it more as a huge arc, curving gently into space, keeping not only the future just out of sight, but the past as well. You never really know what might have caused something to happen, and the effects ripple outward in ever widening circles.

Like losing my contact lens, for instance. I was supposed to be off this whole weekend, my last free weekend before the season gets crazy. And then Juana calls on Thursday to tell me Patrice stepped off a curb and broke her ankle and they need me to work a party Friday night.

"Pinnacle Gallery on Canyon Road," she says. "Lots of people. Big tips."

Friday morning she calls me again. "Hey, *chica.* Party is changed to DeGraf's house—"

"The what house?"

"DeGraf. Mister DeGraf. You know San Tomás?"

As it happens, I do. It's one of those narrow, unpaved roads that winds south off Canyon Road. I've wandered past it lots of Sunday mornings, clutching my coffee from Downtown Subscription and peering in the gallery windows. One time I turned at the corner and walked a little ways, hoping for a glimpse of one of the huge homes behind adobe walls. I got chased by a Doberman for my curiosity, while the owner hollered, "Stand still, miss! He won't bite you."

I didn't trust him or his dog, so I ran like a jackrabbit back out to Canyon, fully expecting to feel the hot breath, the sharp teeth sinking into my leg at any minute. But when I looked around the dog was gone.

It's late April in Santa Fe, but at 7,000 feet, spring is slow to take hold. In the daytime, fierce winds blow out of the west, and the inside of your nose feels like it's lined with Cap'n Crunch. At night the air is sharp and cold, still laced with piñon smoke from hundreds of kiva fireplaces.

Tonight I'm racing the clock, and my breath makes little puffs of steam as I half walk, half jog down the narrow sidewalk. My white shirt's already damp under the arms, I know my tie is crooked, and my hair is about to come loose from its knot.

Worst of all, I'm late. Again. While we were getting ready, Rita knocked a bottle of perfume off the shelf and she tried to catch it before it hit the tile counter, but she just ended up knocking my contact lens off my finger into oblivion, and the bottle smashed all over anyway and then we started yelling at each other and here I am. It's not my fault, but I don't imagine Dale will give two hoots about that.

Then as I round a curve I see lights. *Farolitos,* those little brown paper bags with candles inside that people in this town love so much, line the top of a wall. Except these are probably the new version, *electrolitos.* Plus lots of little twinkle lights twined in the tree branches. This is it.

The address—505 San Tomás—is spelled out in Mexican tiles over a massive blue door, set into a wall the color of chocolate ice cream. A couple of guys with clipboards and walkie-talkies lounge against the wall smoking and looking bored. I give them my name. Apparently

Kirk has neglected to change Patrice's name to mine on his list, so they have to ring up Dale on his cell phone to be sure I'm not an international jewel thief, before they let me in.

"Kitchen door's around to the left past the pool," the older one says. "And stay on the path. Mr. DeGraf don't like people cutting through the garden." He flicks his cigarette away.

"Mr. DeGraf probably don't like cigarette butts all over his yard either." I smile at him as I step through the gate.

The house is a pueblo-style adobe, fashioned with the rounded corners and soft silhouettes of the Pueblo Indian dwellings, not the more boxy, territorial adobes like the Anglos built later on. It's a lighter shade of chocolate than the wall, with the traditional blue doors and windows that are supposed to keep out *brujas,* or witches. I follow the stone walkway past a huge old lilac bush, its branches drooping under the weight of fragrant purple clusters about to explode into bloom, and cut across the patio. A swimming pool sparkles aquamarine in its underwater lights.

The kitchen is in the usual preparty state of controlled chaos. It's small but elegant, with granite countertops and the kind of appliances favored by people who can afford to hire kitchen designers. When the screen door bangs behind me, Dale makes a big show of looking at his Rolex.

"Avery. So glad you could join us." His dark eyes give me a once-over. "Polished and pulled together as usual, I see." The guy standing beside him rustles a wrinkled yellow invoice. "Thanks, Tom. Put the wine over there. Under that table."

I try to secure my hair. "They didn't have my name on the—"

"Jesus Christ, you reek. What did you do, take a bath in Opium?"

"Eternity. I'm sorry. Rita broke the bottle and it went everywhere, and I didn't have time to—"

He gives me The Look. "Never mind. Fix your tie and run out to the—shit! Where's your eyes?"

"My eyes are in my head, Dale. I lost my contact."

I notice the muscle in his jaw twitching. "Well, try not to look at anybody."

"Right. In fact, why don't I just walk around with my eyes closed."

"Don't you have some sunglasses?"

"Sure. You can say I'm blind." My arm sinks up to the elbow in the big, brown backpack and I pull out my *Men in Black* shades.

"The guesthouse . . ." Dale shuts his eyes briefly, as if praying for strength. ". . . is just the other side of the pool. Get six trays of baby *rellenos* out of the fridge, okay? And try not to make any stops along the way."

Juana is arranging vegetables into a sunburst of color around a bowl of chili aioli. She rolls her eyes at me as I slip out the door, squeezing against the wall to let two guys with giant arrangements of weird-looking flowers pass by. Rita's right, I need to get another job. The problem is, Dale and Kirk have one of the best catering companies in Santa Fe, and it would be hard to make as much money with anybody else. That's even assuming I could get on.

I take a big gulp of fresh air. I can get through this. I'll just have to be on full battle alert all night. And I can't see a thing with these damn glasses. I take them off, fold them up, and hook them on the second buttonhole of my shirt.

Steam lifts into the air from the pool's glassy surface, and I find myself wondering how warm they keep it. What it would feel like to glide through the water with crisp strokes, then climb out into the cold air, disappear inside a huge soft towel, and sit in the garden drinking good red wine and listening to the crickets. It's a pretty stupid fantasy for someone who can't even swim. My steps crunch in the gravel.

The guesthouse is private, screened from the big house by coyote fencing and a cluster of aspens. When I open the arched door, I hear voices coming from another room, but I ignore them, poking my head into a bathroom and a coat closet before I find the tiny kitchen. In the refrigerator, I pull out six stacked trays of mini *chiles rellenos* and start to back out. Now the voices are closer.

". . . get rid of some of this stuff. It's like a damn shrine. Or you could set up a collection box and some candles and—"

A man's laugh. "Come on, admit it. It's one of his best."

She sniffs. "If you like that sort of thing. It's too goopy. Blatantly sentimental."

"If I didn't know better, I'd say you were still jealous."

"My ass."

They stand side by side in the hall, a man and a woman, oblivious to my presence, absorbed in the outsized oil painting on the wall. I didn't notice it on my way in and I probably would've walked right past it again, but the energy of their focus draws my attention.

It's a portrait of a woman. Wearing some kind of exotic costume. My gaze climbs from her sandaled brown feet to the long white dress hemmed with a wide geometric border design in black and turquoise. The loose sleeves drape softly just to the elbows, and a black sleeveless tunic clings to the outline of her hip.

Then I get to her face.

I've heard the phrase "shock of recognition," but I never understood what it meant till now. It's not the simple recognition of a person you might know or a place that looks familiar. It's the recognition of a truth that shines in your eyes like a bright light, whiting out everything else. It's that recognition that makes your knees shake and your mouth go dry. The recognition that empties you of yourself.

I take two steps straight backward to stand and stare while my heart bangs against my ribs.

Long dark hair, pulled austerely away from her face, tumbles loose down her back. The mouth—full lower lip and narrow upper lip. The long, straight nose. Eyes—one dark brown, one amber. Her face is a mirror image of my own.

The air feels suddenly thick and shimmery, like heat waves rising from a road. My eyes burn, too big for my head, which in turn is too big for my body, too heavy to hold up.

The conversation beside me has dwindled into silence. Have they stopped talking or am I not hearing? The first sound to cut through is the little plopping noises of baby *rellenos* hitting the Saltillo tile floor.

"Miss? Are you all right?" His words are muffled but real enough to anchor me and keep me from drifting away. I turn in their general direction just as the trays are lifted from my hands. Concern becomes surprise, and surprise deepens into shock when he gets a straight-on look at me.

"You'd better sit down," he says.

Then the woman's voice. "Ho-lee shit."

A straight wooden chair materializes under me. "Lindsey, get her a brandy. Over there on the desk." In a minute he's putting a glass in my hand, guiding it to my mouth. I suck in too much at once and it explodes in my head, making me cough, filling my eyes with tears. He takes the glass away.

Through the blur I see two intact trays of *rellenos* on the table under the painting. The rest are in a heap on the floor. Oh God. Dale's going to shit pink fuzz. I have it in my mind that I can salvage some of them, but when I try to get down on the floor, my head swims.

"Better not make any sudden moves just yet." The woman comes out of the bathroom holding a washcloth. "Put this on the back of your neck, honey." She's sort of pretty, with ash blond hair and a smoker's voice.

I lay the cool cloth on my neck, as directed, and it does make me feel somewhat more in the moment.

"I'm sorry," I manage.

The man, who's been watching me intently all this time, suddenly comes to life. "I can't believe it," he says. "This is beyond—"

The woman clears her throat noisily. "Well . . . I think I'll just go make myself irresistible and find rich husband number three."

The sound of the door closing behind her is exaggerated in the silence and I sit motionless, eyes fastened on the picture of my mother.

"Where on earth did you come from?" His voice is so soft, I wonder for a minute if I imagined it. I probably look like I don't remember where I came from, so he offers, "I'm Paul DeGraf."

I force my eyes away from the portrait to meet his, which are dark and clear like a lake at night. I half expect to see the moon reflected in them. Tall. Or maybe it's just that he's standing over me. The way he's dressed—all in soft tones of gray—gives him the look of a shadow in one of my dreams. My eyes focus naturally on the beautiful silver and bone bolo tie gleaming at the collar of his shirt.

"I'm . . . Avery James." My throat is raw, and my eyes are still leaking from the brandy.

"You need some water." He disappears into the kitchen and I hear cabinet doors opening and shutting, like he can't find the glasses.

I go back to the portrait, and the details begin to crystallize, to sharpen, to register in my brain. I want to memorize the way her hands rest gracefully on some kind of stone table or half column, the way her pale mouth barely curves up, as if she's deciding whether or not to smile. The black tunic, elaborately decorated with colorful flowers— beaded or embroidered—very stylized and precise, like some South American wall hanging. It strikes a chord that echoes deep in my memory.

I know that vest. I saw it once, eight years ago.

Abruptly, the front door flies open, hitting the wall behind it with an angry crack. "Avery, what the hell are you *doing* out here? It's a bit early for a break, don't you—Shit! My *rellenos*—" Dale looks like he might burst into tears. His hair stands up in that little ridge above his left ear where he runs his fingers through it when he's upset.

"Dale, I'm sorry—"

"Damn right," he snaps at me. "You're about the sorriest thing I know. You're also fired. Get your lazy ass out of my sight."

"Fire her, and you won't be working for me again." My head whips around. Paul DeGraf stands in the kitchen doorway.

"Paul . . . I didn't realize . . . I hope there's not a problem." Dale backpedals with his ever handy, shit-eating smile.

DeGraf doesn't smile. "She's sitting down because she fainted."

"I didn't faint, for God's sake."

But neither of them is listening to me.

"Oh, Avery . . ." Dale's thin black eyebrows knit together in faux concern. "We can't have you working when you don't feel good."

The threat of unemployment has cleared my head like a whiff of ammonia. "I'm fine. Just give me a minute, okay?"

"Take all the time you need, of course," he purrs. "If you feel up to it, come on back to the kitchen. If not, I'll get Horacio to take you home. We can manage." He flashes his teeth again. "Well. No rest for the wicked." He picks up the two intact trays of *rellenos* and vanishes, leaving the door standing open.

DeGraf hands me the water, frowning after him.

I drink about half of it and hand the glass back. "I'd better get going while I still have a job." I start to get up, but his hand on my shoulder stops me.

"Are you going to be all right? You don't have to do this. I'll talk to Dale and I'm quite sure—"

"No!" It comes out too loud. "I mean, you don't need to talk to him. I'm fine. Just . . . kind of startled."

I slide off the chair onto my knees and start gathering up the *chiles*. There's nothing wrong with most of them, except cosmetically. For a few seconds I debate whether it would be unforgivably tacky to ask for something to take them home in. I hate to see food wasted.

Paul DeGraf says, "That's understandable. It's not every day you come across a Tom Hemmings portrait of your mother."

I look up. "How do you know she's my mother?"

"Leave those." Something in his voice makes me comply. He takes my arm and pulls me to my feet gently but definitely. "It's fairly obvious," he says.

"Can you tell me—" I turn for a last look at the portrait. "Who is she?"

He clears his throat. "Her name was Isabel Colinas."

"*Was?*" My head swivels around and I try to hold my expression in neutral, but his face says it all too clearly.

"God, what am I thinking? I'm sorry. I should have— She . . . passed away. Some years ago."

"Oh." I nod. And I keep nodding, like one of those dolls on a car dashboard. "Well . . . finding her was a lot to ask. I guess finding her alive was a bit much."

"I'm sorry," he says again. "Look, this has to be difficult for you. I can have someone take you home—"

"I never knew her." I blot my forehead with the now warm washcloth. "I don't harbor a lot of daughterly feelings."

He reaches into his shirt pocket, holds out a card. "I'd be happy to talk to you about her," he says. "Call me when you're ready."

"Thank you." I stick the card in my pocket without looking at it and head for the door. When I pull it shut behind me, Paul DeGraf is kneeling on the floor picking up *chiles rellenos.*

Rita wanders out barefoot in the blue terrycloth robe that makes her look like a little kid. Mascara is smudged under her eyes; her hair is a blond haystack. Coffee vapors float up from the clear glass mug that she stole from the Ore House.

She squints at her watch. "Ave, what the hell are you doing? It's not even light out."

I laugh at her. "Nobody said you had to get up."

"I got up to pee and couldn't go back to sleep."

She drops onto the couch, an overstuffed, high-backed lump in a yellow green color that makes me think of motion sickness. But it was cheap, and Rita's managed to camouflage it with an Indian patterned blanket that she found at a garage sale. She's actually done a pretty fair job of camouflaging the whole apartment—an ugly white box of a place—with nothing more than a few quarts of paint, some fabric remnants, and a lot of upwardly mobile ideas from Martha Stewart. Considering what rents are in Santa Fe and what we might have got stuck in, it's not so bad.

The term "funky" could have been coined to describe our neighborhood on the unfashionable west side of town. The streets are lined with the curving forms and earthy shades of adobe houses, shoehorned in elbow to asshole. Some with crumbling corners, peeling trim, a mattress propped against the wall on the *portal,* the odd pickup truck on blocks in the yard. Some painstakingly restored to mint condition and landscaped with desert plants by preservationist yuppies who couldn't afford to buy on the east side. Others simply maintained at the status quo—walls painted, gardens tidy—by people just trying to keep their heads above water.

There are also a few commercial enterprises—a grocery and *carniceria,* a video rental place with a window full of lurid posters for Spanish-language action movies, a small tailor shop, a coin laundry, and us. Our apartment's upstairs and Alma's Casa Blanca, a two-chair beauty salon, is downstairs. Behind the building there's a narrow strip of gravel with space for five cars and a big old *álamo,* or cottonwood, to shade our rickety balcony.

It has its advantages. I mean, if you have to live over a business, at least a beauty shop is relatively quiet—not like a bar. They open late and close early because Linda and Alma, the beauticians, both have families to take care of. And they give us half-price haircuts because we pay the rent on time.

"How was the party?" I sip at my coffee.

A smile lights her face. "It was fun. I wish you could have come. I met this cute guy named Rick . . . something. It'll come to me as soon as I wake up. He's a reporter for the *New Mexican.*"

I shake my head. "Forget it. Reporters drink too much and don't make nearly enough money."

When she wrinkles her nose, she looks like one of those little fluffy white dogs that rich ladies carry around under their arms. She blows on the coffee to cool it. "Soler. That's his name. Rick Soler. Well, actually it's Enrique." Without waiting for me to comment, she asks, "How was your night?"

"Interesting."

She looks at me over the rim of her cup. "What's 'interesting' mean?"

"I saw a painting of my mother."

She swallows what's in her mouth, then sputters, "Shit! You made me scorch my tonsils." She sets the cup on the table and leans forward, now fully awake. "Tell me what happened, pronto!"

I have to be selective about what I tell Rita. She tends to get fixated on certain details and she can drive me nuts wanting to know more. So I try to explain what happened in very general terms.

"Oh, my God, Avery. This is incredible. How the hell can you be so calm? How could you come home and go to sleep? Why didn't you wake me up? Who is this guy? Are you going to talk to him again?"

"He gave me his card—"

She rips it out my hand and studies it briefly.

"*Paul DeGraf?* Jesus God, Avery. Do you know who he is? He owns Pinnacle Gallery and Buena Vista. He's got money out the wazoo." She looks up at me. "So what did he say about your mother?"

"Nothing, really. Except that her name was Isabel Colinas."

"That's it?"

"Just about. We didn't have time to talk. I was working, and Dale was worked into a major frenzy."

"Well, you're going to call him today, aren't you? This morning?"

"I need to think—"

"You've had twenty-five years to think. Now you can know."

"It's not that easy."

She folds her arms, daring me. "It's not that hard, either. You've got the questions, he's got the answers. What's the problem?"

"I don't know. I just want to think about it."

. . .

C*all me when you're ready,"* he said.

Until now, it's never occurred to me that I might not be ready. But suddenly I'm procrastinating. Maybe just because it's the end of the quest. Once I know who she was, The Truth becomes simply more information.

Or maybe I'm afraid of what I'll find out. But how could it be any worse than what I already know? That my mother didn't want me. That she dumped me in the basement of an institution and never looked back, never tried to find me, never knew—or presumably cared—whether I lived or died.

While I, by contrast, have spent the better part of my twenty-five years wondering about her.

People who live their lives surrounded by family never give it a second thought. They know their eyes are blue because their mother's were, that they're pigeon-toed just like Aunt Sue, their musical talent came from their father, and their tendency to hold up gas stations when the moon is full is from Great Uncle Carl, the train robber.

Obviously I had a mother and father. But I have no idea who they were. Where they were. If they loved or hated each other. Or whether they'd even recognize each other if they passed on the street.

M onday morning I go back to Eyes Right and order another brown contact.

D ays pass, then weeks. Somehow it gets to be May. I can always think of an excuse not to call DeGraf. I haven't had a chance to sort things out. I don't have time to meet him, and I don't want to talk about this over the phone. It's too early—he won't be there; too late—he'll be gone. Midday, he'll be busy. And so on.

Work is getting more frenetic every day as summer season revs up, rushing headlong toward the climax of *Fiestas de Santa Fe* in early September. There are cocktail parties and dinners and gallery openings, picnics and barbecues. Opera season starts in July with preperformance tailgate parties and postperformance dessert buffets. During the day I take bookings and do site surveys and client hand-holding. Juana and I have the coveted full-time slots, so we help with bids and kitchen prep, too. Most nights I work as a server. My schedule rarely coincides with Rita's, so I don't have to offer any explanations for the fog that seems to surround me.

When I do have some free time, I'm usually so tired that it's all I can do to feed myself before I stumble off to bed. The frenzy of activity keeps the shadow of my mother at bay for a while, but then late one Saturday night when I'm tossing hollow-eyed in my bed, too exhausted even for sleep, the past comes looking for me.

two

I read where some famous doctor said that babies are like little blank slates, waiting to be written on, waiting to be made into whoever they will be.

This, as any baby knows, is a load of horseshit. Babies are born with the seeds of who they'll be already inside them. When you plant a sunflower seed, you get a sunflower. If it gets too much water or not enough light or the soil's too heavy, it might grow scrawny or droopy. The leaves might shrivel and drop. It might die. But it's not going to come up a columbine.

Babies can see and hear and smell and feel. They know all kinds of stuff they're not supposed to know. But they can't tell anyone. And by the time they learn how to talk, they've forgotten what they knew.

So it was no big surprise to me the first time I heard the story of how I was found. After all, I was there.

Alamitos, Colorado—in English, the name means "little cottonwood trees." It's a small farm town in the San Luis Valley, down by the New Mexico border. High and dry, flat and windy, ringed by mountains—Sangre de Cristos to the east and south, San Juan, La Garita, and Conejos-Brazos to the north and west. White frosted in winter, dirt brown in spring, green in summer. The cottonwoods that it's named for turn gold in autumn, and the air is thick with the damp earth smell of potatoes, piled at the edges of fields, stacked in bins and boxes, truckloads and railroad cars full.

Besides potatoes, the valley's other big claim to fame is the Great

Sand Dunes—fifty square miles of sand, dropped when the prevailing westerly winds run into the Sangre de Cristos. I lived in Alamitos for the first thirteen years of my life and only saw the dunes once. I knew without being told that they were a freak of nature, didn't belong there—a pale and shifting ocean, high in the Rockies.

San Juan Avenue runs straight through the middle of town. There's the square brick post office and the El Azteca movie theater with its pink and green neon sign, a couple of banks, Corie's Café on one side, Tina's Cantina across the street. There's a hardware store and Raymond's Corner Market, where we used to go in the afternoons to drink lemon slushees and watch the older kids from the public high school smoke and make out. By the time I left Alamitos, Raymond's was closed, and everybody was hanging out at the new supermarket north of town on the Del Norte Highway.

Crossing San Juan Avenue at perfect right angles are ten streets— San Luis, Cerrillos, Hatcher, Selden, Laguna, Sixth, Seventh, Eighth, Ninth, and Tenth. It's like they ran out of ideas for street names. Seventh, Eighth, and Ninth Streets, that's where the poorest people lived, behind crumbling adobe walls, or in wood frame houses with peeling paint and tarpaper roofs. Rusting cars bloomed among the weeds, and skinny mongrel dogs laid on porches.

Up at the other end of town, the streets were wide. There were sidewalks and tall, arching cottonwood trees and big old houses. On Selden Street was the biggest house of all, a red brick building called the Randall Carson Foundling Home.

That's where I made my official debut in the basement one frigid January night, wearing a soiled diaper and an undershirt embroidered with flowers; I was wrapped in a bath towel from the Stardust Motor Inn.

The story goes that the janitor, a nearsighted Arapaho named Charlie Elvin, was in a hurry to lock up and go home to his nice warm trailer where his wife and his dinner waited. Without his glasses, he thought the bundle he bumped with his work boot might be some stray dog that had crawled into the relative warmth of the furnace room to die.

Charlie might have been half blind, but his ears were sharp. He heard a jerky, gasping sound. The bundle was breathing. Crouching down, he found himself looking into a pair of small, dark eyes. Eyes, he later told his wife, that were somehow not right, although at the time, he couldn't say why.

He picked up the baby, and just as quickly set it down. It smelled like his chicken coop on a summer afternoon. He ran to the door. Then back to check the baby.

"I'll be right back," he blurted, sprinting for the night duty station.

Annette Colby, the nurse on duty that evening, was a plump, sensible young woman with short brown hair. When Charlie burst into her tiny office, babbling about a child in the basement, her first thought was that one of the children had fallen down the steep stairs. She lunged for her black bag.

"I've told the board a thousand times to put a gate in front of those stairs—"

"No ma'am." Charlie shifted his weight impatiently. "It's a baby. Poor little thing looks half froze."

She narrowed her pale blue eyes at him. Charlie'd been known to take a nip, but he'd been going to AA for nearly five years now. "That's not possible," she said calmly. "How would a baby get in the furnace room?"

"Damned if—'scuse me. I don't know, lady, but it's there. I'm tellin' you. Come on with me."

Her own panting filled her ears as she followed Charlie down the stairs and through the long, dim hall that smelled of floor wax, taking two steps to his one. Through the high windows she could see huge, silent snowflakes drifting between naked tree branches. The wind had stopped momentarily.

"I don't hear anything," she said as he pushed the door aside for her. "Is it . . . ?"

"Was when I left."

"Did you bother to—" The baby interrupted her with an impatient wail. "Dear Heavenly Father." She bent and picked up the shivering bundle, tucked it inside her jacket, towel and all, wrinkling her nose at the stench. "Charlie. Run upstairs and call Dr. Tatum. Hurry now."

As she climbed the stairs, lost in her conversation with God, she felt a tug at her blouse. She looked down.

Locked in a tiny, filthy fist was the necklace Annette's mother had given her—a gleaming butterfly—made by a silversmith named James Avery. Annette took it as a sign from God, and she named me James Avery. When in the course of the doctor's examination, they discovered I was a girl, Annette simply inserted a comma.

Name: James, Avery.

The thirteen years at Carson are blurred now, like photographs taken by someone in a hurry to get somewhere else. It's mostly the smells that come rushing back, dragging the images behind them—pine disinfectant is the chilly tile bathroom with its row of white sinks. Chalk dust is the stifling paneled room where we had Bible study. Mothballs—the closet where scratchy wool blankets summered, the heavy glass doorknob and giant key.

And then there's the kitchen. Steam from dried flint corn simmering in water and baking soda. The dusty smell of dried chiles that came from Esperanza Verdugo—a round person with a long gray braid, snapping dark eyes, smooth brown arms, and a gold front tooth. The cook at Carson. Not a housemother or a teacher or a nurse. No degree in psychology or social work or early childhood education. No counseling credentials. If the truth be told, she couldn't read or write, and her English sometimes sent me into fits of laughter.

But of all the Carson staff, it was Esperanza who always seemed to be wading through a river of kids. We'd hang on her arms, grab at her skirts, cling to her legs. She was the one who tied shoelaces, wiped runny noses, smuggled *bizcochitos* into the library. She was the one we called Tia or Nana, Abuelita or Gramma. The one we screamed for when we woke from bad dreams.

There was a chair with one leg shorter than the rest. I used to stand on the seat, rock precariously back and forth, watching her make *posole* on the big black stove.

When I was eight, she let me shell peas and beans. When I was ten, she taught me to pat out *masa* dough by hand into perfect tortillas. She said it was one of those things that's best learned young, before you start thinking about it too much. She brought her own *comal*—a big flat round griddle of unglazed pottery—not like the newer ones of cast iron or stainless steel. It had been her mother's, she said, and her grandmother's before that. She greased it with a little rag dipped in Crisco. She kept a bowl of cold water at her side, and she dipped her hand in the water, pressing and turning the tortillas so they didn't stick. When they were browned on one side, she pressed the side of her wet palm on the edge of the tortilla and flipped it over.

From her I learned that no self-respecting cook would make *frijoles* without *epazote* or *chile colorado* without *canela*.

A
lthough Carson was licensed by the state of Colorado, it was run by the Church of God in Jesus Christ, and the administrators all came from the church, including the director, Alice Ridley. Ridley was a tall woman who seemed to be made of large wooden blocks. She had too many yellow teeth and a shock of steel gray hair with eyes to match. She ended every sentence, even the most mundane, with "If God wills." Or "His will be done."

For the longest time I thought of God as some hyperefficient houseparent, intensely interested in the smallest details of life at Carson Foundling Home. Had I brushed my teeth? Were all four corners tucked in tight on every metal bunk bed? Was the kitchen door latched?

The rest of the staff consisted of mostly indistinguishable teachers and counselors, who did their best to make us ready for foster homes, adoption, school, jobs. Productive lives in the real world. Anyone who stayed off drugs and alcohol, didn't get pregnant or get someone pregnant before they graduated high school, was a success story. They put your picture up in the dining room.

I was not on the fast track for the dining room wall. Not only did I have weird eyes, I was also small for my age. I had trouble with school because I hated sitting still. I was slow learning to read, and when I was called on in class, I always fumbled it.

Once when I was sitting in Ridley's office, copying Bible verses as penance for my latest transgression, I sneaked a look at my file, which was on her desk. A note on the very first page announced that I needed to learn self-control and didn't "integrate well with my peers."

Later when I learned what "understatement" was, I realized that Ridley was a master of it. In plain English, other kids didn't like me. No skin off my nose, because I didn't like them either. The difference was that I never felt like I had to do anything about it, whereas some of them couldn't resist the temptation offered by someone like me.

Not integrating well with my peers meant finding dog turds in my shoes one morning. It meant my books regularly got dumped into the laundry chute so I'd have to go down to the basement and sift through everybody's soiled linens to retrieve them. It meant that after I spent hours painstakingly writing a book report, it would disappear from my notebook during dinner and shreds of it would be seen later floating in a toilet.

I learned to fight. And I learned that fighting isn't a skill; it's an attitude. It's tuning out fear, not feeling pain. It's forgetting about what anyone can do to you and concentrating on what you can do to them.

Head butting was my specialty. I was a natural—small and fast. The advantage was that knocking the wind out of somebody meant that by the time they could get up and come after you, there was usually a houseparent there, breaking it up. The disadvantage was that head butting was mostly effective as a surprise tactic. I had to strike first, as soon as I knew there would be trouble. This led inevitably to my being blamed for "starting it."

With my reputation, I didn't get sent to foster homes very often, and when I did, I never lasted long before they returned me to Carson like spoiled milk back to the grocery store.

I only had one friend there, besides Esperanza.

Lee-Ann Davisen was, without a doubt, the smartest kid at Carson. Now that I think about it, she was probably the smartest person there, period. Some people liked her for that, and some didn't. She was taller than me, not as skinny, and she had brown hair that was thick and curly, and smelled like cinnamon. The thing I envied her for, though, was her beautiful green eyes.

Lee-Ann's story was that her parents—Lee and Ann Davisen—had been killed in a car accident, and her aunt and uncle took her for a while, but they had kids of their own, and I guess they didn't have much money. I also heard once that her parents were druggies who both ODed. It didn't matter. Everybody made up their own story of why they were there, and I learned to believe about half of what I could see and zero of what I heard.

It was just a matter of time before one of the counselors decided that Lee-Ann should tutor me in reading. This meant that on Monday and Friday afternoons from 4:00 until 5:00 P.M., we were closeted in Ridley's study—a tiny room adjoining the director's office, the same place where I spent lots of time copying Bible verses.

At first, I only wanted to sit next to her and smell her hair and study the freckles on her pale cheeks, the bristly dark eyelashes that would suddenly fly open revealing those amazing eyes. And I loved to listen to her read. She had a flair for drama, picking up the pace for action, damping it down for suspense, changing her voice to sound like different characters—Jim Hawkins and Long John Silver, Jo and Beth March, Jody Baxter talking to his fawn. She even read me murder mysteries, which I'm sure nobody knew she had in her possession or they would've been used to start a bonfire.

Pretty soon she started making me read some of the characters' lines, waiting patiently while I puzzled over long words, giving me hints to help me sound them out. I progressed from a few lines to reading whole paragraphs, then pages, then chapters while the late afternoon sun shot gold through the dirty curtains and she sat there, head leaned back against the couch, nibbling thoughtfully on one of the *bizcochitos* I smuggled out of the kitchen.

On a windy spring afternoon when she was ten and I was eight, she announced to me that her number one goal in life was to get herself adopted. We were on the playground swings. I didn't say anything at first, because I was flying like a maniac, bending my body and kicking my feet, trying to get high enough to go over the top and back around.

"Well, what do you think?" she demanded.

I stopped pumping, let my weight slow the swing until it was low enough that I dared to jump out. I loved doing that. For one thing it was like flying. For another, it always freaked her out. Physical daring was about the only arena where I ever felt one up on her. My feet and legs stung from the impact of my dirt landing, and momentum pitched me forward, laughing, onto my hands and knees.

"Did you hear what I told you?" she hollered.

"No. What?" I hollered back.

"Just get your flying butt back over here if you want to know, 'cause I'm not going to yell it out."

I sauntered back to the swings, dusting the dirt from the knees of my jeans. "What?"

"My idea is to get adopted."

"Why do you want to get adopted?"

She gave me a condescending smile. "You don't get it. I guess because you never had a family."

"But then you'd have to leave, wouldn't you?"

"Of course. That's the point of getting adopted. Getting out of here." She was digging her feet into the dirt and pushing herself around and around, twisting the swing chains into a tight spiral.

I tried to be philosophical about it. "Well, maybe they'd take me, too."

"No, that wouldn't work." She wasn't cruel, just practical. "I want a mother and father, but no other children. It's better to be an only child. You get more attention."

She picked up her feet and the chains of the swing began to unwind. She spun faster and faster, like a twirling figure skater, head thrown back, dark curls streaming behind her. When the last twist had popped out of the chains, she sat there, mouth open, gazing up.

"Ohh, the clouds are spinning." She giggled.

Her laugh usually made me laugh, but right then I didn't feel much like it. I just kept kicking the heels of my tennis shoes in the hard-packed dirt.

"Want to know how I'm going to find my family?" Her voice was artificially bright, and she didn't wait for my answer. "I'm going to write letters to the *Denver Post*. Everybody in Denver reads it."

I frowned, pushed my bangs out of my eyes. "You mean you write them a letter and they find you some parents?"

This time she laughed so hard, she almost fell off the swing. "No, silly. There's a page in the paper where they print letters and you can say whatever you want. If I write a letter about living here and how I need to be someplace where I can get a better education, somebody's bound to see it and adopt me."

In spite of my inability to grasp her logic, a part of me was enthralled. Until that moment, it had not occurred to me that you could make up your mind that you wanted something and then set about making it happen.

Lee-Ann was right about me. I didn't get it because I'd never known the splendors or the terrors of family life. She took it upon herself to instruct me, in between writing her letters to the *Denver Post* and reading every book in the Dodd County library.

She told me about her parents. Her father had been a cabinetmaker. Her mother's family had owned a farm. "She was working at Pepper's Steakhouse in Pueblo when they met," Lee-Ann said. "She served him a beer. It was love at first sight."

She talked about going to the Cheyenne Drive-In Movie on summer nights when the three of them would have Cokes and share one giant tub of popcorn, with extra butter and salt.

"Did they have fights?" I asked.

"Oh, sure. He gave her a black eye once and then he cried for an hour." She smiled. "And once they were putting groceries away and they started fighting and she threw eggs at him. He started chasing her around the house and she was carrying the eggs and every few minutes she'd stop and throw another one at him." She wrinkled her nose. "It was a mess. And I had to clean it up."

I was indignant. "Why? You didn't do it."

She sighed and looked over the top of my head. "By the time she ran out of eggs, they were all kissy face, and they went in their room and locked the door."

"What for?" I demanded.

"Nothing you'd understand."

I didn't believe she knew either, or she would've loved telling me.

She showed me the big blue dictionary in the parlor, resting on its own wooden table, made available to encourage us to look up words we didn't understand. She thumbed through the onionskin pages till she came to:

foundling: Abandoned child of unknown parentage.

She explained that "abandoned" meant left behind and "parentage" was just a big word for your mother and father. Even then, I was aware that most of the children at Carson knew all too well who their folks were. And where they were—either in jail or riding the rodeo or drinking or whoring around. Most of those kids weren't abandoned; they were deposited by relatives or taken away by the welfare people.

"Avery," she said, "do you realize you're the only true foundling they've got here?"

I took a certain satisfaction from it.

When I proudly showed Lee-Ann my greatest treasure—my embroidered baby undershirt—she looked at it for a long time without saying anything. It was the first time I'd seen her at a loss for words. That Friday she brought a new book to our tutoring session. It was from the library, and it had color pictures of flowers, their names, and where they grew. We spent the whole hour hunched over it and the shirt. She pointed out the pink roses, yellow and white daisies with a few petals scattered to the side, purple asters, and in the center, one blue flower, larger than the others. It reminded me of a bird with a long, graceful tail. Finally I flipped over a page and there it was.

"*Aquilegia cae-ru-lea,*" she announced. "Rocky Mountain Columbine. The Colorado State Flower." She gave me a significant look.

"Does that mean she was from Colorado?"

She shrugged. "Maybe it just means you were born here."

"Big news." I tried to keep the disappointment out of my voice.

"Well, what did you think? The book was going to tell you where she went? At least you know she was an artist."

"How do I know that?" I looked up at her, suddenly noticing how tall she was. And that she was starting to get boobs. Jesus. She was almost thirteen.

She snatched the shirt up off the table, shook it under my nose. "Look, dummy. These aren't just little colored blobs. They're real flowers. You can see which ones they are. Only an artist could do that."

After that, I kept the shirt under my pillow, running my finger along the tiny stitches and knots while I waited for sleep to come, imagining my mother's hands holding the cloth, drawing the threaded needle through it. I figured someday I'd find her, and I'd show her the shirt as proof of ID, like a dog tag. What if she really was a famous artist? Maybe she lived in New York or L.A. What if there were other clues hidden in the flower design? Maybe it was a test to see if I was smart enough. If I figured it out, I would find her.

School at Carson only went up to grade eight, so after that you had to go to San Luis High School on the orange bus that stopped every morning at the corner of Selden and San Juan. The first morning that Lee-Ann went, she looked a little nervous, but it was me that was sick to my stomach. I followed her out the front door and stood shivering in the sharp morning air, watching her and Camille Rodriguez plod silently toward the corner. A couple times she turned around and waved at me. When they reached the bus, the yellow and black door opened as if by magic. They climbed inside, and the bus rolled away, belching black smoke out the back, red lights flashing.

The thing that stays with me is an image of Lee-Ann. Her face. Framed in a window, because that's what it was like after she started going to high school. She was present, but there was some invisible obstruction between us. So real I sometimes thought I could see my breath on the glass. We could still walk downtown to mail her *Denver Post* letters, have an ice cream, or go to the movies. We still read books together, ate meals together. But at night when she climbed under the covers with me, all she could talk about was leaving Alamitos. She was discouraged because her letters had failed to turn up a suitable family. And then a name began to creep into our conversations. Pat Neeley. It took awhile, but I finally figured out that Pat Neeley was a boy. It made me laugh.

"Why'd his parents give him a girl's name?"

Her face reddened. "His name is Patrick," she snapped. "It happens to be Irish. And you don't know a damn thing about it, so don't act like such a stupid twit, or I'll never tell you anything again."

Stung by her anger, I asked, "Is he your boyfriend?"

She looked over my head, something she'd been doing a lot more often. "Not exactly. We like each other, though."

Then came the night I climbed in bed with her and snuggled up next to a pile of clothes wrapped in her bathrobe.

I had to clap a hand over my mouth to muffle my gasp.

Everyone was used to people climbing into bunks that didn't belong to them, but it would've looked strange for me to hop right back out. In the dark I could hear the rustle of other blankets, moans from other dreams, someone trying to breathe through a plugged-up nose. I was shaking with the cold and my own fear and anger.

She was out meeting Patrick Neeley. They were someplace together. Standing in some cold, blue shadow. Whispering, laughing, kissing. Would he put his tongue in her mouth? My stomach turned over, and I buried my face in her pillow to smell her cinnamon hair.

I thought of staying in her bed till she came back but I couldn't bear for her to know how much it bothered me. I lay as still as I could until the sighs and grinding teeth and little tight coughs of the others had subsided, and then I slipped out of her bed and back into my own.

It was easy to avoid her until dinnertime the next day, and I decided to go late to the dining room. All the seats would be taken and I wouldn't be able to sit by her. When the bell rang at six, I hid in one of the toilet stalls, listening to the stampede of feet down the stairs. When it was quiet, I let myself out and washed my hands. At the top of the landing I paused to hear the tail end of grace, the muted chorus of "Amens." Then I took a deep breath and ran down the stairs, like I was rushing to get there on time. Everyone was already slurping their soup.

Only two faces looked to the door when I clattered across the threshold: Edward Blakey, one of the houseparents, looking mildly annoyed. And Lee-Ann. Hair tied back with one of the pale, sheer scarves she'd taken to wearing. Eyes wide open, searching for mine, and finding them, like a heat-seeking missile. She patted the empty seat next to her.

"I saved your place." She smiled sweetly and I came to her side, like a dog hearing its name.

three

I never confronted her, but she knew. Just like she knew I'd never tell. She made up to me by giving me books she decided she didn't want, buying me little treats with part of her lunch money. Malted milk balls and chocolate-covered raisins, pixie straws, red licorice. All the things we used to get at Raymond's. So she was now one of those kids we used to stare at while they groped each other in the parking lot. Her and Patrick. I hated him. Just thinking his name enraged me to the point where anything I was looking at had white around the edges, like the glare of the sun. Sometimes I wanted to scream at her and hit her. Tell her I never wanted to talk to her again. But I did want to talk to her again, and I was terrified that she would shrug me off if I was too much trouble.

On the day before her fifteenth birthday, she was gone. I didn't see her at dinner, so I looked for her in the dorm, and her bed was stripped down to the mattress. All her books, her hair clips, the sheer scarves, her black plastic watch—all gone from her shelf. Her locker in the bathroom hung open, empty.

How could she just go? Without saying anything to me? Sure I was pissed off about Patrick, but she knew I always caved in and forgave her. All I could think of was that she did it on purpose, to spite me. She got her family and she wanted to rub my nose in it by making me ask Ridley or somebody where she went.

Well, fuck that. It was the first time I'd ever said the F word. Even in my mind. I liked it. The cold flatness, the hard edge of it, like a karate chop. When I said it out loud, it left a metallic taste in my mouth.

I would never ask where she went. I didn't care.

I hid downstairs in the laundry room listening to everyone leaving for class, the older ones going out to the bus. I'd be going with them next year. Not that I gave a shit. When it got quiet, I knew Ridley and her henchmen were having their morning meeting, so I crept back up the stairs and into the kitchen.

Esperanza was sitting in that wobbly chair husking corn. "*Niña*, what's the matter you not dressed? You don't go to *escuela*?"

I sat down on the floor by her feet, picked up some cornsilk she'd dropped, and began tying it in knots.

"Señor Ridley, she not happy to find you here."

It was an old joke between us to call Ridley Señor, but I didn't laugh.

Esperanza sighed, wiped her hands on a towel, and touched the top of my head. "*Pobrecita.* You friend, she go. So sad."

"I don't care," I said. But I laid my head against her knee.

"Come, you help Esperanza make *posole.*" Just as we started to get up, the door to the dining room flew open.

"Miss James, will you come with me please?"

I followed Ridley down to her office, curiously relaxed. Nothing she could do to me would make any difference. I was somewhere beyond all that. She shut the door behind us, shut the door to the conference room where Lee-Ann and I used to read books. Then she sat down in the big brown leather chair that rolled around on wheels behind her desk. She leaned back, pressing her fingertips together, looking at me.

I waited. She was going to give me hell for being in the kitchen, for skipping class, for not living up to my potential, for letting all the people down who were trying to help me. She would assign me extra Bible study, more verses to copy, confine me to the house after school for a few weeks, maybe put me on bathroom detail.

Instead, she scooted forward, leaned over her desk. "It's quite natural to feel sad when a friend goes away," she said.

I was noticing the way the light from the window behind her lit up the fuzz on her face, making her look like she had whiskers.

"However, Miss Davisen has gone and will not be back. It does no good to mope around and miss class. In fact, being in class is the very thing you need. If you keep your mind occupied, you'll have less time to feel sorry for yourself. And I think this would be a good time for you to renew your acquaintance with Jesus. The power of prayer cannot be underestimated as a way to—"

"Please, can I go now?" I said it very politely, inching up from the edge of my chair.

She raised one black eyebrow. There was a gray hair in it that curled up like a horn. "No, you may not. Sit down." She straightened her back. "I said, sit down, young lady."

I sat. She talked. And talked. I thought about making tortillas. The smell of the *masa* hitting the hot griddle. How they stuck to your wet palm just long enough to flip over.

Her tone changed abruptly and I tuned back in. ". . . left this for you," she said. She held something out to me. A blue envelope. My whole name Avery James was written in Lee-Ann's neat handwriting. I picked it up, letting it rest on my open hand. The tissue-thin, crinkly paper smelled like cinnamon.

Ridley was watching me, waiting for me to smile or cry or something stupid. Fuck her. Fuck Lee-Ann. Fuck everybody. The letter felt brittle as a dead leaf when I crumpled it. I dropped it on the desk.

"Can I leave now?"

Her gray eyes showed surprise, but all she said was, "Get dressed and go to class."

That spring when it became clear that my attitude wasn't improving, Ridley decided I needed closer monitoring or more individual attention or something, so I got farmed out to a foster home.

The house was old and painted a dark, yucky green. It sat in the middle of a field by a little dry streambed, and there was a huge old cottonwood tree shading the front porch. It was way out from town, which meant you couldn't walk to a movie or the store. Except for occasional "family outings," the only place I went was down to the end of the long gravel driveway to get on the bus for school. It felt the way I imagined prison would be.

There were four of us. I had to share a bedroom with Marla, who was five years old and had a permanent runny nose. Boyd Stiles was a stocky boy with bland features and dark little pig-eyes, a trashy mind and a mouth to go with it. He shared a room with Jeff, who was about eight and so shy that for several days I thought he couldn't talk.

Jim Humber, the father, had an insurance agency in Alamitos. The mother, Sharon, was tall and plain, with really big front teeth that stuck out over her lower lip, which made her look goofy, but she was okay. She hated cooking, so I did most of it. When I was chopping vegetables or making cornbread in the kitchen, she'd sit at the yellow dinette drinking iced tea out of a can and telling me Bible stories. But she talked so quietly I could hardly hear, which was fine.

At least when I was cooking, I didn't have to put up with the rest of them. Marla was forever wanting me to pick her up, even though she was big for five. Jeff just stared at me. And Boyd pissed me off because he kept "accidentally" brushing up against me. Why, I can't imagine. I had weird eyes and wasn't much to look at, and I sure didn't have anything you could call tits. But whenever it was time to go cook dinner, he wanted to take Marla out of my arms so he could cop a quick feel.

The first time it happened I called him on it. He said it was an accident. The second time, I told Sharon. Big mistake. She sat us all down together and told us that we were all children of God, and as such, should consider ourselves brothers and sisters, treating each other with respect. Even more so, since we were sharing a house.

The third time, I was bending over, setting Marla down on the floor in front of the TV, when Boyd sidled over and stuck his hand between my legs from the back. I shot up reflexively, the top of my head catching him under the chin on my way up. The dumb shit almost bit his tongue off. I told him it was an accident.

·   ·   ·

May was really too early for thunderstorms, but the morning that Sharon had to take Jeff to the doctor in Alamitos started off hot and hazy, with the smell of weather coming. Sharon was running around trying to get herself and Jeff ready, packing snacks—she was one of those people who can't go to the grocery store without a plastic bag full of animal crackers "just in case."

"Okay, people," she hollered. She had one arm in her sweater, purse on her shoulder, keys in her teeth, clutching Jeff's hand like he was going to bolt, a bottle of spring water tucked under her chin. "All of you mind Avery. She's in charge." That was supposed to make me feel important. "Boyd, you are not to wear that horrible shirt out of the house." The shirt in question was a relic of some Metallica concert, which Boyd insisted he'd been to see.

"Yes, ma'am." He smiled and we all knew he'd do exactly that as soon as her car was out of sight.

"Marla, you be a good girl for Avery." Marla was playing with paper dolls, and barely looked up.

I was reading my English assignment when Boyd clomped through the living room and out the front door, wearing the ripped T-shirt that Sharon told him not to wear, jeans that were too small, and black high-tops. He'd tried to slick his hair down straight, but it stood up stubbornly on the sides like little fins. I assumed he was headed for the river to hang out and smoke with his idiot friends, and I was glad.

As the sun got higher, the living room got hot and stuffy. I opened all the windows. I made cheese quesadillas for me and Marla, and right after that, she fell asleep in front of the television watching Vanna White spin the Wheel of Fortune.

I kept looking up from the book, watching her sleep, blond wisps plastered damp against her forehead, tiny drops of sweat like a fine mist on her nose and upper lip. She looked angelic, but she snored because her nose was plugged up. It was pretty funny. Shit. Why did people ever want to have kids? So much trouble. I made up my mind right then that I never would. The world was fucked up enough as it was.

I went outside and sat in a white plastic chair and watched the dark thunderheads pile up over the San Juans. The air was dry and still and felt like very thin glass.

I must've dozed off. When I woke up, the sky all around was black like nighttime, and the wind whipped leaves and papers past the corner of the house. I stretched, sticking my feet out and arching my back, and started to get up, when I suddenly felt the hair rise on my arms and neck. There was a funny smell.

And then a flash and a noise like a shotgun. Pieces of wood flying around me, tongues of blue flame. I was on my hands and knees, breathing hard, head ringing. I looked up at the cottonwood tree, smoking and shattered. A sharp, burnt smell filled my nostrils as I pushed myself up and stumbled into the house. Marla sat on the floor, mouth open in a soundless wail.

"Are you all right?" I yelled at her. "Lightning hit the tree!"

Then I realized she was crying, but I couldn't hear her. Outside, lightning was striking all around, and a solid gray curtain of rain lashed the house. The white plastic chair flew silently past the front window like some strange bird. Marla kept crying and talking and she looked so funny making all these weird faces, mouth opening and closing without any sound.

A cold gust pushed the door open, and three sopping boys shot in, pale and hollow-eyed. I'd completely forgotten about Boyd and his buddies. They stood there dripping all over the rug, all talking at once, but of course I couldn't hear them. One of them pointed at me and said something. For the first time I looked down at myself. I was covered with quills, like a porcupine. On closer inspection, they turned out to be splinters of wood sticking out of my bare arms and legs. At the base of some were little drops of blood.

The three pushed past me and ran down the hall into Boyd's room, closing the door behind them. I started shutting the windows, but then

I remembered something about if there was a tornado and all the windows were shut, the house would explode, so I left them all open a couple inches at the bottom.

I took Marla into the kitchen, set her at the table, and gave her some grape juice while I went hunting for Sharon's eyebrow tweezers and the plastic bottle of rubbing alcohol. Eventually she stopped crying and sat there drinking her juice, huge eyes fixed on the window over the sink. Meanwhile I plucked splinters out of myself and doused burning alcohol on all the red welts. I felt like I was on fire.

By the time I finished, the ringing in my head had stopped and so had the storm. I was even glad to hear Marla's sniffling again. Then I looked up and saw Boyd and his buddies standing in the doorway watching me.

I glared back at them. "What do you want?"

Boyd seemed to suddenly remember that he was supposed to be the bad ass here, not me. He threw his shoulders back. "We're getting something to drink."

"Well, hurry up," I snapped. "Then take it back to your room. And don't make a mess." I picked up my book.

He turned to the other two. "Don't worry about her. She's just a bossy bitch."

"Boyd, get out of here. Sharon doesn't want Marla picking up your potty mouth."

"If Sharon doesn't like it she can blow it out her ass." He was clearly warming to his role, and the other two made a perfect audience. One of them was taller than Boyd, but skinny. He had brown hair down to his shoulders and a thin, cold mouth. The other one looked a lot younger and seemed to find whatever the other two said absolutely hilarious. He laughed like a donkey.

"Fine. I'll let you tell her that." I tugged Marla's hand and led her into the living room. My idea was that we could watch TV, but of course there was no electricity. In a few minutes the three boys joined us, sprawling on the sofa, sloshing their sodas everywhere. I didn't like where the afternoon was heading.

"Avery, read a story." Back in our room Marla was holding out her book of Bible stories. We arranged ourselves on her bed, propped up with pillows. "Read Noazark."

I opened the book to the story of Noah and the ark, holding it at different angles to get better light. That's when I realized it would be getting dark soon, and there were no lights to turn on.

I read "Noah," I read "The Tower of Babel," I read "Jonah and the Whale." By that time, it was too dark to read anymore. Surely there were candles in the pantry. But I was reluctant to go back out there. I kept thinking of this thing I heard one of the counselors at Carson say once. "You have one boy, you have one brain. You have two boys together, each one has half a brain. You get three boys together, you got a problem." Where the hell was Sharon? Better yet, Jim?

"Avery, turn on the light."

"I can't. It doesn't work. The storm took out the power."

"I'm scared of the dark."

"That's silly. The dark won't hurt you."

Then, "Avery, I'm hungry."

"Me, too. But I can't cook anything because the stove's not working. Why don't we just take a little nap and when we wake up Sharon and Jim will come home and we'll all go out and get a hamburger."

"I'm not sleepy. I'm hungry."

"Marla, there's nothing I can do. We just have to wait."

"Can I have a cookie?"

I threw the book on the floor. "No! Will you please shut up?" Marla began to cry. I slid off the bed and looked out the window. The sky was washed clean, studded with stars. It had been quiet for a while, and I wondered hopefully if Boyd's friends had left. Marla was getting really wound up, rocking back and forth, hugging her pillow. It wasn't even really crying anymore, it was like a siren.

I couldn't stand it. "Marla, come on, stop. I'll get you a cookie, okay? You want to come with me?"

"No." She pulled the bedspread up around her chin.

I stood in the hall for a minute, willing my eyes to penetrate the darkness, feeling the worn carpeting under my bare feet. I felt around for the phone that sat on the wicker table outside Jim and Sharon's bedroom and held it to my ear. Nothing. When I could make out the dim shapes of the doorways, the jut of the corner where the hall veered into the living room, I took a step. As soon as I did, I heard their voices. Low, laughing. Probably in the kitchen. I walked loudly so they'd hear me coming.

They'd found a flashlight and it was in the middle of the table. They were taking turns spinning it, making weird moving slashes of light and shadow on the walls and on each other's faces.

"Wow, she came to join the party." Thin Lips.

"I need to find Marla a cookie. Let me use that for a minute." As I leaned across the table, he grabbed up the flashlight, holding it out of my reach.

"Say please."

I folded my arms impatiently. "Give me the goddam flashlight. I just want to find a cookie for Marla and some candles."

"You heard the man. Say please." Boyd's smile showed every tooth in his head.

"Please," I said through gritted teeth. I held out my hand. The two of them looked at each other and shook their heads.

"You have to say it nice. Like you mean it," said Boyd.

"You know what? I'm really tired. Marla's in there crying because she's hungry—"

"Awww, pore little thing," Donkey-Boy piped up.

I wheeled on him. "Shut up! I'm not talking to you." I looked at Thin Lips again. "Come on, give me a break. Let me use the flashlight. I'll get the cookies and then you guys can go back to your games."

"My name's Shawn," Thin Lips said.

I sighed. "I really don't give a shit. Give me the goddam flashlight."

"You forgot the magic word," Boyd taunted.

"Oh fuck you, Boyd." I lunged for the flashlight and Shawn handed it off to Donkey-Boy. Him I could handle. I stepped toward him, but somebody's foot shot out in the dark and I went down hard on my left hip. Two hands appeared in my face.

"Get away from me, you bastards." As I got to my knees I heard the scrape of chairs on linoleum, and by the time I was on my feet, the three of them were around me, pressing my back against the refrigerator door handle. I caught a whiff of Shawn's sour breath.

"You still want the flashlight?" he said.

My mouth was so dry that I nearly gagged when I tried to swallow. "Get away from me." The sudden cold of the flashlight on my thigh made me jump. I tried to swallow the thudding of my heart.

"You can have it if you want it." Now it was Boyd looming over me, his face like some comic book monster in the light shining up from below. I batted out with my hand and the flashlight clattered to the floor. The light disappeared like a match down a well.

A hand tightened on my arm, I could tell it was Donkey-Boy, so I leaned hard, squeezing his knuckles against the refrigerator.

"Ow! Fucking bitch."

I shoved in the direction of the voice and broke away from them, stumbling toward the living room, and suddenly the lights flickered on. In that moment of distraction, Shawn somehow got ahead of me, blocking the hallway.

"Get out of my way." I tried to sound like I was in control, at least of myself. Boyd shifted his weight from one foot to the other, uncertain how far he wanted to go. But Shawn smiled.

"We won't hurt you. We just want to look at your tits."

"In your dreams, butthead."

"Avery . . ." Marla's reedy voice floated down the hall. "Where's my cookie?"

He was taking small steps in my general direction.

"Stay away from me. Don't you know Sharon and Jim are on their way? They're probably going to be here any second. Your ass is going to be in a sling if you lay one finger on me."

Years later I'd discover that you can't talk sense to a guy with a hard-on, but at that point, I still thought reason would work.

"Avery, where's my cookie?" Marla stood in the doorway, wiping her nose with the back of her hand. I could have kissed her.

Then Boyd said, "Oh, forget it, Rainey. She doesn't even like guys."

"Huh?"

Boyd looked disgusted. "That's why they sent her here. She got all bent out of shape when her lesbo girlfriend got pregnant and they sent—"

What happened in the next few minutes is flattened to one dimension in my memory, everything taking place in a certain order, and yet all taking place at once. Me, running at Boyd Stiles, head down. And when he's on the floor, leaping on his chest like a bobcat, clawing at his face, pounding his head, him trying to push me off, and all the time I'm thinking where did he hear this? How did he even know Lee-Ann existed? And at the same time as I'm wondering, I know of course the only way he could know was from hearing Sharon and Jim talking about it. Somebody's pulling on the back of my shirt, choking me, and there are headlights sweeping across the wall, people yelling at me, and finally Jim just picks me up off of Boyd, who's sobbing and cursing and flailing his arms and saying I tried to kill him. Sharon's eyes are round with disbelief.

"What in the name of heaven is going on here?" she says.

The next morning, she brought me my breakfast in the bedroom and told me I could use the bathroom but that I had to come back to my room and wait for Elena from Children's Services.

Sharon acted like I was going on a vacation. She was all chatty, asked me if I wanted help packing. Since my stuff didn't even fill one suitcase, I thought that was pretty stupid. Anyway, I hated her. I'd never

forgive her for talking about Lee-Ann in front of Shit-for-Brains Boyd.
When Elena came that afternoon to pick me up, Sharon stood out on
the front porch, smiling.

"Bye, Avery. God bless you. You're going to be just fine. You're a
good girl at heart."

I brushed past her. "And you're a lying hypocrite."

"Avery!" Elena's voice was angry.

"It's okay," Sharon said. Ever the good Christian, she turned the
other cheek. I guess she forgot that if you do that, you get hit on the
other side, too.

There was a new counselor at Carson. Named Melissa something.
They gave her the job of telling me about Esperanza. She said it was
very peaceful, she didn't suffer or anything. I heard from Charlie Elvin
that her son found her in her bed, looking surprised but pleased to see
the angels.

I thought I was getting sick. Pounding head, trouble swallowing,
eyes burning. I sleepwalked through the day, aching for the dusty smell
of dried chiles that was Esperanza's perfume.

Melissa came up to sit beside me while everyone was at dinner. I laid
on my bed, stared at the ceiling. I missed Esperanza, but there was
nothing I could do about that. What haunted me was Lee-Ann's
letter—every minute of the day I wondered what she might have written to me that I didn't even read. At night I dreamed that I somehow
retrieved it, that the letter would miraculously turn up at the bottom
of a trash bin. Somebody would find it and bring it to me. It would be
wrinkled and dirty, but it would still have her cinnamon smell. Please
God. What if she told me where she was going so I could write to her?
So we could be together someday.

"It's only natural to be sad, Avery," she said. "It's okay to feel angry
that she left."

Silence.

"I just want you to know that you don't have to go through this alone."

Why should this be any different than everything else?

"There's a special doctor coming Wednesday. His name is Dr. Luchkov. He's coming all the way from Denver especially to see you."

I turned my face away.

"But in the next few days, if you feel like talking you can call me. I put my card on your shelf. See? It's right there. It has my home phone on it, too. You can call me any time. Day or night." She got up. Her face hovered over me like a ghost, short pale wisps of hair floating around it. "I'll check in with you tomorrow. Don't forget now. Call me anytime."

I woke up suddenly in the night, not knowing if I yelled or just dreamed that I did. I strained to hear something. There were always sounds—breath, voices, a truck grinding gears out on the highway. But not now. Silence folded around me.

I thought about calling Melissa. That was my intention when my feet first touched the cold floor, but instead I found myself silently pulling on jeans, a T-shirt, sweatshirt. Removing the case from my pillow and stuffing it with clothes, my hairbrush, one book—I didn't even know what it was—and my baby undershirt. I wadded up my money, all eight dollars and twelve cents, pushing it down deep in my right front pocket.

I was meant to leave. If not, someone would have sat up in bed and called my name. It was like angels sat by them, putting hands over their eyes, filling their ears with night breath so they wouldn't see me, couldn't hear me tiptoeing down the stairs.

The doors all had alarms on at night, so that if they opened, a bell would ring at the night duty station. Only I knew the one in the kitchen was broken—at least I hoped it still was. I sat in the rickety chair by the stove, lacing up my tennis shoes, saying good-bye to

Esperanza. Then I let myself out, made my way down San Juan Avenue toward the highway. Should I go north to Denver? No, that's what they'd expect.

Albuquerque. The name blossomed in my mind like a night-blooming flower. I didn't know anything about it. But it was a big city. I could get a job. Cooking. I could disappear.

I inhaled the cold night and slung the pillowcase over my shoulder. My legs refused to walk; they wanted to run. So I ran along the curbless edge of the dark streets, slipping in the soft earth, till Alamitos was behind me. I tried to recall the things I'd heard about hitchhiking. Put your bag between you and the driver. Notice where the door handle and locks are. Don't fall asleep. Try to stop a truckdriver.

The first few cars that passed me slowed down to look but kept going. I didn't stick out my thumb. I wasn't scared, I just had to work up to it. When I was ready, I turned around, walking backward so I could see whatever was bearing down on me.

I saw the lights, high off the ground, and heard the purr of the big diesel at the same time. A semi. I started waving my white pillowcase before he was even close, and when I realized he was slowing down, my heart rose in my chest like one of those hot-air balloons slipping into the sky.

four

Rita likes to say that we were predestined to be roommates because we wear the same size clothes—6 petite. That's where the similarities come to a screeching halt. She's three years older, and even though she can be incredibly naïve at times, she's taught me all the urban survival skills.

We met waiting tables at Pete's Diner when I first went to Albuquerque to go to the university. Before I met her, I'd never even had a checking account. I was living in a house with four other people—an arrangement I hated, but it was cheap and close to campus and I didn't have a car. I didn't even know how to drive. That's one of the first things she taught me.

"Honey, you can't survive in this town without wheels," she said the first day we met. Calling everyone "honey" is one of those little tics of hers that used to irritate the shit out of me, but I finally learned how to tune it out.

She proceeded to bundle me into her rickety blue Plymouth Duster every Wednesday and Thursday afternoon after work and take me to the big parking lot next to Lobo Stadium where I drove in circles, clockwise, counterclockwise. She made me back up with my body twisted over the back of the seat. I was fine with angle parking, but I never really got the hang of parallel parking. I practiced stopping slow and stopping fast, making U-turns and three-point turns. She showed me where the blind spots were in the rearview mirrors. After graduation from the Rita Harmon school of driver ed, the MVD driving test was a piece of cake.

She took me to the hospital supply store to buy surgical scrub pants, which are cool and lightweight and absolutely the only thing to wear in Albuquerque in the summer. She showed me how to use makeup without looking like a hooker, and she talked me into cutting my hair, which was almost down to my waist by then, dark and thick and straight. When Rita's hairdresser lopped it off at my shoulders, it suddenly had body and a nice way of curling under at the ends.

Rita's from Sundown, Texas. When I asked her where that was, she said the nearest big town was Levelland. She's tried really hard to lose her accent, even going so far as to take speech therapy in college. Partly because New Mexicans aren't exactly fond of Texas, and partly because she's got it in her head that a west Texas drawl is somehow uncool. It only surfaces when she's upset or when she talks to her family on the phone.

I've heard so much about her family over the years that I feel like I know them. Her father's a rancher named Cade Harmon, which sounds like a character out of a Larry McMurtry novel, and her mother, who she calls Momma Jen, is a rancher's wife and stay-at-home mom. They still live in the house where Rita and her two sisters grew up. Rita's the oldest, and the only one who's left Texas.

They don't call each other a lot, and I only recall Rita going home for a visit once, years ago when her sister Rhonda had her first baby. I personally think she's afraid that if she ever goes back, she might never escape again.

Mostly the Harmon girls communicate with cards. The family could probably keep Hallmark in business all by themselves. They send cards for every holiday on the calendar, and I'm not talking about just Christmas and Easter. I'm talking about Halloween and Columbus Day and St. Patrick's Day and Easter and everyone's birthday. And of course, everyone's wedding anniversary, and those always serve to remind Rita that her family thinks it's real sad that she hasn't found Mr. Right yet.

If there's an argument they send apology cards. If Rhonda has a problem with her husband, she gets a "coping" card. When her parents' old dachshund died, Rita sent a pet sympathy card. And when there's no other reason, there's always a "thinking of you" card. If the postal service goes bankrupt, it won't be because the Harmons aren't doing their share.

Two weeks after I met Rita she sent me a "thanks for being my friend" card.

My contribution to our household has always been cooking. Rita's idea of fixing dinner is to open some cans, mix the contents together, and serve it over pasta. And apparently green vegetables don't show up on the menu in west Texas—at least not until they've been deep fried into crunchy anonymous nuggets or spent several hours boiling in the company of a hunk of bacon.

When I first moved in with her we alternated weeks of cooking dinner, but I could never eat the stuff she put on the table, and a lot of times, she couldn't either. We made a bargain early on that I'd do all the cooking and she'd do all the cleaning.

The other thing I do is treat all our minor illnesses—colds, flu, upset stomach, headaches, and hangovers—with herbal remedies. Most of them are in an old book that I've carried around with me for years. The spine is cracked and the pages are made out of some kind of paper that no one uses anymore—instead of getting dry and brittle, they get softer and fuzzy—like old cloth. Some of the corners are so soft, they've almost disintegrated. Over time I've tried some variations on most of them, so they've sort of evolved into my own personal recipes.

Rita's hands-down favorite remedy is the women's tea. With a little shot of whiskey, it works wonders for cramps. Straight up it's good for PMS. The recipe says it's good for whatever ails a woman, that it keeps your female plumbing in good repair. Plus it tastes good, as opposed to most of the stuff you find in health food stores. Rita takes a cup every night the week before her period because she swears it keeps her from bloating up and feeling like "a bitch with her tail caught in a La-Z-Boy." She calls it UMS tea—UMS meaning Ugly Mood Swings. She's gotten to be sort of a walking advertisement for the stuff, and at one time or another, I've ended up supplying it to most of the women who drift in and out of our lives.

In Santa Fe the best jobs never make it into the classifieds or employ-ment agencies. They get passed along by word of mouth, through family or friends, over a cup of coffee or a beer, across a bin of apples at the market or walking the dog down by the *acequia*. I don't make friends, so it was probably good that Rita decided to come with me when I left Albuquerque.

After leaving Pete's Diner, Rita wanted nothing whatsoever to do with food. She said she was tired of smelling like deep-fryer grease and chiles. She wanted to work in a gallery or upscale boutique where she could meet what she called "a better class of people." Meaning men who had enough money to take her out for something more than a beer and line dancing. Men with long-term potential. After all, she was pushing thirty with a very short stick.

As it turned out, the combination of her blond china-doll looks and unabashed friendliness got her the job of her dreams—sales associate at SunDogs, an upscale jewelry boutique on Don Gaspar. Her knowledge of jewelry could be summed up in three words: "I love it." But the owner took a shine to her and apparently decided her presence was worth the trouble of educating her.

I just wanted a job. I've always had a touch of paranoia about being out on the street, so I would've scrubbed toilets if necessary. Rita to the rescue again. Through someone she met at SunDogs, she heard about a job opening at Dos Hombres, the trendy caterers of the moment. She even had the brass *huevos* to press for a personal introduction for me from her boss. That's how I found myself facing the tall, thin, dark-eyed man seated behind a gleaming black desk.

He picked up a piece of white paper with a few scribbles on it and frowned.

"I don't hire students." Those were Dale's first words to me.

If it had been up to him, I know I never would have gotten the job. Something about me rubbed his fur the wrong way from the start, but he's not the kind of guy who comes out and tells you what's on his mind.

Instead he tried to discourage me by telling me I was too young, too small. He said my eyes were "interesting." He sneered at my experience working at Pete's Diner. And then he asked if I'd ever had a background check.

It did make me think back for a minute, if there was anything in the past I wouldn't want to discuss with an employer. I've done some things in my life that I'm not real proud of, but as far as I know, stupidity's not illegal.

"We require background checks for all our employees." He obviously hoped that would scare me off. "We work in the finest homes in Santa Fe. And other venues—that means locations, by the way—"

"I know what a venue is." Suddenly I was conscious of the little pills that I'd tried to razor off my black sweater, and that my only good pair of black pants were probably a bit shiny at the knees.

He leaned back, clasping his hands behind his head. "Would you be available to start Wednesday morning?"

I held my breath. "Yes."

He smiled too happily. "I have a couple of other interviews this afternoon, but we'll be in touch." He opened his black leather appointment book as an indication that I was dismissed.

When I didn't move, he looked up. "Was there something else?"

"I don't think you have my phone number," I said.

He scribbled it illegibly on the piece of white paper that I knew was bound for the circular file, and then I was out on the sidewalk.

I found out later when Kirk called to offer me the job that they had offered it to someone else first who'd gone to work at Bishop's Lodge.

I was too relieved to have a job to worry about not being their first choice.

· · ·

Rita says that Santa Fe is the third-largest art market in the country. While I've never thought in terms of "markets," I've always known about the Santa Fe art scene. It's probably been in the back of my mind for years as a possible starting point if I ever got serious about looking for my mother, although I had no idea how you would go about locating somebody when you didn't even know their name.

After living here for almost two years, I can't help wondering what all the fuss is about. Some of the art is good, I guess. To me, a lot of it is bad, and even more is beside the point. Artists might have to struggle for their success, but a lot of them around here look pretty fat and sassy. Dealers and gallery owners and art critics all strike me as navel contemplators who've probably never survived for three days on ketchup and saltines and wouldn't have any idea where to find an eight-dollar retread tire.

It's kind of interesting walking down Canyon Road, or around the Plaza, looking in the windows, but I rarely go inside a gallery voluntarily. I get more than enough of their conversations about exhibits "inhabiting their space" and "interacting with their environment" just from the jobs we do for these people.

Of course, here in the third-largest art market in the country, that's a minority viewpoint.

It's Friday, and I can't believe my luck. First, I'm not working a party. After eight days straight, I figure I've earned it. Second, Rita's not home when I get here. I never know what to expect when I walk into the apartment. Will she be making awkward small talk on the couch with some new guy, her nervous laughter cutting the air like a chainsaw? Or will I open the door to the sounds of Patsy Cline or the New Age stuff she calls jazz that sounds like background music for group therapy?

Tonight it's quiet. I take my shoes off, open all the windows, and curl up on the couch with the stack of paperbacks that I just got in trade at Book Mountain. I'm only on page five of the well-used copy of *The World According to Garp* when Rita blows in.

"Ave, I've got an invitation to a show at Dream Weavers Gallery."

I look at her over the book. "Have a good time. And leave your MasterCard here."

"Oh, come on, Avery. You've been working your butt off. Go with me. It'll be fun." She pulls the invitation out of her purse and waves it under my nose. "They have gorgeous stuff—"

"That neither of us can afford."

"Well, we can check out the men—"

"The nice ones are ugly. The cute ones aren't nice. If they're cute and nice, they're gay. If they're cute and nice and straight, they're married. Or they're divorced and every penny they earn goes to the ex—"

She bursts out laughing. "So what? You have other plans? Scrub the toilet? Bleach your mustache? Jesus God, you're the oldest twenty-five-year-old I've ever met. Come on, go with me. It's Friday night, honey. Or maybe we should go dancin' at Cowgirl. . . ."

I groan. "Absolutely not."

I turn the book upside down on my stomach and look at the ceiling. Rita interprets the slightest hesitation as a sign of weakness, and she closes in for the kill.

"Then it's settled. Dream Weavers it is. You can wear my new silk shirt." She's already heading down the hall, her mission accomplished. "That teal color's gonna look so good on you. . . ."

I knew this would happen. Rita's flirting her brains out with two guys—they look like the kind who hit all the Friday night openings so they won't have to buy drinks.

I can't stand to watch her desperation, so I pick up a glass of wine from a passing tray, grab a brochure, and wander off through the gallery's rooms. Dream Weavers is housed in a rambling old adobe that's been gutted, but in a pleasing way. The structure itself is intact—the floors wear the burnished glow of very old wood, the pure white walls show off the curves and shadows of *bancos* and *nichos* and foot-thick doorways, and the ceiling rests on sturdy, age-darkened *vigas*. Everything extraneous has been deleted, creating the perfect space for a gallery.

And the display is dazzling. There are weavings—scarves, shawls, ruanas, coats in rayon chenille the colors of desert and ocean and sunset. There are kimonos and wraps, handpainted and stamped and stenciled with petroglyphs and nature motifs and fossils. Long silk scarves with hundreds of narrow pleats that conceal spectrums of unsuspected color. Sweaters with architectural motifs and geographic patterns that dissolve into one another, and quilts made with sheer silks and organza and beads and ribbon.

In spite of the artsy bullshit of the brochure, most of the work on display is oddly fascinating to me. I've never been that interested in clothes—probably fortunate, since I've never had the money to buy anything more than the basics—but I can imagine wearing these things.

When I look at my watch, it's 7:00. I can't believe I've been here for an hour. I retrace my steps, looking for Rita, but without success. I could walk home, but the soles of my boots are worn thin, and walking any distance in them isn't comfortable. Instead I duck under the velvet rope into a back room, where the light is dim and the air is cool and noise from the front is muffled.

I flip idly through racks of shawls and dusters and sweaters—nice things, more utilitarian than spectacular. Suddenly I'm tired and hungry and pissed off that I can't find my roommate. I make a quick loop of the room and head back, past half a dozen glass-fronted *nichos,* lit by soft spotlights.

In the next to last case, a blaze of color stops me. The vest. The one my mother wore for her portrait.

"Hey, I spent all afternoon cleaning these cases. Do you mind not fogging up the glass?" I wheel around, hitting a little frog figurine that holds a tray of business cards. I manage to retrieve it before it goes over the edge.

"Sorry. I was looking for someone."

"Well, I don't think he's in there. Good save, though." The face is almost childlike, small and delicate. Her smile reveals a chipped front tooth and dimples. "I was kidding about breathing on the glass. Relax. I'm not so crazy about these soirees myself." A thatch of sandy hair falls just above huge dark eyes. She holds out a small, blunt-fingered hand with nails bitten down to the quick. "Elaine Cumming." I rearrange my purse and shake her hand.

"Do you work here?"

"You'd best believe it. Twenty-four/seven. I own it. Half of it, rather. See anything you can't live without?"

"On my income, the only thing I can't live without is food."

She laughs, a surprisingly hearty laugh for such a fawnlike creature. "I hear you. Of course there's always layaway."

My eyes go back to the vest. "Do you know the artist who did this?"

"I did know her. Isabel Colinas. Unfortunately she passed away a number of years ago. She was a fabulous artist. And a very nice lady."

"Was she from around here?"

"Not originally. I think she was from up in Colorado, but I wouldn't swear to it. We bought this place ten years ago, my partner, Suzanne, and I. So we only worked with her for a year or so before she . . ." She looks from me to the vest. "Isn't it exquisite?"

"It's beaded, isn't it?"

"No." She shakes her head. "She used this technique of knotting metallic threads so that it does look almost like beading, but it isn't. It's just incredibly fine needlework. And look at the design. She did it pretty much freehand. If you'd like to see it up close and personal, I can get the keys . . ."

"No, that's all right. I'm sure it's not in my price range. Just out of curiosity, do you have anything else by her?"

"No. Getting this piece was a lucky accident. When an artist dies, it's very good for business. Too bad we can't learn to appreciate them when they're still around."

"Well . . ." My voice trails off. "Thanks. I guess I should get going." She falls in step with me, and we both duck back under the velvet rope.

"Don't rush off in the heat of the night. Have you had a glass of wine?"

"Yes, I did. Thanks."

"Well, have another one. What's your name, by the way?" She slings the end of a gorgeous cerise, gold, and green scarf back over her shoulder like a dishtowel.

"Avery James."

A leather-clad couple glides past and she says, "Hi, Mary. Hi, Sid." They nod graciously, like nobles acknowledging the greeting of their tenant farmer. "What do you do?"

"I work for Dos Hombres Catering."

"Really?" She gives me an appraising glance. "Do you cook?"

"In my dreams. Mostly I take bookings, do site surveys, work parties, and kiss ass."

"Do you like it?"

I shrug. "I'd like to cook. But you have to pay your dues."

She sighs. "Ain't it the truth? It's tough in Santa Fe. Just to survive takes so much time and energy. Have you had anything to eat?"

"Um, actually . . . no. I—"

She takes my arm and maneuvers me over to the hors d'oeuvre buffet. "Might as well, it's free."

"Do I look malnourished?"

Again the big laugh. "Only slightly."

"Elaine, excuse me for interrupting, but Petra Crispin's here. From *Fiber Arts Magazine.* She wants to ask us a couple of questions about the show." A tall, dark-haired woman smiles at me. "I'm Suzanne Rose and I just need to borrow her for a minute."

Elaine winks at me. "Back in a flash."

I turn my attention to the buffet. Not a terribly imaginative presentation. Using serapes and quilts and scarves to decorate was undoubtedly meant to be in keeping with the ambiance of the gallery, but the food is lost against the mishmash of colors and styles. The serving pieces are pretty basic. Dead white platters, lots of cutesy little bowls and pitchers. Dale may be obnoxious as hell, but he's a former ad agency food stylist, and the man is a genius at plating food.

I take a polenta cake with sautéed mushrooms and pop it in my mouth. Polenta's a little soggy . . .

"Are you hungry, or just scouting the competition?"

Paul DeGraf.

He's got the monochromatic look down pat. Tonight it's black, from the knit pullover shirt that hugs his body and black jeans that look like he hasn't sat down in them yet, to the soles of his black cowboy boots. On his wrist is a narrow band of silver inlaid with turquoise and coral and white shell.

I wash the polenta down with room temperature white wine. "Both. Although I have to say I don't think the competition is very competitive."

"I agree."

There's an awkward silence while I try to decide where this is going. "I've been meaning to call you," I say finally.

"Then why haven't you?" He insists on looking right into my eyes.

"It's just been so busy. This is my first night off in weeks." I pick up a small plate and study the buffet. "And, quite honestly . . . it just feels weird."

He says, "If you were to pretend we've never met, would you be more inclined to tell me about yourself?"

"So you're having trouble sleeping?"

"I doubt that you could put me to sleep—" He smiles charmingly.

"I wouldn't bet the adobe on it. Anyway, you already know most of that first-conversation stuff—my name, what I do for a living, where I work. You even know who my mother is. Was."

Over his shoulder I see Elaine break away from a knot of people admiring an elaborately patterned quilt and start toward us. A few feet away she slows abruptly. A shadow crosses her face—not even a shadow, really just a flicker of something, and then it's gone and she joins us.

"Hello, Paul."

"Elaine." When he bends to kiss her cheek, she doesn't lean toward him.

"Well. It's been a while. How are you?"

"Busy," he says.

She smiles. "Still bringing things up from Mexico?"

There's a pause that's just slightly wrong, like a picture hanging crooked on the wall. Before he can say anything, a large red-haired woman swathed in a multicolored cape waves frantically from across the room. "Elaine, where's the catalog?"

She rolls her eyes at me. "I'm sorry. Obviously I'm going to have to actually work tonight. It was nice to meet you, Avery. I hope you'll come back sometime. Bye, Paul." She whips the scarf back over her shoulder and walks away.

He pushes his shirtsleeve up to look at his watch. "I'd like very much to sit down and have a real conversation with you. Have you had dinner?"

He's just zeroed in on my greatest weakness. "Well . . ."

"Let me buy you dinner. We can go to Café des Amis over in Burro Alley. It's quiet, and we can talk."

I hesitate. "My roommate's here someplace. I should tell her I'm leaving."

"Go ahead. I'll meet you outside."

Café des Amis is a restaurant where the plates as well as the walls have paintings on them—landscapes, portraits, still lifes. It has a low ceiling, white walls, dark wood floor, white lace curtains at all the windows, white paper over the white tablecloths. A small fountain in the middle of the floor gurgles over fake stones, lit from below. A little girl of about ten years old is carefully placing flatware on empty tables, lining up the end of each piece along the edge of the white paper.

When we come through the door, a short, dark woman plants herself in front of us chattering in French and kissing Paul on both cheeks. Then he's talking French to her. Suddenly a bear of a man in chef's whites strides out of the kitchen and *he* kisses Paul on both cheeks and claps his shoulder. Then Paul introduces me and they both beam at me till I feel like I'm standing naked in a spotlight on a dark stage.

The woman, whose name is Claudette, shakes my hand and says she is happy to make my acquaintance. The guy, Etienne, bends over my hand, barely brushing his lips against it and murmuring, *"Enchanté, mademoiselle."*

Finally we get to sit down.

While I study Paul, he studies the menu. Or appears to. He probably comes here so often that he knows it by heart. A slight frown of concentration wrinkles his wide forehead. His face is long, narrow jawed, the skin smooth and dark. When he looks up and catches my stare, he smiles. I look quickly at my own menu. It's all in French with no helpful hints.

"Do you know what you'd like?" he says.

A glance tells me that I don't have the faintest idea what most of the dishes are, so I tell him to order for me.

He was right about one thing—it's quiet. Most of the tables are occupied by couples. The older ones look married and most of them aren't talking because they've already heard everything their spouse has to say—probably several times. The younger ones look like they're madly in love, and they just sit there staring at each other in the flickering candlelight till their eyes glaze over, because they're saving their energy for after dinner.

The first thing that happens is Madame brings one of those standing wine coolers and a bottle of Champagne. I can tell by the look on Paul's face that he didn't expect it.

"From Etienne and me." She smiles as the cork pops gently.

"Are you French?" I ask him after we touch our tall, fluted glasses together.

"I went to school in Paris. My father was French. My mother was American."

"Indian?"

He looks puzzled.

"I sort of thought you looked part Indian."

This makes him laugh. "No. I'm Jewish. Same general idea, though. Just different tribes."

I take a sip of the pale straw-colored wine, savoring the fizz. I've only had real Champagne once or twice, but that was enough to know I love it—not just the citrus taste, but the way it fills your head with toasty bubbles. It's like holding bumblebees in your mouth.

"So how did you end up in Santa Fe?" I ask him.

"My mother lived here. After she divorced her second husband. When she died, I came to settle the estate." His shoulders lift just slightly. "By the time I was finished with all the legal business, I was in love with the place. I only went back to Paris long enough to pack up my apartment. That was twelve years ago."

The bread is pale yellow and chewy, and there's a fruity green olive oil for dipping and a small dish of olives in a chile-spiked marinade. I almost forget that the true purpose of this outing is something other than having a great meal, till he says, "Why do you wear contact lenses?" He leans back, one arm draped over the chair next to him.

I swallow too quickly and the fizz goes up into my sinuses. "Because most people find my eyes . . . distracting."

"What's wrong with being distracting?"

"It's not my style. I like to blend in."

The intensity of his stare makes me fidgety. "There are so many things I want to know—it's hard not to bombard you with questions."

I smile queasily. "Well . . . you're buying. Go for it."

"Where did you live before Santa Fe?"

"Albuquerque."

"What did you do there?"

"Worked as a waitress."

"Where did you work? I know quite a few of the restaurants there."

The thought of Paul DeGraf on a stool at the counter of Sneaky Pete's Diner makes me smile. "No place you've ever been, I promise. I was working and going to school."

"The University of New Mexico?"

"Yes."

"What did you study?"

"Whatever I felt like."

"What was your major field?"

"Didn't have one. Didn't graduate."

Claudette is standing beside us with bowls of a pale green soup. *"Potage de courgettes,"* she announces, setting them on the table.

I pick up my spoon. The soup is like cool silk on my tongue, fresh and peppery.

"It's unbelievable," he says suddenly. "How much you look like her. Where did you grow up?"

"Colorado. A little town called Alamitos."

"I know the place. Near Wolf Creek. Did you ever ski there?"

"No. They weren't into skiing at the Randall Carson Foundling Home."

He seems embarrassed. "You grew up in a—what was that like?"

"Carson? Basically, I think of it as survival training."

He frowns. "It was that bad?"

"Of course. Why would you think being in an institution would be anything else?"

"Were you . . . abused or—" He looks startled when I laugh.

"Nothing like that. At least not by the staff. I didn't get along with the other kids. I was always getting in fights. 'Does not integrate well with peer group' was how they put it."

"Why? I mean, what did you fight about?"

"Oh, typical kid stuff. They made fun of me because I was little, because I had weird eyes. Because I was dumb."

"Dumb?"

"I had trouble with reading. Till my friend tutored me."

"So you did have friends."

"Friend. Singular. When I was thirteen she got—she left. Then the cook, who was the only other person I liked, died." I shrug. "I had enough to eat and clothes to wear and a rudimentary education. It was just lonely, I guess. And strange. Not knowing who I was. Who my parents were."

"I see."

"No offense, but I doubt if you do."

A young busboy picks up our soup plates, and Madame reappears immediately with our entrées. Set in the middle of each huge white plate is a skinless chicken breast, sliced crosswise into five pieces and napped with a pale green sauce. Tiny perfect carrots and small ovals of zucchini nestle around it. Like the soup, everything is slightly chilled.

"It's light," he says, watching me cut a bite. "I thought because of the heat . . . If you're still hungry after this, they have a wonderful tarte tatin."

The chicken has been poached in white wine, with herbs. Mostly tarragon, I think, and it's meltingly tender. More herbs flavor the sauce—tarragon, parsley, thyme. There's something else, too.

"Walnuts?" I look at him.

He smiles. "Very good. Yes. Ground walnuts and a little walnut oil in the sauce. Do you like it?"

"I love it." For a minute I wonder if Kirk and Dale would be interested in this recipe, then common sense kicks in. Why would I want to give them anything this good?

DeGraf eats European style, and it fascinates me, the way he uses the knife in his right hand to cut small pieces and position them on the fork in his left hand. The only other person I've ever seen who ate like that was a German girl in my student housing in Albuquerque.

Abruptly, he's talking again. "I have to admit that I'm a little bit puzzled. I thought that as soon as you got used to the idea of knowing who your mother was, you'd want to know all about her."

"I don't think I am yet. Used to it."

"Do you hate her?"

"I can't hate a stranger."

"Well, then." He wipes his mouth carefully with the white napkin. "Why not approach it from the perspective that she's a very interesting stranger that you might want to know about."

I twirl my Champagne flute around and around, watching the bubbles materialize in the bottom and float upward to disappear again. "Listen, I know you're trying to be nice, and I appreciate you wanting to tell me about her, but I can't help wondering what the hell difference it makes now. Especially since she's . . . I mean, I know my life doesn't look terribly exciting, but the thing is, I don't have a lot of unrealistic expectations to make me miserable. It's taken me a while to get to this point. Where I'm reasonably content. I'm just not sure I want to rock the boat."

He sets down his knife and fork. "But I can't understand your reluctance to even know about her. I want to give you information. I'm not asking for anything from you."

"I'm not quite clear on your interest in this."

He glances distractedly at the candle, sputtering in its own meltdown, then looks directly at me.

"I loved her," he says. "We were to be married."

A tremor jiggles my knees, and my purse slips from my lap onto the floor. When I reach down to pick it up, I find my hands are shaking.

"Oh. I'm . . . sorry."

He inclines his head slightly. "She was an artist, you know. Very gifted."

I lean back slowly into the chair, release my stranglehold on the napkin, and try a normal breath. "Actually . . . I did know that. Sort of. They gave me—the nurse on duty that night—gave me this little shirt. It's what I had on when they found me. It was embroidered with flowers. I still have it."

"I'd like very much to see it sometime."

I don't respond, but it doesn't matter. He's already launched into the story of their first meeting.

"It was at a party," he's saying. "After a gallery opening. Typical Santa Fe. Everyone dressed to the nines. Loaded with jewelry, scarves, fringe—all the usual suspects. Isabel was wearing this plain red dress. Long skirt, high neck, long sleeves. All covered up. But the way it fit her . . . the way she moved in it. People would stop talking, stop eating and drinking, stop looking at the paintings, and just watch her."

He's looking at me, but seeing her. Moving through a gallery in her red dress. I used to think that once I knew who my mother was I'd never feel invisible again.

"I saw some of her work tonight," I say. That seems to bring him out of the dream.

"The Malinche vest."

"What's a Malinche?"

"Malinche was the Indian woman who served as the interpreter for Cortez during the Spanish conquest. That vest was one of Isabel's favorite pieces. One of the few things she made that she wore herself. I've tried a number of times to buy it, but Elaine won't part with it."

"Because she doesn't like you?" It's out before I have time to think.

"I wouldn't say she actually dislikes me . . ."

"I would."

"You know what it's like."

"What what's like?"

"This town. The politics, the gossip . . . who's doing what to whom. That's all it is." He leans forward, resting his elbows on the table. "Look, Avery, I'd like us to be friends."

"Why? Because you loved my mother? Who didn't know me and who I didn't know? It doesn't seem to make a lot of sense."

"Maybe not. At least not right now. But I hope it will later on."

I look at my watch. "I've got a long day tomorrow."

"You haven't finished your dinner."

"I'll take it with me."

He reaches for his wallet.

In the fountain, some poor black bug is fighting for his life in a foaming whirlpool.

The dashboard clock of his white Mercedes reads 10:35 P.M. I can see him looking at the place, the overflowing Dumpster that some kids have pushed out of the alley, the crumbling plaster on the corner of the stairs, the dented sign for Alma's Casa Blanca.

"Welcome to the west side," I say.

He turns off the engine and it gets very quiet. I look up at our window, the glimmer of light as the curtains part just a fraction of an inch.

"Did she ever tell you about . . . me?"

He shifts in the seat to face me. "She told me she'd had a child. When she was very young. That the father was married. He wanted her to have an abortion, but she refused. She said she gave the baby up for adoption."

Angry heat crawls up the back of my neck. "So dumping me in the furnace room of an institution was her idea of giving me up for adoption?"

"I think she was young and alone and frightened."

"That makes two of us."

"She didn't tell me much more than that. I think it was a very painful thing for her to talk about." His smile is just awkward and defenseless enough to be oddly comforting.

"I have to go." I fumble for the seat belt release.

When he pulls the key out of the ignition, I touch his wrist, then snatch my hand back. "That's okay, don't get out. I'll just run up." My hand is on the door handle.

"Avery, I'm glad we had a chance to talk. May I call you?"

Without overexerting my memory, I can be pretty sure no man has ever said anything like that to me before. I turn to look at him. He's got to be forty-five. Rita says with men it's harder to guess age. She says it's because shaving exfoliates their skin and makes them look younger than they have any right to. His face is smooth all right, but there are a few gray hairs at his temples, squint lines around his eyes, and deep smile lines from nose to chin. I think of tracing them with my finger, and my stomach turns over.

"I have your card," I tell him. "I'll call you."

Sleep has never come easy for me, even at the best of times. Tonight I can't seem to find the right place for my arms and legs. My shoulder hurts. I'm thirsty. The room is too warm. And when I finally manage to drop off, I keep jerking awake.

Like something's about to happen in a dream that I don't want to see.

In the morning I can still taste garlic. I'm dried out from too much alcohol and not enough water. I smell coffee brewing before I hear Rita tiptoeing down the hall. I roll out of bed, throwing the covers aside.

She's in the kitchen nuking a cinnamon bun from Cloud Cliff Bakery and looking mournful.

I open the dishwasher and pull out my coffee mug. "What's wrong?"

She shrugs. "Nothing. I'm just depressed because Rick didn't show last night."

The microwave timer dings.

"Was he supposed to?"

"Well . . ." She sighs and slathers butter on the hot roll. "I talked about it. I mentioned that I was going. I thought he might come. Since he knew I was going to be there."

"When did you mention it?" I fill my cup and add whipping cream, my big indulgence.

"Last Friday," she says around a bite of the roll.

I take a sip of coffee. "You know how guys are. Unless you drew him a map, it probably didn't register. Besides, he doesn't sound like your type."

Another sigh. "Maybe that's why I like him. He seems different."

"None of them are different," I say flatly.

She yawns, pushing her bangs back from her eyes. "Listen to you. The voice of experience."

I open the refrigerator and take out a carton of vanilla yogurt. "By the way, what time did you go to bed last night?"

"I don't know. I hung around Dream Weavers till eight, hoping news-boy would show up, and then I came right home. I had one more glass of wine and then I read for a little while—then I guess I just zonked out. I didn't even hear you come in. What time did you get home?"

"About ten thirty. So you weren't peeking out the window when we drove up?"

Silence. Two spots of color stain her cheeks. "Well, what am I sup-posed to do? You never tell me anything. For God's sake, I'm about to croak. So . . . ? What happened? What did Mr. DeGraf say?"

"That's Paul. We're close personal friends now. It seems that Paul DeGraf was in love with my mother. He said they were planning to get married."

"Jesus God. How did she die?"

I stir the yogurt around and swallow a spoonful. "He didn't say."

"And you didn't ask?"

"No."

"Why not? How could you not want to know how she died?"

I can feel the top of my head getting warm. That's what happens when I get pissed. "Because I don't care. Because it couldn't possibly make any difference. Okay?" I put the lid back on the yogurt and lick the spoon clean, then I turn on the faucet.

"I swear, girl. You're crazy as popcorn." She stuffs the rest of the roll in her mouth and heads for the shower.

I refill my coffee cup, top it off with more cream, and sit at the table tracing the gold pattern in the red Formica. I don't care, and it couldn't possibly make any difference. So why am I wasting time thinking about it? DeGraf probably thought it was strange that I didn't ask, but who cares what he thinks?

His card is in a cigar box that I keep on the floor by my bed. It's where I keep everything I own that's worth keeping, which admittedly isn't a lot—two or three photos, a tiny locket, an old embroidered handkerchief, a circle of turquoise on a leather cord. My baby undershirt.

I know I put the card in here. Then my fingers brush against something cool and weighty, and my heart gives a tiny shiver. I pull out the small heart made of gold nuggets, hung on a flat gold chain. I rub it against my shirt but it still looks dirty. Needs a real cleaning. The last time I took it off, I promised myself I'd never put it back on, but on this morning, I find myself drawn to it. The chain has a strange kind of clasp that looks like a question mark. I know there's a special name for it, but I can't call it up just now.

Instead of opening the clasp, I slip the chain over my head, and the heart nestles comfortably against my chest. As the giver intended, I think. I look into the box and see DeGraf's card, standing flat against one of the sides. That's why I missed it. But instead of taking it out, I close the lid and crawl back under the covers, rubbing the gold heart gently against my T-shirt.

"Ave? Are you asleep?" Rita calls.

I sigh. "Not anymore."

"Sorry. I'm leaving. See ya later."

The front door bangs and I lie still, eyes shut tight, taking shallow breaths.

Will Cameron. Jimmie John. Cassie. Florales. The names pop in my brain like those flash cards they used to teach reading with. The tightness in my chest moves up in my throat, and my face gets too warm. I should just get up and get busy doing something.

Thinking about it serves no purpose. I'll never go back to Florales. Cassie's dead. So's Jimmie John. Will Cameron might as well be. Those years are a blank. Like the hole that's left after you lose a tooth. When you poke your tongue into the space, it seems oddly tender.

Like yes, once there was something there. But it's gone now. And it's never coming back.

PART TWO

florales

May 1988

five

Florales, New Mexico, was no place to be coming off a ride, hungry and flat broke. If you turned the entire population upside down and shook them hard, you might end up with a couple of bucks and some change.

Being a thirteen-year-old runaway didn't help either.

I wasn't good at panhandling. Not cute enough to make people sorry for me, too small and skinny to be intimidating. And of course, there was my eyes. A lot of people took one look and got so creeped out that they forgot whatever kindly impulses they may have had.

The ones that didn't turn away somehow felt entitled to ask a lot of stupid questions. Even people who'd never dream of staring at a cripple or asking some guy how he lost his arm think nothing of getting right in my face and asking me where I got the weird eyes. Like maybe I picked them out at Wal-Mart.

I worked the three shabby streets of downtown in the morning, coming away with enough change to buy a candy bar and a Coke. By noon I was thinking about another ride south, but I was so hungry I could practically feel the sides of my empty stomach rubbing together.

I was sitting on an upside-down bucket in a service alley between a hardware store and a feed store, watching the dust settle and feeling sorry for myself when I saw my deliverance across the street. A man stepped out of Mami's Café holding a white sack of take-out food. He looked like a big rooster with little twiggy legs and a gut that hung over his belt like he was eight months pregnant.

He carried the sack carefully over to an old green pickup truck angle-parked at the curb and stood there for a minute looking around.

He patted one pocket, then switched the sack to the other hand and patted the other pocket. He touched his shirt pocket. Obviously he'd forgotten something—keys, glasses, wallet. He set the food on the truck's driver-side fender and followed his stomach back into Mami's.

As they always said at Carson, For what we're about to receive, Lord make us truly grateful. I started to run, eyes locked onto that sack like radar. I barely slowed when I passed the truck, and I was well into the next block clutching his lunch before I heard him yell,

"Hey! You come back here! Somebody grab that kid!"

As it turned out, nobody had to.

In my imagination I was already digging into tacos—that's what it smelled like—and he was too far behind me, moving slow, maybe already given up and gone back inside to order some more. I was past most of the little stores and feeling suddenly spacey from no food and not much sleep, but I put on one more burst of speed. I needed to make it to the big weedy yard by the cottonwoods at the edge of town where the last driver left me off. It was full of decrepit RVs, empty flat-bed trailers. I figured I could duck in there long enough to inhale a taco or two.

I was flying so fast my heels were kicking my butt. Then I turned my head just to glance behind me and when I turned back, something loomed up in my path like a brick wall. I saw stars.

Bags went sailing, spilling cans and boxes. White powdery stuff was everywhere, including up my nose. I coughed and sneezed. I sat up, brushing my face, and I winced when I touched my forehead.

"Cassie! You okay?"

"Fine, Delbert. Just let me get my breath. See if that child's hurt."

Even though I was choking and half blinded with flour or whatever it was, I knew that was my cue to leave. I got as far as one foot and one knee before a big hand latched onto the back of my shirt.

Apparently the two things I'd just rammed were an old lady and a very husky Indian.

"Easy there, kid. Nobody's gonna hurt you."

"That's what you think, Delbert Begay. That little shit stole my lunch." The pregnant guy wheezed as he came limping up. I was rubbing my eyes, which only made them worse, but I didn't have to see him to know he was pissed.

"Missin' a meal or two won't hurt you none, Harlan." This from the old lady, who was still sitting on the ground. I thought her hair might've been pinned up to start with, but it had gotten knocked loose by our collision, and some wiry gray strands hung around her face.

"That ain't the point, Cassie." He bent to help her up and the Indian held out the hand that wasn't bunched in my shirt, and between them, they got her to her feet. "It's a wonder you're still in one piece. She could of broke your leg or something."

The old lady brushed herself off. "Well, she didn't."

"Maybe not," he insisted, "but she stole my lunch."

"She was probably hungry. Is that right, child?"

I just nodded, looking at the ground.

He walked over to where the sack was laying, miraculously intact. "Lookit that, wouldja."

The Indian said, "No harm done, then, Harlan." But he didn't loosen his grip on my shirt.

Harlan lifted his cowboy hat and smoothed his greasy hair back, replaced the hat. "Reckon we oughta call Austin. Think I saw his cruiser go by awhile back."

"What on earth for?" The old lady rubbed her hip, like it was sore.

"What d'you mean what for?" His voice rose. "She stole my lunch. She ran you down . . ." I didn't like the way he was looking at me out of the corner of his eye. "And she looks pretty young to be out on her own. Probably a runaway."

"The way I see it . . ." The woman picked up a sack from the ground. "You got your lunch back. I'm in one piece . . ." She looked me up and down. "As to her being a runaway, whether she is or she's not, she needs to get a decent meal in her regardless."

When she smiled at me, I noticed she had a lot of wrinkles, but her cheeks were firm, and she didn't have old lady whiskers like Ridley had. She bent down very slowly and started picking up cans and boxes and putting them in her sack. "So . . ." She looked up at him. "Why'n't you just go on back to your lunch, Harlan, and let me and Delbert take care of this."

"You suit yourself, Cassie, but you're gonna be sorry for taken up with the likes of her." He rolled the top of his lunch bag closed and limped off muttering, "Sick and tired of these goddam kids runnin' wild and stealin' . . ."

The Indian laughed. "She's a regular one-girl crime wave, Kemosabe."

Harlan turned back. "Yeah, you go on and laugh, Begay. Wait till she starts stealin' stuff out of your store."

Self-righteous booger. When he'd shuffled his way out of earshot, the Indian said, "Cassie, what the sam hill are you going to do with this kid?" Like I wasn't standing right there with his hand on my collar.

"Take her home and feed her, of course."

"You think we should call the sheriff, try to find out where she came from?"

I nearly bit clear through my tongue. If the sheriff started making some phone calls or plugged me into his computer, I'd be back in Colorado by tomorrow night.

"Plenty of time for that after she's got a decent meal in her."

"Well, come on, I'll give you a ride. How's that hip?"

"A little sore, but I've had worse. We'd appreciate the ride, wouldn't we, child?"

I stared at the toes of my sneakers.

"You ought to thank Cassie for helping you, girl."

It was the first time they'd said a word to me, and they were already telling me what I should be doing.

. . .

Isat between them in the old flatbed truck and stared at the red rock mesas through the windshield, picking absently at the white stuff erupting like cottonwood puffs from a crack in the bench seat. Delbert shifted the black gearshift knob between my knees while he and Cassie chattered about whether it was going to be a drought summer; he said his nephew had gotten a part-time job as a fire spotter over by Magdalena and he told Cassie he'd give her some eggs if she'd make a poultice—whatever the hell that was—for his father's arm.

Meanwhile, I was looking around, trying to figure out how and when I could get myself out of here. By the time he turned off the highway onto an unmarked dirt road and rattled across a dry wash, I was starting to get scared. Nobody could really live out here. The old lady might be crazy. They could kill me and no one would ever know. What if Tonto was one of those people Ridley used to tell us about who sell girls as slaves to black drug dealers?

"Where the hell are we going?"

They both looked at me like they'd forgotten I was there.

"To my house, child."

"Don't call me child."

"Then suppose you give us your name."

I chewed on the inside of my cheek.

The truck ground to a halt and Delbert flicked off the key.

I'd make my move the second he was out of sight. The old lady could never catch me. But when I jumped down from the cab and tried to stand up, my head got hot and my knees started shaking and things got suddenly dark.

When I opened my eyes, I was on a couch, covered up with a dusty-smelling blanket. The room was dim and cool. The old lady was standing by a window with a ragged lace curtain over it. Just standing there, watching me. When I sat up, a wet rag fell off the egg-sized lump on my head.

She picked it up. "Feel like eating something now?"

She looked pretty harmless. Probably just some old do-gooder, but I'd keep her in my sight, watch everything she put in the food.

She fed me a bowl of thick stew that had no flavor except hot. It brought out a sweat on my face, made me conscious of my own stink—three days of walking and thumbing, four nights of sleeping in gas station restrooms and drainage pipes. She seemed not to notice. Just kept my glass full of water and my plate piled with dry cornbread. Compared to Esperanza, she wasn't much of a cook.

"They call me Cassie Robert," she said finally. When I didn't answer, she said, "What's your name, child?"

"Avery James." I knew I should make up a name, but I was too tired. My brain wasn't working right.

"Where you from?"

"Montrose." It was the first town that came into my head.

"How long you been traveling?"

"Four days."

"Made darn good time, didn't you?" She gave me a sideways look, which I avoided. "How long since you ate?"

I was starting on the second bowl of stew, and my mouth was full, so I just held up two fingers.

"Won't your people be worried about you?"

I swallowed something so fiery that my eyes watered. "No."

"Where you headed?"

Nosy old toad. "Albuquerque."

"You got family there? Friends?"

"Yeah."

"Which? Friends or family?"

No answer.

"What're you lookin' to do there?"

"Get a job."

"A job doing what?"

"Cooking."

"I see." She leaned her elbows on the table and peered at me.

I stared right back, folded my arms, waited for her to mention that my eyes were pretty unusual. But she just got up, carried the empty bowl and spoon to the sink, washed them.

"Thanks for the food." I shifted uneasily on the hard chair.

She nodded at the window. "It's dark now. Won't be many rides out there for you tonight. Might as well sleep on the couch and start out fresh in the morning."

"I should get going."

"Suit yourself." She dried my bowl and put it back in the cupboard. Then without turning around, she said quietly, "Nobody's gonna come lookin' for you here."

I hesitated. Having a full stomach didn't really put me in the mood for walking. Not to mention that it was dark and I had no idea where I was. She was puttering around, wiping crumbs off the table, setting the soup pot in the sink. Finally she dusted off her hands and said, "I'm goin' to bed. If you leave, be sure to latch the door behind you."

She disappeared into a little room off the other side of the door. I could hear her getting undressed, shoes hitting the floor, then a long, tired sigh, the rustle of bedcovers.

I knew I should get up, but I couldn't move. My arms and legs were too heavy. Like in those dreams, where you're running, but you're not getting anywhere. I sat there staring at the flame of the oil lamp till I could hardly hold my head up. When she started to snore, I kicked off my shoes, blew out the lamp, and laid down again on the couch. It was saggy and hard as a damn rock, but I closed my eyes and that was it.

I jolted awake with the sun full in my face, needing to pee so bad I thought I'd explode. Smells of bacon and coffee and biscuits made the saliva pool in my mouth. I'd leave right after breakfast. I got up reaching for my shoes.

"Better shake 'em out first," Cassie warned. "Make sure there's no scorpions or black widows." She pronounced it "widdas."

I shook them hard upside down, then wiggled my feet inside. "I need to use the bathroom. Please."

"Out there." She jerked her head toward the door.

"Outside?"

"Yep. Just follow the path around back. And mind the snakes."

The eggs were laced with mild green chiles, the bacon was crisp, and the biscuits were a little chewy, but there was some kind of spicy honey for them. She gave me coffee with sugar and milk. Esperanza used to give me sips of her coffee sometimes. They never let us have it at Carson. They said it was a stimulant, and one thing that Christian young ladies and gentlemen didn't need to be was stimulated.

When I couldn't eat another bite, I sat back and looked at the old woman across the table from me. Steel gray hairs like little bent wires poked out of the knot at the base of her neck. Her face was as wrinkled and faded as her dress. She had a thin mouth and a pretty big nose, and eyes that kind of reminded me of Esperanza, black eyes that could look smiley and sharp at the same time.

"Why do you want to help me?"

"I help you, then you help me," she said.

She surprised me. I was expecting some goody God bullshit about Samaritans helping strangers like they used to put out all the time at Carson. But given the fact that she'd fed me two meals and let me sleep in her house, I figured I owed her.

"How am I supposed to help you?"

"Garden wants watering and I need some herbs cut. It's a small patch."

Well, it wouldn't take long, and then I'd be back out on the highway. Hitchhiking to Albuquerque. If I could figure out where she kept her money, I might even have a couple extra bucks in my jeans.

It was a small patch of garden, all right. But there was an amazing number of plants in it. Cassie tied on an old-timey sunbonnet, sat on a dented blue metal stool, and watched me haul buckets of water from a sink on the back porch.

The only flowers I recognized were sunflowers—the little wild ones that grow along the roads. There were some pink pompoms and some orange ones.

"Those marigolds." She pointed at the orange ones. "Cut about a half dozen of those. No, child, at the base of the stem, not right under the flower."

She had me snip a bunch of silver weedy-looking stuff, soft and silky to the touch. "Wormwood," she said. "Mexicans call it *agenjo*. Good for arthritis and headaches."

"Yeah."

"This one's feverfew. Altamisa. For upset stomach." It looked like miniature daisies. She pointed at a pretty green plant. "This is bas—"

"*Albácar*." The licorice scent filled my head with a memory of Esperanza.

Cassie shot me an odd look. "How do you know basil?"

"*Albácar*," I said again.

"Same thing. Have you used it for tea?"

"Just for soup and stuff."

She nodded. "Brings good luck, too." She pulled off a leaf and tucked it into my shirt pocket.

By now the sun was beating down on the top of my head till I could just about keel over.

"Gonna be a hot one today."

I squinted up at her. The sweat that kept popping out on my face evaporated before it could drip off. What was your first clue, lady?

"You might want to have a bath before you leave. Probably easier to get a ride if you don't smell like a nanny goat."

Before I could think too much about it, I was on the back porch up to my neck in a metal tub of barely warm water, my hair fat with shampoo suds. I closed my eyes and almost fell asleep. Except Cassie was making a lot of noise with pots out in the kitchen.

Then she hollered, "Seems a shame to put those filthy clothes back on. Now that you're all clean. Might want to wait till they're washed and dried."

This made me nervous. I should've been out of here a long time ago. I should've left right after I ate last night. This morning at the latest. They could be looking for me. Never know who Tonto might be talking to. And old fat-ass Harlan obviously couldn't be trusted.

I paddled my hand back and forth in the water and the ripples washed over my stomach like tiny waves. But Ridley probably thought I was headed for Denver. Trying to find Lee-Ann. Ha. I snorted and the little explosion of water made me laugh.

One more night wouldn't hurt. One more free meal. Maybe there was something else she needed done—as long as I was going to be around for another night.

When I stood up out of the filthy water, a little breeze hit my wet skin, raising goosebumps on my butt. I wrapped the rough towel around me and started dragging the washtub toward the edge of the porch, water sloshing out all over.

"Don't do that, child!" Cassie's voice startled me and I straightened up.

"Don't you want me to pour the water out?"

"Lordy, no. We don't waste water around here."

I looked down at the brownish scum floating on top of my bath. "It's dirty. What else can you do with it?"

"The garden don't mind dirty water. Leave it be for now. I'll show you later what to do with it. Get dried off and let's find you some clothes."

She gave me a plaid dress to wear, faded and soft like it'd been washed about a million times, and big as a tent. We had beans and rice for dinner. I saw peppers and tomatoes in the garden, but they weren't ripe yet. She had *masa,* so I made tortillas. She didn't say anything, but I could tell she was impressed. Patting out the dough, slapping them in her big old black frying pan, I felt for a second like I was back at Carson, kneeling on that chair next to Esperanza, smelling the cumin and chiles on her skin. I remembered her stories about how her whole family made tamales at Christmas. She said she was going to teach me, but we never got around to that.

After dinner Cassie boiled water in the blue metal coffeepot, threw in a handful of coffee and let it steep. She called it cowboy coffee. When she decided it was done, she dropped in pieces of shell from our breakfast eggs.

"Makes the grounds sink to the bottom." When she smiled, she looked like a little kid. Well, a wrinkly little kid. She fixed two cups with sugar and that canned milk that smelled like the can.

We spent the evening tying plant cuttings into bundles by the soft yellow light of two kerosene lamps. Then we hung them to dry on nails hammered into the low ceiling beams. She gave me a pair of scissors and had me cut squares of a coarse material for teas and medicines, tie the packets with kitchen twine. Her hands were all knobby, with swollen knuckles, and I wondered how she could do this at all.

"Where'd you learn all this stuff, Cassie?" I'd started off calling her Miss Robert—I always had pretty good manners for a girl with no mother, and I believed you were more likely to get what you wanted that way—but she said I could call her Cassie.

Her eyes glinted behind the metal-frame glasses held together with white tape. "My momma taught me."

"Where'd she learn it?"

"From her daddy. He was a doctor up in Minnesota."

"That where you used to live?"

When she shook her head, the glasses slipped down her nose. She pushed them back up with her thumb. "No, I been here my whole life. My momma came here before she had me."

"How come?"

"Because my daddy was a Chippewa Indian."

I set down the scissors. "Really?"

"Yessum." She punctuated it with a little jerk of her chin. "It was a big scandal in her little town. A tempest in a teapot, she used to say."

"Because she was white?"

"Because she was white and her daddy was rich and the family was lily pure Lutherans."

"What's Lutherans?"

"It's a kind of Christian. Like Baptist or Catholic."

I dumped a spoonful of dried rosemary—what Esperanza called romero—on a white muslin square, gathered up the corners. "Like the Church of God in Jesus Christ?"

Cassie cocked her head to one side. "I don't know that particular bunch. That what your people are?"

The packet dropped from my hand, sending tiny needles everywhere. "Oh shit."

"Never mind, child. Leave 'em on the floor. When we step on them, they make the place smell good."

"So what happened with your momma?" I asked quickly.

She sighed. "Her and my daddy left North Prairie and moved down to Colorado. He was a cowboy. It was about all the work he could get. Momma started makin' the remedies she'd watched her daddy make back home, sold 'em to folks. They came down here 'cause he heard he could make better money workin' in the Bisti Oil Fields, over to Farmington. He did, too. Till a rig blew up and killed him."

"Why didn't your momma go home to Minnesota?"

"Lord, child, I don't know. I was just a little thing. Probably her family wouldn't have her back there with her half-breed daughter. She just kept sellin' her remedies, teachin' me how. Then there was some influenza goin' around and we both caught it. I got better and she didn't. I was just about your age when I lost my momma."

I thought about telling her that I didn't lose my momma. That she lost me. On purpose. But what the hell.

I picked up the scissors and started cutting again. "You ever been married?"

She looked startled for a minute, then said, "Had a man once. Railroad roustabout. Not even worth tellin'."

"What was his name?"

"Martin." She didn't look at me when she said it.

Two days turned into three. Suddenly a week was gone, and I was still there. Every night I made plans to leave the next day, promised myself I would. But every morning Cassie asked if I'd mind doing one more thing before I left—hang up some washing, deliver a medicine, water the garden. Then she'd say that I really should eat something. And then after lunch—or dinner, as she called it—the sun would beat down, till the heat shimmered off the ground in waves and she'd say that I should wait until the cool of the next morning.

Finally one night after supper, we were sitting at her table, stripping dried sage leaves off their stems, and she looked over at me. "Since you got no kin in Albuquerque, you might as well stay here awhile."

I said very businesslike, "You know I can't pay you anything."

"You could help me with the garden and deliver the medicines. If you help out, that's payment. Besides . . ." She reached into the cardboard box under the table for more muslin. "I kinda like your company, child."

six

Cassie Robert was like nobody else I'd ever encountered. She was always making her teas and cures. She had a lot of weird little poems and sayings that she muttered continually to herself. When I asked her about them, she'd say, "Oh, they're just prayers." But they weren't like any prayers I ever heard at Carson.

Weird as she was, I sort of liked her. I saw something of her in myself. Here was someone who was truly alone, like me. Had been for a long time. And she'd not only survived, but she looked to have things under control. She didn't have lots of friends hanging around, but people respected her medicine. She didn't seem to need any more than that.

Before I came to her, I didn't know that anybody still lived the way she did. Her old, three-room wooden house squatted at the end of a dusty road a couple hundred yards off the main blacktop. She said it wasn't quite three miles from Florales, but when you walked it in the midday sun, it seemed more like thirty.

She had a well for running water—although sometimes it ran kind of rusty looking. The propane gas tank out back worked the water heater and fueled the kitchen stove and a teensy refrigerator, but there was no electricity, no phone, no flush toilet. I knew what a privy was, but I'd never seen one till that morning I used hers, and the first time I had to evict a snake from the place before I could go about my business, I gave serious thought to getting back on the highway with my thumb out.

Naturally she didn't have a car. Never even drove one, she said. After I'd been there with her almost two weeks, she woke me up early one morning and we set off to Florales, dragging this old wooden wagon, to shop for supplies. That was what she called anything she couldn't grow, find, make, or get in trade for medicines.

I wasn't very excited about going to town. I was still leery of making myself too conspicuous, but she insisted that she needed my help, since she had to buy twice as much food as usual. Or maybe she was afraid if she left me there alone I'd take her money and run away.

Old Highway 323 stretched out in front of us like a black ribbon winding through an ocean of blue-green greasewood bush with islands of brown-gray grama grass, silvery chamisa, dark filigree globes of tumbleweed. Hawks floated on the thin air, hunting prairie dogs and mice. The soft breeze carried a faint smell of woodsmoke from cooking fires, the screech of a piñon jay.

Cassie wasn't one for a lot of pointless talking, and for that I was grateful. She walked silently except for the flopping legs of her baggy overalls, her eyes focused on the pavement, watching for potholes and the occasional rattlesnake, snoozing on the warm asphalt. A pickup truck honked as it sped past us and got lost in the orange ball of sun.

When we rattled into Florales, the noise of the wagon's rickety wheels seemed to echo from one end of town to the other, and the few people out on the street turned to wave when they recognized Cassie.

She gave me the grocery list and sent me into Begay's while she headed for the hardware store. Stepping over the yellow-brown dog sprawled in the doorway, I looked around the shadowy interior. Delbert, or whatever the guy's name was, was nowhere to be seen. A Navajo girl about my own age sat on a stool at the cash register head bent over a comic book, straight black hair falling around her face like a curtain.

She didn't look up when I pulled the dirty handle of an even dirtier shopping cart and started down the first aisle. I grabbed a bag of *masa*, one of sugar, a tin of coffee and four cans of evaporated milk, a box of rice, a jumbo plastic sack of pinto beans, and then headed toward the refrigerator case for a pound of bacon. There was a stack of newspapers on the floor by the dairy case, and I picked one up. I'd lost all track of time. I didn't even know what day it was.

The paper was from Española, dated Tuesday, May 27, but the pages looked yellow and tired, like they'd been here a few days. There was a big story about the ongoing drought, another about a bank robbery in Farmington. I flipped the paper over and threw it back on the stack. When I bent over to reach for a package of cheese, my eyes landed on a small headline in the lower right corner of the page, and I froze.

HUNT INTENSIFIES FOR MISSING COLORADO GIRL

I felt this tightness in my chest like I used to always feel if I got called to Ridley's office. If Cassie saw that, she'd know it was me. She'd find a way to sneak off and call the sheriff, and they'd come take me back to Carson.

Then I read the first paragraph, and my knees just about buckled from guilty relief.

> *Volunteers joined local authorities here today as efforts continued to locate little Connie Morales, the toddler who wandered away from her family's camper at Bandelier National Monument yesterday morning. With temperatures expected to dip into the thirties tonight, Sheriff Gus Gilmore voiced fears that the child may already be suffering from exposure and dehydration. . . .*

"Don't dawdle, child." Cassie's voice blared, making me drop the paper on the floor. "Put that cheddar back and grab some Long Horn. It's cheaper." She reached down for the newspaper and tossed it in the cart. "You got everything else?"

"Yes." I said weakly. "I mean no. I didn't get bacon."

She marched off toward the meat case, leaving me staring after her.

Suddenly it came to me like a singing telegram. Nobody was looking for me. They never had been.

Cassie's living was mostly in her garden, so that was where she
needed my help. Easy to see why she wanted me to stay, never mind
enjoying my company. As weeks passed and the sun moved higher in
the sky, it needed watering more often. Two barrels were supposed to
collect rainwater from the thunderstorms that weren't happening often
enough.

We used it to bathe in and wash our hair, and then we poured it,
bucket by bucket into this contraption she had rigged up with a fifty-
five-gallon drum full of stones and sand and charcoal. When it came
out the other side, it was clean enough to use on the garden. This had
to be done in the evening or early in the morning while it was still cool,
so the water wouldn't evaporate before it could soak into the ground.

Cassie showed me how to clean the kerosene lamp chimneys and
keep the wicks trimmed so they didn't smoke. How to split logs for the
woodstove and stack them on the *portal* for winter. Not that I was planning to be around that long, but I didn't mind helping her out. It was
hard work, and it felt good—the heft of the maul, the cracking sound
when the logs came apart, the dark, sharp resin smell that shot up like
a fountain.

We took turns with meals—although we were both happier when I
took her turns—and with washing clothes in the deep sink on the
porch. I always hung them on the wire line she had strung between the
house and a scraggly juniper tree, because she couldn't reach over her
head without her shoulders hurting.

There were medicinal plants in the garden, but lots more grew wild
in the low scrub hills around the house. Gathering those got to be
one of my favorite chores. We collected juniper needles and berries for

digestives and teas for pregnant women, male saltbush flowers to treat ant bites and make soap, the delicate white petals of Apache plume for upset stomach, broom snakeweed for rheumatism, big sagebrush for purification.

She taught me which plants were poisonous—like the beautiful white-flowered jimson weed and narrow-leafed milkweed. She said how it was important to take only the tops of the amaranth and bee plant greens, so the plants could keep growing. When we dug yucca roots to make shampoo, Cassie buried the seedpods, to make sure there'd always be more yucca plants.

I delivered medicine to her customers, figuring out on my own the mostly unmarked roads and rutted dirt tracks that ran around and between the low, scrub-covered hills. Sometimes they paid in cash, but more often it was eggs or fruit or a chicken or a rabbit that I hauled back home.

It bothered me, killing the animals. In fact, the first time Rick Chee gave me a rabbit I turned it loose. Its ears were soft, and when I held it against me, I could feel its heart beating about a million miles an hour, like it knew it was going to end up in Cassie's big iron pot. When I put it on the ground, it sat there and looked at me for a second, too stupid to run, or maybe too surprised. So I stamped my foot, and it took off like a shot.

When I got back to the house, Cassie was folding clean clothes. She looked up.

"What'd he give you?"

I swallowed the dust in my throat and told her the truth. I expected her to get pissed off and say I couldn't have any supper, or some such. First thing she did was laugh. Then she shook her head and said I was a "caution." Whatever the hell that meant. She didn't say anything else about it.

Later while we were eating our beans and rice—for the third night running—I started to feel pretty stupid.

I said, "I guess I shouldn't have let the rabbit go."

She set down her spoon. "There's no sin in killing for food, Avery. Truth to tell, that rabbit probably made some coyote a meal this very night, while we're eatin' beans. But that's okay. Coyote needs to eat, too."

The next time we got a rabbit, I made myself watch Cassie kill it. She was all business—just picked it up by the hind legs and clubbed it right behind the ears with the flat side of our kindling ax. It made a thunk noise and the little body went limp. Okay, so there was no pain, but when she flipped it down on the log splitter stump and chopped the head off, I had to turn around and go in the house. I couldn't look at it again till it was flour-coated and sizzling in the big iron skillet.

Eventually, my muscles stopped aching, and I could actually feel my body getting stronger. Our food wasn't fancy, but there was plenty of it, and I could tell I'd gained weight. One morning when I was yanking weeds out of the garden, I looked up to see Cassie watching me.

"Skin's gettin' dark," she said. "You got any Mexican blood in you? Or Indian?" After that first night, she'd never asked me about anything about where I came from or who my people were. She never acted like my eyes were different from anyone else's.

I sat back on my heels, making lines in the baked earth with the old trowel. "I don't know."

"Your folks never talked about their kin?"

"I never knew my folks."

She just nodded. "So you don't know who had them eyes like yours."

"No," I said. And then I got back to weeding.

It wasn't just herbs Cassie was selling. Sometimes strangers showed up at odd hours, looking for a different kind of medicine. The first time it happened, I answered the door one night after supper because Cassie was out in the garden. I was just getting used to her doing stuff like burying pieces of hair and fingernail clippings out there after dark to keep away gophers and make sure no raven got any of your hair. She said if a raven made its nest with a person's hair, that person would die young. Then, too, she'd sprinkle osha root around the house at night to repel rattlesnakes.

A woman was standing on the creaky wooden porch—not as old as Cassie, but not all that young either. She had shoulder-length brown hair and she was wearing a faded plaid shirt and black stretch pants. She seemed pretty surprised to see me.

"Is Cassie around? I need to see her right away."

I stepped back from the door, and she walked right in and sat down at the table, like she did this all the time. "I'll get her," I said.

When Cassie saw the woman sitting there, she shook her head. "Evelyn, Evelyn. Not again?"

Evelyn bit her lip and looked embarrassed. "Just this one time, Cassie. If it doesn't take, I'll leave him go." She laid a five-dollar bill on the table.

Cassie opened a cupboard and took out a cardboard box. She sat down across from Evelyn, while I hovered in the background, hoping she wouldn't notice I was eavesdropping. Cassie picked up the money and stuck it in her shirt pocket.

"Let's see, what's today? Thursday? Not good. You need to do this tomorrow. Friday night and it's a waxing moon, so that's good. If this don't work, Evelyn, it wasn't meant to be."

Evelyn kept biting her lip. It was getting red and swollen looking. "Should I come back tomorrow night?"

"No, I'll give you what you need and you can do it yourself at home. Just don't forget. Do it right after moonrise tomorrow night. If you forget, you should wait till next Friday."

Cassie took out a small white candle and gave it to her. Then she took a box and fished out two straight pins, one with a plain silver head, one with a blue head. She put them in a little brown envelope like the kind the nurse at Carson used to put pills in.

"Now, tomorrow night just after moonrise, you go out on your porch. Stick the blue pin in the candle like this, left to right. Then stick the silver one in right to left and make sure they cross. Then get you a saucer and set the candle in it and light it, and let it burn down till it goes out of its own, all the while thinking of Tommy and sending the message to come home. Then bury the pins in your garden."

"Okay, I'll do it just that way. Thank you, Cassie." She gave Cassie a little hug. "Pray for me."

"I will," Cassie said. "Now run along home. And if he comes back before tomorrow night, do the candle anyway. Can't hurt. Might help."

After she left, I glared at Cassie. "I can't believe you take somebody's money for hokey stuff like that."

She acted like she didn't hear me. She put the box back in the cupboard, pulled out an old beat-up cookie tin, and rummaged in it for a dried wand of big sagebrush that she lit off the stove. She held it under her nose and inhaled, pulling the smoke up into her nostrils while I watched, fascinated. It was something she did nearly every night after supper. "To ward off melancholy," she said. I didn't know about that part, but I'd come to love the smell of burning sage.

After one good snort, she turned her mild gaze on me. "What do you mean, hokey?"

"Lighting candles, burying pins in the garden by the light of the moon," I said scornfully. "How's that going to make some guy come home?"

"You know for certain that it won't?"

"How could it?"

She shrugged. "People been using this energy for hundreds, maybe thousands of years, Avery. Seems like if it didn't work, they'd a stopped doing it a long time ago."

She took another hit of sage smoke and closed her eyes with a small smile of contentment.

One day in August I came running into the house, my face on fire and streaked with sweat.

"Cassie, look! Old Lady Many Goats gave us peaches! We can—" The rest of the sentence evaporated in the dry air.

A stranger sat with Cassie, coffee cups on the table in front of them. Ribbons of sage smoke seemed to connect the two old faces. We stared at each other till I remembered to lower my eyes.

"Avery, this is Señora Sanchez." Señora was fat, and even though she looked as old as Cassie, her hair was black and so shiny it seemed to give off blue sparks.

"*Buenos días,* Avery." She had some missing teeth that made her lisp.

From they way she was looking me over, I knew I was the topic of the conversation that I just interrupted. Señora wiped her hand across the faded green skirt stretched tight over her thigh, and she reached out to touch my chin, tilting my face up.

"She's my *comadre.*" Cassie drank the last of the coffee from her cup. "My friend."

When Señora Sanchez started to make the sign of the cross on me, I jerked back.

Cassie got up, reached for the chipped blue enamel coffeepot on the stove. "Avery, there's clothes in the sink need hangin'." She took the sack of peaches from me and stuck her nose in it. "Mmm. Those smell just fine."

I went out to the porch. The clothes still felt soapy to me, so I filled the sink for another rinse, wrung them out, and dropped each one into the galvanized bucket. All the time, I was straining to hear the women in the kitchen. The hum of their voices came through, but I couldn't make out any words. I slipped the strap of the canvas clothespin bag over my head and took the clothes outside.

. . .

It was a warm, still morning at the end of summer that I woke up feeling something sticky between my legs. Surely to God I hadn't peed in my sleep on Cassie's couch. I yanked the covers off and my heart stopped when I saw a patch of half-dried blood on the sheet. Jesus. I touched my finger to it and sniffed it just to be sure. It was blood all right. That sick, sweet smell. I was still sitting there trying to figure out how much longer I had to live when Cassie came out, dressed for garden work in her baggy denim overalls and a high-necked white shirt.

"What's the matter, child?"

I was holding my finger out stiff, so as not to touch anything else. "I think I've got cancer."

"What?" She looked down at the sheet, then smiled broadly. "That's not cancer, Avery. Didn't anyone ever tell you about men-stru-ating?"

Immediately I felt stupid. This was what the older girls at Carson giggled and whispered and complained about in the bathroom. That was why I knew the smell. I smelled it plenty of times when I went in a stall that one of them had just used.

She beamed at me. "Your first moon cycle." When she reached out and touched my forehead, I shrank back, but she didn't seem to care. She just closed her eyes and said, "Avery James, respect your body like the blessing it is. Honor your blood that comes with the moon. Let it flow gently, without pain. Remember the circle of life you hold in you."

Then she went into the kitchen, turned on the oven, and started cutting big squares of leftover cornbread for our breakfast, humming softly to herself.

I hugged my knees to me, placing my feet carefully to avoid the reddish-brown spot. "Cassie?"

She raised her eyebrows at me over her shoulder.

"What kind of—you know—thing was that?"

"Thing?"

"You know. Prayer or whatever. I never heard anything like that in church. I mean it didn't sound very . . . Christian."

"That's because it's not."

She put the cornbread in a pan, slid it into the oven. I waited, but she didn't say anything else. That was the damnedest thing about old people. When you didn't want them to tell you stuff, they just couldn't wait to jam it down your throat. When you did want to know something, they weren't talking.

She opened the refrigerator and got out butter and milk. "I thought you weren't interested in God."

"I'm not," I said quickly. "I was just curious, that's all."

"There's other ways of thinking about God than the Church of God in Jesus way, you know. Or the Lutheran way. Or the Catholic way." She pulled two mugs out of the cupboard. "Just think, Avery—how many different kinds of Christians there are. Then you got your Hindus and your Moslems—" She waved a spoon around like she was conducting a band. "And all kinds of other religions in places you and me never heard of. And every darn one of them thinks that they're the only ones doin' it right. What's that tell you?"

"That they're all wacko." I got up and pulled the dirty sheet off the couch.

She laughed. "What else?" She edged the coffeepot under the faucet, filled it, and set it on the stove.

"I don't know."

"Every one of them outfits has got themselves a little old piece of God and they act like they got the whole thing. In the meanwhile, the real God's going about taking care of business, and not paying a bit of attention to what everybody's saying."

"So then, what difference does it make what you believe?"

She smiled. "That's your answer, same as your question."

. . .

If I was expecting any special treatment because I had got my first period, I found out different right after breakfast. I finished washing the dishes and I went and curled up on the couch with my knees tucked up to my chest to relieve the strange ache in my low abdomen.

When Cassie turned around and saw me, she said, "Don't get too comfy. We got work to do."

I shifted uncomfortably, the wad of material that she'd given me feeling like a saddle inside my underpants. "I don't feel good."

"You probably got cramps."

She put water on to boil, pulled a blue tin off the shelf, and scooped some stuff out of it into a mug. After she poured the boiling water in and let it steep for a few minutes, she added some honey and a squeeze of lemon, gave it a quick stir, and handed the cup to me.

When I brought the cup to my mouth, a pungent smell hit me. I looked at her suspiciously.

"What's in this stuff?"

"It tastes a lot better than it smells. Go on, try it. If you don't like it, don't drink it."

I held my breath and sipped cautiously. At first it was really sour, but the honey smoothed that right out, and it went down pretty easy. There was a surprising fresh aftertaste with just the tiniest tang of salt.

"Not bad," I said.

"It's better if you don't hold your breath," Cassie said.

I drank some more without holding my breath. I sloshed it around in my mouth. She was right, but I didn't have to tell her everything.

"So what do you call this stuff?"

"Women's tea."

"What's in it?"

"All kinds of things good for women."

"Like what?"

"I'll show you sometime," she said. "When you're ready."

"If I'm ready to have my period, I'm ready to know what's in some silly tea."

She narrowed her eyes at me. "Any fool can have a period, Avery. You didn't have a thing to do with it. It takes some time to become a woman."

"How old do I have to be?"

"It's not how old you are, it's what you understand."

I felt the top of my head getting warm. "Oh, bullshit."

"Nope, there's not a bit of that in it," she said.

Fifteen minutes later I was out back, turning over compost with a pitchfork, watering it, then turning it again, while Cassie pulled weeds and picked off grasshoppers that were stiff and sluggish from the cold night. Whatever was in her women's tea had made me feel pretty good in short order.

When we were walking between the rows, picking the plump, red-shouldered tomatoes and swollen green and yellow peppers, she looked over at me.

"Avery, you and me need to have a little talk."

"What about?"

"Some folks call it the birds and bees." She plucked a yellowed leaf off a bean plant and studied it. "I call it sex."

"I already know about that," I said quickly.

"If you thought blood coming from your womb meant cancer, you got some more to learn. I think we'll pick some of these green tomatoes and put them up. That way if we get an early frost . . ." She handed me her basket and said, "Put these on the *portal* and bring me an empty basket. Then you can start watering."

I picked up the old galvanized watering can and put it under the rusty fifty-five-gallon drum.

"Your cycle's based on the twenty-eight-day cycle, just like the moon. When you bleed, it means you're not pregnant. Which is what I want to talk to you about. Now that you're having these 'periods,' it means you can get pregnant—"

"Not without a guy."

She sighed and pushed the shirtsleeves up higher on her bony arms. "I see you already know this part."

"Yeah. So you don't have to worry. There's no guys hanging around me and there never will be." I pulled the cork stopper out of the drum and water began to gurgle out rhythmically, hitting the bottom of the watering can with a metallic thunk. It smelled flat and stale, but Cassie always said the plants didn't care.

"Now why would you say a thing like that?"

"Because I don't like them. And even if I did, they wouldn't notice me. Not that way. I'm too weird looking."

"You're not weird looking at all, chil—Avery. You're a pretty little thing."

"Don't you think I see how everyone looks at me?"

She sighed again, deeper this time. "I know you're probably not going to believe anything I say about this, but things will change. I guaran-dang-tee you they will. Lots of times when we're young, we only see what's on the outside of somebody. And the folks that look best to us look pretty much like ourselves—"

"Grownups look at me that way, too. Not just kids."

"Not all grownups. You get older, you're gonna meet some boys that think you're pretty nice. And that's where you need to be careful."

I folded my arms and glared at her. "Why don't you just say, 'don't have sex'?"

"For one thing, you wouldn't listen to me. For two, I done it myself, so I know how it happens. Look to your water."

I stuffed the cork back in the hole and picked up the overflowing can.

"It's a force, Avery. It's a force so powerful—well, it's what creates life. It's not to be sneezed at."

I poured some water in the shallow trench running next to the row of tomato plants, my arms shaking from the strain of holding still, pouring slow, and trying to imagine Cassie having sex. "So what's the point?"

"The point is to be careful. Think about what you're doing. And no matter what or why, take precautions. You're a smart girl, and if you work hard, you can do all kind of things. But it ain't gonna be easy if you get pregnant."

"Cassie, I'm not going to get pregnant."

"Well, then, we'll consider it settled."

She put two more green tomatoes in the full basket and shuffled off toward the house.

seven

By September I knew I was staying. We never really talked about it; it just felt okay. The only thing we disagreed on was my attendance at school. I was adamant about not going. She was equally determined that I would.

She sat down on the couch next to me. "You got to learn things I can't teach you, child. Sorry. Avery."

"Like what?"

"Like how to live in the white world."

"No, I don't." I hated the way my voice sounded—all whiny like a little kid. "I'm staying here with you. I'll be a medicine woman like you."

"No, Avery. You got your own way to go."

"You said I could stay here with you."

"You can, for now. But you won't be stayin' long."

The hair at the base of my neck began to rise. "You mean they're going to come take me back?" I tried to see her face in the shadows.

"No, it ain't that. You're just bound to go tryin' to find your momma."

I looked at her sharply. I'd never said a word to her about that.

"If I go to school, they're going to want to know where I came from," I said.

"Don't you s'pose I been thinking on that very thing? I got a plan, Avery. I'll take you to the school. I'll say you're the child of my cousin who died. I'll say I'm taking care of you now. You got no records because your momma was home schooling you." She looked pleased with herself.

"That's not going to work. Delbert knows I'm not your cousin's kid."

"Delbert keeps his own counsel, like most Navajos. He's not going to go talking about you to anyone."

"What about that Harlan guy?"

At that she laughed, loud and long. "Harlan don't care, Avery. Long as you don't get between him and his lunch. And he's such a horse's patoot, nobody pays him half a mind anyways. Most people around here are busy just trying to make a living. Once you're in school, nobody'll waste a minute wonderin' where you came from."

The uniform of the day at Florales County High School was stiff, dark new jeans, cuffs rolled up about three inches. The girls who had boobs wore sweaters or nice blouses if they could afford them. The rest of us wore whatever was on sale at Nina's Bargain Fashions. Guys weren't supposed to wear T-shirts with anything written on them like club names or beer labels, but a lot of Florales County was so poor, teachers were just happy if everyone had a shirt to wear, and as long as you didn't have things like FBI, which everyone knew meant Fucking Big Indian, on your back, you could pretty much get by.

One thing I knew for sure, it didn't matter what I wore, I'd never be like any of these kids. First, they all thought Cassie was a witch, so that meant I was the witch girl. Second, I was smarter than them. No bragging; it was just a fact. I never raised my hand in class, but the teachers called on me anyway, because they knew I'd have the answer. Or at least I'd be one of two or three who'd done the homework.

And then of course, there was my eyes.

I walked by myself, sat alone, ate lunch on a far corner of the ball field. I looked straight ahead, ignored the giggles, concentrated on the fact that I could now kill a chicken by wringing its neck quickly so there was no pain. That even though I was small, I was stronger than most of those fat Indians, quicker than the lazy Mexicans, smarter than the stupid Anglos. Eventually they'd forget about me; I'd become invisible.

For the first few weeks it worked okay.

The last Friday in September was one of those high desert autumn days when the air was so clear it made your head buzz, and the leaves of the giant cottonwood tree in front of the school burned like a gold fire.

There was a football game that night against Rio Arriba that everyone was all high about. Why, I don't know. There can't be any dumber sport in the world than a bunch of guys banging heads and chasing each other up and down that pitiful grass field after a little brown pellet.

I shouldered my backpack, pushed open the heavy door, and stepped outside. The buses were gone, but I didn't mind. I preferred walking back to Cassie's by myself in the crisp fall afternoon.

A shout of laughter drew my eyes out to the street. Two pickup trucks sat at the curb side by side, and a bunch of guys gathered in a loose knot in front of them. A couple of them still had their football uniforms on from the "spirit rally." Even the name of it was silly. It just meant everybody working themselves into a frenzy so they could kick Rio Arriba's butt tonight.

The circle of guys grew and shrunk and moved, like the amoebas we saw under the microscope in biology class, and with roughly the same IQ. Then one of them spun away, and I saw what was in the center.

His name was Jimmie John, and he was a Navajo. He was actually older than me, but he was in my class because he was what they politely called "slow." He stood there, looking goofy in his too small, faded green T-shirt. A roll of soft flesh draped over the waistband of his baggy jeans. Around him, the hard-muscle macho boys in their tight pants grinned like monkeys. He looked from one to the other, like he couldn't figure out their game.

The pretty girls sat on the low stone wall that ran across the front of the school yard, comparing fingernail polish, too cool to notice what was going on. I pushed past them and started across the street, happy to be ignored.

And then I heard Jimmie John say, "I need my book back."

"You have to say please." Kevin Gonzales, the handsomest, stupidest football player in school, held the book just out of reach.

"Please."

Kevin passed the book to Toby Jones. "Didn't hear ya."

"I said please."

"Please what? I forgot what you want."

"Please my book." Jimmie gave him a gap-toothed smile that would have broken my heart, if I had one. But I didn't, so I kept walking, but slower now.

"Please my book." Toby mimicked him and tossed the book to Josh Rainey.

"Give me," said Jimmie. His smile was fading, and I was trying not to watch.

"Please my book give me?" Josh shook his head. "Boy, you got to learn English if you're goin' to get anywhere in this world. 'Sides, you don't need this book. You can't read." He tossed it back to Kevin.

"Please give me my book."

I stopped in the middle of the street, shaking my head against memories that elbowed their way in front of me. Memories of my books hidden, my papers flushed down the toilet. Boyd Stiles and his buddies holding the flashlight just out of my reach. Anger flooded my stomach, overflowed into my chest, somehow familiar and comforting.

I wheeled around.

"Give him the goddamn book, you assholes!"

The entire group turned to stare in surprise, and for a few seconds, it was quiet. Then the morons fell out laughing.

"I said, give him the book." I was walking back now, wishing I wasn't, feeling really stupid. What was I planning to do? Martial arts?

Kevin wasn't laughing then. "Hey, Witch Girl, suck my dick."

I stopped about two feet from him.

"I hope it's bigger than your brain."

This brought on a whole new uproar. His face turned scarlet. "Fucking bitch." He took a step toward me, but somebody grabbed his arm.

"Forget it, man." It was Will Cameron. The one they called Cam. "She's not worth the trouble." The voice was good-natured, reasonable. "Save it for Rio Arriba."

Kevin hesitated. It was obviously straining his brain to decide if what he wanted to do to me would be worth the shit he'd get into. Finally his shoulders relaxed. He shook off Cam's hand and threw the book at my feet. "You give it to him. Witch Bitch."

He turned and strutted off to where the girls were sitting, and the others followed him, making stupid little kissing noises as they passed me. Except Cam. He didn't even look at me.

I picked up the book and handed it to Jimmie John, who followed me across the street. I couldn't feel my legs under me. When my chest started to ache, I realized I was holding my breath, and I let it out all at once.

"They won't bother us no more." Jimmie said cheerfully. His voice had the odd, flat intonation I always associated with Navajos speaking English. I nodded and kept walking; to my dismay, he fell into step beside me. "Want a Coca-Cola?"

"No. Thanks."

"I would buy you one."

"I have to go home," I said.

"You're my friend now."

I turned abruptly. "No, I'm not."

"Well, I'm your friend." He lumbered in silence for a few minutes, occasionally pushing the thatch of black hair off his forehead. When we passed Begay's, he peeled off like a fighter plane from formation and disappeared inside.

About a half mile outside of town, I heard this commotion like a herd of cattle stampeding behind me. I looked back, half expecting to see Kevin Gonzales and his buddies coming to beat the crap out of me. Instead, there was Jimmie John, running as fast as he could—which wasn't very fast. When he got closer, I saw that he had two Cokes in his hand. Open. They were about half empty, and he had Coke all over his arms and on his T-shirt.

Panting hard, he held one out to me. I took the warm, sticky bottle, and he grinned.

"You sure walk fast," he said.

W hen I got back to the house, Cassie was sitting at the table peeling a small apple. I poured the warm Coke down the drain and sat down across from her, watching the spiraling apple peel grow while I told her about Jimmie John.

When I finished she just shook her head. "Truth is medicine for ignorance. But there's no cure for stupidity." She sliced the apples in half and rubbed a cut lemon on them.

"And now this Indian kid thinks I'm his buddy."

Cassie sliced the apples in half and rubbed a cut lemon on them. "It's good to have people like Jimmie around."

"Why?" I sat back in the chair.

She scuffed over to the stove, turned on the heat under the skillet, and dipped two spoons of sugar out of a mason jar. "Keeps you from feelin' too sorry for yourself."

She dumped the fruit in and stirred gently with a bent wooden spoon, and the heavenly smell of caramelized apple began to fill the room. After a bit she scooped the apples into two dishes and we sat at the table in the long afternoon sun, eating our snack. When we were finished, she pushed her chair back and went over to the door. She lifted something off a hook in the wall and brought it back to the table, holding it out to me. It was a leather cord. When she slipped it over my head, I saw the small, rough oval of blue stone, veined with a goldish green.

"What's that?"

"Turquoise. To protect you," she said. Then she closed her eyes.

"In this stone, before my eyes,
Bless and make its power rise.
She who wears it, safe is she.
This I ask, so may it be."

"You really believe that?"

"It's turquoise." Like she thought I didn't hear her the first time. "A circle stands for all creation, child. A circle within a circle like this . . ." she fingered the stone, "makes it double powerful."

I held it up in front of my face, rubbing it between my fingers. It was cool and smooth. "Where'd you get it?"

"It was waiting for me in the desert," she said.

"You mean you found it someplace?"

"No, I mean it was waiting for me. I was walking in a place where I'd never usually go, and it was because I was meant to have this stone. And now you need it, so it's meant to be yours."

I rolled my eyes. "Cassie, sometimes don't you think things just happen?"

"Nothing just happens. You think your coming to me was an accident?"

"What else? You just happened to be walking out of the store when I was running away from Harlan."

"Oh, Avery, don't you see the plan in it? I needed someone to help me. You needed a home. You think it's happenstance that I stepped out that door at that very moment?"

I started to take the necklace off and tell her she might as well keep it because nothing short of a well-placed hand grenade would protect me if Kevin Gonzales decided to kick my ass, but she looked so serious and intent. And no one else had ever wanted to protect me from anything before.

The next morning when I got to the end of Cassie's dirt road, Jimmie John was standing there, waiting to walk to school with me. That afternoon he was waiting outside the school doors to walk home. And the next day. And the one after that, till finally we became friends by default. We had nothing in common except that neither of us had any other friends—me being the witch girl and him being the retard.

He was always bringing me junk. Rocks, mostly, but sometimes it would be a piece of glass worn smooth by wind and sand, a twisted chunk of metal, a Y-shaped twig from a cottonwood branch with a few shriveled leaves still clinging to it.

He was most proud of the gearshift knob. It was teardrop shaped, but flat on one end, like a Hershey's Kiss. The other end was threaded where it would screw on to the stick shift. It was a pretty turquoise blue and on the flat side, under a thick round of clear plastic, the gear diagram was etched in black, like a little map: R, N, 1, 2, 3.

I was reluctantly and oddly touched by these offerings, but I didn't have a lot of storage space. I put the rocks in the garden, and Cassie gave me an old metal cook pot to hold the rest. I kept it on the floor next to the couch.

It was a funny thing about JJ. Sometimes he'd ask me to help him with homework. We'd sit at Cassie's table, while he stared unblinking at whatever he was having trouble with until I lost patience and ended up doing it myself. But one thing he knew was the stories his grandmother had been telling him since he was born, and he could recite from memory without any hesitation or stumbling about how Changing Woman created the Dineh from the dust of her own skin and how the Twins killed Yeitso the giant and how Coyote got to marry the maiden.

He also told me about his mother. How she loved the *todilhil*— water of darkness, as the Navajos called booze—and it made her sick. So he spent a lot of time at his grandmother's hogan, past Cassie's place by another mile or so. And he had his Black Mesa clan—aunts, uncles, cousins, et cetera. Navajos are big on this.

Of course, the shitheads at school liked to think I was laying down for him, which was pretty funny. He was big as a grizzly bear and he would've crushed me, not to mention that he was totally nonsexual. I don't think he knew there was anything else you could do with a penis besides pee. That didn't stop Kevin and his buddies from making little sucking noises when we walked by or poking their fingers in their mouths and bulging their eyes.

At those times, I didn't see how I could wait three more years to get out of Florales. But then I'd remember that was how I'd felt about Carson, too. I thought if I could just get away from there, things would be different. And here I was doing the same things, listening to the same whispers, the same laughter, seeing the same looks on their faces.

October.
The air was noticeably thinner, sharper. I slept with the blankets tucked under my chin, one arm thrown back over my head. Cassie's hand on my shoulder in the early morning darkness caused me to sit up abruptly, fully awake. I never liked being touched while I was asleep.

"Time for school?" I squinted at her.

"Not today," she said.

I pulled my knees to my chest, looping my arms over them. "What then?"

"Dress warm."

"Why?"

"We're off to the mountains. We got harvesting to do."

I slid out of the blankets. "Harvesting?"

"Can't stand around jawin', child. Señora Sanchez'll be here soon."

"Why does she have to go?"

Cassie laughed. "She's probably wonderin' why you have to go."

"She makes me feel funny. Like she's always watching me." I stepped into my old, soft jeans and pulled a long-sleeved T-shirt over my head, then a sweater.

"Probably 'cause she is."

"What's she watching for? She think I'm going to take off and fly?"

"You can ask her later. Now get busy and brush your teeth."

Amalia Sanchez drove the hulking brown pickup truck like she was born in the driver's seat. One hand on the steering wheel, elbow resting on the open window. The other hand draped over the black shift knob. She and Cassie shoehorned themselves into the cab, chattering in Spanglish. Their laughter pealed out across the desert.

I rode in back with the gear, periodically slammed against the rear window of the cab, choking in the clouds of dust that the truck kicked up.

I wasn't unhappy about going camping with them, but Cassie was so big on school, I couldn't imagine why she would let me miss. All I could figure was that maybe she didn't trust me. Maybe she still thought I'd take her money and run away.

At the Florales River, we veered northwest off the highway onto a narrow, unmarked strip of pavement that burrowed into the foothills of the San Juans. I leaned against Cassie's bedroll, letting the sun warm my face and watching the landscape of greasewood bush and chamiso give way to dark clumps of piñon and juniper nestled in the folds of the hills. Higher up the flanks of the mountains, splashes of yellow and orange signaled stands of aspen. There were other pickups on the road, heading in the same general direction, back ends sagging from the weight of dogs, children, tools, camping gear.

Each time Amalia pulled out to pass one, there was a moment of stillness—it felt like paralysis—in the path of oncoming traffic. I closed my eyes and imagined the sickening impact, broken glass, twisted metal, blood on the pavement. Then the engine would groan, dig in, and we'd fly past the other truck, Amalia honking and waving.

After a while, we turned due west on an unpaved road, leaving the other vehicles behind. When the truck's bald tires finally slid to a stop at the edge of a small canyon, I was thirsty, covered with dust, and bruised from the bouncing around. All business now, the two women jumped down, moving quickly to unload the gear and set up a campsite.

Cassie handed me a pair of old canvas gloves. "We'll need a good pile of firewood. Why don't you stack it by them rocks." As I wandered off into the trees, she called, "Mind where you put your hands and feet."

All day long we gathered the small piñon cones, stopping only briefly for apples and water. Some cones were on the ground, some still clung to the branches. Amalia knocked the tiny brown nuts out, her hands greased to avoid the sticky pitch. The cones that hadn't yet opened we put into sacks to take home and lay out in the warm autumn sun. She showed me how to find and loot the *ratoneras,* the leaf-and-stick-covered caches of industrious little mice who stockpiled the nuts for the winter.

Cassie disapproved of this practice. "Mice worked for their *piñones,*" she said. They argued stubbornly for a few minutes, then compromised by taking only half the nuts. From the relaxed sound of their bickering, I figured that they had this same discussion every year.

When the sun was low in the sky, they tied the ends of the bags shut and threw them in the truck bed. Cassie dug a pit, started a fire with some of the empty, pitchy cones, and began heating a cooking pot full of oil. Meanwhile Amalia took the top off a plastic tub that probably once held margarine, but now held flour. With her fingers, she scooped Crisco from a can, working it into the flour. When it was crumbly like coarse meal, she added water, little by little, from a can that had sat on a rock in the sun all day. Dough emerged between the stubby brown fingers.

She kneaded it on a plastic plate and divided it into six pieces, humming tunelessly to herself.

She looked up at me. "A stick would be good, *niña.*" She held her hands about a foot apart to indicate length.

When I brought back a slender twig, stripped clean of leaves, there were six flat rounds of dough on the plate, each with a hole in the middle. Hooking the stick through the holes, Cassie dropped them, two at a time in the hot fat, turning them till they were golden.

Amalia smiled at me, patting the blanket on the ground with her chubby hand. I sat down. When the bread was done, Cassie wrapped it in a scarf and set it on a rock near the fire while Amalia heated beans and Cassie chopped peppers and tomatoes and crumbled *queso fresco*. I lay back on the blanket, eyes shut, drifting at the edge of sleep. The smell of the fry bread mingled with piñon juniper smoke and their voices were like the soft buzzing songs of insects, telling stories—the ones about *brujas* (witches) and magic.

Actually Amalia was doing most of the talking. Cassie talked offhandedly about magic all the time, but I don't think she actually believed all the spooky stuff about witches changing themselves into coyotes who can run beside your truck at night doing fifty miles an hour and you don't dare stop because they'll kill you. Amalia swore she had seen them. I shuddered, remembering how JJ told me the Navajos believed that just saying the wrong thing can draw evil to you.

At Carson, they taught us that Christians didn't believe all that superstitious nonsense. But they had their own stories—Jonah and the whale, Noah's ark, loaves and fishes—that seemed just as far-fetched to me. I always figured the best thing to do was act like you believe everything, but don't believe anything.

After dinner there was coffee. Amalia pulled out her pipe, filled it, tamped it down, and lit it with a stick from the fire, drawing deeply. She passed it to Cassie and they smoked, absorbed in their pleasure, barely noticing when I left the circle to pee behind a rock.

Starting back from the darkness, I stopped, struck by the picture they made. Two old women, wrapped in their blankets, white pipe smoke curling up around the darker smoke from the fire like a climbing vine. Orange flames flickered up through the trees, silhouetted black against the midnight blue sky.

Amalia's eyes were closed, but she heard me come back and sit down next to Cassie.

"Avery," she said without opening her eyes. "What will you do after school?"

"I don't know. Maybe go to Santa Fe."

They looked at each other and then Cassie said, "Why Santa Fe?"

"I don't—I'm not sure."

Amalia took the pipe from Cassie and drew on it slowly. "There are good *curanderas* in Santa Fe. My sister could tell us."

I looked at Cassie. "What are you talking about?"

"Amalia thinks you have a gift," she said.

"You have the sight, *niña*."

"No, I don't. It's just that my eyes are weird."

Amalia smiled. "There is nothing wrong with your eyes. I was born with a veil on my eyes. My *tia* Yolanda, she cried in her mother's womb. These things are signs, *niña*. Your eyes are a sign that you have the *don*, the gift—"

"I do not!" I dug my heel into the blanket. I didn't say what I was thinking, which was, *If I have this stupid "sight," why have I never been able to see my mother?*

Cassie turned to look directly at me. "Don't you sometimes know things and can't figure out where the knowing came from?"

"No," I said.

"There are dreams," Amalia said.

"I don't have dreams."

Cassie picked up a long stick and poked at the fire until the top log rolled, turning its flaming belly up to the sky. "But we have dreams about you, Avery."

"So what?"

She drank the last of her coffee and set the cup on a flat rock. "Sometimes when a person refuses what comes to them, why then, that knowledge has to go someplace else. Other folks start picking it up. I felt that power in you as soon as we met, Avery."

"It is a gift from God," Amalia said.

"Well, He can have it back."

Amalia looked about to scold me, but Cassie cut her off. "What you do with it's up to you. But there's no denyin' that you got it."

Snow came the Tuesday before Thanksgiving. I sat in the stuffy classroom after lunch, listening to people cough, smelling their menthol cough drops, watching the first big, wet flakes dissolve into the pavement. By the time JJ and I were heading out of Florales, the snow was clinging to our coats and frosting the adobes till they looked like a Santa Fe Christmas card. Gray slush clumped on the side of the road, and then the flakes started coming down so thick and fast the horizon disappeared.

We stopped at Cassie's road, and I said, "Can you find your grandmother's place okay?"

I don't know why I even bothered to worry. JJ wasn't mighty of brain, but he had some kind of homing device inside his head. He wandered all over the desert between his clan's houses and he never got lost.

He grinned at me, black hair plastered to his forehead like bars on a jail window.

"JJ, where's your hat?"

He pulled it out of his pocket, the red stocking cap Cassie had knitted for him. "Don't want to get it all wet," he said. "Bye now." He turned and walked into the swirling white wind, waving over his shoulder.

Cassie didn't celebrate Thanksgiving like other people. She said she didn't believe in spending one day doing what you should be doing all the time. Holidays didn't mean a lot to me either.

Thanksgiving dinner with Cassie consisted of beef stew with cornmeal dumplings, and it was better than any turkey I ever had. For dessert, there was vinegar pie with roasted piñones. Afterward we washed up, and then settled in by the woodstove, drowsy and stuffed.

I was doing about half a job of reading *A Tale of Two Cities,* which I was supposed to write a paper on before the semester ended, and Cassie took up some mending work, holding it at arm's length to focus on the tiny stitches. She kept telling me I needed to learn to sew, if only to do repairs, but up to that point, I'd managed to avoid it.

I was nodding off again when she set down her work and said, "What's your birthday, Avery?"

"December fifteenth, I think. Nobody knew for sure."

"Probably a bit later than that, if you was four weeks when they found you. Maybe like the twenty-first."

I closed the book in my lap and looked over at her. "It was just a guess. What difference does it make? They're not going to make it a national holiday."

"December twenty-first is the winter solstice," she said.

"What's that?"

"It means standing-still sun." She looked out the window into the dark. "It's the day every year when the sun's furthest away from the earth. The shortest day. And the longest night."

"I don't see what that's got to do with my birthday—"

"Be more 'n happy to tell you, if you quit interruptin' me." She took a sip of coffee and made a face. "Put the pot on, please, child. This is stone cold."

While I filled the pot with water and put it on the stove, she launched into a long, rambling story about ancient people being afraid the sun would go away and never come back, so on the longest night there were all kinds of ceremonies designed to convince the sun to come back.

I sat back down by the woodstove and pulled up the blanket to cover my legs. "You been listening to Delbert Begay too much," I said.

She frowned. "Got nothin' to do with Delbert. I'm not talkin' about just Indians. People all over the world doin' the same thing at the same time. Don't that strike you as more than a coincidence?"

"Never thought about it."

"It's a powerful day," she said.

"A day is a day. They're all alike."

A soft sigh. "Not by a long shot. There's forces in the earth, Avery. To make plants grow and animals be born. Seasons die and change. Wind and clouds and rain and fire—"

She got up to scoop the coffee into the boiling water. The can opener made a plonking noise in a new can of milk. "A person born in that time when the forces are strong, well, it'd be only natural for 'em to be a tad different."

I thought about this for a few minutes. "So what do you know that I was supposed to know? Does it have anything to do with my mother?"

She looked stern. "It don't work that way, Avery. You got a gift, but you have to accept it. Take the responsibility that goes along with it. Treat it with respect. If you want the knowledge it brings you, you got to work for it. Like making a living. You can't refuse to work at it, then expect other folks to give you their money."

I looked down at my book again. "I don't really care. I don't believe in things I can't see, anyway."

I could feel her eyes on me. "You ever seen the ocean?"

"No, but—"

"Me neither. But I'm pretty dang sure it's out there."

eight

Floyd Chamaco owned Florales Hardware. Tall and bony, big knuckled. Mouth thin and straight, always had stubble on his chin. Smelled like a goat. The way he looked at me—at all the girls—made you want to go take a bath.

It was bad enough going there with Cassie, but sometimes she sent me by myself to get something while she was off on another errand. I always tried to find whatever we needed without asking him for help, because if he got you back between the aisles at the end of a row, he'd stand too close and accidentally brush against you. Cassie snorted when I complained about him.

"World's full of people, Avery. You got to learn to handle all kinds. Just don't let anyone do you bad."

One day in the summer before my senior year I walked in alone, and I saw right away another reason to hurry up and get out of there. Will Cameron was squatting on the floor in front of a row of shelves, sifting through a bin full of bolts.

He was the one who'd kept Kevin from pulverizing me that day in the street, and he was the only person at school besides Jimmie John who ever said hi when I saw him in the hall or in the cafeteria. We'd been in lots of classes together ever since I came to Florales. Sometimes I could feel him looking at me and when I looked up, he'd smile, and I'd look away. It got to be almost a game.

He wasn't handsome, but he had these blue-gray eyes like the sky when a storm's just breaking up. Not that I spent a lot of time looking at his eyes. I just happened to notice them once, that's all.

He didn't play sports or belong to any of the Mickey Mouse

groups like 4-H or Chess Club that met in the afternoons after class. His family owned the Cameron Ranch, which was pretty famous for their cutting horses, so most days by three-fifteen, he was gone. Back to the ranch, mucking out stalls or whatever you have to do on a ranch.

During long sleepy afternoons I'd stare out the study hall window and daydream about those horses. About watching him ride one, the way cowboys do, cutting out the cows that have to be branded from the rest of the herd. It seemed absolutely real, like if I went outside and looked on the ground, I'd see hoofprints and horse shit.

I started past the aisle where he was, figuring he didn't see me, but he said, "Hi, Avery," and smiled without looking up.

I said hi and kept walking. Past the screwdrivers and wrenches, past the different hammers and utility knives and saws, back to where the different sizes of twine and rope sat in neat stacks off by themselves. I measured the three yards of nylon cord that Cassie wanted and took it up to where Floyd sat perched on his stool.

"That it?" he said.

I practically threw the money at him, grabbed my sack, and headed for the door.

"You want your receipt?"

"No thanks." I didn't look back.

When I heard footsteps coming behind me, my grip tightened on the brown paper bag.

"You might need it. If you want to return anything." The voice was Will's. I never thought of him as Cam. Since we weren't friends officially. I wondered what it would be like to have a nickname that wasn't insulting, like Witch Girl. For one thing, it meant that people liked you.

He was walking next to me, acting completely normal and relaxed, and all of a sudden, I was having trouble breathing. He took the bag from my hand, dropped the receipt in it, and handed it back to me.

"Thanks."

"No problem." His boots made a hollow tapping sound on the section of sidewalk where a gaping hole was covered with planks. "School starts in a couple weeks.

"Yeah." The word cracked in my dry mouth.

"Guess I'll see you then."

"Okay." I could only look at him sideways. He was looking down the street and I noticed his nose was a little bit crooked, like maybe it was broken once. Suddenly I was imagining this whole story about him getting in a fight with one of his brothers. He looked over at me and grinned, white teeth against his tan face, then he turned on his boot heel and walked back toward the hardware store.

When I looked up, I saw Cassie in the doorway of Mami's Café, talking to Anna Marion and pretending like she wasn't watching.

The snake bit me because I broke the rules Cassie'd taught me. Watch where you put your hands and feet. Don't gather wood in the dark.

But I was in a hurry and it was cold, and it was just the woodpile on our back porch. I even hesitated like you do when you're about to do something you know is wrong, but you think this one time won't hurt. So just about when I'd decided that this one time wouldn't hurt, I heard the warning. It started with three slow *crick, crick, cricks,* like a Spanish dancer warming up, and accelerated into a nonstop warning rattle. Instead of freezing the way Cassie always said to do, I jerked my hand back, but the snake was lots quicker than me.

At first I didn't feel it and then I did. My inner arm about six inches above the wrist started to tingle and burn.

"Shit!" I swore, backing slowly away from the woodpile. I stared at the two beads of blood, embarrassed at my stupidity. Then I ran inside. Cassie was stirring a pot of beans that simmered with a ham hock on the stove. She turned off the flame.

"Damnation, child!" It was the first and only time I ever heard her swear.

She ran into her bedroom and came back with a small white cardboard box. "I don't s'pose you got a look at him?"

I shook my head. At the kitchen sink, she let it bleed into the drain, then washed my arm with soap and water.

"Do you have to cut me?" I remembered seeing that in a movie once. They cut an X over the puncture marks and this guy sucked out the venom.

"Course not." She held my arm up to the light, peering at the red place that was beginning to swell. "Sit." She motioned to a chair at the kitchen table. "Let your arm hang down at your side."

My throat tightened with fear. Or was it poison? From the box, Cassie took a white tube with a suction cup on one end, placed it over the bite and pumped. Other than a slight sucking, I felt nothing but the throb of the wound.

"Cassie, am I—will I die?"

She rolled her eyes. "Lord, no, child. You're far too ornery for that. The snake might, though."

She was trying to make me laugh, but I could tell by her jerky movements as she grabbed her black quilted jacket from its hook and the way she didn't meet my eyes that she was worried.

"Where are we going?"

"You're not going anywhere. You're going to sit right in this chair."

"Should I lay down?" I asked.

She shook her head vigorously. "Keep the bite lower than your heart. And don't . . ." She was unwinding the stretchy bandage that she sometimes wore on her right wrist, then rewinding it around my arm a couple inches above the bite. "Don't take this off. No walking around. I'm goin' to get Amalia." And she was out the door.

If I'd thought hard enough about it, I would've been a lot more scared than I was. Here was Cassie, this old lady, running off in the dark to Amalia's a couple miles away. She could fall and break her leg. She could have a heart attack or get hit by a car as she dashed along the road. She could lie in the desert all night and not be found. Even if somebody found her, they wouldn't know about me sitting primly in my chair, arm resting carefully on the table, inflated with poison.

Even if nothing happened and she got there okay, how long would it take? How long did I have? I felt almost like crying, but it seemed pointless, not to mention shameful. For the first time in my life, my fate was truly bound up with someone else's. It was a strange and unpleasant sensation.

Rattlesnake bites were common enough around Florales that I'd heard talk. I knew that most people didn't die from them, but I also knew that being small, I had more to worry about than a normal-sized person getting the same amount of venom. I'd heard people say that it was bad to get all upset and scared, because the faster your heart was beating, the faster the poison would circulate.

I looked cautiously over at the wound, now fiery red and puffy. My arm was starting to tingle. From poison or just from holding it still for so long. How long? How long had Cassie been gone?

Finally I heard Amalia's truck rattling down the arroyo. In the next minute she and Cassie burst in the door, followed by a man. He pushed past them and came close to me, lifting my arm, touching the area around the puncture with surprisingly gentle fingers. He peered into my face, pulled up my eyelids, and beamed a tiny flashlight in my eyes.

I squinted at the light.

"How ya doin', Avery?" I could tell he wasn't expecting an answer. He had bushy eyebrows and dark stained teeth, and his breath stank of tobacco. Without another word, he picked me up and carried me outside to a dirty white car. He put me in the front seat, Cassie and Amalia climbed in back, and we took off in a spray of gravel and dust.

When we got out to the main highway, I asked him where we were going.

"Darby," he said. He never took his eyes off the road as his foot pressed down on the accelerator and the orange bar inched across the speedometer past 50, 55, 60.

"How come?" I didn't know exactly how far Darby was, but I thought it was a pretty good ways from Florales.

"Because that's the closest clinic with antivenin. How you feelin'?"

"Like I might puke."

"Amalia, give her one of those blue things." The blue thing turned out to be a cold pack. "Hold it on your forehead," he said. My arm felt like a roasting hot dog being held by tongs over a flame. That's where I would have liked to put the ice, but I did what he said.

Cassie and Amalia murmured in the backseat, but I couldn't make sense of anything. Little orange and purple shapes like puzzle pieces hovered in front of my eyes, and when I blinked they fell away, to be replaced by others. The headlights searched for something to illuminate in the endless black tunnel we were speeding through. I lost all track of time, all sense of the wheels on the road; it seemed like we were flying, and I kept expecting one of Amalia's shapeshifting coyotes to appear and claim me.

I wasn't exactly asleep when the car stopped under some bright yellow lights, but I don't remember much about what happened. I was in a big bed and there were nurses in white gowns that rustled coolly. When they stuck needles in my arm I knew it should hurt, but I couldn't feel it. I remember Cassie's face hovering over me in a blue cloud, then her hand on my forehead. I could see her mouth moving.

Another nurse was coming with a needle, but instead of sticking it in me, she shot it into a brown tube that was hanging next to me. I was afraid that if I fell asleep I might never wake up, but my eyelids kept falling and every time it got harder and harder to open them, till I didn't care if I died or not, I couldn't force them open again.

I dreamed. Not the old bad dreams I was used to having, the one about falling down the stairs into the dark or the one about running from something in the dark. These were new and more frightening. I was in water. It was dark and cold and I couldn't breathe. I could see something white above me and I kept trying to grab it and pull myself up, but my arm hurt so bad I couldn't grip anything. There was something over my mouth, and my chest burned like fire.

I opened my eyes to find my hair splayed over my face. It wasn't going to suffocate me, but I couldn't get it off. My snakebit arm was too painful and swollen to move, and the other one was taped to a board with a needle stuck in it. I jerked my head back and forth, trying to shake the hair away, and then a cool hand pushed the strands of hair back from my forehead. When it was off my eyes, I didn't see anyone. Not Cassie or Amalia. No nurses.

It was still dark, and I wondered what time it was. I started to call for a nurse, but the sound died in my throat. A woman was standing in the doorway. She was wearing a black dress with white sleeves. The multicolored beads on her dress caught the dim light from the hall and made it sparkle. She had long black hair and her face was shadowed. I figured she was an angel, and that seeing her meant I was going to die. Except I didn't think angels wore black, so maybe she was a bad angel and I was going to Hell for not believing. I stared harder, trying to see her face, but I couldn't. She just stood there like she was watching me.

All at once I knew, and the knowing made the hair rise up all over my head.

She was my mother.

I must have shut my eyes for a second with the effort of trying to sit up, and when I opened them again, she was gone.

Two days later I was back at Cassie's. She wouldn't let me do anything except sit in bed and read while she and Amalia watched me for signs of serum sickness—rashes and hives—and chanted over me.

Poison, come out of the blood, into the flesh
Come out of the flesh, and upon the skin,
Off the skin and into the hair,
Out of the hair, into the air.
Sink from the air into dry sand.
Go disappear into the land.

After a couple days of this, I was going nuts, but they said if I didn't behave they'd send me back to the hospital, so I tried to ignore them and concentrate on whatever book I was reading. Out of self-defense, I started reading out loud to them. They liked it, and it kept them from chanting nonstop.

We plowed through *Anna Karenina,* which I was supposed to have read over the summer for senior English. To my surprise, they loved it, and they both bawled like babies at the end when she threw herself in front of the train.

Personally, I thought it was a fitting end for someone who abandoned their child to run off with a lover.

By the time I went back to school, the wound was small enough to be covered by a gauze patch taped to my arm. I wore it proudly, my medal of honor.

I read one time that the reason cannibal tribes eat their enemies isn't so much a taste for human flesh, but because they want to take their enemies' characteristics, their bravery, skill, cunning. In that same sort of way, I felt altered by my encounter with the snake. Stronger, less worried that I wasn't like the others. More accepting of myself, where I came from, what I might become. I hesitated to call it "optimistic," because that was one thing I'd never been, but I allowed myself to be a little bit hopeful.

As for the other thing—seeing my mother—I kept that locked away in a secret part of my mind. When I did think about her, it was more to puzzle over why she suddenly appeared that night—never before or since. It would have been nice to believe that we had some kind of psychic link and she showed up because I was in trouble, but I figured that was pushing it.

And it wasn't like I got a good look at her. I could've probably still passed her on the street and not known it. The whole encounter was sort of indirect, like something you see in a mirror, something standing behind you, and when you turn around to look at it straight on, it disappears. So I didn't tell Cassie, but sometimes I'd catch her looking at me and I'd wonder if she knew.

No matter how different I felt, in reality, nothing had changed. Everyone had heard about my run-in with the snake. Jimmie John asked me if the snake had told me anything. There was apparently a legend about witches kissing a snake who was really Satan, so that's what I'd been supposedly doing. And of course, the fact that I survived was taken as further proof that I was a witch girl.

nine

When Amalia invited us to go to the *posada* with her family, I was torn. In most ways, the less I had to do with other people, the happier I was. I didn't need anyone but Cassie. Actually I didn't even need her, but we'd sort of gotten used to each other.

On the other hand, there was this feeling that crept up on me once in a while. In Alamitos, I used to walk along Selden Street in the early winter darkness, when I could see in the lighted windows of the houses—pictures on the walls and mothers cooking dinner and kids with TV shadows flickering on their faces. Sometimes I let myself believe that if I could just live in a house like that and have my own family, I could get to be like those people.

Even then I must have known better, but whenever something came up like this *posada* thing, there was a part of me that wanted to fit myself into it. So when Cassie told me we were invited, I sat on the fence.

"I don't care," I told her. "We can go if you want." I didn't really think she would because she was definitely not into the Christian thing.

"All right then, we'll go." She gave me one of her sly looks. "Food's always good."

Esperanza had told me all about *posadas* in the village where she came from down by the border. It was an old Christmas custom for the people of a church to gather on an evening during Advent to reenact Mary and Joseph's search for shelter.

When Amalia picked us up at 6:00 P.M. it was already dark and very cold, with a dry, keening wind out of the west. She and Cassie gossiped all the way down the valley. We had to park a long way off and walk down a winding dirt lane to the little pink church of San Seferino because so many people had showed up for the *posada*. We met up with Amalia's daughter Juanita and her family in the parking lot, and I was surprised to see a lot of kids from school milling around. Cassie and I walked with Amalia and Juanita and her two youngest kids while Raphael and the three older ones trailed along behind into the church.

Juanita muttered darkly about *turistas* coming to the *posada* or locals coming just for the free food. I shot a guilty look at Cassie, but Amalia hushed her daughter.

"It doesn't matter why they come, *mija*. Only that they are here."

After the mass was said and the offering baskets got handed around, and everyone said their *Demos gracias a Dios,* we all filed outside where two men with guitars were playing songs that I figured had to be Mexican Christmas carols because I'd never heard any of them before. People gathered in little clumps and moved from group to group, greeting friends. Children ran and laughed until they got shushed by their parents.

Then all of a sudden a donkey appeared out of nowhere, ridden by a girl who looked about thirteen. She had on jeans and a heavy coat and a long white scarf draped over her head. The donkey was led by a bearded guy who looked like he'd rather be at some biker bar down in Española. He wore a serape over his shoulders, and his long hair was held in place by a scarf rolled and tied around his forehead.

With Mary and Joseph leading the way and the musicians right behind them, everyone else fell into line and began to walk slowly down the narrow blacktop, singing. The night was clear and moonless, so the stars winked overhead like thousands of eyes. I forgot about being cold and hungry as I fell into the swaying rhythm of the guitars and voices.

We stopped at four or five houses, each time the guitarists stepping up on the *portal* and singing the *posada* song, which began, *"En nombre del cielo, os pido posada."* In the name of heaven, I ask of you shelter. The door would open a bit, and from inside other voices answered, *"Aquí no es mesón. Sigan adelante."* This is not an inn. Move along, you. And we would move along, now joined by at least some of the people from that house.

Finally we came up to the community center building across from Lupe's Coin Laundry, and this time when the singers asked for shelter, the doors opened wide and those inside sang, *"Entren santos peregrinos!"* Enter, holy pilgrims.

As I stood with Cassie and Amalia waiting for the crowd to funnel through the narrow door, I heard a snort behind me. I turned around.

Stacey Lord shook her long blond hair and whispered, "Hey, look out. It's the witch's daughter."

Randi Klein said, "I didn't know they let witch girls in church."

Giggles all around. "Don't piss her off, Klein. She'll make your hair fall out."

Cassie was seemingly in the middle of talking to Amalia, so I don't know how she could possibly have heard them, but she suddenly wheeled, her long shawl flying, and fixed them with her fiercest old lady stare. No words were necessary. They eased themselves out of line and disappeared while I bit my tongue so as not to laugh.

No wonder they thought she was a witch.

Every available surface in the huge room was decked out with sweet-smelling evergreens and red plastic bows. At one end a fire burned in a fireplace big enough to stand up in. On the opposite wall, tables sagged under the weight of the feast prepared by the parish women—pots of *posole* and green chile stew, pans of tamales, enchiladas smothered in white and yellow cheese, beef with hot red chile, platters of ham and roasted chickens, baskets of tortillas and bread, washtub-sized bowls of salad. One whole table was covered with desserts—*capirotada* and *bizco-chitos,* puffy *buñuelos* drifting in sticky brown syrup, chocolate cake, raisin and walnut pie, cookies covered with colored sugar.

The priest was invited to begin and everyone else lined up behind him, holding their plates out to be filled, then finding seats somewhere among the rows of long tables with benches and folding chairs. Between us—Cassie and me, Amalia, Juanita and Rafael, and the five kids—we took up a whole table. I was glad that I didn't have to sit with anyone I didn't know.

As people warmed up, shed their coats, and filled their stomachs, their voices got louder and more expansive. Pretty soon you couldn't have heard a gunshot in the room. Children ran around playing tag, screaming and laughing, wound up like tightly coiled springs with the excitement of Christmas and the sugary desserts. I was dimly aware that the guitarists were playing again, and around them people were dancing.

Amalia and Juanita and Cassie were gossiping about people in town; Rafael had gone outside to smoke (and probably drink) with his *compadres;* the kids were off with their friends. Suddenly the noise and the heat and the loneliness hit me all at once. I stood up and pushed my way through the crowd and out into the cold night.

When the door banged shut behind me, it all vanished like it had been sucked out of the atmosphere by some monster vacuum cleaner. All I could hear was the low voices of men gathered near their trucks. I drew in a lungful of the crisp air, scented with wood smoke, and pulled my coat around me. Down at the end of the building in a circle of white rocks was an old buckboard wagon. There was a metal marker on the ground, but I couldn't read it in the dark. It probably said STAY OFF THE WAGON. I climbed up and settled myself on the wide wooden seat.

This would be my last Christmas in Florales. It would be hard to leave Cassie, but I felt like I had no choice if I ever wanted to make any kind of life for myself. If I stayed here, I'd always be the witch girl. In a city as big as Albuquerque, no one would care that I didn't know who my mother was. People would be too busy with their own problems to worry that my eyes didn't match.

"Avery, hi." I turned abruptly. It was Will Cameron. "What are you doing here?"

"Cassie wanted to come," I said.

He held out his hand, full of *bizcochitos,* and I took one. It was warm and damp from his hand. "You want some punch or something?"

"No, thanks."

"Where's JJ?"

I looked at him sharply. "He's a Navajo. What would he be doing at a *posada*?"

He dusted off his hands and thrust them down into the pockets of his jeans. "I guess I'm just used to seeing him wherever you are."

I couldn't think of anything to say.

"He really likes you, I guess."

"I'm the only person in school that treats him like a human being."

He rocked forward onto the balls of his feet, then back on his heels. "You ever been to one of these things before?"

"No."

The shadow of his Stetson falling across his face made him look handsome and slightly mysterious. "We've been every year since I can remember. We used to come with my grandparents. When I was a little twirp." He hesitated. "My grandma was Spanish."

Since I had no family stories to share, I didn't say anything. He stood beside the wagon awkwardly. The crunching of the cookie between my teeth sounded like gravel under car wheels.

"You cold?" he asked.

"No."

"You're kind of a funny girl," he said.

"So why aren't you laughing?"

"Not that kind of funny. Not funny at all, really." He put one boot up on the metal step and climbed in beside me, easing himself down on the bench. "Just different."

"I'm the witch girl."

"Why are you so scared to be with anybody?" His voice was quiet.

I looked up at the stars that gleamed like chips of ice. "I'm not scared. I just don't like people, that's all."

"Nobody?" The bench creaked as his weight shifted slightly.

"Nobody."

"Even me?"

I turned, angry. "Why don't you quit making fun of me? Leave me alone or I'll put a spell on you."

His look was aimed right into my eyes, and it stole the breath out of me. "I think you already did that." I looked away first. "If you want me to leave, I will."

I did want him to leave. Why couldn't I say it?

"But I'd rather stay here and talk to you."

"About what?"

He laughed. "I don't know. Nothing special. I just like being around you—"

"Why?"

"Because you're smart. And strong. And brave." He turned a little more toward me, ignoring the fact that I refused to look at him. "I remember the first time I saw you. Standing in the middle of the street giving Kevin hell for teasing Jimmie John." He smiled. "You looked so little next to him and all those guys—"

I glared at him. "Somebody needed to stop them. I didn't see you doing anything."

"I was in the truck."

"But you saw them."

Silence. Then, "I didn't like what they were doing. I wasn't doing it. I just didn't know how to stop it."

"You didn't even try," I said.

He exhaled. "No. I didn't. You did what I should have done. I never forgot that." A slow grin spread across his face. "I did save your bacon, though. Didn't I?"

I had to smile just a little. "Yes. You did."

"When you smile like that, you look so pretty."

Suddenly my teeth were chattering.

"Sure you're not cold?"

I shook my head. My heart felt so big in my chest that I could hardly breathe. He reached over and hooked my hair behind my ear, then ran his fingertips along my cheek.

"What are you doing?" My voice came out a whisper.

"What I'm doing is, unless you stop me pretty quick here, I'm going to kiss you." And that's what he did, turning my chin with one finger. The brim of his hat grazed my forehead.

Forked lightning ran down the ridge of my spine. He took off his hat and he kissed me again, barely touching my mouth with his. I knew that I shouldn't be doing this, but I never wanted to stop.

"Will, what are you—?"

I jumped like a rabbit. We both turned to the tall woman silhouetted against the open doorway, blond hair a halo in the yellow light. Nora Cameron was beautiful.

"The Kleins had to leave early. Randi's mother's sick." She talked only to him; I was beneath her radar. "I told them it was silly to make Randi miss the party, so I said you'd bring her home. Aren't you cold out here without—"

He stepped out of the wagon. "Mom, this is Avery James. Avery, my mother."

I mumbled something that came out like nice to meet you.

She smiled with her mouth closed, a small, pained, grudging smile that barely crinkled her face. "Nice to meet you . . . Avery, you said? What an . . . interesting name. Is it a family name?"

My face was so hot I thought it must glow in the dark. "No," I said. "It's not."

Silence.

"Well, it's chilly, isn't it? Don't stay out here too long, Willis."

"I won't."

I got up and stepped out of the wagon, brushing crumbs off my jacket. "See you later. Willis."

"Avery, wait a second—" His hand touched the scar on my arm from the rattlesnake bite, making it ache.

"What's the point?"

"The point is I like you. And I think you like me, even if you'd rather walk barefoot in a cholla patch than admit it. That's about all the point I need."

"It's not going to work."

"How can you be so sure?"

"I'm a witch, remember? I can see the future."

"Avery, cut the crap. Just for a minute."

The door opened again.

"Son."

"Ah, shit." Will said it under his breath.

Asa Cameron stepped outside, tall and narrow hipped. He closed the door behind him, shutting off the yellow light and the sounds of music and voices. "Evening, Miss James." He didn't smile. "I do hope you'll excuse the interruption, but I need to talk with Willis." He continued without a pause. "Son, your mother asked you to come inside. She needs you to do something for her."

I was already walking away.

After Christmas, Jimmie John got sick. He seemed to always have a runny nose or a cough, but this time it was more serious. His grandmother had brought in a hand trembler to try to figure out what was wrong. He was diagnosed and a sing was held, but still he didn't get well. Finally they took him to the *biliga'ana* clinic where the white doctor said he had pneumonia and promptly clapped him in the hospital in Darby.

That's why I was eating lunch by myself that day at a table in the back of the cafeteria—by the kitchen where it was warm and humid from the steam table and the dishwasher, and where everyone who bought lunch had to bring their tray back when they finished. I had my nose in a book, oblivious to the shadows of kids who passed my table on the way to bus their dishes. So I didn't notice at first that one of the shadows had stopped and was hovering a few feet away.

"Hi."

I looked up cautiously.

"Are you busy?" Will smiled at me. We hadn't said more than hi since the *posada*.

"No." I closed the book on my index finger to mark my place. "I was just . . . reading some . . ." Did I really want to tell him I was reading ahead in English because I didn't have anything else to do?

"Is it okay if I sit down?"

"If you want."

He pulled out a chair, turned it around, and straddled it.

"Why do guys always do that?" I said.

"Do what?"

"Sit like that. Like they're on a horse."

He grinned. "I don't know. I've just always done it."

I watched people's heads turn as they passed—surprised to see anyone talking to the witch girl. More surprised when they saw who it was.

"How's your arm?" he asked. "Where the rattler bit you."

"It's fine. I don't even think about it anymore."

He scuffed one cowboy boot along the mud-streaked linoleum. "How was your Christmas?"

"Pretty tame. Cassie doesn't celebrate Christian holidays." My eyes swept the room, catching and holding on the table where Stacey Lord, Randi Klein, and all their hangers-on sat staring at us. I opened my book and looked down at the blurred page. "I need to finish this," I said.

"What is it?" He reached for the book, but I pulled it back.

"Will, I can't be your friend."

"Why not?"

"It's too much trouble. For both of us."

He turned in the chair, his eyes moved unerringly to the table where the girls sat. He smiled at them, waved, and they burst into collective giggles. I wanted to disappear.

"Please stop it."

He turned back to me. "What the hell do you care what they think? Bunch of silly bowheads."

"What's a bowhead?"

"I'll tell you if you come to Mami's with me after school tomorrow."

"I can't." It was automatic.

"Why?"

"I don't date."

He ran a hand through his short brown hair. "It's not a date."

"Is too."

"Is not. In fact you don't even have to come with me. I'll meet you there. You can just be minding your own business having coffee, and I'll come in and sit down and pester you." His grin spread. "I'll even let you pay for your own coffee if it makes you feel better."

"Will—"

"Please." His smile disappeared. "I just want to talk. That's all. No harm in that, is there?"

So that's how it started. A January afternoon at Mami's, sitting in a red plastic booth by a window that fogged with our breath as the words poured out and the coffee sat cooling in thick white mugs and the early winter darkness closed in. We talked slowly at first, then faster, words tripping and stumbling over other words, rushing to say everything we could.

Suddenly the clock over the pass-through window to the kitchen said five thirty. I grabbed up my jacket and scarf from the seat beside me. "Oh, God, I've got to go! Cassie'll think something's wrong."

"I'll drive you," he said.

"No, that's okay. I'll—"

"Avery, come on. It's colder than a witch's—" We laughed in tandem. "Let me drive you. I'll worry about you walking in the dark."

So there I sat, buckled into the passenger seat of his white Bronco, wondering how this had happened and how much the Bronco cost and if I'd said too much and if I'd ever talk like that again in the rest of my life and harboring a dark suspicion that he'd be laughing about me to his friends later.

We were silent all the way to Cassie's except for me giving directions and him saying "okay" or "turn here?" When we got to the top of the arroyo, I said, "You can just let me off here."

"No, I'll take you all the way home. I want her to know you were with me."

He stopped the car a ways back from the house, the way I'd learned was backcountry etiquette, and turned off the engine. I unbuckled the seat belt and picked up my books, reaching for the door handle.

"Avery," he said. When I looked over, he kissed me. A no-nonsense kiss, awkward because of car seats, console, and steering wheel. But even I, who had no experience at all of kissing, could sense the current that ran between us like a promise. "I want to talk to you again. Okay?"

"Okay."

The windows of the little house glowed amber from the kerosene lamplight and piñon smoke puffed cheerfully out of the metal chimney. I opened the door and we went in.

Cassie was sitting at the kitchen table, which was set for dinner with two bowls, two spoons, and two glasses. Whatever kind of soup she had on the stove filled the room with a haze of garlic and chiles. Her expression didn't change when she saw him standing behind me.

"I was about to start worryin', child."

"I'm sorry," I said quickly. "We were studying for a test and it got pretty late, so he drove me—I'm sorry, Cassie, this is—"

"I know who he is. Hello, Will Cameron." I watched her eyeballs move under their nearly transparent lids, and I was suddenly aware of how old she was.

"Evening, Miz Robert. I apologize for bringing Avery home so late."

"No harm done. Will you stay to supper?"

"Thank you, ma'am. Some other time. I need to be getting home myself. 'Night."

And just like that, he was gone.

ten

We started meeting at Mami's on Wednesdays after school. That was his one day off from his chores at the ranch, and I was just as glad it was only once a week. I tried not to let it change my routine too much. I was already steeling myself against the day when I would sit in the booth waiting till darkness fell and he wouldn't come.

The third time there, he asked me to go to a party on Saturday at somebody's house. I tried to make him understand why I couldn't. I said that the other kids at school didn't like me and it made me uncomfortable. I told him Cassie would be upset, which wasn't true.

What I couldn't say was, I only wanted to see him as he was with me. I was afraid that if I saw him around all those kids and he acted like one of them, it would spoil everything. I wondered if he'd ask someone else, but I didn't really want to know.

The afternoons at Mami's were enough. More than enough. More than I ever expected to have.

He talked about growing up on the ranch. He was crazy in love with horses—training them, riding them, grooming them—even mucking out their stalls. He told me about all his favorites. Their names—Driver and Lady, a gentle mare, and a bay stallion called Tombstone.

He told me how his grandfather Charles Cameron had come down from Colorado with a few head of cattle and bought twenty acres in the Florales River valley, married Estrella Cortez, the daughter of a wealthy old New Mexico family, and kept buying more land, more cattle. Then

he realized that it was the horses he used for working the cattle that
were his real passion.

Charles and Estrella produced six children, of which Will's father
was the only one who survived beyond childhood. Unable to please his
father no matter what he did, Asa found solace in the ranch, and he
turned out to be a better judge of horses, a better rider, a better trainer,
and more astute in business matters than the old man himself.

"I think that kind of pissed off my grandpa. But what really pissed
him off was when my dad married my mom."

I didn't think she was much of a catch, either, but I just smiled.
"Why was that?"

"For one thing, she wasn't from around here. She was a flight atten-
dant. He met her at a party in Santa Fe one weekend, and he just married her and brought her home. I guess my grandparents went nuts. All
the cowboys were laughing at my dad and taking bets on how soon
she'd be packing up and heading back to the friendly skies." He
smiled. "But she showed them. Learned to ride and muck out stalls. A
couple years ago she delivered a foal."

Although she'd made it plain that she didn't consider me fit company for Willis, I had to admit to a halfhearted respect for her then, for
her daring. I couldn't conceive of gambling like that—giving up a life
you'd built for yourself to run off and marry some cowboy who was
probably good in bed but might or might not be lying about the family ranch.

Asa and Nora had three boys. Chuck, the oldest, was their father's
favorite and Braden, the youngest, was his mother's baby boy.
Will didn't have to say where that left him. I understood how he must
feel standing in that middle-child shadow, but I still had a hard time
feeling sorry for anyone with a whole family, plenty of money, and a job
they loved waiting for them after graduation.

I'd never seen Braden, who was just ten years old. Will said he was artistic, always drawing something, and that their mother kept him safe from most of the hard physical work on the ranch so he didn't mess up his hands.

Chuck, I knew. Well, I'd seen him at school—handsome, smart, serious. He'd gone off to Texas A & M last fall on a football scholarship. Amanda Albert was working at the bank, just waiting for him to come home so they could get married and make beautiful blond babies.

"Is it Chuck that broke your nose?" I asked once, then pretended to look at some kids splashing in a muddy puddle of melted snow on the street. Where the hell did that come from? And what a stupid thing to say. Suppose he'd never broken his nose?

He looked at me for a silent minute. Finally he said, "How did you know that?"

I shrugged and tried to laugh. "Well, I mean it's logical, isn't it? Brothers are always fighting, aren't they? And he's bigger than you . . . just a lucky guess."

"He jumped on me one time when we were kids. Pulled me off my horse, and I landed with my nose on his elbow." He laughed. "My mom wanted me to go to a doctor and have it set, but my dad wouldn't hear of it. He said it made me look like a man, so I thought that was cool."

For my part, I recited the official story about me being the child of Cassie's cousin. He asked me if my parents were both dead, and I said yes. They might as well have been. I guess he figured it made me too sad to talk about the time in Colorado, so I let him think that. He didn't press for details.

I told him mostly about life with Cassie. He knew her by reputation—most everybody in Florales did—but he'd never met her until that first night he took me home.

"Some of the guys that work for my dad have gotten remedies from her before. Especially the Spanish guys. They really believe in that *curandera* stuff—"

"Is that what they call her?"

"Sure. It's like a healer."

"I know what it means," I said with a trace of impatience. "I just never heard her say that about herself." I watched him out of the corner of my eye as I added, "She's always joking with Amalia about being a *bruja*."

He laughed. "My grandma used to say that *brujas* use their power for evil, and *curanderas* use it for healing. So I think we can rule out Cassie being a *bruja*."

"Well . . ." I turned my coffee mug around, first one way and then the other. "Cassie does other things besides medicines . . ."

"Like what?"

"She does charms—you know, like spells or prayers—to draw good luck or to bring someone back that's gone away. Or to bless a house. Things like that."

He studied me for a minute. "Do you believe in that?"

It crossed my mind that most people, especially most guys, would have rolled their eyes and said something like, "You don't believe in that shit, do you?"

"I don't know. When I first came to live with her, I thought she was a little bit . . . nutso."

He took a sip from his mug. "But now you don't?"

"Now I know she's not crazy. I'm just not sure about all that . . . magic stuff." I folded my hands in my lap.

It would have been easy to end the conversation there, but he said, "Does she teach you?"

"I'm trying to learn about the remedies. I like that part. The herbs. I like making the teas. It sort of goes with cooking."

"Are you a good cook?"

I laughed. "I'm a lot better than Cassie."

Cassie's remedies seemed to intrigue him, and I found that I liked explaining them. Other times I told him about books I'd read, because even though he wasn't much of a reader, he said he liked hear-

ing me tell the stories. It reminded me a little of those afternoons in
Ridley's office at Carson, Lee-Ann and me, sitting on the sofa, eating
cookies and reading stories. Once when Will and I were talking about
books, I blurted out that I might go to the university after graduation.
After I'd said it, I thought lightning would surely strike me down for
telling such a whopper.

I'd never gotten a valentine from a boy. Except in grammar school at
Carson, which didn't count, because we all had to make valentines for
everyone in the class. And they were supposed to have a religious message like, "I love you, my brother in Jesus." Not terribly romantic. And
in spite of the many rules and guidelines administered under the
watchful eyes of the teacher, I still managed to collect some from
anonymous admirers that said things like, "Roses are red, violets are
blue, Your left eye is shit, your right one is glue."

So when I opened my locker on February 14 and a square pink envelope fell out, I was first surprised, then embarrassed, then suspicious. I
stuffed it quickly in my notebook to check out later. After second
period, I barricaded myself in a bathroom stall and opened the envelope
with shaking hands.

The card I pulled out was simple and elegant. A square of palest
pink, with darker pink hearts overlaid by a thin, shimmery parchment
that crinkled softly when it moved. All it said was "Be mine." He
signed his name "Will" in deference to the fact that I never called him
Cam, like everyone else.

I held it carefully, like the paper would burn my fingers. I imagined
him picking it out at a store. I could see him chewing on the end of his
pen like he did in class when he was trying to decide what to write.

Then a chill crept up my neck like a spider. This wasn't from Will.
It couldn't have been. He wasn't even here yesterday, and I hadn't seen
him today. I'd gotten used to him missing the odd day for reasons like
mares foaling or a colicky colt or someone coming to the ranch to buy

or sell or breed their horse. He couldn't have possibly put it in my locker.

A white glare of rage blinded me. This was somebody's idea of a joke. Let the witch girl look like an idiot, get all moony thinking she got a valentine from Will Cameron. It was a trick, and I fell for it. Like a fucking ton of bricks. The paper made a rasping sound as I ripped it in half and tore it again and again until it was just dark shreds circling the toilet bowl.

When I walked into social studies I surveyed the faces that looked up and then, seeing me, looked away. Back to their conversations, down at their homework. One of those ignorant assholes had done it, but I would never give them the satisfaction of thinking that for one breathless minute, I'd believed in Valentine's Day.

The sky was already going purple gray when I walked out the double doors and looked around for JJ. He was nowhere in sight. Well, he walked slower than a desert tortoise; I was bound to catch up to him. Then I saw the white Bronco at the curb, Will lounging against the fender. He smiled when he saw me. He looked tired, and his face was burnished from the cold wind.

"Where have you been?" I asked.

He reached for my hand. "We had to take a filly up to 3D yesterday. Got back last night and then this morning Bubba was off his feed and my dad had to go to Kerrville, so I stayed home to meet the vet. I'm getting so far behind I'll be lucky to graduate on time. I was just on my way over to Darby, but I can give you a ride home."

"That's okay. I was falling asleep last period. I'll just walk."

He studied me for a minute.

"Well, okay then." He turned about halfway to the Bronco, then back to me. As if he expected me to say something else. One eyebrow inched up in a question.

I smiled. "See you tomorrow."

But he stood there. "Did you get the valentine?" he said finally.

I felt the blood leave my face. "You?"

He laughed. "Shit. How many guys do you know named Will that are crazy about you?"

Confusion turned to anger. "Why did you—? How—"

"What's the matter?"

"You weren't even here!"

He smiled. "I know. I drove over last night when I got back and put it in your locker. So you'd have it today."

"Goddamn you!" I felt the tears behind my eyes but there was no way I could cry.

"What? Avery, what's wrong?" Standing there in his denim jacket and black jeans, hat clutched in one hand, he looked like a guy in a cowboy movie—the one who could run the bad guys out of town with the sheer force of goodness.

He should have known I'd never believe that anyone would do that. I'd let him get close enough to hurt me and himself, and it made me wild with anger. I turned and ran down the street, my breath spewing in jagged puffs of steam while he stood staring after me. He called my name once, but I kept running.

By the time I got to Cassie's the knot in my chest had dissolved. My hair was all over the place and I had stitch in my side and shinsplints from running down the blacktop. She didn't say a word when I burst through the door. I'm sure she could see by my face that I had a tale, but I wasn't going to be telling it to her. I made myself breathe slow and deep while I took off my jacket and hung it on the hook by the door. I got a glass of water and sat down at the table to lose myself in homework.

"I made spaghetti for dinner." She was obviously proud of herself for trying something new, but I was in no mood to admire her cooking.

"Fine," I said.

"How was school?"

"Fine."

"If you're in some kind of trouble—"

"I'm not."

"You feelin' poorly?"

"No!" She looked at me long enough to make me ashamed of yelling at her, and I mumbled a half-assed apology. "I just need to get this paper written."

After dinner we sat by the woodstove, and I picked up a book I'd gotten from the school library. Cassie was knitting, and the only sounds in the room were the cracking of dry piñon in the fire and the faint clicking of her needles, so I heard the Bronco coming a long way down the road. I was sure Cassie heard it, too, but she didn't give any sign.

It was quiet for so long I wondered if he'd just turned around and driven away, but then I heard him outside. When he knocked, Cassie looked at me.

"Tell him I'm busy. Tell him I'm not—"

"I'll do no such thing!" she hissed at me. "If you don't want to talk to him, have the courtesy to tell him yourself." She got up and went to the door. "Hello, Will."

"Hi, Miz Robert. Is Avery here?"

"She is. Come on in, now, and close that door. You're lettin' the heat out." She paused. "Give me your coat. And your scarf, too. Otherwise you'll catch your death when you go back out." I heard him slip out of the jacket.

Then she turned and disappeared into her bedroom.

He came over and sat down next to me. The tip of his nose and the edges of his ears were red with cold, and I could see the faint rim where the hatband had pressed into his sandy hair. He unbuttoned the cuffs of his gray wool shirt and rolled the sleeves up two turns each, like he was getting ready to chop wood or something. I could hardly look at him.

"My mom went over to Kerrville to be with my dad," he said. "So I can sit here all night if I have to. Till you tell me what I did that upset you so bad." His expression was serious, but perfectly relaxed, like he just might sit there all night waiting for me to tell him something.

I stared at the woodstove, the way the heat rippled off the top in little waves. Like the heat rippling off the blacktop in the summer, making you believe the lie of a thin blue lake on the horizon. He took the book out of my hands, laid it on the floor. He leaned back against the old sofa pillows and crossed his arms.

"Don't you know I'd never do anything to make you feel bad? Not on purpose, anyway." I could feel his eyes on me. "But there must have been something. I need you to tell me what it was so I can make it right."

When he put his hand up to my hair, all those tears I thought I'd left out on the road came rushing back, and they brought all their relatives with them. I couldn't stop. He didn't tell me not to cry or that everything was okay. He just waited till I was through and then he asked me again what was wrong.

"It's stupid," I said, miserable.

"Maybe. But it still bothered you."

"The valentine. I ripped it up and flushed it down the toilet."

"Why?" As if that could be a perfectly reasonable thing to do if only he knew the reason.

"I thought it couldn't be . . . from you."

"Why? Because I wasn't in school?"

"Yes."

"Who did you think it was from?"

"Someone who wanted to laugh at me. Someone who wanted me to think that it was from you—and then . . ."

"Okay. Now I get it."

How could he get it when I couldn't?

"I want you to promise me something," he said gravely. "I want you to promise that when you get upset, you'll tell me. Even if you think it's stupid. Even if you don't really know why. Tell me. Don't run away from me. Promise?"

I took a breath. I pulled a thread at the hem of my sweater. Then I looked in his eyes and I made a promise I knew I couldn't keep.

At the end of February the weather turned bitter. We plugged the chinks around the windows with old rags, but you could still hear the wind whistle as it rounded the corners of the house, and any water left in the sink or the washbasin overnight grew a brittle skin of ice. Cassie kept the woodstove burning continuously and a couple of mornings, she even lit the oven on the cookstove, propped it open and sat in front of it, rubbing her knotted fingers.

Will hadn't been in school for several days—whether he was sick or it was something about the horses I didn't know. I thought about using the pay phone at Mami's to call him, but the chances were his mother would answer the phone and I didn't want to go there. I hadn't seen JJ in about a week, either, but I figured his grandmother was keeping him in because of the cold.

Wednesday morning, I started feeling "poorly," as Cassie always said. Not bad, just not good. It persisted as the day wore on, sort of a weird feeling, like I'd swallowed food without chewing it. I sat in study hall trying to read the New Mexico history assignment, but the words didn't make sense.

By the time the bell rang at 3:15, I couldn't wait to get outside. I knew it would be freezing, but I felt like I couldn't breathe in here. I was standing in front of my locker, winding my scarf around my neck when Mr. Hanover came lumbering up with an armload of books. He was one of two teachers that I actually liked. Probably because he was always giving me books.

"Avery." He was short and chubby with thick blond hair and a penchant for polyester western-style shirts. "Avery, have you seen Jimmie John?"

I shook my head. "His grandmother won't let him out when the weather's bad."

"I know." He frowned. "But he's getting way behind in my class, and I assume all his others. I'd hate to see him get held back again. He's getting too old for high school." He held out three heavyweight books. "I've written out my assignments and so has Mrs. Ortega. I know he lives out your way . . . Do you think you could take him these books?"

I walked quickly till the sidewalk ended at the edge of town. The last thaw had left a lot of mud on the road, and now all the ridges and holes and tiremarks were hard as cement. Frozen weeds and sprigs of grass along the shoulder crunched under my numb feet as I stumbled and slid on the icy patches. When I pulled my scarf up over my mouth and nose, I suddenly pictured Jimmie John, wandering through the falling snow, his cap stuffed in his pocket to keep it from getting wet. It made me smile.

To me, he still looked pretty much the way he did the first time I saw him three years ago, standing in a circle of taunting football players. His face was still childish and smooth, his body overstuffed and round. He was still the same person, too.

He still didn't worry about graduating from school and getting a job. He still didn't have enough sense to get pissed off or offended that people laughed at him. He never thought about money, where he was going to live or what he was going to eat, what clothes to wear. He just took whatever you gave him and smiled his dopey smile. Maybe instead of being a retard, he was really a sort of a higher life-form.

About halfway home, something halted me in the middle of the road, and I bunched my fingers together in the palm of my gloves for extra warmth. The sun had just dipped out of sight, backlighting the tall ragged outline of Silver Butte. The whole valley was hushed, expectant, the way children are when they're waiting for Christmas or to see a parade pass by. Suddenly the air was filled with noise—honking, crying, squawking, calling—and I raised my eyes to a twilight sky full of birds—a sprawling, animated cloud of white and silver wings.

I arched my neck to watch as they passed. My scarf fell away and the humidity of my breath dried on my lips. My cheeks lost feeling and my eyes ran with warm water that turned cold. But the tightness in my chest was gone—in one deep exhalation of dust and smoke. At least that's what it felt like. And in that instant I knew two things.

One, I knew that Jimmie John was dead. I couldn't have been more certain if I'd seen him laid out, still and silent.

And two, I knew that Amalia and Cassie were right. I did have some kind of ability, some sight that wasn't usual. I wouldn't go so far as calling it a gift. A gift was supposedly something you wanted. And I didn't want this. Particularly since it seemed that I had no control over it. It was depressing to think that for the rest of my life, I might never know the things I wanted to know, but that without warning, at random intervals, some vision was going to be stuck in front of my face. Whether I wanted to see it or not.

When I asked Cassie if we could go to JJ's funeral, she said, "No, child. There won't be one. Navajos don't want nothing to do with the dead. Even Delbert—and he's not your traditional Navajo— he won't go near any house where anyone's died. Used to be, they'd just punch a hole in the north side of the hogan so the spirit could get out, and then nobody ever goes in that house again. Even now, most of 'em won't speak the name of a dead person, 'case the spirit's still close by."

"But how could anyone be afraid of JJ's spirit? He was so . . ." I groped for words, startled by the knot of tears forming in my throat. "Harmless. Like a puppy. He just wanted to be . . . friends."

I started to cry. For the first time since I'd come to live with her, Cassie came over and put her arms around me. And I let her.

Will slid into the booth at Mami's on Wednesday, and the first thing he said was, "I'm sorry about Jimmie."

By then everyone in town knew, but other than a listing in the obituaries of the *Florales County Sentinel* and a tiny mention in the student newspaper, his dying had barely created a ripple.

Lia, the afternoon waitress, came over with two cups of coffee and two little pitchers of milk. "Hi, kids." She didn't even bother to give us menus anymore. She knew we were going to sit there for two hours and drink our free refills. After she went back to the counter, he said,

"How are you?" It wasn't something he asked very often, but when he did, I knew he expected a real answer.

"Okay, I guess. I can't stop thinking about JJ."

"I know. It's hard."

"It's worse than hard. It makes me furious that no one cares."

His thumb rubbed gently over my knuckles. "I just think that nobody knew him like you did. It's not that they don't—"

"Of course it is." Angry tears pricked my eyes. "Especially at school. All he was to them was somebody to make fun of. Honest to God, Will, you have no idea what it's like to be the school weirdo. I do."

"What are you talking about? You're not the school weirdo."

"Not now, I'm not, but don't you know why? It's because of you."

"Me?"

"Of course, you. Nobody wants to piss you off, so they leave me alone."

"Avery," he said patiently, "Jimmie was . . . He wasn't normal—"

I pull my hand away from him. "And neither am I. In fact I'm probably more like JJ than you."

"That's not true."

"It is true. If it wasn't for you they'd be taking my books and flushing my papers down the toilet and putting cow pies in my locker—"

"Avery—"

"It's happened before. You don't have to be abnormal. All you have to be is not like them. Open your eyes, Will."

"When?" His voice was quiet.

"When what?"

"When did that stuff happen to you?"

I turned to the window. "A long time ago."

In a few minutes he reached for my hand again. "I used to be kind of jealous of him, you know."

"Of JJ?" I frowned. "Oh, please. What could he have that you'd want?"

"A lot of time with you."

Color rose warmly in my face.

"You always seemed so comfortable with him. And then whenever I came around, it was like you couldn't wait to get away."

"Well," I said, not daring to look at him, "It's obviously not like that now."

Sometimes a silence between two people is empty, and sometimes a silence is so full of words that you're afraid to break it for fear of spilling every single one and losing some in the process.

I decided to make my own marker for JJ. Even though he wouldn't be buried under it, I felt better knowing he had a place that was his. It was in the area where he used to wander around visiting his Black Mesa clan. Will and I found a tiny *bosque* where a cottonwood tree and a couple of scraggly willows hung on in dry times and thrived when rains filled the narrow streambed.

In March there wasn't any water, but the sandy stream bottom was damp.

Will helped me take the material out there, driving the Bronco as far as we could, then hauling it the rest of the way in Cassie's old wagon. I made it from all his little presents, the stones, scraps of metal and glass, twigs, a bird's nest, an old sneaker with no laces that he'd found in the road. It was just a mound, like the cairns Mr. Hanover said explorers used to build to mark where they'd been. And on top I put the gearshift knob, the narrow end down, wedged between rocks to hold it steady. Cassie gave me a wreath that she made of herbs to lay at the base of it— tansy for life, big sagebrush for comfort, and rosemary for remembrance.

eleven

On a glorious Saturday in April, I was working in the garden, pulling the beginnings of weeds, breaking up the still cold red clay, working in a wheelbarrow full of composted manure from Jaimie Rodriguez's henhouse that Cassie got in trade for a charm to keep his freeloading cousin away. I told her it was an even swap—chicken shit for bullshit.

It was only about ten o'clock when I heard the Bronco bouncing down the rutted road. The slam of the door echoed slightly and then he must have stopped to talk to Cassie because it was awhile before he ambled around the corner of the house. When I saw him standing there in his faded jeans, the white T-shirt with the Cameron Ranch brand on the pocket, my heart fell straight to the ground.

"You look like the earth goddess," he said.

I recovered myself and laughed. "You mean the chicken shit queen. What are you doing over here on the poor side of town?"

"I came to steal you away. Get cleaned up and let's go."

"Where?"

"On a picnic. To a special place I know."

"Oh, Will, I can't leave now. There's so much to do—"

"Oh yes you can." He took the hoe out of my grasp and heaved it like a spear.

"What are you doing, you crazy boy?"

"I already asked Cassie and she said it was okay. So go wash the shit off you and let's go."

We headed south on Highway 84 between the mesas and buttes carved from thick beds of dusty red, purple, and yellow sandstone.

Gnarled juniper trees clung to the slopes in seemingly impossible places. He turned west onto a gravel road and right again onto a dirt track where a sign said RIM VISTA TRAIL, stopping in a small parking area.

"Should we walk first or eat first?" he asked.

"I'm starving. Let's eat."

We sat on the Bronco's tailgate, and he produced a willow basket that contained a feast. We fell on it like starving coyotes—guacamole, tortillas still faintly warm and wrapped in foil, an earthenware casserole full of shredded chicken in a spicy/sour tomatillo sauce, and tiny perfect *empanaditas* filled with apples and cinnamon and raisins.

"Who made all this?" I asked him with my mouth full.

"Sofia, our cook. She's great." I had to agree.

When we'd eaten way too much, he repacked the basket, took my hand, and led me, protesting strongly, out onto a trail marked NUMBER 15, that dropped into and just as quickly out of a small arroyo. I hadn't noticed from the car, but now I saw that the wildflowers were blooming—red Indian paintbrush, magenta bee balm, white jimson-weed, yellow clusters of yarrow, and pink puffs of Apache plume—all the more spectacular because of the rugged earth that they sprang up from. The smell of sagebrush was thick in the air.

"I used to come out here with my grandfather," he said. "The whole area's full of fossils. This was all a huge inland sea."

We climbed around the end of a small ridge and up the south flank, following blue diamond trail markers across a rocky slope through juniper piñon forest. The trail flattened out over a broad sagebrush ridge and, after a few sharp turns, veered north to parallel a sandstone cliff rising above us. Barn swallows darted and swooped, and the high-pitched calls of swifts bounced off the cliffs where they nested.

There was no shade, but the day was pleasantly cool, and we plugged along for another mile or so, not talking much, just enjoying the views that got bigger with every step. I took off my sweatshirt and tied it around my waist.

Suddenly we emerged at the top of the mesa, and an immense sweep of a view opened up at our feet—Abiquiu Lake, the rocks of Ghost Ranch, the Jemez Mountains, and the Sangre de Cristos, all laid out like a painting. I felt myself gasp involuntarily.

"Pretty amazing, huh?" He said it like it belonged to him and he was presenting it to me. At that point, I wouldn't have doubted it.

We spread our sweatshirts on the ground and sat down. It was quiet except for a gentle spring breeze, and it was almost like we were alone in the world.

I sat there, hugging my knees to me while he stretched out in the sun, closing his eyes. I jumped a little when he rested his hand on my back, but he didn't take it away. His fingers began to move up and down a short stretch of spine above the small of my back. Gently. Following the contours of bone and cartilage. I laid my cheek on the tops of my knees, closed my eyes, and listened to my own heartbeat, the rush of blood through my veins like wind through a canyon.

Then suddenly he said, "Who are you?"

My stomach contracted on the food I'd just eaten, making me slightly nauseous.

"I'm nobody."

"Bullshit. That's just how you keep people from finding out who you really are."

"People don't want to know who I really am."

"I do," he said. "I want to know everything about you—where you come from. What happened to your family. How you ended up here."

I turned enough so I could see his face. He wasn't smiling.

And so, I told him who I was. I told him the story that I'd never told anyone except Lee-Ann. Not even Cassie. As I talked, my history gathered around me, entangling me like Cassie's knitting yarn sometimes did when she made me feed the strands out for her to roll into a ball. I felt like I might turn my head and catch a glimpse of Esperanza's

braid or Ridley's ugly teeth or Charlie with his glasses or chubby little
Annette. I had to stop then. Before it got too real.

Will didn't say anything at all. He took my elbow and drew me
gently but firmly down beside him on the smooth red rock. He tangled
his hand in my hair, pulling my face down to his and he kissed me. The
way I'd always wanted him to with no steering wheel in the way, no
seat belt or console between us. In fact there was nothing at all between
us and he was holding my body flat against his and I felt like I'd swallowed fire.

If I'd thought about it beforehand, it never would've happened. I
would have convinced myself that it shouldn't happen, and I would
have summoned all my defenses and carried them with me.

But there was no thinking, no planning. At least not by me. He just
showed up and whisked me away to this magic place, and I left all my
defenses back in Cassie's garden. Even as it was happening, I wondered
if he'd planned it. When I heard the crackle of the plastic-covered con-
dom, I realized that of course he had, but it didn't matter. Everything
he did to me I wanted him to do, had been wanting him to do for
weeks, and couldn't get enough of.

Afterward, he wanted to hold me. I was the one who pulled away,
scared and disgusted with myself. Not because I'd had sex, but because
I wanted him so much that it made me forget everything else. Who I
was and where I came from and what I wanted, and what could happen
to my life if I made one mistake.

I pulled my jeans back up, but I didn't bother to zip them or put my
bra or shirt back on. I just sat there, head bowed to my knees. The sun
and his hand lay warm on my back while my stomach roiled in the
silence.

He sat up. "Avery." His hand smoothed my hair off my cheek, and
he bent to kiss my shoulder. "You're not sorry, are you?" He drew back
and looked steadily in my eyes, something very few people had the
stamina for.

"I don't know yet," I lied.

. . .

I couldn't wait to get back to Cassie's. I wanted to take a bath, to wash the smell of him off me so I wouldn't keep remembering. I wanted to curl up on the couch with a book and a cup of tea and pretend the whole day didn't happen. But it wasn't going to be that way.

When we drove up, Cassie was outside sharpening and cleaning her garden tools. Of course he insisted on helping her and then she asked him if he wanted some tea and to my surprise, he said yes. The two of them sat there for an hour yakking like old buddies. Then she asked him to stay for dinner and thank God, he said he had to get home.

"He's a good boy," she said after he'd left. "Not strong as you, but he's got a big heart. Maybe he'll grow into it."

I didn't say anything. I got up and took the cups to the sink. Just as I turned on the water, she said, "I hope he used a rubber."

One of the cups slipped from my hand and broke into three pieces in the sink. "Got to get us a new cup, I guess," Cassie said.

He wasn't in school Wednesday. For the next ten days we only saw each other in class or at lunch. We didn't talk about what happened, but the way his eyes would hold mine made my knees shake. Every night I fell asleep thinking about him. Lying next to him, running my hands along the contours of his arms. His fingers exploring between my thighs, the way he touched me, how it made my breath stop. I really didn't expect it to feel like that, the dark pleasure of it, the way my body arched up involuntarily to meet his.

The following Sunday he took me to the Cameron Ranch.

The first few times he'd asked me, I made excuses. Then, as I got more comfortable with him, I simply refused to go. Then he said he didn't care if I wouldn't go to parties or basketball games, but I had to see the horses. The day he told me that his parents were going to Santa Fe to visit friends, I knew there was no getting around it.

It was the kind of raw spring day that proves April really is the cruelest month. Even though I knew his parents were gone, I was too nervous to talk as we bounced over the gravel county road. I stared unseeing as the gray landscape slid past, conscious only of wiping my damp palms on the legs of my jeans. What if they came home early? What if some of the ranch hands mentioned to them that Will had brought me there?

And then suddenly we were passing through a wooden gate with a sign that said CAMERON RANCH, QUARTER HORSES, and I could see the big white house with black shutters at the end of the drive. He stopped the Bronco on a patch of gravel bounded by logs where a couple of pickup trucks were parked. One had a bale of hay in the back.

Will left the keys in the ignition and jumped out. When I didn't move, he looked back. "Come on," he said impatiently. He was already walking toward the barn. I breathed deeply, popped my seat belt, and got out.

The barn he led me into was prettier than most houses in Florales. The air was filled with dust and the scent of damp hay and pungent manure and the sharp tang of horse. We stood in the pale sunlight by the door until my eyes adjusted to the dimness of the interior and when we started to walk between the rows of stalls, he laughed.

"You don't have to tiptoe. We're not going to bother them."

At first I couldn't see any horses, but I heard their breath, the creak of floorboards, scrape of hooves. He said they were eating. Then a huge black head shot out from one stall, and I sucked in my breath.

"Hey, Driver."

The horse made that funny little whickering noise as we approached, stretching to nibble at Will's pocket. "He's looking for carrots." He pulled one out of a bucket on the wall and handed it to me.

"Go ahead, he won't bite you. No, not like that. Hold it on the flat of your hand and let him take it." I stretched my arm out as far as I could without getting any closer to the horse.

The head moved to my hand, and Driver delicately picked the carrot off my palm with a surprisingly dry and pleasant nibbling sensation.

"See, he likes you." Will urged me forward. "Talk to him. Call him Driver. Blow in his nostril a little bit."

I looked at him strangely. "Blow in his nose?"

He nodded. "That's like saying hello. He can get your smell." He slipped a blue halter over the horse's head, grabbed a rope off a hook, and clipped it to a ring on the halter.

I took a couple steps backward. "What are you doing?"

He slid the wooden gate back. "I'm bringing him out so you can look at him."

I backed up some more. "I can see him just fine where he is."

He ignored me, and suddenly this giant animal was walking out of his stall, right up to me. Like he might walk right over me.

"Hey, not so close." I tried to laugh. "He's a lot bigger than me."

"Move over here to his left," Will said. I was so nervous I started to the right, then corrected myself, and stepped over next to him. "That's good. Now he can see you. Pat his neck."

"What do you mean, now he can see me? I was standing right in front of him."

"He can't see what's right in front of him. Because of the way his eyes are on the sides of his head. He can see almost a hundred eighty degrees on both sides, but right there in front is his blind spot."

When I looked dubious, he added, "It's because horses are prey animals. They need to be able to see predators sneaking up on them."

He took my hand and put it under his on the rope, and we walked Driver between two posts. Will fastened him with what he called cross ties that clipped to the halter.

I was having a hard time thinking of this massive, muscled thing next to me as prey, but I just asked, "Where'd he get the name Driver?"

"Actually it's Taxi Driver, but that's too much trouble." He reached down into an open box that looked like a toolkit and pulled out a brush. He handed it to me. "Brush in the direction the hair grows, start here up on his neck. Yeah. Hold the mane up so you can get under it and just work your way down."

The heat of Driver's huge body reminded me how close I was to about a thousand pounds of horse. "What if I hurt him? Will he kick me? What if he decides to lay down?"

"He can't lay down. He's cross tied. And you're not going to hurt him. Just make nice short strokes. He likes it."

Little clouds of dust rose off the black coat as I brushed, and the horse stood quietly. I did his left side, then crossed under his head. Somewhere between mane and tail on Driver's right side, I stopped being afraid. I quit thinking about how he could squash me like a bug, and I started to enjoy the power I could feel under my hands, almost a vibration. I don't know what I'd expected, but I couldn't get over how warm he felt. At some point I found myself standing with my face pressed against the horse's neck, breathing in the wild, earthy scent of him.

"Damn," Will said softly. "You put a spell on him, too."

He showed me how to clip the rope to the halter and release the breakaway clasps on the cross ties, and then he let me lead the horse back to his stall. "Walk him in and turn him around before you unclip the lead rope."

When Will took my hand and led me out of the barn, I felt like I was floating. He showed me the arena, the turnouts, another barn, and the house. When he started up the front steps, I stopped. "It's okay," he said. "Nobody's here."

"I know, but I just don't feel right." I looked over at the blue pickup truck with the horse trailer parked by the pipe corral. "Somebody might see us. Your parents wouldn't like it."

He sighed. "You know, you're making a big deal out of nothing. They don't hate you."

"Maybe not, but they sure as hell don't like me. And they don't want you hanging out with me."

He laughed then. Picked me up and spun me around till I was laughing, too. "Hanging out," he said. "Is that what we're doing?"

"Of course. What else?"

He stopped and his face got very serious. I could see the little bits of hay that stuck to his shirt. I started to pick one off, and he covered my hand with his and said, "Avery, I love you."

For one second I believed him, and the world stopped while I squinted into the glare of shining possibilities.

Then reality intervened like clouds across the moon.

Because I hadn't said anything, he asked, "Do you love me?"

"I don't think I can."

"Why not?"

"Because I don't know how. I don't even know what it means."

"You love Cassie, don't you?"

I looked straight ahead. Did I? I never really thought of her in those terms.

She took me in when all my choices were for shit. She taught me to survive. She accepted me exactly as I was, never asked me for any more than I could give. But did she love me? Did I love her? We never talked about it. Maybe if I'd come to her sooner. Letting another person get close enough for love has to happen first when you're a child. Before your heart gets fossilized like those little fish in the rocks.

When I still didn't say anything, he sighed and pulled me against him. "It's okay. You don't have to say it." But disappointment was thick in his voice.

We're out." He gave me a sheepish look. "That was our last one."

We were lying on the blanket he carried in the back of the Bronco, looking up at the startlingly blue sky. I wasn't too surprised that we had no more condoms. We'd been going through them at an amazing rate.

I rolled away from him. He tortured me with a trail of kisses down my arm.

"Will, stop it."

"When was your period?"

I pulled away sharply. "I said no, and I mean it. I have no desire to get pregnant."

He flopped back down and exhaled very slowly. "Would that be such a terrible thing?"

"Maybe not for you." I jerked myself to my feet, pulling his shirt around me, glaring down at him.

"Avery, I told you I love you." He got up, still hard, and reached for me. "Worst-case scenario is we get married."

I stepped away. "Will Cameron, use your head for something besides a Stetson holder. We can't get married."

"Why the hell not?"

"Wouldn't your parents just love that? Their precious Willis marries some little no-name white trash—"

"Stop it!" He grabbed my arm roughly. "Don't say stupid shit."

"It's true and you know it." I pulled a strand of hair out of my mouth. "They'd disown you so fast your head would spin. Besides, I never want any kids."

"Okay. Then it'll just be you and me. Happy ever after."

"Stop it!" I put my hands over my ears. "It's not going to happen, so just shut up about it."

He put his hands over mine and pulled them away from my head. "You're pretty smart, girl, but you don't know everything."

"What do you mean?"

"I talked to my dad last night."

"About what?"

"What do you think, about what? About us. You and me."

"Jesus, Will. What on earth possessed you?"

"You." He kissed my knuckles. "I told you I love you, Avery. I know you didn't believe me, but my dad did."

"You told him that?"

He nodded, never looking away from me.

"Was he pissed off?"

"He was kind of upset at first, but I just kept talking. I told him all about you. I told him I couldn't be happy without you." He laughed. "I reminded him how Gram and Grampa acted when he brought Mom home."

"What did he say about that?"

"Nothing. But he thought about it for a while." His voice got husky as he pressed against me. "He said he'd talk to Mom. He said maybe it was time they got to know you."

I wanted to believe it. I knew he did. I could tell by the way he held me that he actually thought we could make it work. "Tell me you love me," he said.

I bit my lip. "I do, Will."

He held me away and looked in my eyes. "Not like that. I want you to say it."

I took a deep breath, holding it to steady myself for a minute, and then I said, "I love you."

His smile sometimes was like sunrise in the desert. You could see the light on the horizon forever before the sun finally showed up.

It was nearly dark when we got home, and there were no lights on at Cassie's. I didn't worry; she was probably out back or with Amalia. Or tending someone sick or working one of her charms somewhere. I said good-bye to Will on the *portal* and went inside, trying to think what there might be for dinner.

The first thing I noticed was the smell. On my travels with Cassie around to her clients, I'd come to know the stale, flat scent of illness in a house. My chest contracted slightly. Cassie'd been fighting off a cold for the past couple days, but she'd been all right when I left. Or had I just been so intent on going off with Will that I ignored the obvious?

I lit a kerosene lamp and went to her doorway.

Cassie lay in her bed, blankets pulled up under her chin. I stood there quietly, wondering if she was awake, till finally she seemed to sense me and her head turned a little. The soft glow of the lamp lit her face—strangely smooth and sweet. Her eyes were questioning.

"Momma?" she called softly.

The plaintive sound of it made my scalp prickle. "Cassie, it's me."

She frowned. "Who are you?"

I stepped into the room. "It's me. Avery."

"Where's my momma?"

"She's . . . not here."

"Where is she?" Her voice curdled into tears.

Fever. She must have a high fever.

"She went to get herbs, Cassie. To make medicine for you."

"Then she'll come back?"

I swallowed. "Yes. She'll come back. How about I make you some tea while we're waiting?"

"Okay." She rolled over on her side, her back to the door, and I went to the kitchen, ran water in the kettle with my hands shaking. I didn't know what to do. I wished for Amalia. I thought about going to get her, but I was afraid to leave Cassie alone. For the first time ever, I wished we had a phone.

I thought about how Cassie took care of me when I got bit by the snake. Now she couldn't take care of anybody, even herself. She was a child in an old woman's body. I was going to have to try to take care of her, but I didn't exactly know how.

Everything. I would just do everything I knew to do, and maybe something would work. But other than filling the kettle and lighting the stove, I was paralyzed with indecision. What should I give her? I knew that a lot of her remedies had one or multiple uses, some had side effects. Some were even poisonous in large enough quantities.

I tried to make my brain kick in, to think about the different herbs for fever. Some would induce fever and sweating for cleansing. I didn't want those. I knew she kept quinine in the kitchen. It would reduce fever, but even a slight overdose could cause dizziness and diarrhea and a lot of other problems.

Borraja was pretty harmless, but only moderately effective. The same for linden. Oh God, why didn't I pay more attention when she was talking about all this stuff? By the time the kettle was whistling, I had decided on *álamo sauco,* the narrow-leaf cottonwood tea. Cassie always said it was good for lots of things and nearly impossible to OD on. I put a little honey in the cup, let it cool slightly, and then took it to her.

She drank most of it, never saying another word to me, but she kept looking around the room, like she was expecting someone. Like her momma. I tried to remember some of her charms to drive away illness. I thought about the one she and Amalia had chanted over me when I got bit by the snake, but it seemed like a different kind of thing.

Then I thought of a really simple charm that she did for a little girl with chicken pox. I remembered the words—more or less—and all I needed was blue cord, like the kind she kept in one of her many boxes in the kitchen. I had to rummage through three boxes before I found it, and then I cut three equal lengths of it and sat cross-legged on the floor. Cassie always went through some cleansing thing in the area where she worked, but I didn't really know how to do that, and I was hoping that good intentions would count for something with whatever powers were listening.

I tied the three pieces of cord together at one end, and I began to braid them, repeating "In these cords send healing power, let it grow with every hour." I said it over and over while I braided slowly, not allowing myself to think, because my natural skepticism would no doubt ruin everything, and I couldn't take any chances right now.

When I finished, I tied the two ends together and tiptoed into Cassie's room.

She was asleep, her mouth open, breathing heavily. I could hear the congestion in her chest and it scared me. Gently, so as not to wake her, I put the necklace around her face. I didn't want to raise her head because it would wake her up, so I just laid it on the pillow and hoped she wouldn't strangle herself with it.

I brought in one of the chairs from the kitchen and sat there watching her sleep, listening for any change in her breathing. I could pray. Yes, for Cassie I'd even do that. Couldn't hurt, might help, as she always said. The only words I could think of were, "Please don't let her die." I sat in the chair by her bed and repeated them endlessly till I fell asleep.

At some point I opened my eyes in a gray daylight. I was twisted in the chair like a screwbean. Then I remembered what I was supposed to be doing and I looked at Cassie. She was looking at me, eyes wide open and clear.

"Scared you, didn't I?" she said weakly.

"Yeah, you did." I felt like the horse that had been standing on my chest all night had got up and gone to pasture. "I don't want you to get up today," I said sternly.

"Who's gonna take care of the medicines?"

"I will. You just tell me what to do."

"You got school," she said.

"No," I lied. "It's a teacher workday. We don't have class."

She looked skeptical. "Every day's a teacher workday."

"Not like this. They get together and yak about curriculum."

The way she immediately caved in let me know she must be feeling worse than she let on.

twelve

At lunch the next day, I told Will I had to study. I took my peanut butter sandwich and a carton of milk and my history notes down to the far end of the football field, where Jimmie John and I used to eat. I never would have guessed I'd think of him as much or miss him as much as I did. He'd been gone for two months, and sometimes I still expected to see him standing patiently at the end of Cassie's road.

Even though it was early May, the sun was high and white, blazing down out of a clear sky like some giant misplaced star. A couple of young cottonwoods just the other side of the home bleachers made a little pool of shade, and nobody ever went there except me and JJ. So I wasn't expecting it when I rounded the corner of the bleachers and I heard voices. Not words exactly, but moaning and laughing—that kind of tight, sharp laughing that you do when you're scared or excited.

Kevin Gonzalez and Randi Klein were sprawled in the grass, playing tonsil hockey. I just stood there in the shadow of the bleachers, too surprised to move. It wasn't like I'd never seen kids making out back here, but Kevin was supposed to be going with Stacey. Kevin got to his knees, fumbling with the big ugly belt buckle at his waist. That's when he looked up and saw me. "Goddamn son of a bitch—what the fuck are you doing here?"

Nothing came out of my mouth. Randi rolled over on her stomach and stared at me. "The witch girl." She pulled her skirt down and got to her knees. They looked so stupid, kneeling there side by side, like at the altar.

I didn't want to get physical with Kevin. He was lots bigger than me. Meaner, too. I was trying to figure out if I could outrun him when, Randi said, "Oh, shit," and burst out crying.

"Don't tell, Avery. Please don't tell."

She had black eye makeup all over her face now, and snot dripping down her upper lip. Little pieces of grass stuck out of her shiny dark hair. "Promise, Avery. Don't tell Stacey. She's my best friend."

I just looked at her, not hiding the fact that she made me sick. "I don't have to tell. She'll find out anyway."

Kevin leaped to his feet, trying to look menacing, and succeeding pretty well, in spite of his king-size stiffie. "You listen to me, you little bitch. Nobody's gonna find out anything. You keep your damn mouth shut. If I hear anything, I'll know it was you, and you'll be real sorry. You hear me?"

I turned, walking away on rubber knees, kitty-corner into the middle of the football field so I'd be in plain sight if anyone cared to look.

He didn't follow me.

Two weeks later on a Friday morning I went out early to water the garden and when I came back, Cassie was dead. I knew it before I opened the door.

She was curled up on the sofa in the early pinkish light like a sleeping child, one arm hanging awkwardly over the edge, fingers slightly cupped. The garden basket was tipped over, filthy canvas gloves and rusty trowel spilling onto the floor. The scene looked like one of the black-and-white photographs Miss Paz liked to show in art class. This one would've been called Dead Woman with Basket.

At first I couldn't move. I watched the dust floating in a shaft of new sunlight between the edge of the curtain and the window frame. The herb bundles suspended upside down from the rafters gave off their pleasant, dry-grass smell. There was another scent in the room. Familiar. Flowery.

Finally I got down beside the couch, and my knees cracked in the stillness. Her face looked the same as always, except her eyes were about half closed.

I rubbed the tiny fingers with their swollen knuckles, the protruding blue veins, brown spots. She seemed delicate and papery, like the skin discarded by snakes, ready to crumble and blow away in the dry spring wind.

"Avery."

My head jerked around to Amalia, standing in the doorway, ugly purple shawl wrapped around her shoulders. "I am sorry, *pobrecita*."

I scrambled to my feet, shrugged off her embrace. Except for the shawl, she was dressed in black.

"How did you know?" I asked.

She reached back, shutting the door behind her. "You don' remember?"

"Remember what?"

"You come to my dream, Avery."

"What?"

"You come to my dream last night. You tell me, Cassie she is dead tomorrow."

"Stop it. You're giving me the creeps. Look at that." I showed her one goosebump-covered arm, but she just dabbed at her eyes with the shawl.

Between us, we got her laid out properly on the couch, eyes closed, hands folded over her stomach. I lit some sage and carried it to the corners of the room, trailing the smoke for purification, the way Cassie taught me. Then I laid the bundle on a plate and let it smolder while I ran water into the coffeepot and lit the burner.

We sat at the table with our chipped cups full of coffee and Cassie stretched out dead on the couch. Amalia looked so sad, I felt awful that I wasn't crying or something. It wasn't that I didn't feel bad. Cassie was about as close to family as I was ever going to get. I guess I just kind of expected it. After this last time she got sick. When she forgot who I was.

"I send Juanita and Rafael. They make her ready for—"

"She wouldn't want a mass or any of that stuff. In fact I want to bury her in the garden."

"I know, *niña*, sure. We bury her nice. Put big rocks on top to stop *los coyotes* from dig up the grave."

"Oh . . ."

"You come to my house, Avery. You stay with me."

The thought of living with Amalia and her daughter and son-in-law and five grandchildren put me in mind of a kitten in a burlap sack.

"Thanks, but I want to stay here." I leaned across the table. "You can't tell anyone she's dead, Amalia. They'll come and put me in a home because I'm not eighteen."

"I not telling. Juanita and Rafael, they not telling." One tear rolled down her cheek, unnoticed, splashed on the table. "She want to see you graduate. She is so proud."

"She'll know." I didn't really believe that, but it seemed to make Amalia feel better.

"And now where you go?"

"I don't know. Maybe Albuquerque."

A spitting noise. "Too big, Albuquerque. Why you don't stay here? You can go to Señora Jaramilla. Learn from her—"

"Amalia, I can't be a *curandera*." I said it emphatically, hoping she'd listen this time.

She put her rough brown hands over mine. "You listen to me, *niña*. You have the gift. And someday you will have need—it will come to you."

She tilted the cup back, draining the last of her coffee, pushed away from the table. She made the sign of the cross over Cassie and kissed her forehead and left me alone.

About noon Juanita and Rafael showed up. They wrapped Cassie in a blanket and Juanita sat by the couch murmuring her rosary while Rafael and I attacked the ground with shovel and pick. The earth was already baked hard, so we were both grateful that she was pretty small. We didn't need much of a hole.

Cassie and I grew most of our food out here for the last four years, and who knows how long she worked it before I came. With the sudden notion that we were planting Cassie in her own garden, a weird laugh bubbled in my throat, and I had to bite my tongue to stop it from coming. I knew Rafael wouldn't understand.

I'd only been in her bedroom a few times in the whole time I lived here—just to leave her clean clothes on the bed. Or to take her a cup of *álamo* tea when her arthritis was so bad she couldn't get up in the morning. It occurred to me now that I didn't even know how old she was. I asked her once and she sidestepped it, just like she did all my questions that she didn't want to answer. In that way, we were pretty much alike, Cassie and me. We lived together four years and then some without really knowing much about each other. I guess we knew what we needed to know.

Her bed was covered with a patchwork quilt so old that all the colors had faded to a pale blue. There was a tall chest that she called a highboy, made of some fancy wood, and it had brass drawer pulls. I figured it belonged to her precious momma.

I felt like a robber going through her stuff, but there was no one else to do it—at least no one I knew about. I opened the drawer that was waist high on me. It smelled like old paper and the osha she used to repel moths. It was her underwear drawer—five pairs of those white things she wore that look like men's boxers except with no weenie flap in front. She got them out of some catalog from back east. Three sleeveless undershirts. Cassie hated bras, and even when I first came, she couldn't reach behind her back to fasten them anyway.

The next drawer down held two pairs of baggy jeans, a crocheted black sweater, and some floppy slippers with holes worn in the bottoms. I thought I should give her clothes to Amalia.

When I opened the bottom drawer, I smelled it—faint, but definitely the same flowery perfume I smelled in the living room. The liner paper had pictures of pale flowers in clusters almost like grapes. The only thing in this drawer was a wooden cigar box. I flipped the top open.

Right on top was a blue satin ribbon wound into a neat coil. Under that there was a handkerchief that probably used to be white, but now was all motley yellow. It had a bunch of flowers embroidered in one corner and the words.

> When this you see.
> Remember me.

In the bottom of the box were three photographs, brown and brittle, corners crumbling off. I lifted them out carefully. The first was a wedding picture. I don't know how I knew this, because the couple wasn't exactly dressed for the occasion. The woman was pretty—delicate and dreamy, blond hair pulled back tight, lots of little ringlet curls on her forehead and by her ears. She was wearing a light-colored dress with embroidery on the front. The man was obviously an Indian—dark skinned, his black hair in two braids. He wore a plain, round-collared white shirt. Cassie's parents. They didn't look very happy for newlyweds. Maybe they knew what life had in store for them.

The second picture was a child about five years old, dark curls all over her head. Wearing a very dirty white dress. Probably Cassie, but all kids looked alike to me. There were no names or dates on the pictures.

The last one was a guy. Good looking as all get-out, dressed like a cowboy in chaps and a dark shirt, a bandana knotted around his neck. His white cowboy hat was pushed back sort of cocky on his head. He wasn't smiling, just looking pleased with himself. This had to be Martin. Martin who wasn't worth talking about, but whose picture she kept till her dying day. Martin who may or may not have married Cassie, but who for sure broke her heart. The snake.

I was about to lay everything back in the box, when I saw one more thing scrunched into a corner. A necklace. A disc of pink gold no bigger than the tip of my little finger, on a chain black with tarnish. You could just barely see a flower engraved on one side. I held it between my thumb and index finger, rubbed it a bit to wipe off the grime.

A sound reached me, not exactly an echo, but barely loud enough to hear over the wind. A woman crying.

I dropped the necklace like I'd been electrocuted. I threw everything in the drawer, slammed it closed, and ran outside.

It was about ninety in the shade and I stood there sweating through my goosebumps.

On Monday morning I went straight to the office before class. I sure as hell didn't need anybody coming out to look for me. Miss Huerfano, the secretary, smiled like she did at everyone, even me.

"Avery, hi. We were worried about you Friday. Were you sick?"

"No, ma'am. Cassie had a touch of flu or something. I stayed home to take care of her." Tripped off my tongue like the truth.

"Did she give you a note?"

"No, ma'am. You know, her hands are so bad now, I would've had to write it myself anyway."

"Oh, that's too bad." She traced the outline of her lips with one finger. "Mr. Meyer, though, he's going to want a note."

"Okay, I'll bring it in tomorrow."

"That's fine. You just write it and have her mark her initials at the bottom." She smiled again and I went back to breathing. "And you tell Cassie I hope she's feeling better. Flu is nothing to fool around with, especially at her age."

"Yes, ma'am. I'll tell her."

Will had been absent for two days, but that was nothing new. It was always something to do with the ranch. He'd been trying hard not to miss school now, though, because graduation was so close and there were tests and papers and projects due—something almost every day.

I wanted to see him, but I was dreading it, too. I still hadn't decided whether to tell him about Cassie. I didn't want him getting all protective, and I was afraid he might tell his parents and try to talk them into letting me live over there.

After class Wednesday he was waiting for me in the Bronco. He didn't get out and come to meet me, and when I climbed in, he turned his face to me, pale gray beneath the perpetual tan. His eyes were raw edged and puffy.

"It's my dad." His voice cracked. "He had a stroke."

I knew then that if there was a God, I was probably damned to all eternity, because my very first thought was for myself. That it was over. Asa Cameron was a vegetable, and his wife hated me. There was no one on my side now but Will, and he was no match for his mother.

"Oh, Will, I'm so—sorry. Oh, God." I took his hand and held it between both of mine. "Is he—I mean, will he—"

"They don't know yet. He's still in the hospital in Darby." He dashed at his eyes, embarrassed.

"When did he—"

"Sunday night. He went down to the big barn after supper to check on Juniper's leg, and we were all sitting around watching TV when Corey came running in yelling that Dad fell down. We don't . . . ." He swallowed hard. "We aren't even sure how long he was laying there before Corey found him."

Two kids walking by waved at him and then peered in the car, when he didn't wave back. Suddenly he turned the key in the ignition and backed into the street. "I've gotta get out of here. I don't want to talk to anyone else."

He drove out one of the county roads, hatched with cattle guards. Here and there a white cross poked out of a tangle of plastic flowers, in memory of someone who ended a Saturday night by wrapping their car around a utility pole or rolling their pickup into a ditch. We passed the little village of San Seferino, and I remembered the night of the *posada*. Only six months ago and everything was changed beyond recognition. Cassie was gone, which I hadn't told anyone, including Will. Now, less than a week later Asa was in some strange place between alive and dead, like what the Catholics call limbo.

In science class we learned that for every action there is an equal but opposite reaction. At Carson they taught us that for every sin there is a punishment. In my mind it worked out to something like this: for every good thing that happens, a bad thing happens. For everything you are given, something will be taken away.

And if, by some chance you ever got something really great—sooner or later you'd lose everything.

He stopped abruptly under the canopy of an ancient, twisted cottonwood. The tears had dried, leaving barely visible silvery tracks to prove that he had cried. For a few minutes we sat there watching the wind chase dust across the fields. I thought about how Cassie said that New Mexico was just the place that Arizona blew through on its way to Texas.

"I had this idea," he said abruptly. "He was going to let me break a horse my own way. I wanted to try riding him bareback first, instead of putting a saddle on him. I thought, you know, that if you could get the horse to trust you first, then the saddle and bridle would be a piece of cake. Of course, Chuck says I'm crazy. He says you've gotta show the horse who's boss. Make him submit to the saddle and bridle and then he'll accept you as the rider . . ."

His voice floated away. He was waiting for me to say something, do something, and I was totally useless. In my seventeen years, nobody had ever looked to get comfort from me.

"The last time I talked to my dad, that's what I told him. He always listened to me. He always tried to understand what I was saying. Now we don't know if he's ever going to listen or talk or think . . . or walk. Or even if . . ."

Finally I reached over to touch his face. "I'm sorry. I don't know what to say."

With one swift motion, he released both of our seat belts, pulled me halfway across the console, and kissed me. His mouth was hot and dry, and he tugged at the buttons of my shirt like some psycho rapist.

"Stop it, Will." I squirmed out of his grasp. In a movement that was more reflex than plan, I opened the Bronco door and jumped down.

"Avery, wait." He jumped out and ran around to my side. "Don't look at me like that. I'd never do anything you didn't want me to. You know that, don't you?" His hands were on my shoulders, pressing me against the car.

"Then stop hurting me."

That backed him up. "I'm sorry. I'm just—" His eyes were brimming again, and I felt like dog meat for being scared, for acting so stupid. This is Will and he's in pain and what do I do? Run away.

I looped my arms around his waist, laid my head on his shirt, and felt him relax against me with a shuddering sigh. I listened to the thudding of his heart and stared over his shoulder into the long, blue twilight while he buried his face in my hair and cried like a little boy.

Amalia stood in for Cassie at my graduation. I told her not to come, but she showed up anyway. I spotted her purple shawl in the middle of all the metal folding-chaired parents when we marched down the center aisle to "Pomp and Circumstance." I suddenly remembered how JJ always said he was going to come to my graduation and clap for me. It was just as well. He had a pretty short attention span.

Late sun filtered in through the high windows in the gym. If you sat absolutely motionless, you could feel a half-assed breeze, but it was still hot enough to bake bread in the gym. Why couldn't they have had the ceremony at night when it would've been cooler?

I hated the stifling black gowns and ridiculous hats—mortarboards, what an appropriate name—with these stupid tassels that everyone played with. They said we were supposed to wear the tassel on one side before the ceremony and then flip it over to the other side after we got our diplomas. All I could think of was that the whole thing would've been a lot easier if they would've just mailed us the damn piece of paper.

Stacey had found out about Kevin and Randi, and the two girls had a hair-pulling, kicking, and screaming fight in the girls' bathroom on Monday. They hadn't even looked at each other since, and all their friends had chosen up sides. Kevin was absolutely sure that I told, so I'd spent the last few days of class avoiding him.

They had us segregated now, boys on one side, girls on the other. The girls whispered and giggled about Stacey and Randi, and the guys were all kicking each other's chairs and pushing each other's mortarboards crooked, and everyone was drowning in a river of sweat. During the prayer you could hear the programs flapping as people fanned themselves, and one pregnant lady had already fainted.

From where I sat, I could see Will's back, stiff as a post. He turned once to catch my eye and smile, then he looked at his mother, sitting with Chuck, who was home from A & M, and Amanda Albert sitting primly on the other side of him, her hand looped through his arm.

Next to me, Linda Jaramillo was using her program to swat the flies that kept landing on the chairs in front of us. There was a lot of shifting and squirming going on behind me, where Randi and her friends were sitting, but I tuned it all out, along with the windy speeches about how the world was out there just waiting for us—all us future farmers and truck drivers and waitresses and pregnant brides.

Finally. Finally. The diplomas. We were supposed to stand when our row was called and walk up to the stage together. I was so bored that I'd sort of dozed off, when Linda poked me.

"We're next," she hissed.

Miss Huerfano was beaming and nodding, the parents were all smiling, and when our row's time came, I couldn't stand up. I couldn't move. My gown seemed to be caught in the chair. I rocked forward, managed to jerk myself up, and the chair came with me, hanging on my back like a turtle shell. The whole row behind me busted out laughing, and I knew what had happened. Randi and her friends had somehow fastened the sleeves of my gown to the chair.

A little frenzy of activity erupted, a couple of the teachers came running over, but by that time, I'd unzipped the gown and stepped out of it, letting the whole thing, chair and all, drop with a clatter.

People were trying not to laugh, but you could hear those explosive little snickers breaking out all over like brushfires. I really didn't care. I didn't mind standing up there in my jeans and T-shirt between Tammy Irwin and Linda Jaramillo in their gowns. When Miss Huerfano called my name, I clomped across the wooden stage in my old boots, took the diploma from Mr. Meyer. And when he shook my hand and said congratulations, I could fix my tassel now, I just ripped the goddamn thing off my head and threw it like a Frisbee into the audience.

There was a little gasp from the teachers and then some of the kids started cheering and clapping. Like they had any idea what I meant. I just walked down off the stage, clutching my diploma, my ticket out of this shithole, and I walked right past the chairs, out the door under the red EXIT sign, and I hit the highway back to Cassie's.

The house was dim and silent when I got home. It was weird. Not that we were always having big conversations, but there were just the noises of another person always in the background. The way she scuffled across the wood floors, banging pots and pans, running water, even the way she'd set her coffee cup down with a little thump. And her old lady smell, dry and powdery and grassy like the herbs. The place still smelled a little like that.

I took some beans out of the refrigerator and set them on the stove so they'd heat faster when I got hungry. There were books in Cassie's room that I wanted to look at, but I hadn't been back in there since that thing happened with the necklace. It was enough to make you wonder if the Navajos didn't have the right idea about dead people.

Still, I wanted to look at the books, and I knew I wasn't going in there after dark. I was standing in the doorway talking myself into it, when I heard the Bronco driving slowly up the wash, the engine cutting off, the slam of the door. I stepped outside, shading my eyes from the sun.

He came straight to me and put his arms around me. "I'm sorry," he said. "Those goddamn bowhead bitches."

I had to laugh, remembering that he never did tell me what a bowhead was, although I had a pretty good idea. "It's not a big deal." I sat down on the steps and watched the dust settle over the Bronco. "We can't go inside. Cassie's asleep. She's been really sick."

"Yeah, I wondered why she wasn't there. Too bad she didn't get to see you graduate. What's she got, anyway?"

"Some kind of virus or something. She'll be okay. It just takes time."

He sat down beside me. All at once I noticed the small, square white box in his hand. He straightened the blue ribbon that held the top in place and thrust it at me. "It's your graduation present."

"Will, I wish you wouldn't do things like this."

He looked exasperated. "Why can't you just say thanks? For once, why can't you just enjoy getting a present?"

"Because I didn't get you anything. It makes me feel weird."

"You don't have to get me anything. I just saw this, and I thought it would look great on you."

I wanted to tell him how it felt taking presents from him, that it was like being paid for with his family's money, but he'd never understand in a million years.

The bow fell loose with one pull of the ribbon and I lifted off the top, folded back the flap of tissue paper.

"Oh . . ." was all I could say.

It was a heart, only about an inch across, made of odd-shaped small nuggets of gold. I lifted it by its chain of flat S-links, let it settle into my palm, feeling its coolness and its weight.

"It reminded me of you," he said, obviously pleased with himself. "Pretty but strong."

"It's beautiful. It's really . . . so beautiful." I was afraid if I said anything else, I'd cry. For some reason, I'd been getting all teary over any little thing lately. He took it out of my hand and fastened it around my neck.

Then he pulled a piece of paper out his shirt pocket. "I need to give you this, too."

I unfolded it. A phone number. Area code 303. Colorado. A coldness settled over me. "What's this?"

"That's where I'll be this summer—"

"What? Why? I thought because of your dad, you'd be—"

He took my hand. "It's just for the summer."

"But who's going to run the ranch?"

He looked away awkwardly. "Chuck."

Of course. This is how it works. Chuck and Nora send Will away for the summer. It suits Chuck because it lets him be in charge of the ranch, and it works for Nora because it keeps him away from me. Out of sight, out of mind. Surely the boy will come to his senses after a summer away. When he has time to consider the consequences of marrying some little—

"—be working with this guy Darryl Hutt. He's a trainer and a farrier and he's been making a lot of waves with this new way he has of training horses. And he's been working with some of the wild horses, tagging them and testing their blood. He thinks they're descended from the original horses the Spanish brought over."

My head was spinning with admiration for her cleverness. How perfect. The one thing he couldn't resist. Oh, Will. My sweet, stupid Will.

"And he's trying to get some land set aside as a historic preserve just for them. It'll be great for me to work with someone like that." He finally stopped talking and looked for a long time into my eyes. "It'll be hell being away from you, but it's only till August. Then I'll be back."

He'll be back. Of course he will. He lives here. But it won't be the same. Not without Asa. Will's too afraid of rocking the boat, afraid to cross his mother, scared of what Chuck thinks. He'll say he loves me, but he can't upset them right now. It's not a good time.

Hell, when would be a good time to give up the Cameron Ranch for Miss Avery James—named after a necklace?

"You can call me collect whenever you want. As soon as I get up there, I'll make arrangements. We can make up a name for you to ask for, and then I'll call you back."

"When?" I said. "When do you go?"

The tops of his ears reddened.

"There's a guy from 3D down here to pick up Tombstone and take him back, so I'm going to go back with—"

"When?" I said it louder.

"Tomorrow." He mumbled it. "Avery, I know what you're thinking." He took both my hands. "But you have to trust me. This is good for us. What I can learn from Hutt, that'll make me worth something to the ranch. Chuck won't be able to just blow me off. He'll have to listen to me. As soon as you turn eighteen we can get married—Avery, goddamnit, look at me!"

I did, but I couldn't seem to focus. He looked blurry and very far away. Halfway to Colorado in his mind.

thirteen

The next day I took Cassie's social security check to Begay's and ran into Delbert. I had to buy enough so he wouldn't get suspicious, but I hated spending the money on food that wasn't going to get eaten.

"Hey, Avery." He smiled at me. "How's Cassie getting along?"

"Not too bad. She's just got kind of a cold or something."

"Still?" His brow creased. "She's been sick for a week or two, hasn't she? Maybe we ought to get Doc Parsons out there."

"I told her that, but you know how she is. She doesn't want him poking around on her."

"Yeah, but it's been too long. At her age, she could get pneumonia or something. You let me know if she's not up and around by the first of the week. The doc might have to just stop by and talk to her."

"I will, Delbert."

Two mornings later I woke up early. I pulled on my jeans and a T-shirt, stuffed the rest of my clothes in a canvas bag. The floorboards in Cassie's room creaked as I stepped around the big box that contained all her clothes. Amalia said she'd come by soon and pick them up.

I opened the drawer and took out the cigar box. I didn't look inside; I just slid a rubber band over it to hold it closed and threw it on top of my clothes. Then I turned to the books. When I picked up the old clothbound herbal, a bunch of papers slipped out and scattered on the floor. I bent down to retrieve them.

They were covered with writing, some in Cassie's cramped scrawl, some either written by someone else, or written by Cassie a long time ago before she got arthritis. I laid them gently back inside the front cover and wedged it along the side of my sack so they wouldn't spill out accidentally. There was nothing else here that I wanted.

In the kitchen I cut two pieces of bread and some cheese, wrapped them in a handkerchief sprinkled with water. I washed the knife, dried it, put it away. I made up my cot and started out to water the garden. Then I realized I was stalling. That garden was going back to the desert, whether or not it got watered today. Cassie was dead and Will was gone. There was nothing here for me. I felt bad about not telling Amalia I was going, but I figured she'd know.

She had the gift, after all.

It was still early, probably not even eight yet, when I ambled up to Dollar Gas. Things were quiet but there was a mud-splashed blue Ford Ranger truck at the pump, a guy in a dusty cowboy hat filling the tank. A fast glance around confirmed that this was not just my best bet, but my only bet.

I slipped the gold heart on its chain down inside my shirt and walked over to him. "Where you headed?"

He was tall and bowlegged. He had on faded jeans and the low heel, Dan Post kind of boots that working cowboys wear, not those pointy-toed, high-heel ones like you see on drugstore cowboys. He looked like one of those guys who never takes his hat off, and if he did, his head would look funny.

He shifted the toothpick from one side of his mouth to the other. "Gallup."

The pump clinked and stopped. He gave the trigger two quick squeezes to top it off.

"I'm going to Albuquerque. Any chance of getting a ride?"

He looked at me again, no expression, then passed his hand across his whiskers.

I looked up at him under my eyelashes and there it was—that flicker, the silent double take that happened whenever they got a look at my eyes for the first time.

"I can give you some money for gas."

When he grinned, deep lines fanned out around his eyes. He didn't exactly look old though—just like he'd been rode hard and put away wet, as Cassie would've said.

"How much is some?"

I pulled my folded bills out, peeled off two tens and held them out.

He took the money. "Okay, little sister. Hop in."

The bed of the truck was full of junk—one suitcase, a toolbox, a beat-up saddle, a Styrofoam cooler, some cardboard boxes full of canned food and breakfast cereal. I threw my sack in with it and climbed up in the cab. As he headed for the cashier's window, I hollered, "Get me some Marlboro Lights, okay?"

The inside of the truck was at least as dirty as the outside. It smelled like dust and old leather and stale beer. The windshield had a big crack running from a rock crater in the center all the way to the upper-right corner. Some kind of religious medal dangled from the rearview mirror. Kind of a weird thing for a guy who looked like him. I hoped he wasn't some kind of born-again lunatic who was going to try to save my soul all the way to Albuquerque.

I hate the taste of cigarettes, but they come in handy when you're stuck in the cab of a pickup in the middle of nowhere with some guy you don't know. For one thing, smoking gives you something to do. Between that and the radio fading in and out, there wasn't much need for conversation. For another thing, a cigarette can be a good thing to be holding sometimes. Some guys can't keep their hands to themselves till you plant the business end of a lit cigarette on one of them.

This guy didn't seem like that type, although you never know till you know. He told me his name was Ed Farrell and he was a bronc rider. I must've looked like I didn't believe him, because he mumbled, "Not that I done much ridin' lately, but I used to be . . . pretty good."

I looked straight ahead at the landscape divided by the crack in the windshield. Scrubby hills, some fields of dry grass where skinny cattle grazed, red sandstone bluffs on either side, framing the valley like parentheses. "So what have you won?"

His laugh rumbled. "A bad back and a bum knee and a foot that can tell you if it's gonna rain. And some belt buckles that I lost playin' poker." The radio crackled with static. "What's in Albuquerque? You know people there?"

"I'm going to school."

"Smart girl. You'll be glad you did that."

He fiddled with the radio knob for a minute, but nothing came in except a Navajo station, with a guy doing that singsong talk that they do, interrupted every few minutes by commercials for "Calhoun's Auto Parts."

"You like Willie Nelson?"

I shrugged. "Sure."

When he leaned across me to rummage in the glove compartment for a tape, his hand brushed my knee and I jumped.

"Easy, kid. I ain't like that."

I glared at him. "That's what they all say."

"Can I steal one of them Marlboros?"

I hit the pack against my left hand to shake one out for him. I pushed in the lighter, but he pulled a pack of matches out of his shirt pocket. He opened it, bent one forward, closed the cover behind it. Then with his dirty, ridged thumbnail, he scraped it along the sandpaper till a flame jumped up. A grin split his face.

"Pretty good trick, huh?"

I folded my arms. "Won any belt buckles with it?"

He sighed. "You're about as friendly as a rattlesnake on a hot skillet, little lady."

"I'm not looking for a friend. All I want's a ride."

"Okey-dokey." He popped the tape in the tape deck, and Willie Nelson's gravelly voice came grinding out Whiskey River, take my mind.

Ed Farrell responded to the suggestion by producing a flask of Old Crow and taking a couple small sips. He raised one eyebrow at me.

"I don't drink," I snapped. "And don't you go getting drunk. I want to get to Albuquerque in one piece."

"Yes, ma'am." He saluted me with the bottle, screwed the top back on, and set it on the seat between us. By the time Willie got to the last song on the tape, Ed Farrell was singing harmony with him, and I have to say, his voice wasn't half bad.

"You ever been to a rodeo?" he asked me when the tape clicked off.

A memory stirred unexpectedly. Hard wooden bleachers, sun setting behind big, lead-colored thunderheads. The smell of cow shit and popcorn and rain about to fall.

"Once. In Colorado somewhere. It was a long time ago."

"What event did you like best?"

"I don't remember."

He seemed amazed. "You don't remember anything?"

"Yeah. I remember thinking if there's reincarnation, I don't want to come back as a calf."

When he laid his head back to laugh, his eyes closed and the headrest pushed the Stetson down low on his forehead.

"Watch the road, Farrell."

That made him laugh even harder. "You're enough to piss off the Good Humor man. Where the hell'd you come from?"

"Alamitos."

"No kiddin'. I'm from Durango."

I could tell he wanted to start talking names and places, so I reached for my cigarettes. "Never been there," I said.

"Haven't been back in a while myself. I hear it's a regular Coney Island, now. T-shirt shops and fudge factory. Forty-dollar sunglasses and the like." He rubbed the back of his leathery neck and straightened his hat. "Not like when I was growin' up."

With that, he launched into an account of growing up in the fifties in Durango. His father worked at the post office, his mother stayed home and cooked and took care of her boys. His younger brother, Dan, went off to college at Fort Collins and became a geologist for an oil company in Houston.

He droned on about him and Dan riding their ponies, playing high school football and making out with girls in their dad's Chevy truck, stealing the cow sign off the top of the grocery store to decorate their bedroom, getting their asses whipped for it—all the usual growing up bullshit legends. I puffed on my Marlboro, watched the trailing smoke get sucked out the open window, all the time there was this big lump in my stomach like I might barf, only I hadn't eaten anything.

When he finished telling me more than I ever wanted to hear about his goddamn life in Durango, he slapped the steering wheel with his open palm.

"Listen to me, wouldja, makin' more noise than a breedin' jackass in a tin barn. Tell me somethin' about your people in Alamitos. That's big potato country, ain't it? How'd you get down to Florales anyhow?"

Maybe it was because I was starving, or maybe I was remembering Cassie lying there on the couch, or maybe it was knowing that I'd looked into Will Cameron's stormy blue eyes for the last time.

Or it could've been just that this jerk was trying his damnedest to be nice but he was making me feel like shit—but something just broke loose inside, and I started bawling like a little snot-nosed kid.

Thank God, Ed Farrell just kept driving.

When I got through hicupping, he pulled a red bandana out from under the bottle of Old Crow and handed it to me, all wadded up. I swiped my face and blew my nose and tried not to think about what else it might have been used for. I fumbled around for another cigarette.

He said, "You okay?"

"Yeah."

"This your first time away from home?"

I almost laughed. "No. My gram died. That's all."

"I'm sorry. I'm sure sorry about that. Never did know my grannies—either one. Both died pretty young." For one awful minute I was afraid I was about to get some more of his family history, but he said, "I'll try to shut up for a while."

I leaned my head back against the seat and closed my eyes. When I jerked awake sometime later, the sun was high and I had the uncomfortable feeling that we weren't where I thought we should be. Not on 125, for sure.

"You had a pretty good nap," he said.

"Where the hell are we? Why aren't we on the interstate?" I bent my head from side to side, trying to work the stiffness out of my neck.

He frowned. "Relax, kid. We're on New Mexico 14. The Turquoise Trail."

"I'm not interested in scenery. I just want to get there."

"Well, you ain't drivin'. And I'm interested in eatin'. There's a pretty good dive just the other side of Cerrillos. Owner's an old friend of mine."

In my head I was calculating how much money I'd have left if I had to buy lunch.

"My treat," he said, like he knew what I was thinking.

I pulled the cigarettes out, then changed my mind and smushed the pack into my pocket. "I'd rather eat my sandwich. I'll just get a Coke."

"You'll change your tune once you get a whiff of them *sopaipillas* and enchiladas, and Bettina's green chile. That stuff'll take the top of your head off. Man, it's fine."

My stomach was making a noise like a whimper. "I'll just have a Coke." I didn't need to be letting some yokel buy me lunch and then start thinking I owed him something besides gas money.

He whistled tunelessly between his teeth. "Okey-dokey."

. . .

The parking lot at the Rio Bravo Café looked like a used pickup sale. Every truck in Santa Fe County was sitting in front of this little wooden building, and it was barely noon. It crossed my mind that this would be a great thing to do—work in a restaurant, making the kind of stuff you love and having people pack in from Colorado to Texas to eat there.

I abandoned my plan of sitting in the truck while he went inside. I wanted to see what it was like. But I wouldn't eat anything. I'd just look around, buy a Coke, and bring it back out here to have with my cheese and bread.

The wooden steps groaned, and Ed Farrell pushed the door open, swaggered in ahead of me like he owned the place. Inside it was bigger than it looked from outside. The light was low and the noise was high, and the air swirled with roasted chile fumes. Two ceiling fans turned slowly, like they didn't have the energy to go faster. The tables were covered with bright-colored oilcloth in yellow, red, and blue polka dots and green stripes. They were so close together you could lean over and pick off your neighbor's tortillas, and every single one was taken—cowboys with their hats beside their plates, families with little kids in diapers standing on chairs, "bidness" men with string ties and vests pulled tight across their bellies. All eight seats at the little counter were occupied, and people leaned against the walls waiting to pounce as soon as anyone even thought about leaving. We took our place at the end of the line. At this rate we'd be holding up this wall till about two o'clock.

Just then the swinging door to the kitchen flew open and a woman breezed by with plates balanced halfway up both arms. The smell nearly made me high. Blue corn enchiladas with *chile colorado* and a capping of melted jack cheese that looked like snow on Mt. Blanca. Puffy golden *chiles rellenos* with tomato sauce. Refried beans sprinkled with *queso fresco* and snips of coriander leaf, dark red *arroz con tomate*.

The woman was tall, and her black hair was pulled off her face with big silver and turquoise barrettes. She wasn't pretty, but everybody acted like she was, including her. I liked the way she shoved through the crowd, smiling and saying hello to everyone, full blue skirt swishing. When she unloaded the plates, I saw the red burn marks up and down her arms. On her way back to the kitchen, she spotted Ed, and her smile got even bigger.

"Ed! *Corazón!*" She stepped right up and gave him a big kiss on the mouth, which he didn't seem to mind in the least.

Then she noticed me standing there with my hands in my pockets. She raised one eyebrow in a perfect arch, and it was plain what she thought. Ed either didn't have a clue, or he was a good faker. He gave her a big, stupid grin.

"This here's Avery James."

I waited for the moment when she saw my eyes, but she was too polite to stare. She held out her hand to me. "I'm Bettina Jacinto. *Bienvenidos.*"

By the time we got a table it was close to one o'clock, and the idea of a Coke and a cheese sandwich had passed like a bad dream. I felt like I could eat one of everything on the menu. Except Bettina wouldn't give us a menu. She said she'd bring us something special.

In the tiny, one-holer bathroom, I pulled out my money. Two hundred and thirty-seven dollars and thirteen cents. I had no idea what lunch would amount to, but I didn't care. I didn't want Ed paying for mine. I washed my hands and face, smoothed my hair in the cloudy, cracked mirror.

When I got back to the table, Bettina was standing there. I had the feeling of interrupting a conversation. Ed was already working on a beer, and there was a glass of water at my place.

"What else you want to drink, Avery?"

"Milk. Please."

One of the busboys brought a basket of tortillas and a dish of tiny meatballs in a nutty brown sauce. *"Albondigas,"* he said.

I'd had them before, but only floating in a clear broth that Esperanza used to make on Sundays. The tortillas were great, almost as good as mine. I dipped them in the sauce, and when that was gone, I poured honey on them from the sticky-handled syrup container on the table.

Ed laughed. "For someone who ain't hungry, you can flat pack it away."

Bettina glided out of the kitchen and set down our plates. *Chiles rellenos*—roasted poblano peppers stuffed with cheese and raisins, deep fried and sitting on a pool of smoky red chile sauce. One taste cleared out my sinuses like Roto-Rooter, and I was glad I ordered milk.

She sat down next to Ed, hooking her hand possessively in the crook of his arm.

"Avery . . ." She rolled my name around inside her mouth. "Where are you off to with this bad *hombre?*"

"I'm not off to anywhere with him. I'm going to Albuquerque. I'm just hitching a ride."

We stared each other down for a few seconds till I felt her defensiveness slip away.

"You go to *familia?*"

"To school," I said. "Great *rellenos,* by the way."

She smiled. "I'll tell Miguel you like them."

"Is that your husband?" I asked innocently.

Ed looked like he might spit out what was in his mouth.

Bettina laughed. "My brother. I have no husband." She lifted her hair off her shoulders for a second to let the breeze from the fans cool her neck.

"I've never had *albondigas* like those," I said.

"Lamb, not beef," she smiled. "And blue corn *masa.* You want more milk?"

"No thanks." I used my napkin to blot the sweat on my forehead.

By this time the place had pretty much cleared out except for us,

and I was thinking I couldn't eat one more bite if somebody was holding a gun to my head, but then the same busboy took our plates away,
and Bettina brought out dessert—*capirotada*, bread pudding like
Esperanza used to make, and a little pitcher of heavy cream.

She gave me a corner piece, which is the best, because on two sides
you get the little crusty, chewy strings of caramel that harden against
the sides of the pan.

As I was digging into it, she said, "It's late to travel now. There's a
lot of traffic on the road to Albuquerque. You should spend the night
here and drive down in the morning."

I started to protest that I was in a hurry, that I couldn't afford a
motel room, even if there was one nearby, which I doubted, but then I
glanced up and caught her and Ed looking at each other with a look I
knew all too well. That's when I finally got that it had nothing to do
with me. Unless I wanted to try finding another ride, I was going to be
here tonight, Albuquerque tomorrow.

Bettina Jacinto was in love with this burned-out bronc rider. I felt
sorry for her.

fourteen

lbuquerque was a dusty brown cake baking in the hot summer
sun. At least that's what it looked like from up here. Ed had
insisted on taking me up the Sandia Peak tram ride before he dropped
me at the university.

He rested his elbows on the railing of the observation platform
while I looked through the skinny tubes that directed your eyes to different landmarks. "Well, kid, here you are. What d'you think?"

I shrugged. "It's big."

"Yep. It is that."

It was about ten degrees cooler up here, but since it was a hundred
and four down at the base, it was still hot. The dry wind plastered my
hair back. "Could we get a Coke? Then you can drop me off."

"Seen enough, huh?"

I called Fran Talbert, the UNM counselor whose card was in the book
on careers that Mr. Horton had given me. I had to waste a couple of
hours with her, filling out financial aid forms and talking about courses
and majors, but she also gave me a five-page listing of approved student housing.

From that, I found a nondescript yellow stucco house near the campus. The room for rent was cramped and depressingly beige, but it was
cheap; the furniture consisted of a twin bed, small chest of drawers, a
chair, and a table. The resident manager told me meals were served
family style in the dining room, but that I'd missed the head count for
tonight. So I turned on my wheezy window air conditioner, unpacked

my sack, laid down on my bed, and promptly fell asleep. When I woke up, the shadows outside were long. My nose was plugged up from the cold air, and my mouth was dry and stale.

It was just after five o'clock and every street, every sidewalk, every building, every surface that had been soaking up sun all day shimmered with heat. Every car going by blew a parched backwash along with exhaust. The windows of every shop and café glared with reflected sun. Dusty leaves stirred listlessly on drooping plants.

I gave up thinking about what I wanted to eat and opted for the first place that was air conditioned and looked affordable. It was called Sneaky Pete's Diner. The neon sign featured a cartoon Indian peering out from behind a cactus. Obviously his beak nose and slitted eyes were meant to indicate sneakiness, but I was even too hot to take offense. Besides, the menu posted in the window offered *posole* and green chile pie and blue corn bread and stuffed *sopaipillas,* so I went in.

The counter was empty except for a guy with his cowboy hat parked on the counter next to him, and my heart gave a feeble little thump, forgetting for a split second that no way in hell could it be Will Cameron. I scooted into the booth nearest the door.

Suddenly the cowboy, who hadn't turned around or looked up, bellowed, "Rita! Ya got company!" A tiny blond shot through the swinging doors like she came out of a cannon. She placed a menu and a glass of water on the red Formica table and said, "Hi. I'm Rita. Like you couldn't figure that out, right? We got a special tonight of *puerco asado* with black beans and corn salad for five dollars and ninety-five cents. Be right back to get your order."

She reminded me of a little windup toy that somebody wound up too tight.

In a few minutes she was back with a red plastic basket of hot tortillas rolled up in a pink napkin. I ordered the special and iced tea and then asked, "How long have you worked here?"

"A couple months." She shifted her weight quickly from one foot to the other, like she was waiting for music to start.

"You like it?"

"Pretty good." She smiled. "At least the boss is human. Which is more than I can say for the last one. Alien life form, honey. Direct from Roswell, you know?"

"Is he here? The human one, I mean."

Rita laughed. "He's gotta be; he's the cook."

"Do you think I could talk to him?"

"Prob'ly."

When I unrolled the pink napkin, the rich grain smell drifted up to me. I tore off a piece of tortilla, dipped it in the dish of salsa and put it in my mouth just as a tall blond man in cook's whites came out of the kitchen. His fair skin was pink with sunburn and he had pale blue eyes. He didn't seem to go with the food.

"Pete Dimon." His big hand swallowed mine up. "What can I do for you?"

"My name is Avery James. I'm just starting class at the university and I'm looking for a job."

He gestured at the bench opposite me. "Mind if I take a load off?"

I nodded with my mouth full.

"What kind of job you looking for?"

"Waitressing. Cooking. I worked in the school cafeteria. Great tortillas, by the way. You make them here?"

He smiled. "No, they come from Central City Tortilla Factory. It's pretty famous around here." His eyes narrowed. "How old are you, anyway? You don't look old enough to be going to the U." Then I caught that flicker in his expression as he noticed my eyes.

"I'm eighteen. I'm just small." I tried to sound confident. "I graduated last month from Florales County High School."

"So you're looking for a part-time job?" He leaned back in the booth.

"No. A permanent full-time job."

His eyebrows reached for his receding hairline. "How do you think you'll manage to work full-time while you're going to school?"

"I have to work. I'm on my own. I won't be taking a full course load."

"I see."

"And I need to start as soon as possible."

"Well, we can probably use another waitress, but not till fall. Things tend to slack off during the summer. We're doing some shuffling around right now."

I turned to the window, staring through my reflection, into the yellow haze of heat.

"Rita, bring me an employment app, willya? And a Coke."

He sipped his drink while I filled out the form.

"You forgot your social security number," he said.

I hesitated. "I don't have one. Yet."

"Then I couldn't hire you right away, in any case. Everybody that works for me has to have a social security number."

I stared at him. "Even your dishwasher?"

The reddish cast of his skin intensified. "Well . . . I . . . he's paid in cash . . ."

I just kept staring.

"Or the last one was, anyway. He didn't show up today, so I figure he's history."

"I'll wash dishes," I said. "I can start tomorrow."

"Oh, hell no. That's an awful job. Just get your social security card. It's not that hard."

"I don't have a birth certificate. I have to get one. Let me be your dishwasher in the meantime. Pay me in cash. By fall I'll have my card and you can promote me to waitress."

"Have you ever washed dishes?"

"Every day."

"Not in a restaurant," he said.

"Same principle. There's just more of them."

He shook his head, frowning. "It's hot, filthy, backbreaking work."

I held up my hands—brown, strong, scarred. "I think you can see I'm not afraid of that."

He still looked dubious. "You sure you want to do this?"

"Yes," I said. "I'm sure."

Those first couple of years in Albuquerque came with a pretty steep learning curve. Living with Rita sometimes threatened to push me over the edge into certifiable insanity, but I honestly don't know what I would have done without her.

She helped me navigate through the bureaucratic nightmare of getting a birth certificate when you had no clue who your mother was and only a general idea of where you were born. She went with me to the Federal Building to get my social security card and helped me file my first income tax return. Six months later when two feds showed up at our apartment wanting to talk to me about having "forged" Cassie's social security checks, it was Rita who alerted Pete, who called his lawyer, who took care of the whole thing. All I had to do was pay back the money from the last one, the one I'd cashed after she died.

In return for Rita's trouble, I tolerated her intrusion into my life. Her questions and her sticky sentimental brand of friendship. I was an awful friend and I knew it, but I couldn't help myself. I was so indebted to her that I resented it, and my own dependence made me angry. And, of course, I was jealous. Not so much of her conventional prettiness. I was jealous of her general good nature, her sense of herself, the family that she took for granted, the life she'd had.

We'd go along just fine for weeks at a time, giving each other man-icures, going to the movies, quizzing each other for midterms—and then something would set me off. Something really stupid and insignificant, an offhand remark about how her father had taught her to ride or how she had a sleepover party for her "sweet sixteen." And I

would withdraw like a tortoise into my shell. She'd be hurt, not understanding why, and I'd be pissed off and ashamed of it.

From day one of my very first semester, I loved the university. Probably because I could only take one or two classes each session, each
one seemed inordinately significant. Rita and I spent hours poring over
the class schedule at the end of every term, analyzing, debating the
options, deciding what to take next. We felt sorry for the kids that
zipped through in four years and then left. Kind of like the joke Rita
liked to tell about the cowboy sex manual: In. Out. Repeat if necessary.

I could've contradicted her on that, but I never did, since my experience was limited to one cowboy.

Not that Rita and Jennifer, the other waitress at Pete's, didn't try.
They were always trying to fix me up with friends of their current
boyfriends, but it never took. The "possibles," as Rita called them,
ranged from rumpled intellectuals in black T-shirts to short-haired
cowboys in tight jeans to the occasional business school yuppie.

I got pretty good at predicting their political views and music pref-
erence within ten minutes of meeting them. One thing they seemed to
have in common was wanting to have sex immediately. Some of them
tried to loosen you up with alcohol or maybe smoking a joint. Some
wanted to talk you into bed, which was almost worse. The end result
was the same, and you had to listen to a lot of bullshit before you got
there.

For the most part, I was happier alone. I knew by then that Cassie
was right—I wasn't ugly. Not brilliant, but not stupid. Maybe too serious. I didn't laugh enough.

I read the magazine articles that Rita kept pushing under my nose,
about how to get a guy's attention. How to flirt. How to tell if someone
was good "relationship material." So it wasn't that I didn't know how the
game was played, it was more that I couldn't bring myself to unbutton
those top two buttons. To appear fascinated when I felt like dozing off.

To pretend an interest in football or the stock market or politics. So most Saturday nights found me in bed with a book instead of a guy. And when Rita got home, whether Saturday night or Sunday morning, she was only too happy to share the details, and I got my cheap thrills vicariously.

Working at Sneaky Pete's was okay, too. The food was good enough that I wasn't embarrassed to serve it to people. Rita and Jennifer and I got along fine, and Pete assumed the role of our protective, if slightly befuddled, father figure.

I knew there were places where the money would be better—night shift at the convenience store, for example. But there, you never knew whether the next person who walked through the door might stand you up against the wall and shoot you in the back of the head.

A couple of the women I knew from my old days at the house were making pretty good money doing telemarketing. But I could never do that—sit and call people who don't want to talk to you and try to sell them things they don't need? No thanks.

Life just kind of stumbled along, day by day, and happiness wasn't something I spent a lot of time thinking about, one way or the other.

By the same token, leaving Albuquerque wasn't something we planned either—it just happened. After five years, working at the diner was getting old. Rita was between boyfriends and I hadn't had a date in recent memory. Our apartment building was falling apart and the landlord never wanted to do anything but the bare minimum maintenance, so we were already looking for a new place, but rents had gone up a lot. And taking one class a semester at the university had started to feel like being on a treadmill.

So one night when we were killing a six-pack and the TV was broken, we started talking about making a change. Going somewhere new. Somewhere interesting. Sort of exciting. Romantic.

We were sitting there on the couch, and we looked at each other and both of us just said,

"Santa Fe."

PART THREE

santa fe

May 2000

fifteen

Wednesday's a cool, bright morning. Too bright. Which means I forgot to set the alarm clock and I've overslept.

I turn my head to see the clock. Shit. It's 7:30 and I'm supposed to be at work at 8:30. I can still manage, but I'll have to push it. I shower and dive into my clothes, hurry down the stairs, and jaywalk across Guadalupe, turning toward the river.

A few of the homeless are starting to stir in their sleeping bags as I cut through DeVargas Park, past the skateboard area, empty and quiet at this time of day, the NO GRAFFITI sign that taggers have plastered with their art.

My eyes drift over the groups of men sitting on cement picnic tables, drinking coffee out of Styrofoam cups and eating their breakfasts of Twinkies and Taco Bell burritos, waiting for the unemployment office to open. They occupy these same tables almost every day, sometimes whistling or hooting when women walk by, sometimes too busy explaining to their buddies how life as we know it could be perfected if marijuana was legal, or you could buy beer with food stamps. In my mind I've nicknamed them the Bench Boys, and I try not to look at them as I walk by, for fear of inviting return scrutiny.

Crossing at Don Gaspar, I jog left, then right to walk in the shade along the river, and something—maybe the swing of long dark hair down her back—makes me turn my head to see the woman striding away from me toward the Plaza. She turns onto West San Francisco, disappearing around the corner.

Without any conscious decision, I jump blindly off the curb, and a horn blares, accompanied by a squeal of tires as the driver hits the brakes.

"Sorry."

I yell it over my shoulder, not really seeing him or the car or the annoyed looks of the hungry tourists as I shoulder my way through the line outside Pasqual's. I whip around the corner after her and stand for a minute. It's early and the stores are still locked, but the window-shoppers are out. I pass a man and woman dressed in identical khaki Bermuda shorts, plaid cotton shirts, and navy sweaters knotted around their shoulders, looking at a window display of jewelry. The woman raises her head, meets my gaze with mild curiosity, then goes back to the silver and turquoise.

I walk slowly along West San Francisco to the corner of the Plaza, peering in every window. I know I'm going to be late for work, but I can't make myself walk any faster. I keep seeing the long black hair flying out as she disappears around the corner.

Isabel's dead. End of story.

Except I've lived in New Mexico long enough to suspect that the mere fact of death doesn't necessarily prevent someone from walking the streets with everyone else.

Dale looks at his watch when I come in, but he's on the phone murmuring, "Of course, Mrs. Renaldi," so all he can do is give me the *mal ojo.* I put my jacket on a hook, sit down, and get busy deciphering the scribbled notes Kirk tossed in my in-box.

When Dale finishes his phone conversation, he plants himself in front of my desk.

"You're ten minutes late, Avery."

"I'm sorry."

"You're always sorry. I'm writing it up this time and it's going in your file." He's chewing on the side of his face, looking exactly like the weasel that he is.

"Let me know if you need help with the spelling," I mutter after he stalks away.

A few minutes later he's back, tossing a manila folder down next to my keyboard. "Site survey this afternoon at Chris DeMarco's." I have the sense that he's grinding his teeth. "Don't—I repeat—do *not* be late. And it better not take all afternoon."

About the 1000 block of Canyon Road, the shops and galleries start to give way to homes—the kind of places I'd buy, if money was no object. Mostly old adobe estates, behind long brown walls. DeGraf's other gallery, the Buena Vista, is out here, in a rustic wooden building that used to be a stable. A screwbean mesquite partially shades the gravel courtyard where two hitching posts still stand.

I'm curious. At least, that's what I tell myself. I just want to see what he's got there. And since I happen to be in the neighborhood for a site survey at DeMarco's house over off Acequia Madre, I might as well walk by the Buena Vista. I don't even have to go in. I can just look in the window. He probably doesn't go there much anyway. It's sort of away from most of the Canyon Road action.

What I see through the window surprises me. *Santos* and *milagro* crosses and sacred hearts, Hopi kachinas and Zuni fetishes, Navajo weavings and those funny painted chickens, primitive sculptures of women with swollen bellies and males with huge penises. Masks and beadwork, pottery and baskets. Not exactly the sort of art I associate with DeGraf. I duck inside, leaving my sunglasses on.

A woman with frizzy red hair and a diamond stud in her nose sits behind a small, elaborately carved desk, eating a bagel and making notes on pages in a binder. When I walk in, she looks up briefly, pegs me as someone with no money, and goes back to the notebook. "There are two more rooms straight back," she says. "If you have any questions, let me know."

"Do you have anything by Isabel Colinas?"

This gets her attention. "Uh—yes, we do." She lifts off the chair, brushing crumbs off her black knit dress.

"Don't bother. I just want to see them. Are they in back?"

"Yes. The second room. If you decide you want a closer look, call me and I'll unlock the case."

In spite of the aromatherapy oil burners stationed at intervals, the place smells like its past—mellow wood and long dead grass and the ever present dust. I imagine that I can hear the squeak of saddle leather, the horses snorting and stamping in their stalls. Suddenly a huge black horse appears in a shaft of sunlight, startling me so that I grab blindly at the nearest display case, knocking off a stack of brochures.

This brings the redhead running.

"Sorry, I just . . ." I squat down to pick up the brochures, "lost my balance."

"Please don't touch the displays." She leaves me with a disapproving frown.

I stick one brochure in my notebook, replace the rest on the case, and continue toward the last room thinking of Driver, Will Cameron's horse. It was a trick of the light. A scrap of memory. After all, he's the only horse I've ever met. Still, I can't take my eyes from the long shaft of yellow sun where the horse—where I imagined I saw the horse. I walk past it gingerly.

All the way at the back, inside a glass case that runs the entire length of the back wall, I find what I'm looking for.

The Isabel Colinas collection. I take off my sunglasses.

The first item is a white umbrella collage called *Pieces of the Sky,* each pie-shaped section is a different kind of sky—a rosy sunrise, clouds heavy with snow, the towering anvil-shaped thunderheads, summer high-desert cobalt, pale lavender twilight, black midnight with a quarter moon and scattered stars.

Next to that sits *Walk a Mile in My Sneakers,* a pair of black high-tops, the canvas uppers covered solid with beaded rainbows. There's a quilt called *Tribute to M.C. Escher,* an intricate pattern of fish lifting from water to become birds in flight. There's a tiny jacket, called *Coat of Many Colors.* Overlapping circles of different blues and a few white clouds form a backdrop for fantastical multicolored birds.

The last item, at the far end of the case is a square of black cloth with ragged edges, obviously an unfinished piece. In the center is a hummingbird, embroidered with hundreds of "loose" stitches that have exactly the textured look of feathers. The threads on the green head and ruby throat even glint with a metallic sheen that mimics the iridescence of a hummingbird in the sunlight. Amalia used to say that *chuparosas,* hummingbirds, were messengers from the spirit world.

"Any questions I can answer?" The redhead is standing next to me.

"Do you know what time it is?"

She consults her watch. "Ten after two."

"Oops."

"I'm sorry?"

"I have an appointment, and I'm probably going to be late." I turn to look directly at her, and I see the little jolt when she notices my eyes. I smile as I make my way between the displays in the direction of the door.

Isabel was right. Startling people is fun.

Most Saturday mornings Rita works, so I usually walk over to the farmers' market to buy our food for the week. I could drive, but I really don't like driving in Santa Fe. Both natives and tourists drive the narrow streets like traffic laws apply to everyone but them. The sun-strafed yellow Toyota pickup truck that Rita convinced me I couldn't live without sits in its parking space behind Alma's most of the time, while I walk everywhere.

At the train station, I cut through the gravel parking lot. SUVs rumble past, raising clouds of dust. Behind the little depot building, a guy wearing baggy denim overalls and a long gray beard is hosing down a big yellow-and-red diesel engine. I keep walking, past the faded railroad cars from the New Jersey Central and Santa Fe Southern marooned on a siding in the weeds, paint peeling, windows boarded up, the inexplicable warning sign stenciled on the end of each car, DO NOT HUMP.

At the far end of the parking lot in the long shadows of trees and umbrellas, crowds of people mill around the stands of the Santa Fe farmers' market. It's packed this morning, like every Saturday morning, everyone trying to get their shopping done before the temperature rises and the dust becomes a curtain hanging in the air. My first stop is the concession stand in the back for more coffee and a poppyseed pastry that crunches sweetly between my teeth. I stand eating and listening to a woman in a long skirt playing a guitar and singing Spanish folk songs.

Drifting with the crowd, I stop at the organic farm stalls to buy pencil-thin asparagus and white-tipped French radishes and fat, sweet Nantes carrots. At Sweetwoods Farms I sample a couple of sheep's milk cheeses before I choose one to take home.

"*Buenos días, señorita.* Are you well?" Señora Castillo greets me with solemn formality at her tiny table covered with boxes of powders, bottles of syrups and tinctures, bags of teas, and little jars of salve. Over her head is a board hung with all kinds of dried herb bundles.

"*Buenos días, señora.* Yes, I'm well. How are you?"

"I am well." She rubs the mole on her cheek.

"And your sister? Is she well?" These two women, Señora Castillo and Señora Garcia run their herb business out of a family home in Galisteo, bringing things to market during the season. Señora Garcia looks ancient—white haired and so stooped over that she has to look up at people from the corner of her eye—even me. Señora Castillo is younger, although not by much, but she gets around better. They both wear heavy black shawls over dark dresses, no matter how hot it is, and no matter which one is manning the booth on a given day, we always have the same conversation.

"Yes, she is well, also. Would you care for some tea?" She offers me a white paper cup like the ones you pee into at the clinic. "Today is *amo-*

lillo. The finest. Very sweet. My brother, he dig the roots in Colorado on *El Dia de los Muertos.*"

My favorite part of this ritual is that I'm learning the Spanish names for all the herbs. One whiff of this new tea confirms my hunch that *amolillo* is what Amalia called *palo dulce* and Cassie called licorice root.

"You put with *miel,* with honey, to help coughing," Señora explains. "Chew the root for quit cigarettes."

"It's very good," I tell her. "I'll remember that if I need a cough medicine. What I need today is *manzanilla* and *cenizo* and *toronjil.*" She hands me a large bag of chamomile, a smaller one of purple sage. She opens an old tea box and painstakingly measures out enough lemon balm to fill the small-size bag. Then she loads all my purchases into my cloth bag, takes my money, and tells me to go with God.

I'm standing at the Cloud Cliff Bakery table trying to decide if I can afford a loaf of purple walnut sourdough, when a heel grinds down on my ankle.

"Oh, shit. I am so sorry. You know, there are some days when I shouldn't be allowed out in public." The pleasantly raspy voice is vaguely familiar. A hand on my arm. "Are you okay, honey, or will I be hearing from your lawyer?" She sniffles loudly.

It's Lindsey, the woman who was with Paul DeGraf at the party.

When I turn around she recognizes me immediately. "Oh, hi. It's Avery, right? How are you?" Before I can open my mouth to reply, she's talking again, picking up speed as she goes.

"Listen, I've been meaning to call you. Well, not you personally, but your company. I'm having a party in September, and I loved what you did for Paul, and I hope you guys aren't all booked up already, but do you think you could check on that for me?" She sniffs again. "God, this dust is making my allergies go crazy."

"It's hard to say without calling the office. I'm working a party this afternoon. If you want, I could get back to you after that."

But she's already rummaging in her big leather saddlebag of a purse, pulling out scraps of paper and a hairbrush full of blond hair, a checkbook in a red-and-black woven cover, a wallet with the leather strap ripped off, a pack of Virginia Slims, a Bic lighter. Finally her hand emerges clutching a cell phone. She thrusts it at me. "Here, why don't you give them a buzz right now."

The thing is smaller than the palm of my hand, and I fumble with it till it opens to the key pad, dial the office. Juana answers and after a few minutes of back and forth, we book Lindsey Hemmings for the third Friday night in September.

Hans and Eva Klein are from Sweden or Denmark or some such place. All those northern Europeans love the American Southwest in summer. I guess they're so tired of long, dark, bitter-cold winters that it can't be too hot as far as they're concerned. They like to have parties from two to six P.M. Outside. They stand around in their jeans and long-sleeved shirts and matching leather vests, grinning like hogs in shit, puzzled that everyone else is close to heatstroke, especially those of us who are cooking and serving. I feel like I've lost ten pounds in sweat.

It's nearly eight when we finally get the last of the chafing dishes and beverage tubs loaded into the van for the trip back to the kitchen, and I crank up my truck and cruise down Old Santa Fe Trail. The western sky is an explosion of orange, blue, and gold, and I catch myself thinking of Cassie. How she and I sometimes sat on the *portal* in the evening, watching the colors bleed out of the land and into the sky, drinking cowboy coffee with lots of sugar and that nasty canned milk.

When I pull into the parking lot behind Alma's, there's a strange car parked on the other side of Rita's Plymouth. A black VW Beetle. Looks like I get to meet Rick Soler.

The apartment is dark. I flip the hall switch and look around. A man's corduroy jacket is tossed over the arm of the couch, a dark, narrow tie neatly folded on top of it. A pair of runover loafers sits just under the coffee table.

I throw my purse on my bed and head for the bathroom. Rita's bedroom door has never closed properly. I think it's warped or something. No matter how hard you pull, it doesn't shut tight. Now through the inch-wide opening, I hear the unmistakable soundtrack of lovemaking. She's moaning softly. The bed creaks rhythmically.

I scoot back to the living room, where the sounds are faint, but still audible. I pull on a county fair sweatshirt that's folded on top of a stack of clean laundry, pour a glass of red wine in the kitchen, and take it out the sliding glass door.

Some of the supports are missing from the rusted railing of our postage-stamp-sized balcony, and the whole thing is wrapped in chain-link fencing, so I don't lean too heavily on it. The leaves of the cotton-wood rustle in the breeze like dark rain.

The back door of Alma's is open, and I hear Linda and Alma laughing as they clean up the shop. I picture them sweeping the hair into piles on the floor. Black, fine, straight hair. Red hair thick with henna. Bleached blond hair with split ends. Blue hair like fake fur. Music from the radio drifts up to me. I can't make out any of the words except *mi corazón*, my heart.

Light floods the living room behind me, and I turn, blinking in the glare.

Rick Soler. Wow. One order of tall, dark, and handsome; hold the tall. He looks around as he's rolling up his shirtsleeves, spots me out on the porch. An Anglo would be quick with a stupid grin, a wave, an outstretched hand. Rick Soler just stands there, watching me till I step inside. When he does come toward me, extending his hand, he moves with an athletic grace, as if he'd be equally adept at dancing or fencing.

"I'm Rick. You must be Avery." His voice is warm and pitched low. "I've heard a lot about you."

I smile. "Only the bad stuff is true."

Rita appears from the dark hallway, looking astonishingly fresh and neat, considering she's just been rolling around in the sack. She smiles at me. "How was the barbecue?"

"The usual smoke and sweat fest."

She hugs herself. "It's kind of chilly in here, don't you think?"

"Sorry. I was having cocktails on the terrace and I forgot to close the door."

For a few minutes we exchange awkward glances. "You guys must be hungry," I say.

Rick smiles almost shyly.

"We were thinking about going out to get something," she says. "You want to come?" It takes me by surprise. Usually she wants her men all to herself, no distractions. Not that I qualify as a distraction from Rita.

"Thanks, but I'm kind of a mess. I think I'll just cook something here."

"Mind if we keep you company?" she asks.

Rita and I drink our beers out of sweating longneck bottles while Rick sits at the chrome and Formica table sipping a glass of our low-grade Scotch on the rocks. I scoop a spoonful of bacon fat out of a soup can into a heavy iron pot on the stove and light the burner with a kitchen match. While she sets the table, I peel a yellow onion, halve it, and begin shaving off thin slices that sizzle when they hit the grease.

"Did you grow up around here?" I ask him.

"Socorro," he says. "How about you?"

"Florales. Rita, can you put some tortillas in the oven?"

From the cupboard by the sink, I take out the big jar of ground red chile, the smaller ones of oregano and cumin. Rita pulls the two-gallon plastic container of stew out of the refrigerator and sets it on the counter next to the stove. Every time I turn, I see them, Rick watching me cook, Rita watching Rick.

When the onions are soft and translucent, I throw in a tablespoon of the red chile, some cumin, a dash of oregano. I open the plastic container, ladle enough soup for the three of us into the pot of onions and spices. It hisses and spits in the hot fat.

Rick inhales deeply. "Smells like my mother's kitchen."

"One of the benefits of having a cook for a roommate." Rita smiles, first at me, then at him.

When the soup is simmering I ladle it into bowls, and Rita wraps the tortillas in a clean dishtowel and we sit down together. He closes his eyes, smells a spoonful of stew. He sips the liquid, then tastes the lamb, the beans, chewing slowly, thoughtfully. "Who taught you to cook like this? Your mother?"

I take a long swallow of beer, set down the bottle. "I lived in a children's home in Colorado till I was thirteen. I used to hang out in the kitchen with the Mexican cook."

"What happened when you were thirteen?"

"I ran away."

He leans back in the chair till it's balanced on two legs. "Why?"

"The cook died."

Suddenly we're all laughing. It's the kind of laughter called up by absurdity and followed by awkward silence. He takes a drink of water.

"Couldn't they get another cook?"

"Not like Esperanza."

"So why didn't you get adopted? Usually, healthy white babies have no trouble."

"I was pretty sickly and there was no information on my parents. And my eyes scared people, I think—"

"What's wrong with your eyes?" He leans forward, peering into my face.

"They're two different colors. I'm wearing a brown contact right now, but my right eye is kind of golden."

"Seems like a small thing."

"I think everyone was afraid of what other genetic crossed wires I might have," I say quickly. "Or maybe I just didn't come across as grateful enough."

He smiles with a sort of understanding. "How'd you end up in Florales?"

"She was hitchhiking," Rita chimes in. She beams at me like a proud mom who can't resist telling her kid's story. "She was going to catch another ride, but she got hungry and then this old lady took her in and—"

"Rita . . . You're telling him more than he ever wanted to know."

"I don't think that's possible," he says. "I like stories. It's very big where I come from. Every family has its own *cuentos,* its own stories to tell around the fire. I guess that's how I wandered into newspapering."

For the first time I hear the Spanish in him, the soft "s" when he says *cuentos.*

Rita rests her chin in her hands. "You think you'll ever write something besides news stories? Like a book or a movie?"

"Maybe someday." He looks only at her. "You'll have to wait and see."

It takes them awhile to say good night. There's not a lot of privacy in our place, but I try to dawdle over the dishes while they dawdle at the front door. She says she'll walk downstairs with him, but he says no. Every time I move past the door to the hall I see them standing there, wrapped around each other.

Finally I hear the last of the heavy sighs, the thud of the door, the click as Rita slides the bolt into place. She steps into the kitchen. Her face is burnished, glowing, like she's been out in the sun.

"So? What do you think?" She opens the fridge and gets two more beers.

"Killer smile."

She pops the tops with a church key and hands me a bottle. We sit at the table.

"It's serious, hm? Must be. You usually don't bring them around for my approval." I draw one knee up, resting my chin on it, closing my eyes. My obvious aloneness is like a cold wind at my back.

"I don't know," she says. "He's really different from anyone else I've ever gone out with."

"I'll say. He's smart. He's sexy. He's obviously crazy about you."

"Are you implying that my past choices of men have been for shit?"

"Hell, no, I'm not implying. I'm just saying it straight out." We laugh.

And then we sit in silence.

"Are you okay?" she says after a few minutes.

"Yeah." The night seems to press against the window above the sink. I stand up and pour the rest of the beer down the drain. "I'm just tired. I'm going to hit the sack."

sixteen

Camino del Monte Sol is one of the most lusted after addresses in Santa Fe. Running between the galleries of Canyon Road and the more heavily trafficked Old Santa Fe Trail, the tree-shaded road is only about a mile long, but it boasts some of the most beautiful homes and gardens in town.

Lindsey Hemmings lives on this road.

Down at the far end on the left, she tells me when I call for directions. She says if I come to the turnoff for St. John's College, I've gone too far.

I find the gravel driveway with no problem, and as I come around a stand of dusty green Russian olive trees, the house, a dark brown pueblo style, looms up suddenly in front of me. It seems like if you were going too fast, you might drive right through the front wall. A taxicab-yellow Mercedes with vanity license plates that say ARTLVR sits in the shade, top down.

Lindsey's standing next to it, wearing running shorts and a baggy T-shirt with the sleeves rolled up. At first I think she's been watching for me, then I see the dog—one of those goddamn Yorkie things that look more like large hairy rats than small dogs. Before I even get out of the truck, he's running around and around it, yapping like some midget Indian war party circling the wagon train.

"Oh, Paco, *do* shut up," Lindsey sighs. She dabs at her nose with a pink tissue. "Hi, Avery. Come on in."

I grab my purse and my file folder off the passenger seat and follow her inside.

The tiled entry widens into a semicircular living room with a back wall of glass framing a view of the Sangre de Cristos. A *zaguan*, or wide hall, branches off to either side, the white walls serving as a backdrop for numerous artworks.

"Great house." I pull a pen out of my purse and open my file folder to a fresh event estimate sheet. "What kind of party did you have in mind?"

She waves a hand at me. "Let's have a glass of wine while we're talking about it."

"Nothing for me, thanks. I have to go into work this afternoon."

She opens a cabinet, which turns out to be a mini refrigerator, and pours herself a glass of white wine. "I find I do my best work after a couple glasses of wine."

"What do you do?" I ask, more polite than curious.

"I'm a juggler." She laughs. "Investments."

"So is this a cocktail party? Dinner? How many people are you thinking?"

"It's probably going to be more of a cocktail reception. Sort of an open house. I have a friend, maybe you've heard of him—Andrew Halvorsen. He's a documentary filmmaker. He's going to be showing his film on Kosovo at the Lensic. To raise funds for several relief organizations. Basically I want some wonderful food, but it all has to be easy to eat standing up and not messy, you know? Can't write checks with greasy fingers. For about a hundred and fifty people."

"This area seems a bit small for that number."

"True, but let me show you . . ." She walks over to the wall of windows, pushes something and slides one whole panel aside. I follow her out onto a broad flagstone patio that wraps around both sides of the house. It's furnished almost like a room, with groupings of bent-willow tables, chairs, loveseats, even a fireplace. Just beyond the patio is a sandy little arroyo and beyond that, the piñon-dotted foothills begin.

"Over here is the door to the kitchen." She leads me around to the right and back inside through French doors to a kitchen that Julia Child would be happy to call home, complete with pickled pine cabinets and a blaze of orange-and-green Talavera tiles.

"Okay, this should work." I'm sketching a rough layout on my pad. As we head back down the hall to the main entrance, I become aware that several of the paintings on the walls seem vaguely familiar. One of a bull rider sitting on a split-rail fence was used as a state rodeo poster last year. I look at the signature. Thomas Hemmings. Of course. No wonder they look familiar.

I look at Lindsey. "Are you married to Thomas Hemmings?"

"Not at this current running moment." She chuckles unpleasantly. "All the paintings you see here were part of the divorce settlement. Actually . . ." She looks at me through narrowed eyes. "I had the one of your mother, too, but Paul begged and whimpered till I sold it to him." She pauses. "I don't suppose he told you about the picture. What happened with it, I mean."

"Well . . ."

"No, he wouldn't. Well, you're bound to hear about it. As soon as people find out you're her daughter."

"Hear about what?"

"About your mother and my husband." She gives me a brittle smile. "I hope I'm not going to shock you."

"I'm not easily shocked."

"Good. Are you sure you won't have a glass of wine? At least have a seat." She gestures toward one of the cushioned *bancos*. "You look like Lois Lane standing there with your pencil and paper."

I sit down, pushing aside some suede throw pillows that I know cost more than our couch. She folds herself down cross-legged on the floor.

"I've known Paul for a long time. We actually met in Paris. We were both living in the Marais." She pronounces "Marais" with a French accent, gargling the "r" at the back of her throat. "I was separated from my first husband, Jay—he ran off with the nineteen-year-old au pair. It just about killed me. I mean, do you have any idea how hard it is to find a good au pair?"

It's a few seconds before I realize I'm supposed to laugh.

"Anyway, I was living there with my little girl in a horrible old building that smelled of urine and cabbage. Waiting for the divorce to come through, living on checks that Jay sent when the spirit moved him, and selling the odd story to the English-language publications there. Paul, of course, had a wonderful flat very close by—that's the way it is in Paris. I met him in the *boulangerie* one day. I was trying to explain to the witch who ran the place that I wanted some day-old bread—because it was cheaper—and she was acting like she didn't understand me. Paul overheard me and realized that I was American. I don't know what he said to her, but she got very red-faced and gave me exactly what I wanted.

"He was very kind. He had a lot of contacts in the English and American ex-pat communities. He introduced me to Tom—who was studying art restoration—and a number of people who bought my articles and gave me other writing jobs—"

"So you're a writer?"

"Oh, I've dabbled in almost everything. These were just what they call 'puff' pieces. You know, features about interesting people, new restaurants, things to do that were not the typical tourist places." She waves her hand. "Anyway, eventually Paul came back here to settle his mother's estate, and he decided to stay, and we lost touch. Until Tom and I came to Santa Fe. We walked into Pinnacle Gallery one day and there was Paul. He's the one who convinced us to move here, and he represented Tom's work. And we were friends—the four of us—Paul and Isabel, Tom and me."

She takes a long drink of wine. "Everything was cozy, except Paul and Isabel were always breaking up and getting back together. And during one of their periodic skirmishes, Tom decided he just had to paint Isabel. By the time she got through sitting for him, she was also lying down for him. One day Paul came to the studio when I was in Albuquerque shopping and found them together. In what's known as a compromising position."

"So you divorced him?"

She smiles, her eyes like blue glass. "In a New York minute. I wasn't

about to hang around and put up with that shit again." She gives a little sniff. "Do I have bad taste in men or what?"

"I'm sorry."

"Don't be. It's ancient history."

"But Paul and Isabel got back together?"

She laughs. "Isabel knew which side her bread was buttered on."

"But what about Paul?"

She rolls her eyes to the ceiling. "He was too far gone. He couldn't
let go of her for long. No matter what she did."

"Did you ever speak to her again?"

"Well, I had to, didn't I? If I wanted to stay friends with Paul." Her
shrug is deliberately casual.

"What happened to the little girl?"

For a second she looks puzzled. "Oh, you mean my daughter?
Sophie grew up weird, as you might expect. She dabbles in painting.
She lives in Paris part of the time, Greece part of the time, Morocco,
too, I think . . ."

"Are you not in touch with her?"

"You could call it that. Anyway, she doesn't send my checks back."

I don't know what to say, so I revert to the business at hand. "Did
you have any particular kind of food in mind for the reception, or did
you want Kirk to suggest a theme?"

She studies me for a minute. "You know, the physical resemblance is
absolutely uncanny. And Isabel was stunning. You could be, too, with
some makeup. Do something with your hair. Different clothes. Different attitude." She pauses, then adds, "Yes, I think Kirk could suggest a
theme. Maybe two themes, then I could decide. I always do better
when I'm presented with a choice, rather than having to make up
something original out of thin air."

"What time were you thinking of starting?"

She finishes the wine in her glass. "Let's say we start here at nine."

"Are you going to specify a cutoff time?"

"*Bien sûr, chérie.* The people I know could drink Santa Fe dry. I can't afford to finance it. I'll put nine till eleven on the invitations." She gets up and heads for the refrigerator, pulling out the bottle of wine and holding it up to me. "Last chance."

"Thanks, but I've got to get going. I'll have a couple of menus with estimates for you by the end of the week."

In spite of my reluctance to get sucked into some wild goose chase after Isabel, I can't be completely indifferent to the little I've learned about her. I catch myself wondering how Paul DeGraf would respond to a direct question about her and Tom Hemmings. I can't quite imagine myself asking. I hardly know him, but there's a sadness under the high-gloss exterior that makes me hesitate to dig up an old grief just out of curiosity. It's too much like those people who crane their necks when they go by an accident, trying to get a look at a body.

But there is one other person who might be willing to give me some information.

It's past noon when I find the nerve to make the phone call, but I can tell from his voice that I woke him up.

"Is this Thomas Hemmings?"

"Who the hell else would be answering my phone?"

"I'm sorry to bother you—"

"We've now established that you're bothering me and that you're sorry. What do you want?"

"I . . . um . . . you don't know me—"

"So why are you calling?"

"I wanted to ask you about my mother," I blurt out.

"If I don't know you, why the hell would I know your mother?"

"She was a model for you. A long time ago. Isabel Colinas."

The silence lasts till I say, "Her name was Is—"

"I heard you." He stops again. Finally he says, "I didn't know she had a kid."

I plunge on before I chicken out. "I was wondering if I might come see you sometime."

"I can tell you whatever you want to know right now. No need to come all the way up here."

"Please, let me explain something. I never met her. I only found out who she was a few weeks ago. I'm just looking for a little information about her—"

"I didn't really know her," he cuts in. "She was just an artist's model, that's all."

"Mr. Hemmings, please. I promise I won't take up much of your time, I just—"

"You're not going to take up any of my time. There's not a goddamn thing to tell. Isabel Colinas sat for a portrait. I paid her for her time, and that was it. Now leave me alone."

The line goes dead.

When I walk into Dream Weavers at nine thirty Wednesday morning, Elaine Cumming is unpacking two huge boxes from UPS.

She looks up and smiles. "Hi. What can I do for you?"

"Avery James. I was at the show—"

"Oh, right. Of course. Knew I knew you. Can I assume that you've come into an inheritance and you're here to buy us out?"

I leave my sunglasses on and stick my hands down in my jeans pockets to keep myself from nervous fidgeting. "Yes, I have sort of come into an inheritance, but it's not money. And what I'm looking for is a little information."

She holds up an elaborately pieced kimono, shakes it out gently, and lays it over a chair with several others. "Sure. How can I help?"

"That tunic vest, the one by Isabel Colinas," I say.

"Yes?" She tucks a piece of hair behind her ear and eyes me expectantly.

"I've . . . um . . . just learned—or confirmed, I guess—that she's my mother. Or was."

She stares at me for a minute. "Really?" She folds her arms across her chest. "Really?" she says again. "That's . . . What a surprise."

"The reason I came here is because I never knew her. Never even knew her name. The other night you said that you worked with her some, and I was hoping maybe you could tell me about her."

"I don't know what to tell you."

"Basically, anything. I mean, you said she was a nice lady. That's more than I ever knew."

She looks down into the UPS carton as if it might contain information. "It really wasn't a personal relationship. We saw her work and loved it, and we contacted . . . Paul because he was representing her. Suzanne and I both had a lot of respect for her as an artist, but we . . ." Her eyes find mine. "How well do you know Paul DeGraf?"

"Not well. I met him when I was working a party at his house. That's where I saw Isabel's picture."

"He was her agent and her manager and—" She stops, disconcerted. "I don't know what else. He pretty much ran interference between her and the rest of the world. I'm sure he can tell you a lot more than I can."

"I know, but I want to get as much information as I possibly can." Only now do I recognize the truth of those words.

"I understand, believe me," she says. "It's just that it's been almost ten years since she died. Let me think about it." She looks at her watch. "Listen, Drew's going to be here in a few minutes and then I can get out of here. Can you meet me at Starbucks in about an hour? I'll tell you what I can."

Elaine's already got a table when I get there. She waves, then picks up her cup and blows on the liquid to cool it, sending a fine spray of foamed milk all over the table.

"Damn, that's hot." She wipes the table with her napkin over and over.

I get coffee and a scone and sit down across from her. "Thanks for coming."

"Oh, of course, of course." She pushes a brown-and-green brochure across the table at me. "I brought you this."

There's a sun logo in the middle and underneath are the words: Katalysis Partnership, Inc. Bootstrap Banking.

"What is it?"

"It was Isabel's favorite charity. Suzanne reminded me how she was always hitting galleries up for donations. You can keep the brochure; we're on their mailing list. But basically it's a nonprofit organization that makes loans available to small businesses in Central America."

She waits a few seconds while I give the brochure a quick once-over and fold it into my purse.

"I wanted to give it to you because I'm afraid I'm not going to be much help otherwise. After you left, Suzanne and I racked our brains trying to think of what to tell you, but the fact is, we didn't know her that well. She ran with a different crowd. We admired her work, and all of our dealings with her were pleasant, but other than that . . ." Her voice trails off and she stirs more sugar into her cup. "The only time we ever saw her socially was once when she and Paul split up."

"Can you give me any other names of people that I should talk to?"

"Well . . . I can, but . . . most of them are artists."

"Is that a problem?"

"Not exactly. It's just that . . ." She pauses, biting the inside of her cheek. "When you have an artist who's successful, like Isabel was—"

"Which is what? How successful was she? I don't even know that."

"Oh. I'd say maybe she was in the top half dozen fiber artists in Santa Fe. Based on where her things were showing and who was buying them and for how much." She studies her chewed-down fingernails. "When you're successful like that, there's bound to be a certain amount of professional jealousy. A lot of artists are like overgrown children, you know? Some of their resentments can get really petty."

"Like what?"

"Like 'You copied off me.' 'Did not. I thought of it first.' That kind of thing. In truth, it makes so little difference. Even if one artist copies another's technique, it's what someone does with a technique that matters." She rests her chin on her hands and looks at me questioningly.

"Did Isabel 'borrow' someone's technique?"

Elaine laughs. "Not someone. Everyone. She learned from every artist she met. But her work was totally her own. She had no equal as a colorist. It's just that some artists feel like if they thought of something, then no one else is allowed to try it. Which is ridiculous. There's really nothing new under the sun. It's all just variations on a few themes. Know what I mean?"

I nod. "I think so."

"I'm afraid it's not a lot to go on." Then she brightens. "What I can do is give you the names of people or galleries who own works of hers and you can go look at them. Then if you have questions, maybe I can answer some of them for you."

She rips a piece of paper out of her notebook and scribbles: Buena Vista, Full Moon (Cate Mosley), Liza Gardner (Good Earth Herbs), Lindsey Hemmings.

I look up from the list. "Lindsey Hemmings has one of her works?"

"I think she has a ruana. Do you know her?"

"Not well. I mean, we're doing a party for her and I'm sort of riding herd on it, but she . . . her husband . . ."

That laugh of hers that's so contagious bubbles up. "I see you've heard the ballad of Isabel and Tom. Well, Lindsey Hemmings has her quirks, but she'd never get rid of a piece of art just because she didn't like the artist." She looks thoughtfully at her own scribbles. "You know, you might want to give him a call, too. Tom Hemmings. His studio's up in Taos."

"Been there, done that."

"Wouldn't he talk to you?"

I shake my head. "He hung up on me. Of course, I called him at noon, but I think I woke him up."

"Yeah, he's a moody bastard, too. Well, try him again sometime. If you catch him in a good mood, he can be fairly charming." She smiles. "What else can I tell you?"

"What's with you and Paul DeGraf?" The question just pops out, surprising me almost as much as her.

The smile doesn't go away, but it hardens on her face like quick-dry cement. "What do you mean?"

"There's something between you two. Bad blood or something. I feel it whenever his name comes up."

Her eyes slide away from mine. "Nothing as exciting as bad blood. We just have your garden-variety personality conflict. That's all."

"That night at the gallery you said something about him bringing things up from Mexico. What was that about?"

"Oh, I was just needling him a little bit." She chews on the end of her red plastic stir stick. Elaine Cumming is definitely a chewer.

"And this morning you asked me how well I knew him. What did that mean?"

"I just wondered what all he might have told you. About Isabel."

I drink the last of my coffee and set the empty cup in the thick white saucer. "It's hard, talking to people about this, you know." I try to catch her eyes so she can't look away. "I have no idea why, but I'm pretty sure I'm not getting the truth from anybody."

She wets her lower lip with the tip of her tongue. "Well, I guess some of the people involved have their own idea of the truth."

"What's yours?"

"I'm not involved. All I can tell you is what I saw, what I heard. I don't know what relationship it bears to the truth."

I put my arms on the table and lean toward her. "I think lots of people know a little bit. I think if I could just get them all to be honest about what they know, I could figure out the truth."

I can practically hear her arguing with herself. Finally she sighs. "All right." She purses her mouth. "Like I said before, Paul and Isabel ran with a different crowd from Suzanne and me. He was a player in the art scene before we ever got here. When we bought Dream Weavers from the previous owner, she gave us her admittedly biased opinions of everyone that we'd be dealing with. She didn't like DeGraf because he controlled where Isabel's work was sold and for how much—"

"But didn't Isabel have to give him that control?"

She shakes her head impatiently. "I'm just telling you the story as I heard it. A lot of people—mostly Isabel's friends, I guess, mostly women—thought he had sort of taken over her whole life. Supposedly they were Santa Fe's longest-running soap opera. They were notorious for their breakups and reunions. Everybody thought that after the Tom Hemmings episode, it was over, but not long after that, they announced their engagement and she moved into his house. We were all taking bets on how long it would be till they killed each other."

She stops abruptly, her face fiery. "I'm sorry. It was just an expression. I didn't mean it literally."

"I know. It's okay. But what else? What about bringing stuff up from Mexico?"

"I wish to God I'd never said that. I wouldn't have if I'd known—I mean I had no idea you were her daughter." She pulls a face. "It wasn't one of my finer moments, in any case."

I just keep staring at her.

"It's all hearsay."

"I'm not asking for sworn testimony."

Another sigh, this one louder and longer. "There were rumors about him dealing in stolen art. Religious art from churches in Mexico and Central America. Isabel was big into Katalysis, and of course, people said that's what their fights were all about. Hemmings was supposedly involved somehow . . ."

"So what happened? Was it all just rumors? Did he ever get investigated?"

"I don't think so." She shrugs. "Maybe it was just nasty gossip. On the other hand, DeGraf is very well connected. All I know is, he suddenly started getting his picture in the paper with the Mexican consul and receiving awards for repatriating some work called the Santo Niño that was stolen from a church in Guadalajara or something. I don't know. And of course . . ." Her gaze shifts out the window.

"It was a long time ago."

seventeen

Horacio is chopping onions, tears streaming from his eyes. Juana and I are rubbing the blistered skins from charred peppers when the phone rings. I mutter Shit! under my breath, wiping the sticky juice from my hands onto the clean dishtowel.

"Dos Hombres, how can I help you?" I jam the phone between my shoulder and my head.

"Avery James, please."

The phone squirts out of its niche at my ear, and I fumble to hold it. My heart begins to thud in my chest.

"This is Avery."

"It's Paul DeGraf," he says. "How are you?"

"Fine." Unless you count the fact that my hands are shaking.

"I'd like to talk to you."

"Well, I'm busy right now."

"Are you working this weekend?"

"Yes."

"When are you off?"

"Tuesday."

"Don't make any plans. I'll pick you up about ten A.M. All right?"

"It's my only day off, and I have a lot to—"

"Please. This is important."

"All right."

I wipe the receiver, hang it up. I rinse my hands at the little prep sink, dry them, and go back to the stack of blackened peppers, ignoring Juana's inquiring look.

. . .

A small brick bungalow in a former incarnation, the herb shop on Guadalupe is a relic of another time. The faded sign over the door says THE GOOD EARTH. The bell on the handle jingles melodically when I enter, and a pretty olive-skinned woman with golden brown dreadlocks smiles at me from behind an old-fashioned counter filled with apothecary jars. The shelves behind her are covered with more jars and bottles and tins. Bunches of dried herbs hang from racks, perfuming the air with a pleasant, grassy smell that I'll always associate with Cassie.

"I'm Avery James," I say. "I called about talking to Liza Gardner."

"Yes, I'm Cookie. Her niece." Her voice is clipped, but oddly musical. English maybe? "I'll have to warn you, my aunt's on medication that sometimes plays havoc with her memory. I don't know that she'll be of much help to you. She has good days and not so good days."

"I'll try to keep it short."

"Auntie?" she calls, seemingly into space. "You have a guest."

For a few minutes nothing happens, then a movement draws my eye to a wooden door behind the counter. A woman appears, dressed in some kind of green kimono thing. She doesn't look ancient, but she moves with agonizing slowness, as if every step is excruciating. Her wild gray cloud of hair sets off her coffee-colored skin, and the blank look in her dark eyes doesn't give me much hope for her memory.

"Auntie, this is Miss James, the lady I told you was coming to call. Shall I make some tea?"

The woman looks around the room, still not focusing on me. "Oh, yes. I think tea would be good."

"If it's not a good time, I can always come back another day," I say awkwardly.

At the sound of my voice, her eyes find me, and some shadow flickers there. She studies me silently and then she frowns. "Isabel?" Her accent is like Cookie's, but less pronounced.

"She's not Isabel, Auntie. Her name is Miss James. She's Isabel's daughter."

Isabel's daughter. In her gently accented voice, the words sound strange, like a familiar song in a foreign language.

I inch closer and she moves toward me, then stops, gasping.

Cookie is right there steadying her. "Is it bad?" she asks. "You want your medicine?"

"No, not now." She looks from me to Cookie, and a small weary sigh floats from her lips. "When you're young, you can't even imagine all the ways there are to hurt."

But pain seems to sharpen her mind. She looks at me again. "So you're the daughter." I hold my breath. A million questions are pushing behind my teeth, but I don't want to break this delicate chain of thought. "Come over here," she says.

In a few minutes she and I are sitting in big old club chairs in front of the window. From the back room I hear the sounds of tea. Kettle banging on a tile counter, water running, the chink of cups against each other.

It's probably eighty-five degrees in here, but Liza huddles in a corner of the chair, almost like she's cold. I lean toward her slightly. "I'm trying to talk to people who knew Isabel. I'd like to know anything you remember about her."

She lays her head back and closes her eyes and I wait, wondering if she's fallen asleep. Suddenly she's speaking. "Isabel could have been quite a wonderful herbalist, but she wanted to be an artist. Always collecting little bits of things, scraps of material, buttons, ribbons. For her pictures. They were quite beautiful, but I always thought—"

Her eyes open at the sound of footsteps. Cookie hands me a mug with chamomile steam rising and sets one down on a table beside her aunt. "You'll want to let this cool, Auntie."

Liza watches, hypnotized, as her niece stirs in a dollop of golden honey and a squeeze of lemon.

"What did you think?" I prompt her.

"I always thought she would have been happier as a herbalist."

"How long did she work for you?" I ask.

"I don't know. Four years. Maybe five. I can't remember now. There was a lot of back and forth."

The bell on the door jingles again, and Cookie goes to greet a tall, thin man with stringy yellow hair. The minute her back is turned, Liza's crabbed hand slips under the pleated skirt of the chair and pulls out a small flask of something, pouring a healthy shot into her mug. Eyes on her niece, she screws the cap back on and replaces the bottle under the chair.

"World's best painkiller," she says, and when Cookie's head turns our way, she adds, "Chamomile."

"About Isabel . . ." I begin, but Liza's sipping thoughtfully at the spiked tea.

"Impatient. Very like you. I suppose it's a young person's disease. For someone who understood plants so well, how everything happens in its season . . . she was just hell-bent. Couldn't wait to make a big splash with her work. Couldn't sketch her ideas fast enough. Always impatient to get the shop closed and get back to her pictures. Worked like a demon, that one did." A pause. "Maybe she knew she didn't have much time."

"Elaine Cumming said you might have some of her work that I could see."

Cookie is bagging purchases for the blond man, charging them on his credit card. When I look back at Liza, her eyes are closed again, her mouth slightly open, her breathing labored.

"Are you all right?" I ask uneasily.

"Of course." She wipes saliva from her chin and tries to sit up very straight.

I should go. Leave her alone, let her rest. But instead, I sit waiting.

"I have a picture she did. Called *Remembering Yellow* or something." The bell jangles again as the customer leaves. "Cookie, fetch that yellow piece for me, will you, dear? The one over the desk in back."

I run down to rescue him, and she gives me a sly smile as we pull away from the curb.

"I was looking for the other car," I say.

"We'll need this one."

"You know, I really have a lot to do today, so I can't be gone long. It's my only day off, and I need to get groceries and do laundry and . . ."

He turns south on Guadalupe, driving in silent concentration, eyes straight ahead. He's wearing jeans and a T-shirt that looks like it's been ironed and hanging in a closet.

"Where are we going?"

"Bluebird Canyon."

"Where the hell is that?"

"Are you afraid of me?" His voice is casual.

"Should I be?"

"No."

"Then why are you asking?"

He signals for a right turn on Cerrillos. "You seem a little stressed, that's all."

I fold my hands sedately in my lap. "I'm not." I look out the window at the lowrider next to us, decorated with a picture of the *Virgen de Guadalupe* composed entirely of bottlecaps. "Now there is a work of art."

He smiles.

"What did you want to talk about?" I ask.

"Isabel. I know you have questions. I wish you'd ask me. Regardless of what you may have heard, I knew her better than just about anyone. Certainly better than Tom Hemmings."

I swallow silently.

"Santa Fe's a big small town, Avery. Particularly in the art community, there are no secrets."

At the next stoplight he reaches into the console and hands me a key ring with two keys on it—one small, like a padlock key, and one large, like an old-fashioned door key.

"Hang on to those for a while."

We pass the Villa Linda Mall and Santa Fe Factory Outlets. Santa Fe
falls behind us, and he crosses under the interstate and Cerrillos
becomes Highway 14. The Turquoise Trail. I haven't been down this
road since the morning I hitchhiked out of Florales, bound for Albuquerque and the University of New Mexico. He puts a CD on, some
kind of classical music. It doesn't matter to me because I'm not listening. I lean my head back and look out the window.

It's already hot, and the sky is a deep, flat blue, like a painted backdrop for the dark cones of the Ortiz Mountains and the more gradual,
rounded profile of the Sandias. The road curls like a sidewinder
between mottled brown hills dotted with juniper, piñon, and chamiso.
Tall cottonwoods mark the bed of a stream that's invisible from here.

As we crest a hill I see the small brown clapboard building ahead on
the right, an island in a sea of pickup trucks. The Rio Bravo.

Paul turns the music off. "Ever been there?"

"Once. A long time ago."

"It's surprisingly good," he says.

I look at him. "Why surprisingly? Just because it's not in Santa Fe
and you don't have to get a bank loan to eat there?"

He turns the wheel abruptly and we bounce down into the parking
lot, stopping at the far end of a long row of trucks. No doubt so his precious Land Cruiser doesn't get scratched by some careless cowboy.

"Why is it that I can never say the right thing to you?" he asks, but
he's out the door before I can answer.

Faint streaks of gray show in her long black hair and there are a few
lines at the corners of her eyes, but essentially Bettina Jacinto looks
the same. She smiles at us, picks up two menus, then turns back to look
again, her lips parted slightly in surprise.

"Avery," she says, and her smile widens. "I don't remember your last
name."

"James. I'm amazed that you remember me at all."

She laughs, grabbing my shoulders and pressing her cheek to mine. "I don't meet many people with eyes like yours." She steps back to look at me again. "*Dios mio,* it's been a long time." Her smile includes Paul now. "Come in. Sit down."

The place is packed, just like the first time I came here, and probably with some of the same people. Paul studies the menu while Bettina and I catch up with each other.

"Did you graduate from the university?" she asks.

I shake my head. "But I learned some things and had a good time."

She wants to know where I live and where I work. When I ask about Ed Farrell she smiles, but her eyes are sad.

"Oh, he's still the same. He thinks he's never going to die." She flips her order pad open. "What can I get for you?" Paul orders *enchiladas verdes.* I give the menu a quick once-over.

"I don't suppose you have any *capirotada* laying around . . ."

Her eyes twinkle. "I don't think we have any laying around, but we perhaps have some cooling that just came from the oven."

She even remembers to give me a corner piece.

I was talking to Lindsey Hemmings."

Paul stops eating, his fork halfway to his mouth. "And . . . ?"

"She booked a party with us. I went to her house for the site survey and . . . she just started talking. Telling me about how she knew you in Paris and how you introduced her to Tom and . . ."

He watches me stir the cream into my iced coffee.

"She told me about Tom and Isabel. That's why I called him. I thought—" My eyes shift away from his. "I don't know what I thought. I don't know why she told me."

He wipes his mouth with the napkin and leans back from the table. "You have to realize that she was devastated. It was the second time it had happened to her. Her first husband left her in Paris for some young girl. She was jealous of Isabel to begin with, and after that, she was just—"

"What about you?" I cut in.

"What about me?"

"Well, I—I mean she said that you were the one who walked in and found them . . . together. So why are you telling me about how Lindsey felt? How did you feel?"

He takes a deep breath and lets it out slowly. "I was . . . upset. Of course. Angry."

"But you took her back."

"Yes."

I look at him very directly. "Why?"

"First and foremost because I loved her. Then, too . . ." He rests his forearms on the table. "We weren't really together when it happened. We had split up and she was back at Liza's."

"Lindsey said there was a lot of that. Breaking up, getting back together."

He nods. "Mostly my fault. I had this idea that because I loved her, I knew what was best for her. She never seemed to see things that I thought were so obvious. I tried to guide her, artistically, socially, financially—" He shrugs. "She came to resent it."

I drink the last of my coffee to avoid looking at him, but he's on a roll now.

"It wasn't just that I loved her, it was—I was in awe of her talent, the way she expressed herself, not just in her art, but everything about her. She was like no one else I've ever met before. Or since. Half sophisticated, half naïve. Strong in some ways, terribly vulnerable in others. She was passionate about the things she believed in, and she worked incredibly hard, in spite of the pain—"

"What pain?"

"Overuse injuries. Like carpal tunnel. She could work for hours and hardly change positions. Her wrists, her hands, her back, her neck. All started giving her trouble. I used to rub her back and her arms every night—"

He breaks off suddenly, the palpable memory of their nights looming up between us.

"Sorry." He's reaching for his wallet and signaling Bettina at the same time. "I didn't mean to get carried away. Very few people will sit and listen to me anymore without suddenly remembering a dentist appointment or an overdue library book."

Bettina brings the check, eyeing Paul's half-eaten lunch. "How was it?"

"Even better than last time." I smile at her.

"You can pay Rosa up front." She touches my hand. "Don't wait so long to come back."

It's past noon when we step out of the dim café, into a wall of heat. Paul puts on his dark glasses. We walk to the car in silence.

Only a few miles later, he turns off to the right again, but this time it's onto a seriously rutted dirt road. There's a closed gate ahead and he stops in front of it.

"So this is Bluebird Canyon?"

He nods, his hands sliding on the leather steering wheel. "The small key," he says.

I climb down and insert the key in the padlock that secures the rusted chain. It clicks open stiffly. The gate fights me as I drag it back, scraping the hard baked earth of the road. The going is slow now, because the ruts are deep.

"The last few winters have been very wet," he says.

We rise and fall with the road, crisscrossing furrows like small ditches, weaving through grasses and prickly pear cactus and jumping chollas with their menacing barbs. We pass a ruined adobe, walls melting back into the earth, *vigas* protruding like bleached bones. The land begins to rise steadily and outcroppings of rock like dinosaur spines appear on both sides of us, meeting in the distance to form a high ridge that steps up to a range of hills.

"Those are the Cerrillos Hills," Paul says. "Where they used to mine the turquoise."

"It's redundant."

"What is?"

"Cerrillos means little hills," I say. "So Cerrillos Hills is redundant."

He smiles.

It feels like we've been driving forever, but I can see on the odometer that it's just over two miles when we come around a bend and he stops, turns off the ignition. At first I don't understand why we're stopping, but as my eyes adjust to the haze and glare, a tiny, low-slung cabin materializes, nestled at the base of a rock ridge. Built mostly of wood with a little adobe and rock, it blends perfectly into the background. I laugh out loud, and Paul gives me a quizzical look.

"What's funny?"

"I was just thinking about how all that art bullshit like 'inhabiting its space' and interacting with its environment' suddenly makes sense."

He nods. "Welcome to *Querencia*."

A tin-roofed *portal* shades the front of the cabin. The lock is so encrusted with dirt and rust that I can barely get the key in, and then he has to jiggle it and ease it in farther before it will turn, but the heavy wooden door finally swings inward and the cabin's cool, dry breath is on my face. It's oddly fresh, like it was just opened yesterday, but I can see that no one's been here in a long time.

He steps inside, ducking his head under the low doorframe, and I follow him. Surprisingly, the room is full of light. There's a skylight set into the crudely sawn plank ceiling, supported by ancient log *vigas;* the floors look like dirt, but feel hard as cement, and the walls are partly wood plank, partly a grainy plaster. Except for one end wall, which is made entirely of stone, with a fireplace and hearth built in. A modern-looking woodstove is set into the fireplace, its stovepipe disappearing up the chimney.

Three pieces of furniture are pushed into the corners: a small table, a wooden stool, a rusted iron bed with a filthy mattress. The floor is a minefield of pack rat nests and droppings, and glass splinters under a boarded-up window. In some of the corners, the mud plaster has dribbled down, apparently from leaks in the roof.

Gradually I tune into Paul's voice, a soft drone, and his movements around the room.

". . . an old miner's cabin," he says. "She wanted a place to get away from town, to work, to sketch her designs." He touches the wall. "It's very well built. Do you see how the logs are notched, so they fit tightly? The roof is tin. She loved the sound of it in the rain."

"What did you call it?"

"Call what?" He looks like he just woke up from a good dream.

"This place."

"She named it *Querencia*. Do you know what it means?"

I shake my head.

"There is no exact translation," he says. "It's a bullfighting word. It describes the little space in the *corrida*, the bullring, where the bull imagines he's safe. When he's there, he believes nothing can harm him. So the closest translation would be something like a safe haven."

He reaches for my hand, which is bunched so hard that my fingernails have left marks in my palm. He pries my fingers open and presses the cold metal key ring into my hand. "It's yours now."

My head turns in surprise. "I can't. I mean—"

"It's strange for me, too, you know. Eight years after she—you just materialize. It's not as if I knew you were coming." He turns abruptly and walks out onto the *portal*.

I stand motionless, close my eyes, inhale deeply. As if I could draw her in. This was her place. Why can't I smell her? Hear footsteps. See some glimpse of the woman who smoothed the hair off my face that night at the hospital in Darby. There should be something of her essence here. Instead it's nothing but dust and old wood and scraps of curtains and broken glass.

When I walk out, he's checking the supports on the corner of the *portal*. Or going through the motions, anyway. I stand there in the shade imagining a garden—mostly cooking herbs, but some medicinals, too, like Cassie had. And maybe some vegetables and flowers. What I loved about her garden was the haphazardness of it. The way the wild plants would just show up and take over the empty spaces she left for them. Even plants that most people think of as weeds, like dandelion and cocklebur, goosefoot and scorpionweed, were welcome there.

Paul steps off the porch, following an overgrown path that leads away from the road. "Watch where you walk," he says over his shoulder. "Snakes are supposed to sleep during the hottest part of the day, but sometimes they don't know that."

A shiver races down my back. The dark coil of a snake ready to strike, the cricking sound of the rattle. I force myself not to recall, but just to follow him, trying to step in his footprints.

The sun is a hot, flat hand on the back of my neck, and the air is white with glare and dust. We walk slowly in the canyon's stillness, gravel and dry brush crunching underfoot. Tiny grasshoppers start away and a rabbit scampers under a juniper where a bird perches— bluer than any bird I've ever seen.

I see the grave even before he points to it, and I start to run, forgetting to care what might be lurking in the grass.

The small marker is half hidden in the dappled shade of a piñon tree. Umbels of Queen Anne's lace surround it, nodding gently in the parched breeze. I crouch down to read it, brushing aside scraggly branches and brittle weeds and startling a small gray lizard lounging on the stone.

A flower that looks like a columbine is cut into the stone above her name.

Isabel Colinas
Beauty is the impossible coming true

A few steps away, Paul waits, hands in his pockets.

"How long since you've been up here?"

He turns slightly away from me, and his answer careens off into the air. "A long time."

We drive back out to the highway without speaking. I get out and pull the gate closed, wrap the chain, and secure the padlock. When I get back in the car, I say, "Tell me how she died."

The muscles in his arms tense as he grips the wheel.

"She drowned."

"Where?"

"The pool." His voice is flat and quiet.

"Your pool? How could she—it's not even that deep."

"It was an accident. It never should have happened." His hands relax, then tighten again as a faded green pickup truck approaches from the south. He sits preoccupied, waiting too long, finally pulling out just ahead of it. The driver leans on the horn, and Paul's face seems to follow the elongating sound, but his eyes are blank.

"It was a Saturday night. September 7, '91. We had a party every year after Fiesta. To close out the tourist season and just see old friends. It went on very late. We all had way too much to drink. By the time everyone left, Isabel and I were arguing—again."

"About what?"

He shakes his head, but keeps his eyes on the road. "I don't remember. Everything and nothing. It was happening a lot then. That night was particularly bad. She threw a pot at me and it broke a window. It was all so stupid. So futile."

His mouth presses into a thin, straight line.

"I told her we should sleep it off and talk in the morning. She was so angry she didn't want to sleep with me. We argued about that, too. She said she was going to stay in the guesthouse. She kept some things out there.

"She ran into the kitchen and grabbed the keys to the guesthouse. I tried to take them away, but she ran out the back door. I was furious. I couldn't stand the way she looked at me—as if she hated me. I slammed out the front door and went for a long walk."

The road is suddenly and eerily deserted. The green pickup has long since passed us and disappeared.

"If I'd followed her . . ."

He turns the wheel sharply, hitting the brake at the same time. The car slides to a stop on the gravel shoulder.

"I could have saved her." His voice is like a thin sheet of ice over a very dark river.

I can't look at him, so I focus on a row of weathered mailboxes across the road. The engine has died, and the vented air quickly turns warm and stale. "What happened? When you came back."

"I was gone a long time. An hour. Maybe longer. When I came back, I went in the front door. I went upstairs. I went to bed. So I didn't know. All the outdoor lights were off." He turns his face to me. "You see what I'm saying, don't you? It was dark. She'd had too much to drink, she was upset, she fell in the pool. Hit her head . . ." His gaze goes back to the landscape outside the windshield.

"And I went to sleep."

I should say something. Silence has become the third passenger in the car. Beads of sweat are forming on my forehead, my nose.

I see Isabel, facedown in the dark pool, her long gold-and-black skirt tangling around her legs while her lungs fill up with water and Paul tosses, restless in his bed.

.   .   .

At some point he turns the key in the ignition and guides the car back onto the road, gradually picking up speed, now back in control.

When we pull up in front of Alma's, I open the door. I don't turn my head, but my eyes shift to his profile.

"I still don't understand—" I have to stop and clear my throat. "Why didn't she just stand up?"

He doesn't answer immediately. When he does, his voice is oddly inflected, like those phone messages that piece together separately recorded words. "Probably she was unconscious or disoriented. And... because of the pool cover."

I get out and close the door. Before I get to the bottom of the stairs, he's driving away.

eighteen

It's a rare summer Sunday that Rita and I are both off. And today we're both so wired we can't even sleep in, so after a fast cup of coffee, we decide to power walk Canyon Road from Paseo de Peralta out to the Church of Cristo Rey before it gets too hot and then have lunch on the porch at El Farol.

Walking in the shade along the river is pleasant, but a warm dry wind is already gusting across Peralta, and we're both sweating like the proverbial little pigs by the time we turn up Canyon. *Turistas* are out in force, dressed for Art Safari—men in their walking shorts and polo shirts, women looking like giant poppies in their gauzy cotton dresses. Some insist on driving through the narrow streets, and there's the inevitable nonresident maneuvering his Cadillac the wrong way in the one-way zone.

Watching them can sometimes be mildly interesting, but it's not worth a twisted ankle, so I concentrate instead on the narrow, ragged sidewalk, letting the monotony of my steps lull me into a trance.

At some point Rita stops cold.

"Avery, is that—?"

She's staring hard across the street, where someone is just opening a door for business. Pinnacle Gallery. In the window is the portrait of Isabel, with a sign that says, "Works by Thomas Hemmings."

Again. The impact of it overwhelms the memory of seeing it before. I nod. "That's her."

We dash across the street to stand in front of the window.

"Wow," says Rita. "Wow. Ave, she's beautiful."

"*Was* beautiful."

"Can I help you?" It's the guy who was unlocking the door.

"How much is this picture?" Rita asks.

He smiles, his blond hair lying carelessly on his forehead. "I'm sorry, this one's not for sale. It belongs to Mr. DeGraf, the owner."

"Well, how come it's in the window then?" Rita demands.

He gives us a salesman smile. "It's such a spectacular piece, it draws people into the gallery. Then they can see some of Tom's other work."

She nods. "Sort of like bait and switch, huh?"

His laugh shows his teeth all the way back to his molars. "You could say that, I suppose."

She nudges me. A woman is waiting behind us to go inside the gallery. We step out of the doorway to let her by and as the blond guy turns to follow her in, his eyes fall on me. He's already starting his sales warm-up, but there's a tiny blip, a pause as his eyes slide from my face to Isabel's and back again.

By the time we make it out to the Church of Cristo Rey and back down to El Farol, we're exhausted in the way that only a dry, fierce heat can drain you.

We get a table on the shaded porch and order our green chile cheese-burgers. I know I shouldn't have a beer; I'll end up falling asleep this afternoon, but it sounds so good that I order one anyway after Rita promises to drink part of it.

The service is slow here, but that's part of why we like it, I guess. You never feel like they're rushing to turn your table. We sit in silence, the slow breeze ruffling our damp hair, watching the shoppers, tourists, and locals parade past us.

Rita twirls the plastic table card advertising a tasting of El Tesoro Tequila. "You okay?" she asks me again.

"I don't know. I'm so wound up. I feel like I'm skating on the blade of a knife."

She takes a piece of the wheat-smelling country bread and dips it in olive oil. "Don't you think that sort of figures, considering what's going on right now?" She reaches across the table for my beer.

"One morning I actually thought I saw her. I went chasing after this woman on West San Francisco." I press my lips together. For some reason, it seems important to explain myself. "I almost wish I'd never seen the goddamned picture, you know?"

From the way she's looking at me I can tell she doesn't know. She doesn't even suspect. Her forehead creases with concentration.

"Now I'm not saying it's impossible, I'm just saying—you know how when you get a new car, all of a sudden you start seeing lots of people driving that same car?"

I stare at her, lost for a reply, but the waiter saves me, arriving in the nick of time with our food.

Juana is already waiting for me Friday afternoon in the kitchen at Dos Hombres, drinking iced tea and pulling out packets of plastic flatware and napkins, little salt and pepper shakers that screw together cleverly, plastic bottles of Dos Hombres private label hot sauce, which is actually just the cheapest grocery store variety with a few added "secret ingredients."

Together we pack up Mrs. Donovan's tailgate party—cheese and cayenne crackers; hummus with roasted garlic; chicken breasts stuffed with goat cheese, piñons and sundried tomatoes; cold marinated filet of beef; cold poached salmon with raspberry chipotle sauce; red potato salad with snow peas and asparagus; and olive oil cake with orange-strawberry salsa.

"Is it going to her house or what?" Juana asks after we've checked off everything against the job sheet and packed it into one hot carton and one cold, and a basket for plates, utensils, condiments, and glasses.

"No, I'm supposed to meet her in the parking lot at the opera."

"You want me to take it? I'm going to my cousin's in Española tonight. I could drop it off to her on my way."

"Sure, if you don't mind. I'll clean up here." I hand her the delivery card. "Look for a white Mercedes SUV with Texas plates. She's tall, blond, very tan, lots of diamonds."

"That should be easy. There's prob'ly only about five thousand *gringas* there who look like that."

I laugh. "The license number's on the card. Thanks, *chica*. I owe you."

"No, I owe you."

"For what?"

"That stuff you gave me for my mother. The tea."

"Did she like it?"

"Yeah, it was great. I mean, she got some relief from the sweats, and she's not holding water the way she was. Plus I don't have trouble getting it down her, because she likes it. She said her *tia* Lupe used to make some stuff like that. She was a *curandera* down in El Paso. Strange lady—she could tell you what your dreams meant."

She gives me an appraising look. "You ever do any of that? Dream stuff."

I pick up the dirty utensils and turn on the water. "Nope. Thanks again for taking that stuff."

It's hotter than blazes at four o'clock. By the time I walk home, all I want is a cold beer. Maybe some blue corn chips and guacamole. Rita's sitting on the couch with a magazine in her lap, not reading.

"You're home early," she says.

"Juana did my delivery tonight. What are you doing home?" She's been spending so much time with Rick lately that sometimes I only hear her coming and going.

Her eyes flicker. "I just felt like spending some time with you for a change."

"You want a beer?"

"No, thanks. I have a Coke."

I get a Tecate out of the fridge and open it, then plop down on the couch, untie my jogging shoes and kick them off, wiggling my toes. Through the open slider, the words to some heartbreak ballad drift up from Alma's.

"So where's Enrique?"

"He's been offered a job at the *Albuquerque Sun,*" she blurts out. "He wants me to go with him."

For a minute I can only watch her roll the magazine into a tube and then release it.

"You mean, go back to Albuquerque?"

"You could come, too." She smiles hopefully. "It would be just like old times. Sort of."

I drink some beer and try to get a handle on the ninety-degree turn my life has just taken. "Rita, it wouldn't be anything like old times."

"We could live close to each other. We'd see each other a lot. Rick really likes you."

"And I like him. But that doesn't make us one big happy family. Besides, I'm not going back to Albuquerque. There's nothing there for me."

"Well . . ." Her voice drifts away, like it's blown by the wind.

I get up and go in the kitchen. "When?"

She clears her throat. "Two weeks."

"Two weeks?" It comes out almost a gasp.

"I can stay through September. I could—"

"No." I turn on the water just for something to do, just to hear the sound of it rushing into the empty white sink.

"Avery, please don't be mad."

"I'm not mad." Even as I'm saying it, I know it's a lie. A big, black, outrageous, pink-eyed, flared nostril, yellow-bellied lie. I *am* mad. I'm absolutely furious. Seven years, and I get two weeks notice.

"You are too mad." She's standing right behind me.

"Don't start telling me how I feel."

"And don't you start trying to make me feel guilty for wanting to be happy. All I ever—"

I turn around, leaning against the counter. "If you feel guilty, maybe you should ask yourself why. Like maybe it's because you're leaving me high and dry with two weeks notice, to find another apartment—"

"Oh, puh-leeze." Her west Texas twang kicks in. "Avery, you're twenty-five years old. You can find a place to live by yourself. If you don't want to, then come to Albuquerque with . . . us."

"You don't even know him. It hasn't even been—what—four months?"

"Amost five. Anyway, it doesn't matter. I do know him. And I know how I feel."

I cross my arms. The edge of the counter digs into my back, and I focus on that small pain to avoid the big one that's looming. This is a new thing for her. Oh, she's been "in love" before. Lots of times. But not like this. She's never even talked about moving in with anyone, much less moving away with them.

"I'll go ahead and pay my half of the September rent," she offers.

"No, thanks."

"Avery, don't be like this. I know you need the money to stay here till you—"

"I don't need your money."

Her expression softens, and I have to dodge the hand she tries to put on my arm. "Avery, you'll always be my best friend."

"Right."

"You know, so many times in all the time we've been together, I've felt like you didn't care about me the same way I cared about you—"

"Rita, will you please stop talking like a Hallmark card?"

I walk back into the living room, but she follows me. "Listen to me, Avery. This is life. People come and then they have to leave for a while. It doesn't mean they don't care. You don't have to lose touch. This is normal."

She stands there, rubbing her palms together.

"Normal." I repeat the word like a dummy.

Suddenly I can't stand to look at her trembling chin or the water pooled in her lower eyelids like rain in catch basins.

I go in my bedroom, closing the door behind me.

"Avery . . ."

I stretch out on the bed.

"Let's talk about it." Her voice is muffled through the door.

"Not right now."

Even through the door, I hear the long, resigned sigh.

So this is normal.

Then how come it doesn't feel normal? How come it feels like some goddamned black hole sucking me dry?

Juan Largo Street is easy enough to find. It's a pedestrian walkway off the northeast corner of Taos Plaza, and Tom Hemmings's studio is supposed to be on the right-hand side all the way at the end, past the J. D. Challenger Gallery. That's according to my newly purchased *Guide to the Studios of Taos Artists.*

The modest adobe structure has two doors, one at ground level, and one at the top of a rickety flight of blue-painted stairs. I start toward the lower one, but then I notice a long bank of windows jutting out from the brown adobe wall upstairs. Good light for a studio.

At the top of the stairs the smell of turpentine hits me first, then the music. Some wild kind of tuneless jazz. I take a deep breath and open the door.

The place reminds me of that joke about Española—how a tornado touched down and did several million dollars worth of improvements. It's filthy—paint spilled on the floor, spattered on the walls. Paint-covered rags, jars with bouquets of paintbrushes, old pizza boxes, full ashtrays, and empty beer bottles. Canvases in varying stages of completion are propped against everything.

The wall opposite the bank of windows is mirrored, I guess so you can see the fabulous view of the mountain without turning around. But the man in the center of the room, applying paint to a canvas with a palette knife isn't looking at the view. He's focused so intently on the work in front of him that he might as well be working in a closet.

When the music clicks off, he looks up and catches sight of me in the mirror.

"What the fuck . . . ?" He turns around, straightening up from his crouch over the canvas. He's tall and lean with gray hair cut very short and the most amazing blue eyes. Before he finishes swearing, he stops and stares at me, slack jawed.

"Unbelievable," he mutters. Unthinking, he wipes a hand on his baggy white pants, leaving a streak of orange paint in good company with all the other streaks. He walks over to me slowly, looking at me from different angles. "She was taller."

"I'm sorry to just barge in——" I begin.

"Oh, bullshit. If you were that sorry you wouldn't have come. I'm really busy. I should just throw your skinny ass out of here." He's built like a runner, all long bones and ropy muscles. His collarbone sticks out of the gray V-neck T-shirt that hangs on his frame.

"I just want to know about her. Please. If this isn't a good time, I can come back whenever you say, but I have to talk to you."

He snorts. "I told you, she was just a model."

I try to engage his eyes. "And I told you, I know different."

He folds his arms across his chest. "Who've you been talking to?"

"Lindsey."

His laugh is like a dog's bark, short and sharp. "She lies about me all the time. She's my ex-wife. That's her job."

"And Paul DeGraf."

The piercing blue eyes slide away, but only for a second. "He a friend of yours?"

"Sort of."

"I guess that figures." He exhales noisily, looking around the room. "Better find a place to sit," he says. "Unless you're comfortable on the floor."

It takes some doing. Things have to be moved, chairs brushed off, but in a few minutes we're sitting. He pats his pockets till he finds what he's looking for, a pack of menthol Marlboros. He extracts one, holds it between his lips, and lights it with a yellow disposable lighter.

"I can tell you don't approve." He smiles and blows smoke directly at my face.

I wave it away. "I really don't care if you want to kill yourself."

"It's gonna happen," he says. "The only question is slow or fast. Now what do you want to know about Isabel Colinas?"

"Anything you can tell me about her. How she looked and acted. What she was like."

"Well, if you want to know how she looked, just look in a mirror. The resemblance is amazing. . . . What she was like?" He flicks ashes on the floor. "Confident. Of herself. Her talent. She knew what she wanted and she planned to get it—"

"And what was that?"

He frowns. "What all artists want, of course. Money. Recognition. Respect."

"Love?"

He looks at me. "I don't think that was on her short list. Sex, definitely. Security, maybe. But love implies a certain loss of control, and Isabel was never comfortable with that." He smirks. "She liked being on top."

"Were you in love with her?"

He blows another stream of smoke at me before saying, "Oh, she was fascinating. No doubt about that."

I lean back in the chair and notice for the first time that there are radically different styles represented in the paintings stacked all over the place—so different that it's obvious, even to someone like me with no knowledge of art. There are some landscapes that look nothing like New Mexico, all rolling green hills and tall, skinny trees. There's one of roses lying on a table beside a bowl of oranges. There are pictures of saints having their heads cut off, Madonnas with almond-shaped eyes, and fat little Jesus babies. Somehow I don't picture Tom Hemmings painting religious pictures.

"DeGraf was very . . . protective." His voice bites into my thoughts. "She tolerated it, but just barely. You could always tell when she was starting to feel claustrophobic." He chuckles to himself. "She'd practically be hyperventilating. She'd pace sometimes or fiddle with her hair. Sometimes when she was supposed to be sitting for me, I couldn't get her to be still."

"So why did she stay with him?"

"I never asked. I assume it was because of what he did for her career. When she first came to Santa Fe, she was just another small-town girl with big ideas. She had very little training, and no focus. She was from some mudhole town up in Colorado. DeGraf polished her up a bit. Made the right introductions. Promoted her work. Gave her good advice. Artistic and financial."

"Would you say she was smart?"

"She was intelligent enough, I guess." He brings one foot up, propping it on the seat of his chair and draping his arm over his knee. "Although there was a certain naïveté."

"What do you mean?"

"About the consequences of her actions. She'd run roughshod over people and then be genuinely surprised when they got pissed off."

He takes a long drag of his cigarette. "But I guess most artists operate that way—we're kind of a self-absorbed bunch."

"What did you think of her work?"

"Total waste of time. *Fiber art.*" His voice drips sarcasm. "Now there's an oxymoron."

"So you don't think she had any talent."

"That's not what I said. She had talent, all right. Great color sense. She should have stuck to painting. And not those goddamned faggoty watercolors, either." He rolls his eyes in disgust. "I tried to get her to try oils, acrylics. Something with some meat to it. But she was just as pigheaded about that as everything else."

"Why did you paint her as Malinche?" I ask him.

"Her idea." He smiles broadly. "She was fascinated with Malinche. Whore? Traitor? Sorceress? Healer? Lover? Survivor? All depends on whose version you believe. There's not even any agreement on how she died. Some accounts have her dying of old age, some say it was a fever." He looks over my head out the window. "Some even say Cortéz strangled her."

"And Isabel," I say. "How did she die?"

He crushes out the cigarette. The smoke leaves his nostrils in twin streams like a dragon's breath. "Drowned. But I'm sure Paul can give you all the details." He gets up and walks back to his easel.

"Shit!" He picks up the palette knife and scrapes a glob of paint off the canvas, flinging it on the floor.

Looks like our chat is over.

"Thanks for the information." I pick up my purse and head for the stairs.

Just to the left of the door the picture propped on a shelf stops me. It's a *santo,* one of the folk-artsy paintings of saints that are everywhere in New Mexico. This one's a woman with a thin gold halo and the sweetly sexless face of a child. Her cheeks are rosy and her eyelids are delicately shaded under heavy black brows. But it's the eyes themselves—huge, fawnlike, luminous brown eyes—so transparently emotional that you want to laugh, but somehow you can't. The picture is painted on a round slab of wood, still light colored and oozing sap. One drop of resin on the face makes it look like she's crying real tears.

Hemmings's voice turns me around. "Let me know if you're ever interested in sitting for me."

nineteen

Los Lobos blares out of Horacio's boom box in the kitchen, and Juana's rocking back and forth in time, lip-synching to "That Train Don't Stop Here." I smile. Music is a sure sign Dale's not here. So all I have to do is show up, do my job, and go home. No hassles. The season will be over soon; I just need to hang on for a few more weeks. Then I'll have time. To find a cheaper, smaller place. To decide what to do.

"Hey, *muchacha*," she greets me. "What's happening?"

Before I can answer, the door to Kirk's office opens and he looks around the corner. "Juana, tell Horacio to turn that thing down. Avery, I need to see you." Just like that. No good morning, no kiss my ass, no nothing.

"Should I bring my notebook?" I ask hopefully.

"Not necessary," he says. I look at Juana, but her eyes are glued to the papers in her hand.

Kirk shuts the door behind me and motions me toward one of the *equipale* chairs facing his desk. He sits down across from me and spends a full minute rearranging files, pens, laptop computer, carafe of water and glass.

His face isn't classically handsome, but he has a knockout smile, probably the product of lots of time in the dentist's chair. A couple of times I've caught him alone with a mouth full of those whitening strips. His year-round tan is tasteful—not too dark—his brown hair carefully trimmed and groomed, and I would bet that he spends more on clothes than I do on food and rent combined. The overall effect reminds me of extruded plastic, but some people are into that.

Finally he gets through farting around with his desktop.

"As you know . . ." he clears his throat, "Avery, every year after high season, we . . . uh . . . we lay off our temporary staff. And of course, we generally are able to rehire them. Some of them. For Thanksgiving/ Christmas/New Year, some of course not till next spring."

Long pause.

I'm getting a bad feeling, except I'm not temporary staff. I'm permanent, full-time staff. AKA, employed.

"Well, this year, because of the . . . the economy and the state of . . . things, it's unfortunately become necessary for . . . unfortunately . . . more staff cuts . . ."

He won't even look at me. My heart dips into my jogging shoes, but my brain keeps thinking no, no, no. Like I could sway him through mental telepathy.

". . . you and Juana," he's saying. "And based on seniority, she has more . . . seniority, and . . ." He takes an audible breath. "And so, therefore, unfortunately I think, we've decided to actually . . . uh . . . cut your job. Effective immediately."

The bad news percolates through the silence, eventually penetrates my brain.

"I'm truly sorry, Avery."

"Kirk . . ." I shift in the chair. "This couldn't come at a worse time for me. My roommate's moving to Albuquerque and I'm going to need time to find a new apartment, and how am I going to get anything decent to rent with no job?"

"We—I'll be happy to give you a recommendation—"

"Landlords are always impressed with those."

"I'm sorry. It's all I can do. And your two weeks' severance, of course." He gives me what I'm sure he thinks is an encouraging smile. "And you can always check back with us in November or—"

I can't help laughing, but it's more like a groan. "Kirk. Come on. Once Dale gets rid of me, he's not going to be hiring me back."

He fumbles in his desk drawer for the Dos Hombres envelope that contains my check. He holds it out to me, but I just sit there.

"I'm sure you can get on with another caterer—"

"Right. As you just pointed out, it's the end of the season, for God's sake. Nobody's hiring now. Can't I just—"

"No," he says. "You can't. We just can't afford to keep you. And, Avery . . ." He sighs painfully. "Can I be blunt?"

I look at him in amazement. "You just fired me. How much more blunt are you going to get? Do I have dandruff? Bad breath?"

"What you have is bad attitude."

"About what?"

"The job, Avery. And then there's your working relationship with Dale. Or lack thereof."

"That's at least as much about his attitude toward me."

"There's a certain amount of truth in what you say. However, the fact remains that Dale is—was—your boss. He and I are the owners of the company. Therefore, the onus was on you to make an effort to get along."

"He treats me like shit. No one should have to put up with that."

"You were free to leave at any time."

"But I needed the job, Kirk. Listen, what if I promise scout's honor that no matter what Dale says to me that I'll smile and say kick me again."

He leans back in his chair and closes his eyes.

"I'm sorry, Avery. Really."

He offers the envelope again, and this time, I take it.

Swarms of brightly dressed tourists, like exotic birds, hover around the Plaza. Indian Market's already come and gone. The frenzy is building to its annual peak—*Fiestas de Santa Fe*, commemorating the return of the Spanish after the Indians threw them out during the Pueblo Revolt.

I've always thought it's like celebrating the return of the bad guys. Instead of Fiesta, they should call it The Empire Strikes Back. Even more tourists will pack into town for the Arts & Crafts Market, the feasting, the wine tastings, the pet parade, masses and ceremonies out the wazoo, and of course, everyone's favorite, the burning of Zozobra—old man Gloom—who gets burned in effigy at Fort Marcy Park to the wild cheering of thousands of drunks.

Speaking as someone who's never trusted any mass display of sentiment, of course . . . but in Santa Fe, any excuse for a party is a good excuse. If I call around to all the caterers, I might be able to pick up a couple nights' work, but that's not going to pay the rent. With Rita leaving, I couldn't afford the apartment long term anyway, but I was counting on having September to find another one.

My feet have carried me faithfully back home, but I can't make myself climb the stairs. I don't want to see all her boxes stacked in the hall. I don't want to hide in my bedroom—my bedroom that won't be mine much longer. And I don't want to talk to Rita. If she finds out I'm unemployed, she'll hang around feeling sorry for me and guilty about moving, trying to be helpful and generally making me crazy.

My truck sits waiting in the parking lot. I could throw my stuff in the back and hit the road. Just drive till I get tired, pull over and sleep, drive some more. Go someplace I've never been. Find a job. I can change my name, get some fake IDs. People do it all the time. Probably lots of people right here in Santa Fe aren't who they say they are. And I don't just mean the illegals. I've heard there are even some books that tell you exactly how to do it.

Mr. Hanover, the social studies teacher in Florales, used to give me books all the time, old books that people threw out. He gave me one called *The Great Imposter.* About a guy named Ferdinand Waldo DeMara who had the ability to be anything he wanted to be. Or at least to convince other people that he was. He changed his identity, passed himself off as a college professor, a surgeon, a monk, and a prison warden among other things.

For weeks after I gave the book back, I'd lay awake on my cot, feeling the cold dry wind through the chinks in Cassie's walls, listening to the yipping coyotes, and thinking about how you could be whoever you wanted to be. You could invent yourself a whole new life whenever you wanted to. Just like Ferdinand Waldo DeMara.

Except somewhere at the start of it, wouldn't you have to know who you really were?

Bettina seems glad to see me, if not terribly surprised. I'm a little ahead of the lunch-hour crush.

"You off today?" she asks as I take a seat at a two-top in the corner.

"Sort of."

She smiles. "Sounds like a story."

"Can I get a beer?"

"Definitely a story. You want Dos Equis, Tecate, Modelo Negro—"

"Tecate with lime. Please."

In a few minutes a young girl appears and sets down a sweating red can of Tecate and a cold glass. "Bettina say whatever you want. On the roof."

It takes me a few minutes to realize that my lunch is on the house. "All I want is some green chile stew and *sopaipillas*."

"Okay." She smiles and goes back to the kitchen.

I squeeze the lime into the glass and pour the golden liquid down the side. There was nothing in the refrigerator for breakfast this morning, so by the time I've drunk about half a beer, I'm starting to feel high. I'm also noticing that the place is suddenly packed and Bettina is nowhere in sight. The girl who waited on me is running around like a headless chicken, screwing up orders. I don't think this is her usual gig. Except for the counterman, she's the only one working the room and she looks close to tears.

Back in the kitchen, a husky figure in new blue jeans and a white T-shirt under a long white apron is cooking ground pork with onions

and peppers, rolling enchiladas, and frying *sopaipillas*. Bettina is chopping tomatoes at lightning speed. A whole basketful sits next to her
cutting board.

She frowns when she sees me. "Didn't you get your food yet?"

"You're getting slammed out there. You need some help on the
floor? I'm a certified professional."

She laughs. "If you want to sweat. Aprons are over there. Divide up
the room with Felicia. *Gracias,* Avery." She brushes her hair back with
her forearm. "Miguel!"

The guy at the stove turns around. "This is Avery. My brother
Miguel." Then she says something in Spanish I don't understand.

"Mucho gusto." His short black hair is slicked straight up off his forehead, and his shy smile makes him look like a big Mexican teddy bear
with a pencil-thin mustache.

For the next three hours I run around delivering searing hot plates
covered with blue corn enchiladas, tamales with mole sauce, tacos,
stuffed *sopaipillas,* green and red chile, just like old times at Pete's.
Fending off lonesome cowboys and traveling salesmen, chucking babies
under the chin in hopes that their parents will leave a decent tip, cleaning up spilled Cokes, drying glasses just out of the rinse sink, adding
little metal dishes of sour cream, green salsa, red salsa, sprigs of cilantro
to the brown pottery plates, refilling ice tea and water, doling out more
chips and salsa to soothe the ones who have to wait.

For a brief interlude, I manage to forget that I've lost my job and my
roommate, that I have to find a new place to live, that I'm attracted to
a man who's probably old enough to be my father, who was certainly
my mother's lover, and who may or may not know more than he's
telling about her death.

So, Avery. Tell me the story." Bettina brings two bowls of green
chile and two glasses of ice water and settles into the chair across
from me.

First I take a bite of the stew, letting it sear my mouth and throat and bring the tears to my eyes.

"Too long and depressing." I take another spoonful of green, feel the pleasant sweat break out on my face.

She leans forward. "If you don't tell me, how can I help?"

"You can't help, anyway," I say. "That's not why I came. I just needed to get away for a little while."

She gives me an indignant look. "Of course, I can help. You come in here today and see that I need help, so you just get up and help. It's what friends do for each other. But you must first tell me the problem."

I just keep eating and sweating, thinking about Ed Farrell's description of Bettina's green. "It'll take the top of your head off" was what he said. That's a pretty good approximation.

"The problem is, it's not just one problem. It's a lot of problems— some old, some new . . ." I stop and fan the fire in my mouth.

"So you begin with the oldest one." Her tone of voice makes it clear that she's not letting this go.

"Okay." I sigh. Take a drink of water, which of course just makes the chile burn hotter. "It's my mother. I never knew her. She gave me up when I was born."

Bettina nods gravely.

"So I just found out who she was."

"And you have spoken to her?"

"She's dead."

"Oh, Avery, I am very sorry."

"And then there's this guy . . ."

Her eyes go to the ceiling and she stares at the wooden fan turning lethargically. "Always there is a *tipo*. Always."

"It's . . . he was with my mother . . ."

Her eyes get very big. "*Madre de Dios*. And now with you?"

"No," I say quickly. "Not yet anyway."

"This is the man who was here with you." Again it's not a question, but a statement.

I nod into the silence.

"What else?" She wipes her mouth carefully.

I laugh. "Isn't that enough?"

"Not if there is more."

"My roommate's moving to Albuquerque."

"And what else?"

"I got laid off."

"*Que chinga!*" she swears, then blushes. With small damp wisps of hair curling on her forehead, her dark eyes throwing off sparks, cheeks pink, she looks like one of the video posters in the store near my apartment. Ed Farrell's a moron not to have scooped her up a long time ago. "What do those *pendejos* think? Firing you!"

"Oh, you know, high season's over and times are hard. The usual."

She puts her hand over mine. "Maybe we need some help from time to time."

"Thanks." I smile at her worried frown. "It would be fun, working with you. The problem is, driving down here from Santa Fe, just to buy gas would take a lot of what I make."

"So you can live down here."

I sit for a minute, daydreaming pleasantly about *Querencia*. But it would take a lot of work to make it livable.

"Well, it's something to think about," I say.

The Santa Fe Public Library is a rambling territorial-style adobe on Washington Street about a block from the Plaza. I haven't had much to do with the Internet since I was at UNM, and I discover that access has changed a lot. The librarian palms me off on an assistant librarian who acts like I just started walking upright yesterday, but he manages to get me signed in and shows me how to access the *New Mexican*'s archives.

"Thirty-minute time limit," he informs me primly. "Then you must vacate the station if there's anyone waiting."

After he's gone back to the desk, I go to the Advanced Search and type in Isabel Colinas. Thirty-two matches come back in chronological order, beginning with August 20, 1980. I almost miss what I'm looking for because Paul said September 7, and the closest date to that is September 9, 1991. Of course. If she died on Saturday night, of course it wouldn't make the paper till Monday morning.

ISABEL COLINAS, FIBER ARTIST, DEAD AT 34

With the death of Isabel Colinas, Santa Fe has lost, not only a preeminent fiber artist, but a dynamic citizen of the world, as well as the community.

Her body was discovered shortly after 7:30 A.M. Sunday in the swimming pool at 505 San Tomás, the home of her fiancé, Paul DeGraf. Cause of death has not been determined.

Colinas moved from Durango, Colorado, to Santa Fe in 1977, working at The Good Earth on Guadalupe Street while trying to sell her paintings. In 1980 she changed her medium to fiber arts, quickly becoming a respected practitioner, and finding the success that had eluded her as a painter. In the next few years her wide-ranging achievements mounted and the prices of her works soared.

This has been partly attributed to her friendship with DeGraf, art dealer and owner of Buena Vista and Pinnacle Galleries, where her work was often featured. The two were romantically linked, but maintained a low profile socially until she took up residence in his home on San Tomás and they announced their engagement. No wedding date had been set.

In the last four years, Colinas had become active in Katalysis, a nonprofit organization that provided loans to small enterprises in Central America, and last year she was elected to the board of directors.

There is no known surviving family. A memorial service will be announced pending release of the body by the New Mexico Medical Examiner's Office.

Directly below is a thumbnail of the same photograph that was on the brochure at the Buena Vista.

I sit and stare, letting the words slip out of focus. September 7, 1991. Where was I that night? Fall of my senior year in high school. Probably just hanging out at Cassie's. Doing homework. Actually school wouldn't have started that early.

I stare at the picture till it blurs, not sure what I'm looking for, but certain that whatever it is, I won't find it in a publicity photo. Unfocused, her face becomes a mosaic of light and shadow, the image fixed years ago on the backs of my eyes, and the sudden perception pulls me upright in the hard wooden chair. How could I not have remembered? The clinic in Darby. The night I got bit by the rattlesnake. The night I saw Isabel.

That was the night she died.

The morning air is cold. I left my window open last night, and I wake up huddled in a ball under the covers, feet like ice cubes. There are noises in the hall—the kind made by people trying to be quiet—tiptoe steps, whispers. A faint smell of coffee reaches me. I lie there, comfortably drowsy, listening to the oriole whose nest hangs from the highest branch of the *álamo* outside. Till I remember it's today.

Rita's leaving.

I push away the internal coldness that rises from my stomach. No big deal. I've been alone before. When I think about it, I've always been alone. The few people in my life have all been sort of like mannequins in a store window. Just there to pretty things up, give the appearance of normal life for a while.

The question is, do I get dressed and see them off with phony smiles and good wishes? Or do I lie here and sulk, which is really what I prefer? Based on the memory of seven years together, I drag myself shivering out of bed, pull on my jeans and a sweatshirt. Suddenly, for no reason I can explain, I feel ashamed. Rita has a right to this. To Rick. To a life that doesn't necessarily include me.

I hope we didn't wake you up." Rita tries to smile, but her eyes are red rimmed. I feel both touched and disgusted.

"I woke up because I was cold." I head for the kitchen and pour myself a cup of coffee.

It's a lesson I keep learning. Everyone leaves sooner or later. Usually just when you start to wish they wouldn't. Rita's only the latest in a long line of skippers.

The sweet, nutty aroma of piñon coffee floats up from the mug. I sip slowly, listening to the sounds of moving. Grunts, steps on the stairs, whispered questions about time and filling up the truck. She's finally gotten rid of the Plymouth. Rick's driving the U-Haul and she's following behind in his VW. I don't remember when she told me this, but I know.

By the time I finish my coffee, they're done, having loaded all the furniture yesterday. Rick wanders into the kitchen ahead of her. He gives me one of his solemn smiles. "Remember, you're always welcome," he says. Then he turns and goes outside, leaving Rita and me alone. Tears run in rivulets down her un-made-up face. I feel like that, too, I guess, but I don't seem able to produce any evidence of it.

"Avery, I'll miss you—so much." She gulps it, the sound fading in and out.

"Me, too."

"Promise you'll come for a visit soon."

I swallow and nod. "Drive carefully." I intend it to sound caring, but it comes off like some anonymous radio voice saying, "Have a nice day."

When she hugs me, I feel her tears soaking into the shoulder of my sweatshirt. I force myself to put my arms around her and squeeze gently.

She pulls back and lays a piece of paper on the counter. "Our new address. I'll call you when we get a phone number."

"Rita . . ." My tongue feels like it's glued to the roof of my mouth. "Take care."

She gives me another brief hug before she turns and runs down the stairs. I walk out on the balcony just in time to see them pull away through the screen of cottonwood leaves. The U-Haul lumbers out into traffic, and the black VW follows nimbly. I can almost see Rita, seat pushed all the way forward, clutching the wheel with both hands and crying.

twenty

Somebody's pounding on the door. I roll out of bed, thinking about getting my bathrobe, then realize that it won't be necessary. I'm wearing yesterday's jeans and shirt.

Linda lounges against the doorjamb, taking a deep drag of a cigarette. She smiles, blowing the smoke up at the sky. " *'Mana! Qué onda?*" Her eyes take in my rumpled clothes. "A rough night?"

"Sort of. What's up?"

"Alma's got a fish on the line. She wants to show the apartment. Okay?"

"Now?"

She looks at me closely. "You doing okay?"

"Yeah. I was out late, that's all. When does she want to show it?"

She shrugs. "Fifteen minutes?"

I nod.

She studies the end of her cigarette, the print left by her purple lipstick. "I can still cut your hair, you know. For cheap. I don't mind."

"*Gracias.*"

"*Luego,*" she says. Later.

Rita's been gone for a week now, and it's still sort of a shock to turn around and see the apartment empty. Like somebody broke in while I slept and cleaned the place out. The living room is bare except for the unfinished pine chest that I always meant to paint, the old hat rack that Rita found at a garage sale and gave me for my birthday the first year we roomed together, and the rocking chair that she said they didn't have room for in the truck.

Of course, she was lying. She left it because she felt sorry for me, not having any furniture to speak of. Or maybe it made her feel less guilty. I wander into the kitchen. Even barefoot, my steps echo softly in the silence. I wish I could turn on some music, but the boom box was hers.

I open the refrigerator and stand squinting into its bright, cold emptiness. I sniff the contents of the milk carton. Dubious. I pour it down the drain. I settle for peanut butter on a stale tortilla, warmed in the oven, with a water chaser. Looks like a trip to the store might be in order.

I've just finished throwing the blanket up over my bed when I hear voices outside the door.

Alma's prospective tenants are a very young couple. They look still in their teens, and the girl is about seven months pregnant. I watch them walk around, looking at the appliances, checking out the balcony, peering in all the closets. He acts like she's made of porcelain; his hand is at her elbow, guiding her. He smooths her hair back. He opens the doors and lets her look first. Shit. How long will that last? Wait till they've got two or three screaming kids running around here and all he wants to do is go shoot pool with his *'manos* or lay outside in the parking lot tinkering with his car.

My Spanish isn't that great, but I hear him ask Alma when the place will be available. She looks at me.

"September 30, hmm?" She pats my arm on her way out.

Early in the afternoon, I drag the rocking chair out on the balcony and sit rocking, watching the puffy white clouds mushroom into the anvil shapes of thunderheads, silvery on top, blackish purple like an angry bruise on the bottom. Before long, snake tongues of lightning flicker between them, and on the horizon, black streamers of rain straggle to the ground. Thunder grinds in the distance like an old car starting up.

A sudden breeze lifts my hair, and then huge drops begin to splatter around me, on the top of my head, my face, the backs of my hands where I grip the chair arms. Finally a car alarm going off rouses me enough to get up and pull the chair back inside before sheets of rain start blowing across the parking lot.

I dry my face on my T-shirt and go into the bedroom. A file folder is wedged between the wall and the bed under the window. On the tab I've written "Isabel" and inside are some pages I printed off at the library—newspaper articles, mostly stories about her work. I punch up my pillow for support, lay down, and open the folder.

The first page is nothing but a photo dated August 20, 1980. Isabel and an older woman and a very young man standing in front of some paintings. The caption reads,

Isabel Colinas, Elena Chavez, and Abelardo Gonzalez are among the artists whose work will be on displ. y next weekend at Spanish Market.

The next page is a listing of gallery openings from *Pasatiempo*, May 3, 1981.

Elliot-Newnan Southwest Arts—242 Canyon Road
    Watercolors by Isabel Colinas, acrylics by Les Rafferty
    Opening reception 5–7 P.M.

Then another, larger photo. April 20, 1982. This time Isabel is solo, standing in front of a large landscape of some kind, but the reproduction quality isn't good. Caption:

Red Clouds *watercolor by Isabel Colinas*
    Shows at Brier Fine Arts, 125 Grant Avenue through May 15.

In September 1985 there's a review from *Santa Fe Scene Magazine*, featuring a full-page photo of Isabel, dressed head to toe in black, standing beside the yellow piece I saw at The Good Earth.

Painting with Fiber *by Maxine Engels*

Mystery and magic, memories and dreams—the stuff of which Autumn is made. And it's pure gold for Isabel Colinas, who, two years ago turned over a "new leaf," abandoning her work in watercolors for a new direction in fiber arts. If her first solo show at Moon Dancer Gallery is any indication, she's definitely on the right track.

Both technically accomplished and spiritually vibrant, the works elicit an immediate emotional response. Composed of multiple layers and incorporating many techniques, these pieces draw the viewer's attention inward, beckoning him to look below the surface for the truths that are not always apparent.

Central to the collection is the paean to fall in the Southwest, aptly titled In Memory of Yellow. *It's a complicated piece, utilizing embroidery, photo transfer, loop-pile embroidery, collage and silk ribbon work, and it rewards careful attention with fascinating insights into artist, viewer, and the whole Southwest milieu. The amazing part is, Colinas stitches all her designs freehand.*

"Painting the design on first, then stitching over it feels somehow like cheating," she says with a mysterious smile. "I'm drawn to the danger, I think. The risk of committing to a design before I know exactly what it will be."

The show, Memories and Dreams, *runs through Halloween at Moon Dancer Gallery, Galisteo.*

The caption under the photo reads,

In Memory of Yellow—*In high-desert autumn the days seem to shrink down and glow with sun's last heat, like the coals of a dying fire. The wind feels melancholy, as if mourning a loss that is sad, but inevitable.*

There is a sense of anticipation, too, as winter approaches. It is death,
but life waits on the other side.

There's a story about The Good Earth, in which Liza mentions
proudly that Isabel Colinas used to work there, and a feature on Katalysis that lists Isabel Colinas as a new board member. The last one I had
time to print off before I was unceremoniously ejected from my computer station by a determined seventh grader is a sort of gossipy piece
about an association of women artists founded by Yrena Castellano and
Cate Mosley. It quotes Isabel Colinas calling Cate Mosley her mentor,
and there's a picture of a group of women at a restaurant. A woman
with long blond hair stands slightly behind Isabel, hands on her shoulders, as if she's about to present her as a gift to somebody.

I close the folder, letting it rest on my stomach. Then I lie there and
meditate on the patterns of dots in the acoustic tile ceiling. I know I
should get up and do something. I need to find a job, another place to
live. I need to fill out all those stupid unemployment forms—as a
safety net if nothing else. In the immediate future, I need to go to the
grocery store and get some food. Somehow, I can't convert those
thoughts into action. My stomach growls, but I'm not listening.

Ever since I saw the picture of Isabel, I feel like a fly in a
spiderweb—no, it's not that simple. It's more like having those nearly
invisible threads woven around me so that I'm not just the captive, but
part of the web. Cassie told me once how the Navajo weavers leave a
"spirit trail," one thread that leads to the outside border of a rug, sort of
an escape route so their spirit doesn't get trapped in the work. It seems
I've neglected to provide one of those for myself.

Over the next three weeks, I haunt the library, ransacking the *New*
Mexican archives, pulling up still more articles on Google and
Yahoo! I call the people at Katalysis in Stockton, California, where the
friendly woman on the phone suggests I talk to Nancy Wethersby, the

Director of Program Development, who's in Honduras at the moment, but will be back in two weeks.

Elaine helps me track down Cate Mosley and make an appointment to meet her at her studio when she finishes some big commission she's working on.

And I call The Good Earth and ask Cookie if I can come talk to her aunt again.

"I'm so glad you called," she says. "Auntie's feeling really well. When we went to Albuquerque last, the doctor said this new drug they've got her on seems to have shrunk her tumors somewhat. And then the side effects finally sort of petered out, and for the last day or two, she's been absolutely marvelous. Can you come today? I'd like you to see her when she's her true self, and we mustn't count on it—I mean, the doctor said he couldn't predict how long it would last."

Liza still looks like a gray-haired twig, but her face is transformed, alert and relaxed. Her royal purple chenille robe gives her skin a warm glow.

"Hello, Avery." She takes my hand in both of hers. It's like shaking hands with a bird.

"I like your robe," I tell her.

A smile lights her eyes. "Cookie made it for me. Isn't it lovely?"

Cookie settles her in the chair by the window and goes to put on the teakettle while I take the chair opposite.

"Where shall I begin?" Liza adjusts the folds of the robe modestly over her lap.

"Tell me how you met her. What she was like. Did she ever talk about me?"

"I met her when she came to the shop to buy cream for her hands. She was working for a family in exchange for room and board and they were working the life out of her. She was young—I guess eighteen by then. And she wasn't healthy. She had just had you, and it was a very difficult birth. Although I didn't find it out till much later after we became close, I believe she nearly died."

I lean forward, feeling somehow validated.

"We talked about herbs and she told me her mother was a *curandera* in Ortiz, but that she had died—which I found out later wasn't true. Isabel started coming in regularly and we'd chat. That's when I learned about her family—later on she quit talking about them. She said her father was an engineer who was with a mining company and who left Ortiz when she was about three. She was very close to her grandmother, Dona Maria Ebell, who was a shaman—"

"A shaman?"

"That's what she called her. She said her grandmother could touch objects and know things about the people who owned them. I believe she died when Isabel was about twelve.

"At any rate, one morning Isabel came running in all upset, with a very nasty burn on her arm. Apparently the husband of the family she worked for kept trying to corner her in the kitchen, and when she shouted at him to leave her alone, he slapped her and knocked her into the stove."

Liza's head bobs with indignation. "I was furious and I told her she was not to go back there. I moved her in here, in the back room, and paid her to help in the shop with all the people who only spoke Spanish. I sent a man friend of mine around to collect her things, and she never went back to that house." She sighs. "Then, of course, I found out that she was an artist."

I pull the first few pages out of my Isabel folder and show them to Liza. "Yes, back then it was watercolors. She was good at them, but she wasn't satisfied with just being good."

Cookie appears with the tea and a pottery plate of some kind of crackers.

Liza thoughtfully dunks a tiny piece of cracker into her tea. "Oh, yes, then she met this woman who did some kind of textiles. Maybe quilting—"

"Cate Mosley?" I interrupt.

"Yes, I think that's it. She took Isabel into her little circle of friends and of course Isabel became interested in the fiber art that they were doing. Cate started showing her some techniques, but before long Isabel had left them all behind. That was when she started to become rather . . . driven, I guess you might say. She got to be very short with everyone—me, customers, whomever. All she wanted to do was read art books, sketch her designs, and work on her pieces. Several times I came into the shop and customers would be standing around, Isabel nowhere in sight. I'd find her in back working on something."

"Why didn't you fire her?"

Cookie chuckles. "My auntie could never fire anyone. That's why she never hired many people. She always has such a hard time letting them go."

Liza takes a sip of tea. "Well, I don't know what would have become of her if I'd fired her. And I do believe she couldn't help herself. Sometimes I'd come in to open the shop and find her fallen asleep in the chair over a piece of work. She'd never have been to bed. Oftentimes she would forget to eat. Thin as a rail, that one. Finally I decided to move her into my house where I could keep more of an eye on her."

I set my cup and saucer down, lean back in my chair. "But did she ever talk about me?"

Her face softens. "Oh, yes. One evening we had a bad thunderstorm and the power was out, so she couldn't work. We sat at the dining room table and lit candles and drank wine and she told me the whole story of how she got pregnant. Your father was about ten years older than she was. And married, naturally. He was from a wealthy Anglo family. Very handsome, she said."

"Did she ever say—" I hesitate, not at all sure if I want to hear the answer to this question. But this is probably my only chance. "Did she tell you why she left me in the basement of the children's home?"

Cookie looks at her aunt, and Liza frowns. "In the basement? What-ever do you mean?"

"That's where I was found. In the furnace room of Carson Foundling Home in Alamitos."

"Oh, good God." Her voice is calm and quiet; the only sign of agitation is the rapid blinking of her eyes.

"I always thought she must have hated me. I mean, why didn't she just get an abortion?"

"You poor girl." Her bony brown hand covers mine. "That isn't what she intended at all." She shakes her head vigorously. "Your father, who I think was named Michael, wanted her to have an abortion. He even gave her the money to go to Denver and have it done. But Isabel refused."

"Why? It would have been so much easier. For both of us."

"You must remember that her mother was a *curandera,* and a very devout Catholic. That's how Isabel was raised. And although by that time, she was no longer a practicing Catholic, Isabel had a great reverence for life. She never even considered abortion. She took the money and went to Durango, to work as a maid or cook for some woman. Isabel gave her the money, and she was supposed to have arranged for your adoption. Dear heavens. She obviously didn't do what she was supposed to."

I turn my eyes to the window, losing focus in the yellow glare of autumn sun. My head is filled with questions that have no answers. Who was this woman? Why didn't she arrange the adoption? Didn't Isabel know? Or was this whole story just that—a story that Isabel invented to excuse herself?

The bell over the door cracks open the silence, and Cookie gets up to wait on the two women who are flipping through the samples of essential oils.

"Avery, I'm sorry if I upset you." There's a tremor in her voice, and I turn to find Liza watching me anxiously. She looks exhausted, as well.

"I'm not upset. It's just kind of a shock. All this time, I thought . . . something very different. It's just kind of strange."

One gray eyebrow arches. "I know what you must think, but I knew her well enough to know she would never have done that to you, and I'm quite positive she didn't know what happened."

Something prickles my eyes, and I blink away useless moisture. "How can you be so sure?"

"How can I explain Isabel? She was like a little child in many ways. You know the tale about the sorcerer's apprentice? Her talent was like that magic. She was never really able to control it. It overwhelmed her. She made her mistakes, like everyone, but she was a good person."

She takes another cracker and nibbles slowly. "She took care of me one winter when I had bronchitis so bad I couldn't even get out of bed. I couldn't breathe without my chest hurting. I was afraid of taking pneumonia and ending up in the hospital. She made me teas and mustard plasters and herbal steam to inhale, and she sat by my bed all night when the fever got high and sponged my face with alcohol."

Liza's breath is coming faster and her face is flushed. "No, my dear, she was not the kind of person to go around leaving babies in the basement, of that I am certain."

The bell jangles again as the two women leave, and Cookie comes back, casting a watchful eye on her aunt. "You look tired, Auntie," she says. "I think it's nap time."

"I feel fine. I want Avery to ask her questions now, in case—" She breaks off.

"No more questions today." I give her the best smile I can manage. "Cookie's right. Besides, I need to digest all this first. Then I'll come back."

I watch as Cookie gently helps Liza to her feet and guides her, one arm around the tiny figure, to the back room. The curve of their bodies toward each other, the way their heads tilt together, radiates a tenderness that tightens my chest.

. . .

September is unraveling faster than an old sweater.

At last, three days before I'm supposed to move out of the apartment, I shake myself awake. I take a hard look at my assets—a couple of pieces of furniture, a cigar box of memories, my wardrobe of blue jeans and T-shirts, a carton of books, a stack of partially completed unemployment forms, some linens and dishes. My baby undershirt. And Paul DeGraf's card.

Time for drastic measures.

Paul DeGraf." He answers on the first ring, sounding annoyingly chipper.

I draw air into my lungs. "It's Avery."

"Avery, how are you?" A brief pause. "I heard you were no longer working at Dos Hombres."

How the hell did he—oh, yes. Lindsey. They would have had someone else take over her party. She's a great disseminator of information.

"I quit. I just couldn't take Dale's bullshit anymore."

"Are you working for another caterer?"

"No. I haven't decided what I want to do next. I'm just sort of kicking back for a while. Um . . . listen, I was just wondering if maybe you'd like to see the shirt that my—that Isabel made for me. When I was born. You know, I told you they gave it to me—"

"Of course. Yes, I'd like very much to see it. When?"

"I don't know. Whenever. That's the great thing about unemployment. You have lots of free time."

He doesn't laugh. "Unfortunately, I'm tied up all afternoon. Maybe we could have dinner tonight? If you're free, I could pick you up about—"

"I'm going to be out this afternoon. Why don't I just meet you somewhere?"

"If that's better for you, of course. How about El Rancho? Say seven o'clock?"

"I'll see you there." I replace the receiver, rubbing gently at the smudge on it from the dampness of my hand.

When I pull into the parking lot at El Rancho, I see the white Mercedes parked at the end of the row, a little apart from the other cars. Before I get out of the truck, I twist the rearview mirror around for a last-minute inspection. A stranger looks back at me. A stranger with a hair ribbon and makeup. Even mascara.

I try on a carefree smile, adjust the black bow that holds my hair neatly at the nape of my neck. I'm wearing a black dress—the only dress I own. It's about five years old, but it's only been worn half a dozen times, so it still looks like new. It's not exactly a trendsetter, but the guy I was dating at the time said it was a classic, and his sense of style was the only thing about him I could trust. The newly polished gold heart swings from its chain, the barely noticeable weight grounding me every time it thumps against my breastbone.

I open the door and step down, brushing the lint off my skirt. I clutch my brown leather purse and plastic grocery store sack under my arm, and hobble to the door in Rita's old black flats, which are about a half size too small for me.

The El Rancho is an old-time Santa Fe restaurant featuring good steaks and red wine, if you must, but mostly martinis and manhattans, Scotch on the rocks and beer. They probably haven't changed the décor since 1945—mellow pine paneling and black leather booths, photos of cowboy movie stars decorating the walls, branding irons hanging from the ceiling.

Paul is sitting at the bar with a glass of red wine. I can't read his expression when he realizes that the woman in the little black dress is me, but what he sees is obviously not what he was expecting.

"Avery . . ." He smiles at me. "You look . . . wonderful."

"I feel like somebody sneaking out in their big sister's clothes, but thanks."

"Would you like a drink?"

The aroma of prime beef sizzling on a grill has hit the hunger button in my brain. I can't remember the last full meal I had, and I suddenly feel like I could eat a whole cow. "I'd like to eat, if that's okay."

He gives his practiced nod to the hostess, and she hustles us to a booth in a far corner of the room. He orders a Chilean cabernet, and after they bring it and we order filets, rare, I reach into the grocery bag and bring out the undershirt.

"Here it is."

He takes it from me like it's the Shroud of Turin. For the longest time he sits there looking at it, holding it up to the light, setting it down on his napkin to trace the flowers with his elegant fingers.

"This is a wonderful piece." He holds the shirt up to the light. "Charmingly primitive." My gaze steadies on the fabric of the shirt. I try to see it as a collector's item, instead of as the only thing my mother gave me. "Look at the tiny stiches. They're so delicate, but they have that sort of endearing clumsiness of a novice work."

"How much do you think it's worth?" I ask.

He casts me a look that mixes surprise with curiosity and a liberal dose of pity. "Surely you're not planning to sell it?"

I shrug with what I hope is nonchalance. "I haven't decided what to do with it. I was wondering if maybe I could borrow money. You know, use it as collateral."

He folds it carefully and hands it back to me. "You certainly could do that." His tone is very careful. "I'd be more than happy to provide a written appraisal. If you need one."

The server looms out of nowhere, setting salads down in front of us. "Fresh ground pepper?" she asks.

As soon as she's gone, I start shoveling lettuce into my mouth, but he says, "Of course, that's assuming that you have some appropriate credit history."

I swallow. "What do you mean?"

"A legitimate lender—such as a bank—is going to want a track record. Proof that you've had credit before and used it responsibly."

"You mean like credit cards?"

He nods.

"I don't have any of those. I'm sort of a cash-and-carry kind of girl."

"Have you ever borrowed money?"

"I had a student loan . . ."

"That would work." He smiles.

"But I'm still working on paying it back."

"Have you kept up the payments?"

I concentrate on spearing a cucumber. "For the most part."

He takes a piece of French bread, spreads a microscopic amount of butter on it, and sets it on his plate. "I heard you were let go," he says gently.

I set down my fork and take a big drink of wine and just look at him. I know if I try to talk I'm going to cry.

"I told you, Santa Fe is just a big small town."

I take another drink of wine. My voracious appetite is gone. One tear finally escapes. I wipe it away quickly, chase the lump in my throat with more wine.

"Can your roommate carry the flat for a month or two?"

"She's gone." The first word squeaks embarrassingly when it comes out.

"Your roommate's gone?"

I take a deep breath, poke at the salad. "She moved back to Albuquerque with her boyfriend."

"When do you have to move out?"

"Friday."

He chews thoughtfully, dabs at his mouth with the white napkin. "All right, first thing is, you'll move into the guesthouse till you can find a job and your own place—"

"I can't do that."

"Why not?"

"Because I can't pay you anything."

"I think that's the point," he says patiently. "It's only temporary, just till you get back on your feet. In fact, we'll make it a business proposition. I've always wanted a personal chef. You can fill that job till you find one you prefer."

He extends his hand across the table. "Deal?"

I take another gulp of wine.

"It's a fair trade. Your services for room and board. Deal?"

"Okay." My hand is cold and his is warm.

Counting drive time, it takes an hour and a half to move my stuff from Columbia Street to San Tomás on Thursday afternoon. It feels like a parallel universe.

My rocking chair, coat rack, chest, and bed end up in a storage unit where Paul stashes art that's not on display for one reason or another. The rest of it—clothes, shoes, books, linens, dishes—everything I own is contained in half a dozen cartons scavenged from the supermarket.

Paul DeGraf's guests are happy people. You can't stay in this house and not be happy. It's small, maybe even smaller than our apartment was, and has only one bedroom, but it's like everything has been designed and arranged for your comfort and pleasure.

The floors are Saltillo tile, cool and smooth against your feet in the hot afternoons, radiant heated in the cold mornings. Beautiful rugs. Some with a soft pile where your toes get lost, some flat woven, like Navajo rugs. The walls are adobe—well, not real adobe. White plaster or stucco or something, but there's not a straight line or a right angle in the place. It seems to accommodate the human body, inviting you to nestle in.

There's no couch in the living room—just cushioned *bancos* adjoining the kiva fireplace in the corner opposite the door. There's a small table in the kitchen for eating, or you can sit in the one big chair in front of the fire. The bathroom is all Talavera tiles, blue and green and earth colors, and the tub is big enough to stretch out full length. The antique hand-carved Mexican bed with a puffy, weightless comforter is situated directly under an oversized skylight so you can lie on your back and look at the stars.

But the two features that—for me, anyway—raise the place from merely comfortable to unimaginably luxurious are the floor-to-ceiling bookshelves on one wall of the living room, filled with everything from paperback mysteries to ten-pound picture books of European art, and hidden away in a hall closet—a stackable washer/dryer.

After Paul hands me the key and leaves me to "get settled," I spend an hour walking from room to room, reminding myself not to get too comfortable, that I won't be here long, that I need to get busy finding gainful employment.

This, after all, is the place where Isabel died.

twenty-one

By mid-October, I've managed to get four interviews.

Paul insists on lending me money for some new black pants and a lightweight jacket, some black shoes with a small heel that won't cripple me. I wear Cassie's circle of turquoise for luck. Everyone says they'll call me. Eventually they do.

Two of them say, Thanks for interviewing, but we've decided not to hire additional staff at this time. Check back with us in the spring. One says the position's been filled, period. The fourth one calls me in for a second interview with the chef/owner. This makes me breathless and sweaty-palmed—the way some women go off about first dates.

Andy Ross, chef of Casa Rosada, reminds me a little of Pete Dimon—tall, fair-haired, and ruddy-faced. I interpret this as a good omen. I fantasize about saying casually to Rita on the phone someday, "Yeah, the guy I work for looks just like Pete."

We sit at the textured cement bar. My legs hang off the edge of the high stool, feet dangling in space like a little kid—not exactly the image I'm trying to project.

He doodles on the résumé I put together on the library's computer. A little blue-ink race car with squiggles of exhaust coming out the tailpipe.

"Dos Hombres, huh?" He doesn't even try to hide his scorn. "It's a whole different ball game—catering."

"Yes, I know." I smile. "I didn't like it as well as restaurant work, but when I first moved to Santa Fe, that was all I could find."

He rests one elbow on the bar, sipping a mineral water with lime, no ice. "How much notice would you have to give?"

"None." It comes out too quickly, before I consider his strategy. "I quit a couple of weeks ago."

"Why?"

"It just wasn't what I wanted to do."

"Bullshit," he says.

"Excuse me?"

"In this town you don't quit one job till you've got something else lined up. Usually two something elses. Just to be safe." He hops off his stool and walks around behind the bar.

I'm so focused on what he's just said, and how I'm supposed to answer, that I haven't bothered to wonder what he's doing behind the bar.

I swallow. "Well, quite honestly, I had a personality conflict with someone at Dos Hombres and—"

"One of the Hombres, I bet. And I could probably guess which one." He laughs unpleasantly. "And so you got canned." He turns his back to me and pulls a bottle of wine out of the wine rack. Then he picks up one of those pocketknife-looking wine openers and plunks them both down in front of me. "Happens to everyone sooner or later. Open that for me."

A trickle of perspiration rolls down between my shoulder blades. I've watched people use these things, but I've never ever used one myself. At Pete's, when we finally got wine, it came in a box with a spigot, and at Dos Hombres, we had what Kirk called "sissy corkscrews"—the ones that look sort of like a little chrome doll with the two arms that you just push down and the cork pops out.

This damn thing is like a surgical tool. I break a nail opening the little knife part. I manage to cut off the foil without too much trouble, but then I proceed to totally destroy the cork. He just sits there, not saying a word, watching me screw the thing in crooked and try to pull it out three times. When it finally pops out, it leaves a flotilla of cork crumbs sitting on the surface of the wine.

"I guess they had screw-tops at the diner." He peers into the bottle disapprovingly. "What side do you serve from?"

"The right," I say. "Clear from the left."

"Have you done tray service?"

"Yes."

He points to a table where linens, dishes, flatware, and glasses for wine and water are stacked. "Do a setup for me."

I try not to show my surprise. "Don't the busboys do that?"

"Usually. But when it's busy, you might have to pitch in."

I slide off the stool.

I move all the dishes and spread the two cloths, one over the other, turned at right angles so the corners alternate. It's a table for two, and I put the service plates down first, dinner plates on top, then salad plates on top of those. The plates are beautiful—all white, but each different size has its own textured design on the rim, giving them an intriguing look when they're stacked. Bread plates go to the left, glasses to the right. Before I'm through with the flatware, I realize there's a few pieces whose function escapes me, like two long butter knives. Either that, or he's just thrown in some extra pieces as a test.

When I finish, I look at him, and right away I know I've screwed up bigtime.

"First of all, the cloths are reversed," he says. "The finer should be on top, the coarser one on the bottom. You should be able to tell by the feel which is which.

"Second, you never put a dinner plate on a service plate. The salad plate goes there, and then they're cleared before the main course. The fish knife doesn't go on the butter plate, it goes to the right of the entrée knife. But I don't guess that ever came up at Pete's."

My face flares. I want to tell him where I think he should put the fish knife, but I just say, "It's not rocket science. I can learn all that."

"Are there any restrictions on what hours you can work?" he asks.

"No."

He makes a few notations on my application, takes a leisurely swallow of mineral water, and says, "Well, thanks for coming by. We'll keep this on file."

First I feel cold. Then hot. I tell myself I didn't hear what he said. "When will you make a decision?"

"I've already made one. The position was filled yesterday. I'll keep your app on file in case something changes. And you can always check back with us."

I can't move. I stand there, stuck to the floor, while a lot of bad memories pile up from behind like one of those chain reaction car crashes. Disapproving frowns directed at my tacky pilled sweaters, sideways remarks about my size or age, suggestions that I wear contact lenses to make my eyes look normal, the implication that my experience at Pete's Diner was worse than useless.

"If you already filled the job, why the hell did you make me come in here—so you could have fun watching me jump through my ass backwards?"

We stare at each other for a few seconds. Then he says, "I like to keep people in the file in case we get in a bind. What's your problem?"

"I have a life. I don't want to live it in your goddamn file."

He shrugs. "Your choice." He rips my application in half, then in half again. Before he's finished ripping it the third time, I'm out the door, catching the doorknob and flinging it back so hard that the big glass pane shivers and crashes to the ground. He yells something I can hear but not understand, and I just keep walking.

The Good Earth is quiet, not even a bell on the door today. Cookie's sitting behind the counter, a tumbled heap of green material in her lap, and her face opens into a smile when she sees me.

"Avery, hi. How's it going?"

I start to say fine, but something in her dark, watchful eyes makes me blurt out, "I'm unemployed, my roommate's left town, and I've just had the job interview from hell . . . but other than that, fine."

Her laugh bubbles like a fountain. "We're having one of those days, too. Auntie didn't sleep at all last night, so she's napping now.

That's why I took the bell off the door." She frowns. "I hope you didn't need to speak to her. I'm afraid she wouldn't be much help today."

"No, that's not why I came. I don't really know why I came. I just saw the sign as I was driving by, and . . . here I am."

"Well, I, for one, am delighted. I can use the company. Let's move to the comfy chairs."

The bruised-looking hollows under Cookie's eyes are more apparent in the light from the window.

"You must have had a rough night, too," I say.

Her long snaky curls bounce as she shakes her head. "I'm used to it. I don't need a lot of sleep anymore. It's poor Liza that's having a rough go. I'm afraid there's not much more to be done."

"I'm sorry." I never know what to say when people drop that kind of information on you. "But I guess she's lucky to have you here."

"I'm lucky to have her, too. Liza's my mum's younger sister, and she's been like a second mother to me."

"How long have you been here?"

She sighs and leans her head back against the chair's faded flower pattern. "About five years."

"Did you come from the islands, too?"

"I was born in St. Kitts, but then later, my family moved around a lot."

"What did your parents do?"

"They were professional troublemakers." When I look puzzled, she explains. "Political activists. They went to different places to organize political opposition parties, labor unions, voter registration, usually staying just long enough to annoy local politicos. Finally when I was about seventeen, they annoyed someone in Jamaica sufficiently to have a bomb planted in their car."

"So they were killed?"

"My father was killed outright. My mother spent the remainder of her days in a wheelchair. I took care of her till she died five years ago."

"So then you came here, just in time to take care of Liza."

She regards me quizzically. "Yes, but that's what women do, isn't it? Take care of people. And make no mistake, she was the one taking care of me at first. I was in a bad way then, and I came to her because she was my only family, but from the very first she made me laugh.

"When she picked me up at the airport that day I came, she said, 'Cookie, my dear, one thing you're going to have to get used to in New Mexico is their odd ideas on race.' I was rather appalled because I'd heard mostly good things about New Mexico being a very tolerant place. So I said, 'What do you mean, Auntie?' And she explained to me that there are only three races here. You are either Spanish, Indian, or Anglo. She said, 'That means you and I, my dear Cookie, are as Anglo as we can be—just like the Chinese gentleman who owns the dry cleaners.'"

A crash from the back room freezes us both.

"Auntie." Cookie jumps up and disappears through the door behind the counter.

I walk over to the counter and stand, listening. I can't make out any words, just their two voices—Liza's thin and reedy like a wailing kitten, Cookie's lower, soothing, rising and falling like a boat on gentle swells.

In a few minutes she reappears, shaking her head, smiling ruefully. "She's going to make me old before my time."

"Is she okay?"

"For the moment. She was trying to reach the glass of water on her night table and managed to pull the tray off onto the floor. I've told her to call me if she needs something; I've given her a bell to ring . . . she's about the most stubborn woman I know."

I look at my watch. "I've got to get going."

"I hope you'll come again, Avery. I'm not always so scattered. This situation is becoming . . ."

"Is it the pain?" I ask hesitantly.

"Not really, her medications are controlling it fairly well. It's just they make her a bit woozy. She's restless and she thinks she can still do everything for herself. The hard part is knowing what to do with her during the day. I don't dare leave her at home, but I can't very well close the shop. Most of the time she stays back in Isabel's old room, but I have to watch her like a hawk to be sure she doesn't decide to scrub the floors or something." Again the rueful laugh.

I hesitate, but only for a second. "I have something that might help her. It's not a medicine or anything, it's just a tea. The old lady who raised me said it was good for whatever ails you. Worst-case scenario is it just tastes good and doesn't do anything. But I was thinking it might help her relax. You, too."

"What's in it?"

"A bunch of herbs—lemon balm and ginger and anise, fenugreek—and one or two others that I've forgotten. I haven't made any in a while, but I have enough for probably three or four cups. I could bring it by tomorrow . . ."

"I'd love to try it." She frowns. "Unfortunately I have to take Liza to Albuquerque for her med check, so I'm going to have to close the store in the afternoon."

"I could just drop it through the mail slot."

She brightens. "Oh, lovely. It should be a good day to try it, too. She's always rather down after we see the doctor."

By the time I park by the gate on San Tomás, the sky is deep blue and a silver arc of moon is rising in the sky. Crickets chirp happily. I let myself in the gate with the key Paul gave me and crunch through the gravel to the guesthouse. The lights are on inside, and I know I didn't leave them on because I expected to be back long ago.

Paul is sitting in the wingback chair in front of the fireplace. A glass of wine is in his hand. He smiles tentatively.

"That must have been quite an interview."

I pretend to search for something in the depths of my purse. "I guess you could say that."

"I had a phone call from Andy Ross—"

"That son of a bitch." I toss the purse down on the *banco*. "He had my phone number. Why did he call you?"

"I suppose to tell me you broke his door. He saw that I was listed as a reference—"

"And he wanted to warn you that you were vouching for a psychopath."

It's the first time I've heard him laugh—a low, pleasant rumble. "I'm sure all he wanted was to get paid for the door."

I look up quickly. "You didn't tell him you'd pay for it?"

"I told him that's why he pays insurance premiums. I said I'd cover his deductible. He was happy."

"Frankly, I don't give a shit if he's happy or not. And I'll pay the fucking deductible."

His index finger absently rubs the rim of his wineglass. "You can't pay the fucking deductible until you get a job," he says mildly, "and you're not going to get a job if you go around breaking restaurant windows. Sit down."

"Doors." I glare at him. "I don't feel like sitting down."

"He said you were angry because the position was filled, and you slammed the door so hard the glass broke."

"That about covers it." For some inexplicable reason I find myself wanting a cigarette.

"I can understand your being angry, but not that angry. Not about something like that. Why don't you tell me the rest of it?"

"Because I don't feel like talking about it."

"Don't you think I've a right to know?" He sets the wineglass on the floor.

"Actually, no. I don't. But here's the lite version: First, he knew the job was filled, and he let me come anyway. Second, I'm sick of people like him giving me shit because I don't know which side to put the fish knife on. Above the finger bowl or below? In your ear or up your ass? They think they have to explain what a venue is. I get treated like dog poop because I worked in a—gasp!—*diner.* Or because I don't know how to use a frigging surgical corkscrew—"

"Avery, I think you're—"

"I got all dressed up and paid three bucks for parking so he could get off watching me screw up and then, and *only* then, tell me the job's been filled. What's three bucks? Nothing, if you're pulling down a hundred grand a year—"

"Avery—"

"You want to know the worst part?" I start toward the chair where he's staring at me incredulously. "The worst part, the part that *really* pisses me off, is that he enjoyed every goddamned minute of it!"

At this point in the conversation, my foot hits his wineglass, knocking it over.

"Finished?" he says. I can tell he's trying not to look at the wine soaking into the Tibetan rug.

I run to the kitchen, returning with a box of salt.

"What are you doing?" he asks.

I dump salt all over the spreading stain. "Damage control." I look up at him, thoroughly embarrassed. I close my eyes and breathe in deeply. "I'm sorry. Maybe this wasn't such a good idea, me moving over here."

He says. "The rug can be cleaned. Don't worry about it."

I start to say that "Don't worry about it" seems to be his philosophy of life—and one that works best with plenty of money, but for once, common sense intervenes. I don't need to be picking fights with the one person who's standing between me and the street. Instead I take a deep breath, force my face into a reasonable facsimile of a smile and say, "What can I fix you for dinner?" When he looks at me in surprise, I remind him that I'm supposed to be his personal chef.

"I'm giving you the night off. Why don't we go out?"

"Oh, no. We had a deal. I can't stay here if you won't let me earn my keep. You haven't eaten already, have you?"

"No . . . and I'm not even sure what's in the pantry."

"Well, let's go look."

He brightens. "On one condition. You'll have to eat with me."

The cupboard isn't exactly bare, but it's close enough. There's a plastic bag of tortillas in the fridge. From some ends of cheese, I manage to grate enough for enchiladas, and I throw together a half-assed sauce from a can of chopped tomatoes, a lot of chile powder, and a touch of heavy cream. In the vegetable bin I salvage enough unspoiled lettuce and a few mushrooms that can be trimmed for a salad.

"I'm going to the farmers' market Saturday and get some decent food," I say when we're sitting on the couch in his office with a fire crackling in the fireplace. "How can you live like this?"

He shrugs. "I eat out a lot. And on Mondays Mrs. Martinez always leaves dinner for me. She makes so much I can usually eat it for at least two nights. This is great. I can't believe you could make dinner out of the dregs of my kitchen."

"It's not great." I laugh. "Actually it's pretty awful; fortunately, we're both hungry." I sink back into some squishy throw pillows and let my eyes sweep the room. His massive desk is unlike anything I've seen—it's red—a beautiful orangey red that looks about a mile deep. On the back and sides, there are painted scenes in an oriental style, with figures carved from what looks like colored stone. Against the wall perpendicular to the desk, his computer sits on a rough wooden table.

The fireplace is stone, not a kiva, and above it hangs a Tom Hemmings painting of some old farmers staring at a dry *acequia*. You can almost smell their stale sweat, taste the dust in the air, feel the sun beating on their heads through a yellow haze.

He sees me looking at it. "That's one of Tom's," he says. "Amazing, isn't it?"

I nod. "It's so . . . real. But not like a photograph. You can tell it's a painting, but you still feel like you could step into it."

"His brush technique. His use of color and light. His style is very complex, you might even say delicate. Like the old masters."

"In what way?"

"If you look at the paintings by the old masters, they have an incredible depth and richness of color, texture, and transparency. Effects that can only be produced by layer upon layer of paint. Artists like Titian or da Vinci sometimes used forty or fifty layers. Not many artists want to be bothered with that anymore. Tom was trained as a restorer as well as an artist, so he appreciates those older techniques. He understands what can—"

He breaks off, looking sheepish. "What art do you like?" He's only being polite, but the intense way he zeroes in on me, I could almost believe that my preferences matter.

"I like useful art. Like baskets and pottery and rugs."

He nods. "I like those, too. And it's odd, I never thought of them as art until I came to New Mexico. I was educated in France and England, studied painting there—"

"Do you paint?" I ask.

A rueful half smile. "Not anymore."

"Why not?"

"I wasn't good enough."

"Says who?"

"My teachers. One in particular told me in no uncertain terms that if I wanted to make a living in art, I should pursue art history."

"And you let some pompous old fart decide what you could do with your life?"

He sighs. "Of course it was more than that. But he was right. I think the main reason I wanted to be an artist was for my mother, anyway."

"Was she an artist?"

"No. She was like me. Loved art, but didn't have the talent. She worked in galleries in London after she left my father. She lived for art.

And artists. Our flat was always full of peculiar people. It wasn't uncommon for me to wake up in the morning and find some strange man snoring on the floor next to my bed."

"So she wanted you to be an artist?"

"I don't know. She never said as much. I just felt that if I were a famous artist, I could . . . win her back or some such foolishness."

"Back from where?"

His shoulders lift slightly. "Back from the glamorous world where she lived, I suppose."

"But didn't you live with her?"

He peers into the fire. "We lived in the same flat. I don't think we ever lived in the same world."

I get up quickly, stacking our empty plates and shuffling out to the kitchen. "I'll just clean up."

"We might as well finish this wine," he calls after me.

When I come back from tucking the dirty dishes into the dishwasher, the fire is sputtering. He gets up to add another hunk of wood and pour out the rest of the wine into our glasses. He waits by the hearth for a minute until the new log blazes up before settling himself next to me on the couch. His physical proximity sends a pleasantly guilty ripple through my whole body.

"Tell me about that one." I point to a small picture over the computer table. "It's a *santo*, right?"

"A *santo* can be any image of a saint, but it usually refers to a carved wooden figure. These paintings are usually called *retablos*." He smiles slowly. "This one is very special. And very rare. Go over and take a good close look at it. Tell me what you notice about it."

I walk over to stand in front of the picture. It's a woman in a simple white dress with a green mountain in the background. Her halo, which takes up the top third of the picture, looks like real gold leaf.

"Well . . . it's much simpler than most of the ones I've seen."

"Yes. What else?"

I study the woman. "She's different. More native. I saw one similar in Tom's studio, but the woman looked very European. Spanish."

For the thinnest slice of a second, his eyes darken. Or maybe it's just a shadow from the fire. Then he says, "This woman is Malinche. She has the Mayan features, broad cheekbones, prominent nose, full mouth, dark skin."

"What makes it so valuable?"

He gets up and comes over to stand next to me. "Three things. One, the fact that it even exists. For hundreds of years Malinche has been widely considered a traitor who delivered her people up to Cortez. Two, the fact that she was painted as a saint. And you notice the picture doesn't have a cross or any of the usual Christian symbols. Other than the halo. The volcano in the background is called La Malinche."

"Somebody must have liked her then."

"The picture probably came from Tlaxcala. The tribes in that area hated the Aztecs and they became allies of Cortez. Malinche has always been venerated there."

"And what's the third reason?"

He turns away from the painting almost reluctantly. "It was a gift from your mother," he says.

Cate Mosley probably used to be beautiful. She still is, from across the room. But when you get up close, you see that she has that very thin, pale skin that some Anglos have. It wrinkles in this high, dry air like old leather, sagging into flaps under her chin. There's a fine network of blood vessels around her nose, but her eyes are a beautiful clear green, like gemstones.

And they feel as cold as gemstones when she turns them on me.

"Well, there's no mistaking you're her daughter."

She motions me inside her studio, which is cluttered with bolts of

fabric, baskets of ribbon and yarn. Lint is everywhere, balled up in corners like dust bunnies, covering every surface, hanging in the air. It
seems to go with being a fiber artist.

The walls are slick and white, like they were designed to showcase
her work, but there are only a few collages on display. She notices me
looking. "I've gone to soft sculpture." She nods at a form sitting on a
pedestal. It's about two feet tall, black and gray, kind of lumpy, and
there are pieces of what looks like twigs and leaves poking out of a long
fold on one side of the piece. "Freestanding. I find it more kinetic, more
involving, more dynamic than flat work."

I wear my ignorance like a sign around my neck. "It's very interesting."

She laughs and then abruptly remembers who I am. "Elaine said you
wanted information." She lifts one hip and plops it down on a tall stool
but doesn't offer me a seat. "What kind of information?"

"About my mother. I never knew her—"

"Doesn't surprise me," she says flatly. She folds her arms across her
jade green shirt. Her left forearm is covered with silver bracelets that
jangle noisily and flash light off in every direction.

"Why do you say that?" I already don't like this woman, but I try
not to let it show.

"No offense, but she was exactly that kind of person."

"What kind of person do you mean?"

"The kind who'd give up her child if it wasn't convenient to keep
her. No offense."

I exhale wearily. "I'm not offended. I'm just looking for some
answers. I'm sure you can understand." Actually, I'm not sure of that at
all, but I need her to open up a little. "Can you tell me why you say she
was that type of person?"

"Because she was a selfish bitch." Her eyes snap with anger. "There
are takers and givers in this world, babe, and your momma was the
former."

I don't say anything. I read somewhere that if you just keep staring at someone long enough, they'll eventually tell you everything you want to know and then some.

"I mentored her. She didn't know shit from Shinola about fibers or quilting or collage. All she'd ever done was some pretty mediocre watercolors. She was going nowhere fast."

"Then why did you teach her?"

"She had a certain color sense," she says, a smile barely moving her lips. "And she came on so sweet. Told me how much she admired my work. Okay, I was flattered. I felt sorry for her. I liked her. She could be exceptionally charming when there was something in it for her." The smile vanishes. "As I found out too late, she was a user. She learned all she could from me, then dropped me like I was Typhoid Mary. But . . ." When she raises her eyebrows, the skin on her forehead looks like plow furrows, ". . . not before she seduced my husband."

Her word choice strikes me as a bit silly. In her dramatic voice, the word *seduced* takes on overtones of a costumed melodrama—one of those cheesy plays where the audience cheers the heroine and throws popcorn at the villain.

"He thought she actually cared about him—men are so stupid—but as soon as Paul DeGraf appeared on the horizon, Dave got the old heave-ho. Came crawling home with his tail between his legs.

"Of course she found out that life with DeGraf had its own drawbacks."

"Like?"

"You should ask him about that." Her eyes narrow. "Surely you've met him."

Even though there's no reason for it, I feel suddenly exposed. I keep hearing Paul's admonition that there are no secrets in this town. Does she know I'm living in his guesthouse?

"So what did you think of her work?" I ask quickly.

Cate Mosley gives an irritated little snort. "I think she was very good at what she did. Which was to steal a lot of people's ideas and synthesize them into her own hodgepodge style. No offense."

.   .   .

I'm in the kitchen roasting peppers over the burner of the Wolf range when he brings the tray back and sets it on the counter. He opens a file folder that's tucked under his arm, pulls out some papers clipped together.

"You just need to sign this. For the cabin."

I wipe my hands on the towel that's tucked into my belt and take the paper he holds out to me.

It's a pretty simple thing, this Quit Claim Deed. It just says that Paul Julien DeGraf relinquishes all claims and rights to the property in Bluebird Canyon to Avery James, effective October 1, 2000, for the consideration of $1.00.

"Is this legal?" I hate sounding like I just rode into town on the last turnip truck, but I can't believe anything legal could be this simple.

"It will be," he says. "As soon as you and I both sign it, and my attorney records it."

The pen rests motionless in the crook of my thumb and forefinger as I stare at the piece of paper. "Are you sure?"

"That it's legal?"

"That you want to do it."

I would understand completely if he laughed at me, but he doesn't. "Of course. Aren't you?"

"You've heard the saying, there's no free lunch?"

"I have. However . . ." His thumb worries the corner of the file folder. "I'm not sure why you believe it applies here. You think there are strings attached?"

"I think there's strings attached to just about everything."

He looks down at the folder, then back at me. "It disturbs me. That you feel you can't trust me."

"It has nothing to do with you. Not you, personally. I just believe that everything has a price. Cassie taught me that."

"Who's Cassie?"

"The old lady I lived with when I was in high school. In Florales. She was pretty sharp. She said even knowledge isn't free. That if you learn something, it usually means you have to do something about it."

"What do you think you would have to do about the cabin?"

"Take care of it, for one thing. I don't want to own a place and just let it fall apart. And it's not just the money. It takes my time. It takes my attention. It might ask me for something I can't give or don't want to. It's a little scary. I've never owned anything before, except for my truck."

"Are you saying you don't want it?"

"No, I'm not saying that. I'm just saying . . . if you give this to me, if I accept it, I want it to be done . . . mindfully." I break off, my face suddenly warm.

He holds out an envelope. "Maybe this will help you to think about the place in more concrete terms."

"What is it?"

"Open it."

I slide my thumb under the flap, rip it open, and pull out a check. For $25,000 and some change. I stare at him.

"What the hell is this?"

"It's from Isabel's estate."

"I can't—"

"Please. This is something that doesn't require any mindfulness at all. I know she'd want you to have it."

"But you could have just given me the money." I search for some explanation in his face. "You didn't have to move me into the guesthouse."

"I don't want you to live on this. You should invest it. I'll put you in touch with—" He makes an abrupt U-turn. "That is, if you'd like, I can introduce you to a good financial planner."

"Never in my wildest dreams have I ever pictured myself head-to-head with a financial planner."

"It's yours. I hope you'll use it wisely."

. . .

My eyes open as soon as it's light. I roll onto my back and watch the sky turn from silver to blue. It's one of those moments that you want to keep forever. I'm warm, I'm comfortable. I don't have to get up and go to a job where somebody hates me. There's a check for $25,000 sitting on my night table. I'm queen of the world.

twenty-two

I try to settle into my new life. A life so different from anything I ever imagined for myself that I sometimes jolt into full awareness like out of a dream, look around me to see if I'm really where I seem to be, doing what I think I'm doing. Which is mainly cooking for Paul.

Breakfast four days a week—a no-brainer. *Café au lait,* orange juice, a three-minute boiled egg, and a toasted baguette with butter and jam—which he calls a *tartine.* Most nights I cook dinner. He eats alone in that empty dining room at the starkly cold glass-topped table. He eats whatever I want to cook. I have unlimited funds for the best ingredients, a shelf full of lavishly illustrated cookbooks for inspiration. It's a cook's nirvana.

Once in a while he goes out to a restaurant or to someone's house. The following day, he never fails to tell me that he should have stayed at home, since my food is so superior to whatever it was they were serving. Sometimes Lindsey comes for dinner, and when she's here, the temperature seems to rise a few degrees, the lights burn a little brighter, and her laugh makes its own party. She's the only person I've ever seen light a cigarette in this house. He just smiles and waves the smoke away till she leaves, and then he runs around emptying ashtrays into the garbage and opening all the windows.

A pretty good case could be made for the idea that what I really am is not a personal chef, but a paid companion, since he freely admits that I'm the only one who'll listen to his stories. I got an earful the night I told him about my visit to Cate Mosley.

The only indication that he was angry was the color that crept up his neck into his face. Not exactly red, it was more a dark, mottled earth color like a clay pot before it's fired. I could sense him searching for the right words to express his contempt for her. He finally settled on "shrill and insecure. Not to mention a second-rate talent."

It was about the worst thing I'd ever heard him say. Not that he seems like such a Goody Two-shoes, but I have the feeling that for the most part, he can't be bothered discussing anything or anyone who ranks that low in his opinion.

"It was a classic case of the student surpassing her teacher," he said. "Cate never forgave your mother for being more talented than she was."

When I got to the part about Isabel seducing Mosley's husband, he actually laughed.

"David Mosley is delusional. How he could have imagined that Isabel had any interest in him whatsoever is beyond me. He was fixated on her, of course. That's understandable, particularly considering that he was married to the Medusa. But she never gave him any encouragement at all."

"How can you be so sure?" As soon as I said it, I wished I hadn't.

The flicker of doubt was brief, but it was there. "She wouldn't have had anything to do with someone like him."

It was after dinner that night and we were sitting in his office—me on the couch, him at his desk, shuffling papers from one stack to another. It was something he did a lot, and I never saw that anything actually got rearranged. It was just a nervous habit, something he did while talking, the way other people fiddle with their hair or twist a ring round and round on their finger.

"Why are you still here?" I asked him all of a sudden.

He stopped his paper stacking and looked at me. "What do you mean?"

"I mean, why don't you sell this place? Get a new house."

"I like this house." He said it evenly, matter of factly. "It took me a long time to get it just the way I wanted it. Besides, it's close to the galleries and I—"

He was missing the point, maybe on purpose. "What I mean is . . ." I paused, trying to choose my words carefully. "Don't you think it might be easier to get on with things if you weren't living here. Where—everything happened. In a different place, maybe you could—"

"Forget?" The word sort of floated in the air between us.

I shook my head. "I know it isn't the kind of thing you forget. But maybe you could put some distance between the past and present."

He leaned back in his chair, and his eyes drifted away from my face, sweeping the room. As if he might find a trace of her clinging to the walls. When he looked at me again, he didn't exactly smile, but his expression was softer, almost wistful.

"You're not the first person to ask me that," he said. "And it's a reasonable question. I suppose the only answer is that I don't want to." He looked blindly at the stack of papers in front of him. "Or can't."

Highway 14 is empty. The morning sun ignites the cottonwoods, and their tops leap like hot gold flames out of the dusty streambeds. There was a dusting of snow on the Sangres this morning, and long white streamers of cirrus clouds to the west signal another front coming in, although right now the sky is that endless, drop-dead blue of October in New Mexico.

This is the first time I've been to the cabin alone. It feels like some kind of pilgrimage, unlocking the gate, bouncing over the ruts, approaching the house like a penitent approaching the altar. I'm stepping carefully, watching the path, when a grayish brown streak across my field of vision draws me up short. I think of Amalia and her admonitions to never let a coyote cross your path. Except this is no coyote—or at least not entirely.

He does have the pointy snout and long bushy tail, but his eyes are big and dark, not yellow like a coyote. His coat is brownish gray, matted with dirt and weeds, and he's so skinny you can count his ribs. We appraise each other from a distance of about ten feet. It's not clear whether he sees me as a possible friend or potential breakfast. Then he takes a couple steps toward me trying to look ingratiating. He gives a half-assed tail wag.

I stamp my foot. "Go away."

The way he looks at me, head up, ears twitching, I think he knows that sound, the resonance of a human voice. He inches closer, making a wide arc, and I stand perfectly still. When I feel the cool nose sniffing at my hand, I close my fist so he can't bite my fingers. When I turn cautiously toward him, he shies away.

"Okay. I know your type. You're so cute and shy and you come sniffing around and wagging your tail. You let me win you over, then you let me feed you, and pretty soon you're laying down next to me. Giving me that devoted look. And then one morning you get up and go outside to take a pee and you don't come back. So just go away now and save us both the trouble." I stamp my foot and he flinches but doesn't move.

"Go bite a prairie dog. Go on, get!" I bend down and pick up a few pebbles and fling them in his general direction. That's all it takes. He's gone so fast it's like he was never there.

Every sound is exaggerated in the quiet canyon. My footsteps on the wooden floor of the *portal*. The clang of the key in the lock. The squeak as I push the door open. I jump a little when something darts into the shadows of the corner by the fireplace. Probably a rat.

It's not easy for me to picture how the place might look, all cleaned up and snug. I don't have much of an imagination, and I've always believed that what you see is about all you're going to get. It was Isabel who had the vision of *Querencia*. Not me. She's the one who put in the skylight and the woodstove. The curtains that hang from the windows in tatters.

So why should I trust Isabel's vision? More to the point, is there any reason to think I should trust myself? In my whole life, I've never let myself want anything that much. I've never tried to hold anything. Or anyone. Always at the last minute, it seemed easier to open my hands and let go. If I say yes to *Querencia*, do I really mean it?

The Rio Bravo is fairly quiet when I finally get there just after 1:30—maybe half a dozen tables occupied, a few cowboys at the counter. I take a table in the back and order *posole*. Bettina brings it herself, along with the little dishes of sliced radishes, avocado chunks, and lime wedges. The chile and garlic steam rising from the bowl makes my eyes water.

"I need your help with something," I tell her.

She sits down across from me, and her jaw juts forward as she blows a wisp of damp black hair off her forehead. "Of course."

I fish in my purse for the scrap of paper and push it across the table. She reads it while I eat.

"I will call Alonzo tonight. Alonzo Lopez. He is the one to do the roof and the windows and check the *vigas* for dry rot. Maria, his sister, she is an *enjarradora*—one of the last."

"What's that?"

"The *enjarradoras* were the women who once did all the plastering of homes. The traditional way. It was passed from mother to daughter. Alonzo and Maria are the only ones you need."

"You think they might be too busy or something?"

Bettina looks vaguely offended. "They will do it. I will ask them for you. I can get you a better price. This cabin, how did you find it?"

"It was Isabel's—my mother's. Her grave is down there too."

She pats my hand. "Maybe in this place, you can come to know a little more about her."

I rip a tortilla in half and dunk it in the soup. "It's hard not knowing about her, but it's even harder that she didn't know about me. She didn't want to know."

Bettina shakes her head. "There you are wrong, *amiga.* If you think that she didn't spend her whole life looking in the face of every girl child she saw and wondering if it was you, I think you are very wrong."

When I don't reply, she claps her hands together. "Are you too full for *capirotada*?"

I make myself smile. "When hell freezes over."

"Let me just take care of this cowboy, and then I will bring it."

There's something familiar about the cowboy paying his check at the register—the way he stands, rocking back on his boot heels, the way he holds his hat. I know him, and my heart is miles ahead of my brain, thundering in my ears before he feels my stare and turns around.

His eyes find mine, like a needle finding a nerve. Speaking of ghosts . . .

Seconds or minutes or maybe hours pass. Then he's walking over. When he sets his hat down on the table, the gold ring gleams on his left hand.

"Avery."

"Hi, Will. How are you?"

"Okay. Yourself?"

"Fine."

Is it possible that we have nothing more to say?

He clears his throat. "I thought you'd be in L.A. or New York or someplace."

"If you really thought that, you didn't know me very well."

His eyes are flat gray, not at all the way I remember. "I figured that out pretty quick when I came back to Florales and you were gone."

A wave of heat rises up my neck. "I thought it would be best."

"Best for who?"

"Everyone."

The white lines around his eyes contrast with his tan face, and I picture him squinting into the sun. I remember Cassie's appraisal of him.

"He's got a big heart. Maybe he'll grow into it." Maybe he has. Or maybe his heart's gotten smaller.

"Where are you living these days?"

"Santa Fe." I take a drink of my iced tea, gripping the glass like it can save me. "What brings you down this way?"

"Business," he says. "I'm working with Darryl Hutt now."

"I never thought you'd leave the ranch."

"It's a long story." One that he's obviously not interested in telling.

"Well . . . things must've worked out for you. I'm . . . glad. Who's the lucky girl?"

Before he answers, I know. Like a photograph. I see her face the way I saw it that day, dripping with tears and snot, grass stuck in her hair.

"You married Randi Klein?"

His eyes turn to granite. "What difference does it make to you?"

"I'm . . ." I scan the Formica tabletop for something to focus on, stopping on the initials of some lovesick cowboy and his sweetie tucked inside a heart.

"When I came back and you—-" His voice is controlled, like a horse on a very short rein. "I waited. I kept thinking you'd call or write. That we could talk about it. Get it straightened out."

"We could never have—" I start but he talks over me.

"I knew you wouldn't just leave. Without telling me anything. Without even saying good-bye. It took me some time to figure out that was exactly what you did." He hesitates. "And then I went kinda crazy for a while. So don't say a goddamn word about who I married."

"Well, I'm sure it made your mother very happy."

His fingers encircle my wrist as he leans across the table. "You don't know a goddamn thing about it."

I'm pulling my arm away, but he won't let go. "I know they never would've let you marry me—"

"I didn't need their permission."

"And I know that if by some chance you did do something that stu-pid, I would've had to spend the rest of my life being grateful that someone named Cameron was interested in doing anything at all to me." I jerk my arm away at the precise second that he lets go, and my elbow hits the water glass. It rolls off the table.

He looks at the shattered glass on the floor, the spreading pool pouring off the edge of the table like a waterfall. For a minute I think he's going to bend down and start picking it up. That would be like him. But he changes his mind.

"Sorry," he says. He picks up his hat, bunching the water-soaked brim in his fist.

Without another word he turns and walks to the door, his boots making that hollow tapping noise on the wooden floor. He rounds the corner by the cash register and disappears. I hear the sound of the door closing behind him. The two guys at the counter turn back to their food.

I put my cold hands on my hot face and sit staring at the water. Bettina appears with a towel.

"Old friend of yours?" She throws the towel on the puddle and stoops to pick up the biggest pieces of glass.

"I'm sorry."

"Bah! Men." She sits down next to me. "Raoul! Get a broom and get the rest of this." She looks at me with her sad dark eyes. "Our punishment for the sins of Eve. You still want your *capirotada*?"

"No, *gracias*."

twenty-three

November starts off bitter cold and dry. Clothes have to be peeled apart, crackling with static electricity, when I take them out of the dryer, and every time I touch a doorknob, sparks jump. The main house is so cold in the mornings, I can see my breath in the kitchen.

One morning I'm getting ready to grind the coffee beans when Paul walks into the kitchen silently in stocking feet.

"Wait!"

I swing around, startled. "What's wrong?"

He smiles. "Nothing." He's wearing jeans and a nubby cableknit sweater the color of whole wheat bread. His hair is soft and loose, tucked behind his ears.

"Nothing's wrong," he says. "I just thought we should go out for coffee. I have some holiday plans I want to discuss with you."

"Can't we do that here?"

"I want your undivided attention while we're talking. Besides . . ." His grin is appealingly boyish. "It'll be fun. I know that's a difficult concept for you, but let's give it a try. Go on, get your coat."

I can't help thinking that we make a strange pair as we stride down Canyon Road with our breath streaming behind us—him in his black shearling rancher's coat, black cowboy hat, black cashmere scarf, and black leather gloves, and me in gray sweatpants, red wool turtleneck that itches my throat, my navy surplus peacoat, the scarf that Rita gave me five years ago that used to be white, and navy blue gloves with a hole in the right thumb. He doesn't seem to notice.

Being perfectly comfortable in his stylish ensemble, he keeps stopping to look in the windows of the galleries, saying things like, "Look
at this Paul Signac, Avery. Interesting, the palette he uses in this one. It
could almost be here in New Mexico."

"Looks like blue sky over brown dirt, to me. I guess you could say it
resembles New Mexico."

He places his hands on my shoulders and walks me back about five
steps. "Voilà. *The Quay at Clichy.*" Sure enough, from this distance the
gazillion little dots fuse into a picture of an empty wharf. I can even see
trees and the mast of a tall ship in the background.

"He's a pointillist," Paul says. "They used tiny dots of primary color
not only to describe forms but to generate secondary colors. It was an
offshoot of impressionism."

I try to study the picture, but his face, only a couple of inches from
mine as he peers over my shoulder, is a distraction.

I say, "Paul, I'm freezing my ass off. Could we please just walk?"

At Downtown Subscription we carry our lattes and scones to a
table in the packed, noisy room. The chairs are awful—straight and
hard. In the restaurant business they're called thirty-minute chairs
because people don't tend to linger in them and you can turn the
tables fast.

Paul seems oblivious to the noise, the jostling crowd, the uncomfortable seating. He takes his coat off and drapes it carefully over the
back of the chair, neatly folds the scarf, lays it on the table, gloves go on
top. By the time he takes his first sip of coffee, I'm halfway through my
scone. I watch him dip his index finger into the mound of frothy milk
dusted with cocoa and cinnamon, lick it. The gesture is so childlike
and unselfconscious, so unlike him, that it makes me laugh.

His smile warms me. "It's nice to hear you laugh."

Immediately I feel ashamed for all my ungracious thoughts.

"So what do you want to talk about?" I ask. "Not that we'll be able
to hear each other in here."

"I can hear you," he says mildly. "I want to talk about some enter-
taining plans I have."

"I didn't bring my notebook," I protest.

He turns partway, fishing in the inside breast pocket of his coat,
hands me a small pad and a slim gold pen.

"First a dinner party. Next Friday. Or maybe Saturday. I'll have to
check. Intimate. Say two couples."

Something thumps in my chest, and I look quickly toward the rack
of glossy decorating magazines lining the far wall. "Clients?"

He nods, lost in his plans. "Can you do something French?"

I sit up a little straighter. "Of course. What did you have in mind?"

"Bistro style. Country food. A daube, a braise. Something comforting."

My mind is racing. I can braise, but I can't recall for the life of me
what a daube is. Oh well, that's why God created Julia Child.

"No problem," I say. "What else?"

"Christmas Eve supper for . . ." He closes his eyes as if visualizing
the guest list. "Ten. Maybe twelve. After the Canyon Road walk." He
pauses to throw me a questioning look. "Maybe we should call a
caterer. So you can come to the party."

"I don't need to be at the party."

"We can at least hire some servers. I don't want you to be stuck in
the kitchen all night."

I consider telling him that being "stuck" in the kitchen is far prefer-
able to making small talk with a bunch of rich people that I don't
know, but I don't want to come on too ungrateful.

"What about Thanksgiving?"

"I won't be here," he says. "Will you be all right?"

I shoot him a withering glance. "Of course I'll be all right. Where
will you be?"

"I'm going skiing."

I laugh. "If there's any snow."

"Whistler," he says. "British Columbia. They've got plenty already. Tom and I and some other people are going."

I find myself wondering whether the "other people" are male or female people, but he doesn't elaborate.

We eat in silence for a few minutes, while he pretends to read the paper. Then, abruptly, he asks, "What will you do for Thanksgiving?"

I shrug. "Sleep late. Read. Take a couple of long walks. Maybe a bubble bath. If I get really ambitious, I might go rent a movie."

"What about your friend? The one who owns the Rio Bravo."

"Bettina? What about her?"

"I just thought maybe you'd get together with her one afternoon."

"We're not that kind of friends."

"What about your old roommate. Is it Rita?"

"I haven't talked to her."

"I hate to think of you being here alone."

"Why? I don't mind. In fact, most of the time, I prefer it."

"It just seems . . . sad somehow."

I set down my latte. "I told you when we first met that my life might not look like much to you, but I'm content. I don't need sympathy, and I sure as hell don't need you patronizing me."

He looks around. As if anyone could care what we're saying—as if anyone could even hear what we're saying. "I'm not patronizing you—"

"Of course you are. You assume that if I could, I'd be going on a ski trip or having a big dinner with friends, but since I can't, you picture me as Poor Pitiful Pearl standing out in the snow with my nose pressed against the window." I stand up and pick up my plate. "I assure you that isn't the case."

"Avery."

"What?"

"I'm sorry."

I let my breath out slowly and sit down. The whole atmosphere of our "fun" outing darkens abruptly with my mood.

"I almost wish I weren't going," he says.

Having successfully cast a pall over the morning, I'm now determined to salvage it. "You'll have a great time once you're there. It'll be
good for you to have a break."

He pushes the scone around with his fork. "It's just that if I really
think about it—oh, the actual skiing will be fun, although Hemmings
has to make a competition out of everything. But the rest of it—too
much food and booze, listening to him talk about football and how
many times he got laid last month—"

"Are you trying to tell me you don't like football?"

His eyes crinkle when he laughs.

We stand up, shrug into our coats. He, as usual, has stopped to talk
to somebody, and I'm halfway to the door when I hear my name.

"Avery. Over here." My eyes sweep the crowd until they're caught
by a dark hand waving from the other side of the room by the door to
the side patio.

"Cookie, hi." We wade through the tables, chairs, and bodies toward
each other, and she surprises me with her big hug.

"I can't believe running into you like this. I've been trying to find
you, but all I had was a phone number that's disconnected. Where did
you go?"

"I moved."

"But you're still in town?"

"Yes. I feel like an idiot, but I can't remember my phone number.
I'll call the shop and give it to you."

"Right. If I'm not there, just ask Annette to be sure to put it on my
desk in back. She's minding things for a few days."

"How's Liza?"

Sudden tears brim in her huge dark eyes. "Gone," she says. Barely a
whisper.

"Oh, Cookie. I'm so sorry. When?"

"Last Saturday afternoon."

"Oh, shit." My face gets all hot and blotchy, practically glowing
with shame. "I'm sorry, I really am. I meant to come—oh goddamnit

312

JUDITH RYAN HENDRICKS

all anyway." I stand there, frozen in place, and all I can think of is, why didn't I know? I should have known.

Cookie is murmuring quietly. "I miss her incredibly, but she was in pain. At the end, it simply overwhelmed all the drugs. I guess I could have taken her to the hospital, but she didn't want that. She wanted to be at home—oh, that's the other thing I wanted to tell you. When I was cleaning out her bedroom, I came across a—some things that belonged to Isabel. I thought perhaps you'd like them."

"Yes, I do. I'll come by . . . I'm just . . . sorry. I feel so . . ."

She squeezes my arm. "She was very fond of you, you know."

I can't bear to hear myself say I'm sorry one more time. Or anything else stupid and totally inadequate, so I just nod my head.

"I'll see you soon, then." She turns to go back to her table. "Do call me before you come, so I remember to bring Isabel's things."

Thanksgiving Day is gray, the air cold and thin. I wake up early from habit and then, remembering Paul's not here, drift back to sleep, burrowed into the down comforter, thinking about his departure last night. The way he stood in hall, almost reluctant, hand hesitating at the doorknob, eyes lingering on my face. From the street we could hear Tom Hemmings shout, "For Chrissakes, DeGraf, get your ass in gear. Traffic's already a bitch."

Paul's brief, apologetic smile faded as he closed the door.

When I wake up again it's nearly ten o'clock, and I lie still, looking up through the skylight, as if the weather might be the source of the vague but persistent unease that settles over me lately when I first open my eyes.

Is it about Paul? The few simple tasks I do for him couldn't by any stretch of the imagination be considered a full-time job, and yet, for all intents and purposes, I've stopped looking for work. I tell myself it's the wrong season. That I'll get going on the job hunt in the spring. Meanwhile, I'm simply living here, rent free, doing a little food shopping, a little cooking, reading the long mornings away, listening to him reminisce about Isabel.

He's in the habit of coming into the kitchen sometimes in late afternoon, before it's time to get serious about dinner, but I'm usually in there either browsing cookbooks or doing some prep work—roasting peppers, chopping onions or tomatoes, snapping beans, scrubbing vegetables, shelling pecans—the kinds of things I've always enjoyed doing alone, things that don't require conscious attention.

He'll sidle in casually, sometimes with a glass of wine, park himself on a stool, say something like, "I hope I'm not disturbing you," or "What culinary magic are you performing tonight?" Stuff nobody else I've ever known could get away with saying. It would sound completely hokey.

We'll chat for a few minutes, sometimes about a book I'm reading or he'll tell me about some new artist he's discovered, but somehow he always manages to maneuver the conversation around to her. He talks about her like she's still alive, maybe just living in another town for a while. Like she might call some night and say she's coming back to Santa Fe tomorrow.

I can picture his face, the way he smiles kind of understated, but even so it would be with what novelists always refer to as "delight." I can hear him saying to her, "Isabel, the most amazing thing has happened. You'll never guess who's sitting in my kitchen right now."

It's during these afternoons that he imparts the gospel of Isabel to me. The night they met—which I've now heard at least three times, but which he never seems to tire of recounting. The day they went down to Madrid and discovered *Querencia*. The time he found one of her early watercolors and had it put into a beautiful gold frame and hung it at Pinnacle, and she was so embarrassed she didn't speak to him for three days. Their trip to New York for Christmas when he got the flu.

But I think my favorite story is the lead up to their first date. How he found out where she worked from one of her friends and called her at The Good Earth to ask her to have dinner.

"She said no the first time." He gave me a solemn look. "And the second time. And the third. I started calling or going by the shop every day——"

I laughed. "I think that's called harassment."

He raised his eyebrows. "It was nothing of the kind. I bought something every time I went to the store. I was always respectful, and I never stayed long. Just long enough to ask her to have dinner and to get turned down." He laughed quietly with me. "I think Liza Gardner got heartily sick of me."

The knife in my hand slipped, nicking my left thumb.

"Oh, you've cut yourself."

He started to get up, but I waved him off. "It's nothing." I flicked the tiny bead of blood with my tongue. It was warm and salty, and my skin tasted of onion.

"Would you like some alcohol and a Band-Aid?"

"Right." I bit off the word. "That would taste great in the chicken." He frowned.

"I'm . . . sorry," I said. "I was just thinking about Liza."

It wasn't exactly a lie. Although I wasn't thinking about her dying. I was hearing her voice, twisted tight with pain. *He killed her, didn't he? That one who loved her.*

His eyes are nearly black, but clear somehow. You feel like you could see all the way to the bottom. Nothing to hide.

I smiled a little. "So how long did it take?"

"Three weeks, four days, eleven hours, fifteen minutes."

I stared at him, speechless. Finally, I said, "Don't bullshit me."

"It was three weeks and four days later at eleven fifteen in the morning when she finally agreed to have dinner with me." He settled himself on the stool again and took a sip of wine. "I spent the rest of the week getting the house ready. Planning the menu with the chef.

Checking the weather forecasts to decide if we should be inside or on the patio. Choosing the wine, hiring a guitarist, buying flowers—"

"Jesus H. Christ. Do you have to orchestrate everything?"

"It's the only way to ensure that you get what you want," he said, and moved on quickly. "The best part was that night. I sent a limo to pick her up and bring her to my house—I was living up off Artist Road then—and about thirty minutes later the limo came back without her. The driver was beside himself. He said that Isabel asked him to give me a message. The message was, 'You tell Mr. DeGraf that if he wants to take me out to dinner, he can come and pick me up himself.'"

In spite of myself I felt the smallest tingle of elation. Like she would hold her hand up and I would give her a high five and say *you go, girl!*

"So did you?"

"I did. And I felt about seventeen years old, calling on a girl for the first time."

I smirked at him. "So that just proves that even if you orchestrate everything, you don't necessarily get what you want."

The smile he returned was wistful. "She was always proving that."

It's a weird day, all closed and quiet. The rest of the world seems divided into two camps, the ones who are going to somebody's house to celebrate Thanksgiving, and the somebodys who are hosting the event. While I sit at the polished black granite counter eating my oatmeal in silence except for the dull chink of spoon against bowl, I imagine women clustered in warm, noisy kitchens, laughing and gossiping and tasting, arguing about seasonings or whether to add roasted green chiles to the stuffing. The men would be gathered around the TV watching the football games that have probably already started back east, or soccer matches on satellite, telling dirty jokes, shouting when somebody fumbles, and punching each other in the arm the way guys do. And the children. Laughing, fighting, stealing food when no one is looking.

At least that's how I imagine it. About noon the clouds start to break up. I shake off my mood, put on my apron and get ready to make my own Thanksgiving dinner. *Posole.* Or what Pete Dimon used to call "hog and hominy."

There are as many versions of *posole* as there are of barbecue, and the merits of each are hotly debated, but mine is the one I watched Esperanza make while I stood on the rickety chair by the stove at Carson. Basically it's just a green chile stew with pork and hominy. Esperanza didn't serve it with all the little garnishes—avocado and lime wedges and radishes—like Bettina does. She just served it plain with big, thin, soft flour tortillas, and that's how I like it best. So that's what I'm thankful for today.

Friday morning the sky is gray and heavy, and a raw wind out of the north pushes my little truck around on the road. It's not cold enough for snow, but it looks like we might finally get some rain.

Alonzo's do-it-yourself blue hybrid pickup truck with the water tank bolted behind the cab is parked in front of the cabin. He and Maria have been coming here for almost three weeks, and the roof is done, but I still can't get him to quote me a price, and I haven't been able to get a hold of Bettina. It makes me a little nervous.

"So how's Maria doing on the inside?"

"She finish soon." It's what he says every time I ask.

Maria convinced me that the whole interior of the cabin should be replastered, now that the roof's watertight, and she's mixing the plaster with local sand from the creek bed. It gives the walls a wonderful warm gold blush. I also ended up springing for three new windows because Alonzo said the ones I didn't do this year would have to be done next year, and if we have a wet winter they might leak and ruin my new rosy plaster.

Progress is complicated because of the way they operate. They have several jobs going all the time, and they move back and forth from one to the other every few days. It's almost like finishing anyone's job too far ahead of the others would somehow be impolite.

Of course, just because it's my day to have work done doesn't mean the supplies they need will be available. The first time we were supposed to put the new windows in, the windows didn't arrive at the lumberyard.

When I suggested to Alonzo that he should have gone to another job, he regarded me with amused benevolence. "Ah, but it is your day. I cannot work other job on your day." So he passed the time wandering around the cabin, rechecking the roof, remeasuring the windows, examining the interior to see if anything else needed attention.

When I came back that afternoon, he informed me that the pump that brought water to the sink needed to be replaced.

"Great," I said. "Let's do that this afternoon."

He shook his shaggy head. "I order for you the pump."

"How long will it take to get?"

He rubbed one hand over the black and gray stubble on his jaw. "Two days. Maybe three."

I nodded. "Okay. So we can get it in by Thursday?"

"No, *señorita,*" he explained with a patient air. "Thursday is not your day."

This morning, he's just strapping on his tool belt when I walk up.

"Ah, *buenos días, señorita.*" He touches his fingers to the brim of his hat, where several corks bob at the end of short strings. My best guess would be that it keeps the flies away from his face. Although today is too cold even for the flies.

"What will you do today?" I ask him.

"I fix estones," he says.

"What stones?"

"Behind estove. There is bad mortar. I fix."

He crosses his muscular arms across his chest, and regards me with interest. "Bettina say you maybe have a garden? You want I clear the land?"

I sigh. "Maybe. Let's see how the rest of this goes."

There aren't many cars in the Rio Bravo's gravel parking lot. I don't see Bettina's old brown Nova, but maybe she came with Miguel. I park next to the building and walk around back. The rain-smelling wind whips my jacket open, and I hug it around me.

The kitchen is warm and steamy. It smells of chiles roasting, *sopai-pillas* frying. Miguel and Raoul, Felicia's brother, are working with the radio going full blast, so they don't hear me come in.

"Miguel!" I shout over the brassy music.

He waves at me.

"*Dónde está Bettina?*"

"*No se.*" His usual jovial smile is missing.

"She will come when? *Cuándo?*"

"*No se.*" He keeps working, eyes down at the *masa* dough he's mixing.

"Miguel, is she sick? Is she all right?"

He stops and looks directly at me. I can tell he's trying to put the right English words together to make this pesky *gringa* understand.

"She es no here."

"*Sí.*" I nod. "*Dónde está?*"

He chews his thoughts for a few minutes. "She go with the cowboy."

My mouth falls open. "Ed Farrell?"

He just nods and goes back to his dough. I want to know when she left, when she's coming back. Is this just a jaunt for the holiday or something more serious? But I can't make him understand the questions, and I probably wouldn't understand his answers. Besides, he's obviously not happy about this turn of events.

"Miguel, can I have some soup?" When he looks up, I point at the huge pot bubbling on the stove.

"*Sí. Por supuesto.*"

I ladle Miguel's black bean soup into the biggest bowl I can find, add a dollop of sour cream, a sprinkling of cilantro and chopped jalapeños, grab a couple of tortillas with my other hand, and shoulder through the swinging door to the café.

Only a few tables are occupied. Everyone's probably at home eating leftover turkey. Felicia looks up from the cash register, smiles at me as I seat myself at my usual post in the far corner. Some *gringo* has left part of their Albuquerque newspaper on the chair, so I prop it up and flip through it looking for Rick's byline, but I don't find anything.

The barrage of ads for Christmas has already started. Christmas. The first time in eight years I won't be with Rita. Cassie never celebrated it—we celebrated the winter solstice on my birthday—so when I first moved in with Rita, I wasn't prepared for her over-the-top American Christmas. She always decorated the apartment to within an inch of its life, stenciling snowflakes on all the windows, draping ribbons and greens everywhere. We never had a big tree because they were too expensive, but the little misshapen ones that we got for cheap in the last week before the holiday never had a naked branch to their name. Rita had been collecting ornaments for a long time.

The first year I said I didn't want to swap presents, but she said it was part of the deal. If I didn't want to get her anything, that was fine with her—or so she said—but she was going to get me whatever she felt like getting me. Her gift-giving philosophy was "More Is Better." There were several years when the stacks of presents took up more space than our scrawny little tree.

Of course, I was forced to reciprocate, and eventually I had to admit it was kind of fun to open everything Christmas morning while we drank hot chocolate and nibbled muffins. There was usually one nice gift—a new scarf or a blouse or a pair of gloves—and then the rest were homemade presents or joke gifts. Like the license plate frame for my truck that said "Always late, but worth the wait."

Now as I sit staring at pictures of CD players and laptop computers tied with bows and proffered by pretty girls wearing Santa Claus hats, I understand why suicide rates spike during the holidays.

"Mind if I sit down?"

I know his voice. I could pick it out of a roomful of others like the single gold thread in a tapestry. To hear it in the quiet of the nearly empty café shocks me.

Will Cameron is standing next to the table, holding his hat, not smiling but looking considerably more subdued than the last time I saw him. His hair's a little longer, creeping down over the collar of his plaid wool shirt, and it's imprinted with that perpetual line that all real cowboys have—that little indentation just above the ears where their hat sits. I remember how it feels under my fingers, and the thought calls fire up into my face.

"Sure."

He sits down in the other chair across from me, and I have a sudden shiver of déjà vu.

Mami's. The lukewarm coffee in thick white mugs, the two of us stringing words together in ways I've never done before or since, only a vague awareness of the rest of the world, dark and cold pressing against the window. Now we both seem unable to say anything.

"There's too much," he says, reading my mind. "I don't know where to start."

"What are you doing here?"

He tosses his hat on the table next to us. "Having lunch. What about you?"

I look down at my half empty bowl of soup. "I just came to see Bettina, but she's not here."

"I kind of went off last time . . ." His face is ruddy from cold and awkwardness. "I didn't get around to asking you what you've been doing."

Before I can say anything Felicia comes to the table.

"I'll have some of that soup, please ma'am." He nods at my bowl.

"And some corn tortillas and some iced tea." I ask for more water. When she's gone, he says, "Tell me."

"It's a long story."

I pause to give him an opening to say we can do it another time, that he's got to be somewhere, that he understands if there's somewhere I need to be. But I know he's not going to say any of those things, and he doesn't.

"Well, I found out who my mother was."

"Have you talked to her?"

"She's dead." I'm a terrible person for enjoying the shock value of those two words.

"I'm really sorry, Avery."

I shrug it off. "At least now I know. Her name was Isabel Colinas. She was from Colorado, but she came to Santa Fe to be an artist."

"And was she?"

"Yes. A fiber artist. Quilts and stuff like that. I guess she was pretty successful. I've seen some of her work. It's amazing."

Felicia comes back with his soup, sets his bowl down, the basket of tortillas, wrapped in a napkin. I watch him examine the labels on different bottles of hot sauce till he finds the one called "Nuclear Fusion" and doctors his soup liberally with it.

He takes a bite, adds more sauce. "So how did you find her?" he asks.

"I was working for a caterer, and I was at a party at this art dealer's house and I saw a picture of her. A portrait. An oil painting by Tom Hemmings." I can tell he has no clue who Tom Hemmings is.

"How did you know it was her?"

"Because she looked exactly like me." My studied reserve goes out the back door as I lean across the table. "Even her eyes, Will."

Saying his name out loud jangles every nerve ending in my body.

"She had this little cabin," I add quickly. "Not far from here. A place called Bluebird Canyon. It needs work, of course, but Bettina's got me someone to do plastering and fix the windows and the roof—

anyway, that's sort of why I came today. What are you doing down here?"

"Looking for you, I guess."

I stop breathing.

He dumps a whole packet of sugar in his tea and stirs it around. "Every time I drive this highway lately, I stop here. Thinking maybe you'll be here again."

"Why?"

Now he sets down the spoon and looks at me. "A lot of time's gone by, Avery. A lot's happened to both of us. I think we still have some things to say to each other."

I give him the coldest look I can manage under the circumstances. "Whatever you have to say to me, it better be something you wouldn't mind your wife hearing."

"My wife?"

"The former Randi Klein. You remember her."

"Not very well. We've been divorced for three years."

My one boot slips off the rung of the chair.

"Then why are you still wearing your goddamned wedding ring?"

"To remind myself not to do anything else stupid."

I watch him eat, that careful, polite way of his. I watch the tiny beads of sweat on his forehead from the heat of the sauce.

"So," I say. "Tell me what happened with you and Randi."

He leans back in the chair. "Not a lot to tell. I was . . . unhappy. She was, too."

"What was she unhappy about?"

"She hated Florales. Always did—"

"Why did she marry you then? You never looked like you were going anywhere else."

"And Kevin dumped her. He got back together with Stacey." He shrugs. "I don't know . . . one minute we were hanging out at Lucky's, telling each other our troubles, next thing I knew we were getting married."

"So what happened?"

"It was a mistake from the get-go. You put two unhappy people together, seems like it multiplies times four. Her way of dealing with it was to go to Lucky's and drink it away. My way was to hang out with the horses and not talk about anything. One day she just left. Not too long after that I got served with papers from some big lawyer in Denver."

"But why did you leave the ranch?"

"Had no choice. I had to sell my share of the ranch to Chuck. To pay her what she wanted."

"I'm sorry."

"It was probably the best thing that ever happened to me. Getting out from under my brother. I've been working with Darryl for two years now. We've got a ranch down by Pecos Monument."

"Are you happy there?"

"I think it's what I always wanted."

Felicia comes by with a refill for his tea, and he waits till she's gone before he adds, "Work-wise, anyway."

My stomach feels like a knotted rubber band. His eyes are searching mine, and I have to look away. "Things are a lot different now, Avery. I'm not a rich kid anymore. I'm a poor cowboy." He tries to laugh. "We've both been through some changes—I mean I have no idea what's going on in your life right now, but . . ."

I know where this is heading and I want to get up and run away before it gets there. "Will—"

"Wait, Avery. Just wait. You haven't even heard what I'm going to say and you're halfway out the damn door." He puts a warm, dry palm on my arm. "I want to see you sometime. I'm not saying we can pick up where we left off, but now that I know where you are, I can't just walk away."

While I grope for something, the right thing—or anything—to say, he pulls a few pieces of paper out of his shirt pocket and separates a dirt-smudged business card from the rest. "Here."

I take it from him and read: "Stony River Ranch, Darryl Hutt, Will Cameron (505) 435-1227."

"Think about it," he says. "Think about it and then call me. If I don't hear from you by Christmas, I won't bug you again."

I stick the card in my pocket and stand up. "It's good to see you, Will."

I'm outside, down the steps, and at my truck before I think to look at the sky. The clouds are low and heavy as a pregnant woman. While I'm fishing the key out of my pocket I hear the door shut again.

"Avery." Footsteps crunching in the gravel. Before I can get the door open, his hand is there, holding it shut.

He's standing so close to me I'm surrounded by his scent. The cold wind circles my neck.

"I know why you left," he says. At this range I can see the pale stubble of his beard.

I swallow the argument that rises in my throat. It doesn't matter.

One calloused finger slips down inside the neckline of my T-shirt, hooking the flat S-links of the gold chain. He tugs gently but steadily until the heart of gold nuggets emerges.

"You didn't trust me," he says.

For a minute the heart dangles from his finger. Then he lets it fall, silent and heavy against my chest.

"You still don't."

He's already moving away from me when I feel the first drops of rain.

twenty-four

Something wakes me after what seems like only a few minutes of uneasy sleep. Noise—low key, but insistent. Like static. I roll onto my back, open one eye in the cold darkness to stare blankly at the strange pattern of reflected light on the ceiling.

The noise is water.

I sit straight up, shedding sleep like a coat off my back.

I throw off the covers, and my feet splat on the soaking rug. I run, slipping on the wet tiles down the hall to the bathroom, feeling for the light switch just inside the door. The floor is wet, but no water is running.

I splash through the living room into the kitchen, where the water is almost up to my ankles. The sixty-watt bulb over the stove is on, and the whole floor glistens darkly under spreading ripples of water. I open the cupboard under the sink to see water gushing from a small white hose.

Kneeling in the cold water, jostling the plastic basket of cleaning supplies, groping for the oval metal shutoff valve, I turn it first one way, then the other. The flow shrinks to a trickle and stops.

On the pad next to the kitchen phone, he's left the number of the hotel. It's late, but I should call the insurance company first thing tomorrow. Reluctantly, I dial the number, and the hotel operator connects me to his room. The phone rings four times and then a woman's voice says, "Hello?"

I try to think what to say. Have I got the wrong room? There are other voices in the background, laughter and music.

"I can't hear anything," she says, not into the phone, and there's a rustling as she hands the receiver off to someone else.

"Hello?"

"Paul, it's Avery." My voice feels stiff and awkward.

"Avery? What is it? Are you all right? Hold on a minute." He puts his hand over the mouthpiece, and when he comes back on the line, there's silence behind him.

"What's going on? Is everything all right?"

"Just a little accident. A pipe burst under the kitchen sink. In the guesthouse. The whole place is flooded. I'm sorry. I was asleep, and—"

"Oh, don't worry about it." He sounds relieved. "Are you all right, though?"

"I'm fine. I just thought I should call your insurance company and I didn't know where to look for it."

"Good idea. There's a Rolodex on my desk. Look under Travis. Eugene Travis. There are two or three numbers. You can call him on his cell phone tomorrow."

"Okay. I wasn't asleep that long . . . it must've happened pretty fast. It's kind of a mess over there, everything—"

"Don't worry about it. Gene will take care of it."

It's quiet on the other end. I can almost see his frown. The flicker of worry in his dark eyes—that look of quiet concern he's always throwing at me, that I've gotten to expect and even maybe to want from him, even though I keep batting it away. "Are you sure you're all right?"

"I'm fine. Just sleepy and cold."

"You can use my room. There are clean linens on the shelf in the closet."

"Okay. Sorry to bother you."

A sigh. "Avery, you're not bothering me."

"See you Sunday."

My steps echo up the stairs and along the hall toward the only open door. The house is absolutely silent. I'm used to silence, but always in small spaces. A house this big full of silence is overwhelming. I wonder if it bothers him. Does he sing in the shower? Talk to himself? Turn on the TV? Stereo?

His bedroom is small and spare, almost monastic, in spite of the colors—mud walls, a blue quilt on the bed, a weathered red night table, and a bright yellow folk art bookcase set under the blue casement window.

The closet has no door. I think at one time it was a bathroom, but now it's just a large alcove off the bedroom, full of neatly organized racks of black and gray clothes. One shelf holds three sets of towels, all black. Beside them are three sets of sheets, all white.

I make up the bed hurriedly, but I'm cold again, so I don't undress. Instead I lie on my back, rigid as a corpse, blankets pulled up under my chin, thinking about the party that I obviously interrupted. The woman who answered the phone.

When I was a little girl at Carson, sometimes at night I'd suddenly get the weirdest crawling sensation deep in my legs. Like they were walking on their own. I found out later from a nurse at UNM that it's called Restless Legs Syndrome. I outgrew it eventually, but the way I feel now reminds me of it—the sense of movement without intent or even awareness. I get out of bed, move to the window, and open the blue shutters, and look down on the silent, shadowed yard. From here I can see the faint glow of the solar lamps that line the walk, but most of the yard is hidden by the curving bulk of the second-story guest room.

I can't see the pool.

I grab my jacket from the hook on the back of the door, slip into it, pull on my boots, and go out.

Canyon Road is deserted. All the galleries are closed and shuttered, dark except for a few lighted display windows. The trees toss melodramatically in the wind like a group of bad actors, and leftover storm clouds scud across the sky, lit from behind by the moon.

In one courtyard, kinetic sculptures of odd metallic birds circle and flap like ghosts hovering over me—more elusive than menacing, reminders of what no longer exists—or worse, what exists, but is out of my reach. When I'm so cold that I can't feel my feet anymore, I turn and head back to San Tomás.

. . .

At nine Saturday morning Cookie calls to say that the shop is closed today, but she'll be there taking inventory and rearranging the stock, and that she'll bring Isabel's things if I want to stop by.

I show up just after 1:00 P.M. and she greets me at the door with a clipboard in one hand and half a tunafish sandwich in the other. Her hair is completely hidden by a bright green cotton scarf.

"Hi," she says, leaning in for a hug. "I hope you're hungry. I ordered this from Sandwich Board, and it's the size of a small rowboat."

"I could probably be persuaded to eat a piece of it."

"Excellent. See if you can find a place to sit down, and don't mind the mess."

I look around at boxes and tins, jars and paper bags, empty, dusty shelves, vacant drawers with faded paper lining. Two large garbage cans lined with plastic trash bags are well on their way to overflow. "What are you doing?"

"A thorough inventory and general housecleaning." She cuts half of the sandwich in half again, making it the size of a normal sandwich. "Here, if you can finish this, you're welcome to the rest. Would you like something to drink?"

"Just water, thanks. It looks like you've got your work cut out for you."

"Poor Liza. I don't know when was the last time she went through all this. At first when I came, I wasn't that involved in managing the place, and then after she got sick, I never had time to see to a proper cleaning."

"You need some help?"

"Oh, I wouldn't ask it of you, thanks. It's nasty work."

"I don't mind. Really. Paul's gone till tomorrow night and I have nothing exciting going on."

"Paul?"

"Paul DeGraf."

"Isabel's . . . intended?"

I laugh. "Yes. That's where I'm living now—in his guesthouse. Which is currently flooded because of a busted pipe under the kitchen sink."

"So where are you sleeping?"

"In his—in the main house."

One eyebrow goes up, but she doesn't say anything.

"I guess it is a bit strange. But I lost my job at Dos Hombres and my roommate chose that exact moment to move to Albuquerque with her boyfriend, so I was sort of in a bind. Paul said I could live at the guesthouse free if I'd cook for him. It's just till I find another job," I add quickly.

"Doing what?"

I shrug. "Waiting, I guess. It's about all I know."

"You seem to know a fair amount about herbs."

"Only what I learned from Cassie, the old lady I lived with. She had her remedies. They were about half herbal and half voodoo."

Cookie smiles. "Nothing wrong with that. Is that where you got that tea?"

I nod.

"Well, it's damned fine stuff. Maybe you'd think about selling it here?"

I swallow the last of the sandwich. "I never thought about selling it. It wouldn't make much sense, would it?"

"What do you mean?"

"I mean, Cassie grew stuff, harvested wild herbs, traded for some things. If I had to buy the ingredients here, then sell the mixture back to you, wouldn't that make it kind of expensive?"

Cookie laughs brightly. "Well, I wouldn't charge you retail, silly. I think we could work something out, but you don't have to answer now. Just think about it. I'd love to carry it." She wraps up the remains of the food and stuffs it in a white paper sack. "And now, if you're still temporarily insane enough to want to help me, we can start pitching the stuff in those tins. I think it's been here since the conquest."

The afternoon doesn't pass; it crumbles around me like paint off a weathered door. The air is heavy with the dusty scents of dried herbs, the sharper smells of rubbing alcohol, vinegar, volatile oils of rosemary and peppermint and eucalyptus, steam from the teakettle that Cookie keeps going more for it's humidifying effects than for tea. I find it all strangely comforting.

We're both tired and filthy. I'm parched from dusty air, and the icy water from a jug in the little refrigerator seems like the best thing I've ever tasted. I can't get enough.

She picks up one of the old apothecary jars from her aunt's collection, turning it around, looking at the light through the wavy, bubbly, blue-tinted glass.

She frowns. "Of course now that we've washed these, the labels are going to disintegrate. Most of them were unreadable to begin with, but that means I have to sit down and write new ones."

"Maybe you should make them in Spanish." It comes direct from brain to mouth, no more than idle conversation, but she perks up.

"Of course I should. They were all in English and Latin, but hardly anybody uses the botanical names any longer. And lots of people come in asking for them by Spanish names. I can put English and Spanish on the labels and just keep my handy Latin crib sheet at the register. What a wonderful thought, Avery. I know a few of the names—*ruda* is rue, *romero* is rosemary. *Yerba buena*—mint . . ."

"*Albácar,*" I add, seeing Cassie's face. "Basil. *Ajenjibre*—ginger. *Canela*—cinnamon."

We bat the words back and forth. "*Mananzilla, álamo, toronjil.*"

I love the sounds rolling around in my head like a song with a secret meaning.

"*Sabino macho.*" She does a little flamenco dance. "This is all so exciting. I'll have to get a book." She pats her stomach. "But first, pizza. I'm buying. With anchovies or without?"

"With."

"A woman after my own heart."

I don't know what I was expecting. Maybe a shopping bag or a cardboard box full of books or magazines, old clothes, maybe photos— odds and ends left behind when Isabel moved in with Paul. What Cookie drags out of the backseat of her car is a suitcase. A fairly sizable one. Other than a thick layer of dust, it looks brand-new. It was obviously never used. It's locked.

It's heavy, too. She helps me hoist it into the back of my truck.

"How did you know it was Isabel's?"

"There's a tag on the handle," she says. "It's got Isabel's name, but my aunt's address." She's looking at me inquiringly. "I have to say I'm near dying of curiosity. If it hadn't been locked, I probably would have opened it." She looks mildly embarrassed. "After all, it could be some new piece that no one even knew she was working on."

"Thanks for dragging it over here for me. When I figure out how to unlock it, I'll let you know what I find."

Suitcase locks turn out to be almost disappointingly easy. I don't know why anyone even bothers to lock them. A couple of little twists with the ice pick and they pop right open. I lift the lid of the bag and push it back till it's resting against the couch in Paul's office.

The firelight gleams on a blaze of red material. I pick it up and shake it out.

A dress. No, not *a* dress, *the* dress. Long sleeves, high neck, clingy as water. The left sleeve is embroidered with flowers, dense at the wrist,

thinning out as they move up, twining around the arm like some
climbing vine. At the shoulder there's only one—a blue columbine.
Like the one on my baby shirt.

Without hesitation, I kick off my jogging shoes, unzip my jeans,
step out of them, leaving them in a heap on the floor. Pull my shirt off.
Then pull the dress on over my head. The musty smell of storage fills
my nose, and I choke back a huge sneeze.

I can't see myself, but it feels like magic. Like an embrace, softly
skimming my body. I feel like dancing—a ballet or a waltz, something
that would make the full skirt rise like wings—and it's so out of character for me that I laugh out loud at the image of myself in flight. Like the
swing. That's what it feels like. That moment of weightlessness when I
jumped from the swing on the playgound. Before I fell to my hands and
knees on the hard-packed earth. Before falling was even an option.

I pad down the hall to the bathroom, silent in my cotton socks.
Light floods the room and I stop breathing as I catch my reflection in
the three-way mirror over the vanity.

Jesus God. I'm her.

I turn sideways, look over my shoulder. Pull my hair back from my
face, twirl around till I'm dizzy. The dress is a little bit too big, and
several inches too long, but I still feel an ownership of it. An attach-
ment I've never felt to any article of clothing. I stand on tiptoe imagining myself in strappy high-heeled sandals. Or leg-hugging black
squaw boots. Or barefoot, running through the garden by the light of a
pale moon, like those women on the front of romance novels.

Then I remember what happened to Isabel running through a garden.

When I pull the dress off, I notice a hole in the right elbow. I wonder if Cookie could mend it. Shorten it and take it in a little. I could
wear it Christmas Eve. I lay it over the back of the chair.

The rest of the suitcase is full of clothes, naturally enough. I start on
the left side, trying to move them without disturbing everything. Underwear. Jeans. Shirts and shoes. A short red toreador jacket, embroidered in
the style that I now recognize as hers with lots of vines and flowers.

On the right side under some scarves and a few pieces of unopened mail is a green plastic box like the one Rita used to store sweaters in. I lift it out carefully, but not carefully enough. Suddenly the lid is all I'm holding. The box hits the tile with a sharp crack and the contents go everywhere, like a giant fireworks explosion.

Spools of thread—thick, coarse, slender, silky, fuzzy, metallic, iridescent—a flat plastic box full of beads and sequins and buttons and *milagros,* the little silver charms that represent prayers. Ribbons and trims and fringes unwind from their neat coils like ticker tape, and pieces of fabric—wool and cotton, linen, silk, satin, loose knits, lace, sheer organza, leather, and suede—some no bigger than a patch. Solids and stripes, plaids and prints. All over the office floor.

Piece by piece, I fold the material and lay it back in the box, starting with the soft, thick wool and felt and velvet. Next the coarse and sturdy canvas, cotton, denim. Next the knits and synthetics, spilling through my hands like liquid, and finally the lace and silk. I rewind the ribbons and trim, the spools of thread, sift the beads and buttons into their separate compartments. Some of them are so tiny I'll never find them. They've ricocheted under the couch, the desk, or embedded themselves in the Oriental rug. Everytime someone walks in this room, something of Isabel's will crunch underfoot.

When I lift it—from the bottom, this time—to replace it in the suitcase, I see the manila envelope lying in the bottom. The metal clasp has broken off, leaving a sharp stub that scratches me when I open it and withdraw a stack of papers—some blank, some with sketched designs and scribbled notations for materials and techniques. My hands shake slightly as I hold them up, one at a time, and look at the work Isabel had planned.

Some of the sketches are so rough that no one but the artist could see what they are. Others are more detailed and recognizable. One is a long apronlike thing that ties on the sides. She calls it a pinafore, and the design is incredibly intricate, like the view through a kaleidoscope. There's a reversible kimono with a sort of quilt pattern on one side, all straight lines and hard edges, and a lush tropical landscape on the other, full of sensuous curves and graceful flower forms.

The image on the next page immobilizes me for a few seconds. It's a drawing of a woman in a long skirt and hooded cloak. Underneath the figure is printed *La Llorona*. Every child in New Mexico knows who she is—The Weeping Woman. Juana told me her parents used to threaten to leave her out for *La Llorona* to take if she misbehaved. But Esperanza always said the woman who walked by the river at night, crying and calling for her lost children, wasn't scary, just sad.

I lay everything back in the suitcase, as close as possible to the meticulous way that she packed it, hoping I'll be able to get it closed again. Then as I start to lower the top I notice the elasticized cloth pocket inside the lid. I slip my hand down inside and pull out two items.

A blue passport. An airline ticket jacket.

I draw in one long and shaky breath and open the passport. Isabel Marieta Colinas looks back at me, beautiful even in her passport photo. She looks like she's trying to be serious and dignified, but her eyes seem to sparkle with some private joke. Her address is listed as 2501 Rivera Street—Liza's house.

I pull out the airline ticket. Albuquerque to New York. And New York to Madrid, Spain, on September 15, 1991. The return portion says "Open."

I sit back on my heels and stare at the papers in my hand. Isabel was going to Spain, but for what? Was she going alone? Meeting a friend? A lover? Was it a working trip? A vacation? Was she planning to come back at all?

The only thing I'd be willing to bet on is that, whatever her plans were, they didn't include Paul DeGraf.

Sunday night just before eight, I hear him in the hall. The door shuts and a minute later Paul walks into the kitchen where I'm sitting at the work island surrounded by cookbooks and notepads, crumpled lists, and a stack of index cards. He has the skier's tan, complete with white goggle marks.

"Avery." He comes straight to me and for a second I think he's going to hold me, but he puts his hands on my shoulders, plants a chaste kiss on my forehead. "Are you all right?"

"Of course. I'm just finishing up the menu for Christmas Eve. The insurance guy came yesterday and left an envelope for you. I put it on your desk. That guy Travis said you should get a different water purifier."

"I did," he says. "It must have something to do with the water pressure."

So how was the trip?" I ask when we're ensconced on the leather couch with big bowl-shaped glasses of red wine.

He smiles ruefully. "Exactly like I told you it would be. Great skiing, but Hemmings was hotdogging down every run, going much too fast, wiping out on the moguls, shouting that the rest of us didn't have a hair on—" he breaks off and blushes to his scalp. It's really quite charming.

"Three-hour dinners every night—"

"I thought all you Frenchmen were into that."

"Not every night. Not when you have to be in the lift line at eight A.M."

I look at him sideways. "You *have* to be? Because . . . someone's holding a gun to your head?"

"Well, we were only there four days. Of course we wanted to get the most—"

I laugh. "You're so full of shit, DeGraf. Admit it. At heart, you're a down-and-dirty jock."

Then he laughs, too. He leans his head against the back of the couch. Sighs. "You are so good for me, Avery. You really are."

I stare at the yellow flames behind the black fire screen and take a drink of wine. "How was the food at Whistler?"

"Very mediocre." He smiles. "Especially given what I'm used to.

And the bar had the worst selection of brandy and cognac I've ever seen." He hesitates for a minute. "So I bought some *bas* Armagnac and had everyone up after dinner Saturday night."

I want to ask who "everyone" is and why he's decided to tell me this. But instead, I say, "You're probably tired. I should go up and get my things out of your room."

For a second he looks blank. Then he remembers I'm camped upstairs. "I can sleep in the guest room," he says.

"No, all your clothes and . . . it'll be easier if I move."

"Not tonight." He touches my arm. "Let's deal with it tomorrow when Mrs. Martinez comes. Tell me how your holiday was."

"Oh . . ." I have a flash of Isabel's suitcase, stashed behind a pile of dirty linens in the laundry room, and my eyes go automatically to the small picture of Malinche over the computer table. "It was fine. Quiet." I get to my feet. "I'll just go finish up in the kitchen."

"Wait." He stands up, too, suddenly closer now. I can smell his soap—a clean, glycerin smell—and my heart seems so loud to me—not a beat, but an embarrassingly noisy throbbing sound. "Avery . . ." The firelight flickers in his eyes. "I wanted to ask you . . ."

I'm absolutely certain that if I moved two inches closer I'd be in his arms. Not even two inches. All I'd have to do is lean toward him, and it would happen. Part of me wants that. Craves the comfort of it, the resolution of this tension between us. There's a kind of inevitability, like the end of a story or the last line of a song.

But there's another part of me. Something that pulls back, gazing into the distance at a greenish-black line of advancing storm clouds.

For a minute I hover, caught between push and pull. The piñon wood pops in the fire, and the room seems to expand and contract with my breath.

When the phone shrills, I jump.

It rings again, more insistently. Paul waits, frowns, then turns and picks it up.

"Yes, fine, thanks. And you?"

It's the woman who answered the phone in his room Saturday night. I wonder fleetingly if I know because I have "the gift," or if it's just what Rita always called women's intuition. Not that it matters. I pick up the wineglasses and carry them out to the sink.

As I'm washing them, he comes into the kitchen. I turn around. He's looking in my direction, but past me. Over my shoulder, out the kitchen window, into the night.

"What was it you wanted to ask me?"

His eyes rest on my face. "I—I was wondering what your thoughts were about Christmas Eve."

I turn back to the sink, twist the stopper, and watch the water spiral into the drain with a soft sucking noise.

"I think we should do . . . Noël. A French Christmas Eve."

"Really?" He sounds dubious. "But the Canyon Road walk is so traditionally Santa Fe, don't you think everyone will want something more New Mexican? Or Mexican?"

"Not necessarily." I smile stiffly at him over my shoulder. "I think that's what they'll expect. Personally I'm not into giving people what they expect."

It's amazing how much efficiency you can buy if you have enough money. Within a week, the guesthouse is repaired and cleaned and I can move back in. But there's a lingering dampness in the walls and floors that seeps into my bones at night, chilling me so that I wake up cold and stiff in the mornings. The place just doesn't feel the same as it did before.

I drag Isabel's suitcase over there one morning when Paul's at Pinnacle Gallery and push it under the bed, out of sight behind the dust ruffle. I don't want him to see it, but I also don't want to think about why.

I find myself spending more time in the kitchen of the main house, only going back to the guesthouse at night after I finish cleaning up. I'm hardly there at all during the day except to use the telephone.

On the first Friday in December, I finally connect with Nancy Wethersby at Katalysis. When I give her my name, it obviously rings no bells.

"I talked to someone there while you were in Honduras and they said I should contact you—"

"Is this regarding the funding for the knitters in El Salvador?"

"No. Actually it's regarding my mother. Isabel Colinas."

"Ohmigod. Avery James, yes. I'm so sorry. Alice told me you'd be calling. Please excuse me for being so distracted. I'm doing my end of fiscal year reports and I don't know where my head is." She laughs. "I'm really pleased that you called, but Alice didn't say exactly what you wanted . . ."

I sit down on the edge of my bed. "This is probably going to sound a little strange, but I'm trying to find out about my mother."

"To find out . . . what about her?"

"Anything you'd like to tell me. I never knew her."

"Oh. Well . . ."

"She had me when she was very young. Just out of high school. She gave me up for adoption." It sounds so ordinary, so usual, I hardly recognize my own voice, talking about the defining fact of my life. "I just recently found out who she was, and someone in a Santa Fe gallery gave me your brochure."

By this time, Nancy Wethersby has recovered herself. "It makes me very sad that you never knew her. She was a wonderful woman. We worked together on the Katalysis board for several years. She was a very warm, generous person. Very open and giving. She was also, as I'm sure you know if you're in Santa Fe now, an incredibly talented artist."

"Yes, I knew she was an artist. And I've seen pictures of her . . . I was just wondering . . . you know—I realize you might not have known her that well, but . . ."

"I still miss her. We made several trips together—Guatemala, Honduras." Her voice gets slower, loses that "strictly business" edge. "Those were very special times for all of us. All our clients—do you know about what we do?"

"Yes, I read the brochure."

"All the small-business people we worked with, they loved Isabel. She was so beautiful and of course she spoke Spanish fluently. Whenever we couldn't find her, we knew she'd be in somebody's kitchen. Down on the floor playing with their kids. The children were crazy about her—" She stops abruptly. "Have you seen much of her work?"

"Most of it, probably."

"I'll have to see if I can find some of the back issues of our newsletter to send you. There were undoubtedly pictures of her and articles about her work on the board."

"That would be nice, if it's not too much trouble."

"It's no trouble. It may take a few weeks though."

"Did she—I mean, did you guys ever talk about personal things? Do you think she was happy?"

There's a hesitation.

"Well, she mentioned the man she was in love with. I think she was happy with him—I mean, you know—as happy as any relationship is."

"Look, Ms. Wethersby. I know you probably feel like this is an invasion of privacy or something."

"No, I don't," she jumps in. "Not at all, it's just that I don't know you. You say she was your mother, but I feel strange talking about her like this after all these years."

"Believe me, I can relate to that. Well, thanks. And if you could send the newsletters to 505 San Tomás. Santa Fe 87505. I'd appreciate—"

"Avery, wait. I'm sorry. I don't mean to sound paranoid, but you just don't know these days . . ." Her voice trails off. "I didn't know Isabel that well, but there's a certain closeness that develops when you travel with someone, and also the kind of work we do. It can be a very emotional thing for some people. It was for her. I guess I could be totally off base, but I sensed a sadness in her. Like an emptiness in her life. Obviously I had no idea that she'd had a child, but, now it all sort of makes sense . . ." She sighs. "I'm sorry. I hope I've helped somewhat."

"Yes. Thanks very much for your time."

I lay back across the bed. Oh, shit, Isabel. You were just so warm and generous and giving, weren't you? Just not to me.

You had this great sadness in your life, right? You remembered me on December 21, didn't you? Of course, I was wondering about you every day. Who you were and where you were and why you didn't come get me.

In all the fantasies I had about finding you, it never occurred to me that you might be dead. It's not fair. I wanted you to explain it to me, how it happened. So I'd understand how you got to be Isabel Colinas the famous artist, and I got to be Avery James, named for a necklace.

I think I would have enjoyed seeing you cry.

I stuff the Katalysis brochure into the folder and sling it onto the floor in the corner by the fireplace. I consider burning it, but somehow I'm not quite there yet.

The sun pours into the little apartment in back of The Good Earth, making the dust in the air glimmer like gold dust. It haloes around me as I stand in front of the full-length mirror, staring at myself in Isabel's red dress. Cookie kneels on the floor beside me, pins bristling from her mouth like fangs.

I can't believe what she's done with the dress. Unable to mend the right sleeve to her own satisfaction, she's simply eliminated it. The neckline now begins under my right arm and sweeps gracefully up the diagonal and over my left shoulder, setting off the embroidery on the left sleeve to perfection. It's as if the dress should have been cut that way to begin with. She's taken in the darts so it barely skims my waist, molds to my hip.

She sticks a few pins into the dress at various lengths, squinting at me from different angles and spits the rest of the pins into a small cardboard box.

"So what else was in the suitcase? Besides the dress."

"Lots of clothes," I say, avoiding her glance in the mirror. "Stuff for at least a week or two. Plus a green plastic box full of her work. Different kinds of material, thread, trim—all sorts of buttons and beads and doodads. Plus a couple of design sketches."

"So Isabel was planning a getaway, hm? I wonder where."

I shrug, and she admonishes me to hold still.

"Probably just down to her hideout in Bluebird Canyon. She was obviously planning to get some work done."

"I think this will do." She finishes the pinning, and I step reluctantly out of the dress, back into my real-life jeans.

"Do you have time for a cup of tea?" Before I finish buttoning my flannel shirt, the kettle's on the stove, and she's hunting for clean cups and spoons, milk and sugar cubes.

"Where will you wear the dress?" she asks, her head out of sight inside the pantry. She emerges with the faded and chipped ironstone teapot.

"Paul's having a dinner party on Christmas Eve after Canyon Road."

"And he's invited the hired help?"

By now, I'm used to her odd sense of humor. "Not exactly. I'm cooking, but there's no rule that says the chef can't look good."

She wags her finger at me. "Now don't be slopping food on that dress. It's much too lovely to be all grease spotted."

"I won't even put it on till most of the work's done."

The kettle interrupts us with a shriek, and she pours boiling water over the loose tea in the pot while I stack shortbread wedges on a rose-colored plate. We carry everything into the shop, to the chairs by the window.

"I do love shortbread. One of the best things about being an Anglo." She nibbles delicately on the point of a wedge. "So what else is happening at the home of the revolving fiancé?"

"Have you considered stand-up comedy?"

"Is that your avoidance method of choice, answer a question with another question?"

"Sometimes."

"Have you decided yet?" She sits back in the chair.

I inhale the steam coming off the surface of my tea. "Decided what?"

"About that tea. Your voodoo tea."

"God, you're pushy. I thought you island people were supposed to be so laid back."

"We be talkin' business now, Ladyfriend," she says affecting her Jamaican accent, and when I smile, she turns serious. "You need a plan to get where you're going."

"Is that a general you or a specific?"

"Both. You've got lots of talent and brains, and I think you're spinning your wheels over there on the east side."

"I'm learning things."

"Like what?"

"Things about Isabel. I know this sounds weird, but sometimes I'm jealous of Paul because he's forgotten more about her than I'll ever know."

"I understand the feeling of wanting to know about her—"

"Cookie, that's what everyone says to me. That they understand. But trust me, you don't. Nobody who's had a family can understand what it's like to not have one."

"You have a family." She sounds nearly indignant. "Your great-grandmother Dona Maria Ebell was a shaman. Your grandmother Josephita Colinas was a *curandera*. Your mother, Isabel, was an artist. My God, girl, think of the powerful blood you've got in those veins."

I set down my tea. "But I didn't know them. They didn't know me."

"They're still your family. And I believe you can know them to some degree by listening to yourself, your own heart. They're all in there. Waiting to tell you what you need to know. All you have to do is listen."

twenty-five

On the morning of December 21 when I open the door to the kitchen, I smell coffee already brewing. Paul is sitting on one of the tall stools, looking pleased with himself. On the granite counter is a muffin with a candle in it. He flicks the fire starter in his hand, and a flame bigger than the candle nearly engulfs the whole thing.

"Oops." He adjusts the fuel and tries again. The candle sputters and catches, burning cheerfully. "Happy Birthday," he says. "I'd sing, but it isn't really my forte."

"Paul . . ." I swallow. "That's so—How did you know?"

He looks at his watch——the commando one that shows you the date and time in four time zones, temperature, barometric pressure, and probably a recipe for biscuits if you need one.

"December 21. It's the winter solstice, *n'est-ce pas?*" His face softens. "Isabel told me once that her daughter was born on the solstice."

I dive into the refrigerator, rummage in the bin for oranges.

"This is for you," he says, forcing me to turn and look at him. He's holding out a small package wrapped in silver paper and tied with a green ribbon. "It won't bite you, so take it. And it wasn't expensive. And you don't have to open it now. There, I think that covers everything."

My face burns. "Thanks. But I wish you hadn't."

"Well, I did." He smiles. "And this came for you in yesterday's mail at Pinnacle, which I just got around to looking at this morning."

The large square envelope is green with holiday designs covering every available inch of surface, so I know before even looking at the Albuquerque return address that it's from Rita.

"I have to run up to Taos this morning, but I'll be back by noon," Paul says, sliding off the stool.

"Don't you want breakfast?"

"No, I had some coffee. Take the day off, and I'll see you later. Oh, you'd better blow that candle out."

Wax is melting all over my muffin, so I puff the candle out.

"Did you make a wish?"

"I don't like to tempt fate."

He shakes his head at me.

After he leaves, I sit on the stool with my cup of coffee and the part of the muffin that doesn't have wax on it and the green envelope and the package.

The card says "For Your Christmas Birthday, Across the Miles." It's signed "Love ya, Rita and Rick." A piece of paper folded into quarters falls out of the envelope; I open it and read.

Dear Ave,

Where the hell are you????? I sent this card to Columbia St. and it came back stamped no forwarding address. I tried to call and the recording said the phone number was disconnected. Then I tried Dos Hombres and Juana said you were gone and she didn't know where. Not that I blame you for that. I hope you told Mr. Dale Baby to stick it where the sun don't shine on your way out the door. Knowing you, you probably did.

Are you okay? This is my last try at this damn birthday card, then I'm going to call DeGraf, and if I don't get any info from him, I'm going to come up there and kick ass and take some names till somebody tells me where you went. What is going on?

I would've tried to get in touch sooner, but right after we got here, my daddy died, and I went home for that. Rick went too. You should've seen the looks on Rhonda and Ricki's faces when they saw him. If I hadn't been so sad about my Daddy I would of laughed myself sick. Of course Momma Jen was so upset, she barely noticed he was there. Rick was really sweet and ignored all the Remember the Alamo types that came for the party.

My other BIG NEWS is that we got married!!!!! November 10. Can you believe it? I wanted you to come and stand up for me, but I couldn't find you, and besides we decided against a big wedding because of it being so close to Daddy's funeral. And Rick couldn't take any time off for a honeymoon anyway. Not to mention it would've been expensive.

I've got a job as a receptionist at this really beautiful big law office downtown, although I have to say, it's pretty boring compared to Santa Fe. But I hear lots of interesting gossip that I can tell Rick. Make myself useful—ha! He really likes his job. He says, hi, by the way.

Ave, I can't believe I'm so goddamn happy! I just wish I could see you. I miss you more than you probably think. I hope you get this card. Rick and I both really want you to come for a visit. PLEASE let me know where you are and that you're okay. I worry about you more than you probably think. Write me or call me. Our phone number is 505-866-0271.

Lots of love,
Rita and Rick

The card—Rita and Rick. The letter—Rita and Rick. It could almost be one word—RitaandRick. Like some two-headed creature—ugly but benevolent—from a fairy tale. But for some reason, I find myself smiling.

Now I turn my attention to the package, untie the ribbon, and unfold the paper. Turn back the tissue paper that surrounds it. It's a ceramic tile plaque like you'd put outside with your name or street number on it. Or the name of your estate, if you belong to that segment of society where your house has its own name.

The plaque is oval shaped with a crackled ivory glaze and a border of red poppies. Only one word is spelled out in black script—*Querencia*. Underneath it, a blue columbine.

. . .

In Santa Fe, everyone wants and expects snow for Christmas. It happens often enough that a lot of people consider it their birthright. So far this year, what we've got is mostly the same dry, bitter cold that we had all through November. But Christmas Eve morning there are promising clouds in the west. They grow darker and bulkier as they close in on the city.

Then at about two thirty in the afternoon, when I look up from the bowl of chocolate ganache I'm making for the *Bûches de Noël*, I see that the sky has pulled in around the house like a billowing gray comforter. Lacy pinpoints of white drift down and then, caught by the wind, swirl against the windows and walls where they melt.

I go over my checklist for the gazillionth time. The fish guy at Whole Foods obligingly sliced the salmon for me into thin scallops, so all I have to do is arrange it on the plates with the mustard sauce and mushrooms. Oysters have been opened and sit in a pan with their liquid. The plates for the oysters are prepared with beds of cedar instead of seaweed, which I couldn't find anywhere.

The two saddles of venison sit in the refrigerator, the *duxelles* is made. I'm using store-bought puff pastry. I guess that's cheating, but I couldn't see myself in the middle of everything else, making puff pastry, giving it six turns or however many you have to do. The Yule logs are made, filled, and waiting to be frosted. Then all that has to be done is place a few meringue mushrooms artfully around them and dust with powdered sugar.

The lettuces are washed, the vinaigrette made, the coffee ground. The Champagne is chilling outside, the Margaux is in the laundry room.

By the time I finish making the saffron cream sauce, and the pan is sitting in the sink full of lukewarm soapsuds, I'm exhausted and starving all at once. I realize that I've been on my feet since seven this morning and that breakfast was my last meal.

In a corner of the refrigerator where things have been relegated that I don't need for tonight, there's a small piece of leftover baked chicken and one stalk of broccoli still clinging to life. I wolf it down cold, standing at the sink in a daze. I don't know how long I've stood there holding the empty plate when I notice that it's snowing again.

The hand-lettered sign that says PLEASE REMOVE YOUR SHOES is greeted with surprise and dismay, but the grumbling turns to little sighs of contentment as people ease their cold feet into the drier-warmed booties that Juana and Patrice offer them, along with whispered admonitions that Father Noël will leave treats in their shoes if they behave themselves.

Juana's boyfriend, Jesús, has gotten a haircut, and he makes a pretty slick bartender—as long as he doesn't talk to anyone with his lowrider Spanglish vocabulary of colorful obscenities. He's serving mulled wine and hot cider spiked with Calvados at the bar by the fireplace in the living room. Once most of the guests have arrived, Juana leaves Patrice to take the coats, and she carries trays of small cheese pastry cutouts to be nibbled with the drinks.

It seems like everything's under control, so I dash off to the guesthouse to change clothes. As I pull it over my head, I wonder again at the power this dress has over me. When I wear it, I'm beautiful. I can do anything. Nothing can touch me. I brush my hair and pull it back at the sides, catching it with the silver clips I borrowed from Juana. I give my makeup a quick once-over, pull on my new, black deerskin boots, and float through the garden, barely touching the gravel path, to the kitchen.

The first person I see is Juana, loading up another tray of pastries; Jesús is behind her, nibbling her neck.

"Hey, none of that," I warn, only half joking.

They both snap to attention, then Juana's eyes get round.

"Ay, chica!" she breathes. "Bitchen dress!"

"*Hola, Mamacita!*" Jesús grins, shakes his hand like he just dropped a hot potato. "*Muy prendido!*"

Juana smacks the back of his head with her towel.

"Back to work, *baboso.*" She laughs as he disappears into the hall.

"How are we doing?"

"We're just cruising now. Patrice is finished with the goody bags. Shall I tell her to put them in the shoes?"

My nose wrinkles. "I think we should wait till they're having coffee. Probably the less time the stuff spends in some of those shoes, the better."

"Gotcha."

"Avery, have you got the—" Lindsey is halfway through the door and the look on her face is impossible to describe. For a few seconds she can't seem to get her breath. Then she sputters, "Holy shit! Where did you get that dress?"

"I found it in—"

"Oh, dear God, Avery." She looks at me like I'm some kind of gargoyle. "Didn't you have anything else to wear?"

"Sure," I snap. "I have a vast wardrobe of party frocks sitting in my closet. This was just the one closest to the door."

"I'm sorry." She comes over to put her hands on my shoulders. "I didn't mean it. You know me, born with a silver foot in my mouth."

"What's wrong with this dress?" I feel my face becoming the same shade as the material.

"Nothing," she says softly. "It's beautiful. And you're beautiful in it. It's Isabel's, isn't it?"

"No, it's mine."

"Has Paul seen it?"

"No."

"Does he know you have it?"

"Probably not."

She gives about half a shrug. It's a gesture of helplessness. "I hope you won't feel badly if he—"

"Lindsey, Paul DeGraf is a grown man and he speaks English fluently. If he's got a problem with me or my clothes, I'm sure he'll let me know."

She turns away from me. "I'll just go check on everything in the dining room."

Juana bites her thumb at Lindsey's back. "Such a bad case of *envidia* I never saw."

You want to take in one of these things?" Patrice asks me.

"Hey, they ain't 'things,' dummy." Juana winks broadly at me. "They're bushes."

I roll my eyes. "They're not bushes. They're *bûches*. *Bûches de Noël*. Yule logs to you crackers. And no, you guys take them in, light the sparklers, and let everybody get impressed before you start cutting."

"I don't get it," Juana says. "Why you want to get all dressed up and not leave the kitchen once. You look beautiful."

I hold the door open for them and smile at the low rumble of approval that greets the sight of my gorgeous bushes. In a few minutes, Patrice comes back.

"Your presence is requested. Mr. DeGraf asked me to send you out." She pokes me in the arm. "He's pretty cute for an old guy. Rich, too. You better be nice to him, or I might slip him my phone number."

"Knock yourself out, girlfriend. I just work here."

She looks at the ceiling. "Right. And I'm Mrs. Claus."

Juana pushes open the door, hissing, "Avery, get your ass out here. I can't cut the dessert till you come. Patrice, bring me the hot towel and the server."

Suddenly I'm reluctant. Lindsey was right. I should have worn something else. I blot my face with a napkin, lift my hair up, feeling the dampness on the back of my neck.

"You look like a million bucks," Patrice says, "Now move your butt."

The light in the dining room is dim after the brightness of the kitchen.

"Here she is," Paul says, beaming. "Come in, Avery. I think you know some of these gourmands. This is Avery James, culinary wizard and daughter of—"

Now I'm far enough into the room. The dress seems to draw the light from the flickering candles, the dancing sparklers, and burn with its own inner fire. His face freezes. But only for a second. "Daughter of the late Isabel Colinas, as I think you can all see," he finishes smoothly.

Everyone is clapping and smiling at me. Someone says something about New Year's Eve, and another disembodied voice asks if I have a business card. Every face is turned toward me except one. Lindsey is watching Paul, her heart in her eyes.

Why did I never see it before? She's in love with him. Always has been. Since before Tom. Since Paris. Now she's just hanging around, being The Friend, playing part-time hostess, sending him business, listening to his ramblings. Trying to outlast his memory, waiting for him to regain consciousness.

"Thank you." Suddenly the room is quiet. "I'm glad you enjoyed dinner. I think you'll love dessert. And since you've all been such good boys and girls, Père Noël has left you all a little something in your shoes to take home for sweet dreams. Merry Christmas."

When I walk back to the kitchen, I feel Paul's eyes on me all the way down the hall.

After dessert and coffee, the party adjourns to the living room for brandy. Juana, Patrice, and I clear the dining room, extinguish all the candles, load the dishwasher, handwash and dry the crystal and silver. I hand out the checks.

Patrice kisses hers. "Hey, I'm going to quit the Hombres and come to work for you."

"I don't think you can live on one party a year."

"No, but there's going to be more." She gives me a knowing look. "You really wowed 'em, Avery. They'll be knocking on your door now. You should start your own company."

"Wouldn't the old hombres just eat their tails?" Juana giggles. "Ooh, ooh! I've got the perfect name for you, too. Listen to this— Nacho Mama's Cookin'. Get it? Not Yo—"

Patrice screams with laughter. "I love it! I want to work for Nacho Mama!"

"This town doesn't need one more caterer."

"But honey, you'd blow 'em all out of the water," Patrice says, wiping her eyes with the dish towel.

"Look at you," Juana scolds. "You musta been raised in a barn. Now you got your stupid mascara all over the nice white towel."

If I laugh, it will only encourage them. "Will you two take your money and get the hell out of here?"

"What about the pots and pans?" Juana says.

"I'm letting them soak over night," I tell her. "They're too gunked up to wash now."

"Okay, *chica*. You don't have to tell me twice." She's out the kitchen door, hollering for Jesús, with Patrice trailing in her wake.

" 'Night, Nacho Mama."

It's almost two A.M.

The backs of my legs feel like I've been whipped with a rubber hose, and I dig my knuckles into that muscle just below my right shoulder blade that's been in spasm for the last hour. I turn off the overhead lights, leaving only the under-cabinet lamps on.

I pour myself a glass of Champagne from the open bottle in the big

Sub-Zero, and sink into a chair, extending my legs in front of me and letting out an involuntary groan. Twenty-five—no, twenty-six—years old and I sound like Cassie. I take a sip of the Pol Roger and hold it in my mouth. God, I love this stuff.

I think this is where I'm supposed to feel like I've finally arrived. If only—fill in the blank—could see me now. If only who? Rita? Yeah, she'd probably think it was pretty exciting. Cassie? I doubt she'd be impressed.

Then there's all those morons in Florales. Like Kevin—who thinks Champagne is something you pour over your head after you win the football game. *Oh, you can drink it?* Randi and Stacey would probably be jealous—except they'd rather be eating the dinner than cooking it. Will Cameron—don't go down that road.

I prefer to think of Andy Ross, chasing me around the Plaza, not to tell me I broke his door, but begging me to come cook for him.

And what about Isabel?

"Avery? What are you doing sitting here in the dark?" Paul's voice snaps the spell. "Sorry. I didn't mean to startle you."

"Is everyone gone?" I ask.

"Yes. Stuffed and happy." He nods at my glass. "Shall we finish off that Champagne, or are you too tired?"

"You're not going to give me any more presents, are you?"

He laughs. "No, I promise. There's something I wanted to talk to you about."

I smile. "Like New Year's Eve?"

He doesn't answer.

I follow him into the living room, where the fire has died down to glowing logs that radiate a delicious, enveloping warmth. The fragrance of the Christmas fir is laced with piñon smoke. He refills our glasses. I take a meringue from the little plate on the coffee table and nibble at it. The sweet crunch vanishes into nothing.

"Dinner was wonderful. I think if you want a career as a caterer in this town, you could easily build on tonight . . . if that's what you want."

I relax onto the sofa, ease off my boots, and pull my feet up, tucking the skirt over them. "How are you supposed to know what you want?" I say lightly.

He pulls open the fire screen, lights a piece of fatwood, thrusts it among the smoldering logs. In seconds the whole thing bursts into flame and he stands there watching it.

"Maybe it's more a matter of knowing what you don't want."

His eyes drift restlessly from the fire to the tree, to the three miniature landscapes in their gilt frames beside the door. Finally to me. "That dress. It's beautiful on you. I love the one-shoulder effect."

"Cookie," I say quickly. "It was her idea."

It's so quiet I imagine I can hear the bubbles rising in my glass.

Suddenly the room is close and stifling, the dress feels too tight. He sits down beside me. Close enough that I feel the slight breeze on my shoulder when he leans back.

It's not like he's never touched me before. I distinctly recall his hand at my elbow, or resting in the small of my back as we stepped off a curb. We shook hands once. I remember him kissing my forehead, his lips smooth and dry.

And sometimes in the kitchen, I can feel him watching me. The way his eyes follow my hands when I work, as if he's wondering how my fingertips might feel on his skin. The way he looks up and smiles when I bring his breakfast into the office. It's not my imagination that his hand occasionally brushes my arm for no reason. No reason except that he wants to touch me.

But tonight is something else; there's so much electricity between us the air is almost crackling.

Surely to God he knows. It's all right here. In my eyes, in the way my body leans toward him. I feel transparent as water. He could see my thoughts like stones on the bottom of a clear pool. I have a nearly unbearable urge to close my eyes and trace his profile with my fingers, from his hairline down his forehead, the long straight nose, his mouth and chin. I want to rub my thumb across his lower lip, follow it with my tongue. I want him to hold me.

Just now I have the oddest sensation of sailing—or at least the way I've always imagined sailing must feel—like being pushed by the wind. I'm not sure, but maybe my hand is already moving toward him when he says,

"I'm thinking of going away for a while."

Everything stops. The room stills—the fire, our breath. My eyes lock on his face. All I can say is, "Where?" As if that mattered.

He stretches his feet out, resting them carefully on the coffee table. His black loafers look soft, like the leather was buffed to a muted glow by some butler, but I'm sure he did it himself. He puts his hands up behind his head, not looking at me.

"Maybe Mexico for a while. Then I thought perhaps New Zealand. I have a friend in Auckland who collects Maori art. It's quite interesting. It would make a nice change for me—"

I can't listen; I can hardly breathe. I mean to ask when, but somehow it comes out of my mouth as, "Why?" And I'm mortified by the bleating sound of it.

He keeps looking at the fire. "You're welcome to stay on in the guesthouse, of course. In fact, I'd like it if you would. I always feel better knowing someone's around when I'm gone for extended—"

"Someone?" My face burns like the fire. I don't recall getting to my feet, but that's where I am. "That's how you think of me? Someone to stay in your guesthouse while you're gone?"

When I reach down for my boots, he puts his hand on my arm. I jerk away, but I have to go around the coffee table to get out of the room, and by the time I do, he's in front of me.

"Avery, I'm sorry. Let me—"

"Get away from me." I push past him, heading down the hall toward the kitchen.

"Please let me explain." He's right behind me, moving practically in my footsteps.

"It's not necessary," I hiss through clenched teeth. When he touches my shoulder, I start to run. "Leave me alone."

His legs are longer, and he's keeping up without any trouble. "Please don't do this. Just let me—"

"I don't care," I shout at him. By now I'm in the kitchen. I circle the work island, grab the back door knob and jerk it open. I scoot through just as he lunges for me, stepping on the little rug in front of the sink. It slips on the tile and I hear a grunt and a slapping sound as he goes down hard, but that's not what stops me.

What freezes me, one foot on the back step, one in the cold gravel—stuns me into silence and makes every hair on my scalp rise—is the way he shouts,

"Isabel!"

Desperation rasps in his throat, and the sound of it hangs in the air like a physical presence.

I've lost the sense of minutes passing, but eventually, I move back into the kitchen, shut the door behind me. He's lying on the floor, motionless, white as paste under the ski tan. For a second I panic, thinking he's hit his head, but his eyes open and he looks up at me, not moving, his cheek pressed to the Saltillo tiles.

I kneel down next to him. "Are you all right?" My voice is unsteady.

He exhales and it's a weary, defeated sound. "Yes," he says.

I help him to his feet. We check out his arms and hands, shoulders, hips, knees. He takes a few steps, wincing a little.

"You might have sprained that ankle. I'll make you a herbal wrap tomorrow."

He smiles, still a bit shaky. "Is there no end to your talents?"

I smile back. "Actually, no."

"Avery . . ." His voice cracks. "I'm so sorry. I've made such a—"

I touch my index finger to his mouth. "We'll talk tomorrow. It's late. I'll lock up. Do you need help up the stairs?"

"No. I'm fine." He pushes the hair off his forehead. "I'm going to watch the fire burn down first, but you go ahead. It's been a long day. You must be exhausted." He leans toward me, brushing my forehead with a kiss that I barely feel.

"Sleep well, Avery."

Outside the frosty air knifes into my lungs. The garden is silent and dark, a patchwork of shadows. The insulating cover floats on the surface of the pool. The white coping and a few escaping wisps of steam make it look like some bubbling black tar pit is hidden underneath.

I can see my breath in the guesthouse. When I jerk the dress off over my head, I hear the scrape of a seam ripping. I roll it up and throw it on the floor, crawl under the down comforter, swimming over the surface of the sheet to warm it up. I reach for the lamp switch and fall back into the dark.

I want to sleep. Preferably for the next two days, but I dread waking up. That's when reality comes for you and you're too groggy to outrun it.

The illuminated numbers on the clock say 3:02 A.M. Through the partially open curtain I can see the neat row of *electrolitos*, still glowing, still marching uniformly across the top of the roof above the kitchen.

What the hell am I doing here? When did I stop resenting Isabel and start trying to be her?

With a sudden wrench, I recall a different Christmas. The *posada*. Cassie and Amalia—the long, cold walk in the darkness, the music of guitars and voices, candles dripping wax in the church windows, the simple feast in the community center. And the first time Will Cameron kissed me.

With the sound of his name in my head, memories are breaking over me like waves. The smell of Mami's coffee and grease from the griddle, the feel of the plastic booth on the backs of my legs, the pink valentine I flushed down the toilet, the scent of big sage and his jacket, the feel of his skin against mine, the sun on my back, the calls of swifts echoing down the canyon. I clamp my eyes shut against them.

You didn't trust me, he said. You still don't.

One blue plate special order of truth, hold the excuses.

He gave me plenty of chances, plenty of reasons to believe in him. And I didn't even try. All I knew how to do was run away. First to Albuquerque, now to the nether world presided over by Paul DeGraf. A shade, that's what Paul reminds me of—one of those beings that isn't exactly alive, but not quite dead—just existing on some weird plane with his art and his guilt and his memories.

It strikes me now with bone-jarring force that the reason I'm here is because I'm comfortable with that. I'm like him. Not dead, but never fully alive, always letting people get just so close and no closer. From that certain distance I probably looked like a real live person. To Will.

And to Rita. With her Hallmark sentiments and her goofy Christmas presents. How I depended on her and resented her for it. The way I let her do all the hard work of our friendship and then mocked her for doing it.

Even Cassie. Jimmie John. *Lee-Ann.*

I was always the one who pulled back first. Always stopping the music so I didn't have to hear the end of the song.

Landscape shifts around me. Santa Fe. Albuquerque. Florales. Carson. Each year dissolving into the one before, nesting inside one another like those wooden dolls. I hug myself, shivering, feeling suddenly sick. I fling off the covers, run for the bathroom, squat down in front of the toilet, tucking my hair out of the way.

A spasm that seems to start in my toes shakes me, but instead of throwing up, I'm crying—huge, heaving sobs, bone dry at first. I grab a towel and hold it over my mouth to muffle the noise because the echoes bouncing off the tile are frightening. Then come the tears, flooding out of some bottomless reservoir.

I just kneel there and empty myself.

twenty-six

When I finally fall asleep, I go way under. No dreams. Not any that I remember, anyway. I wake up in broad daylight with a pounding headache. It's after nine o'clock. I pull on my gray sweatpants and a long-sleeved T-shirt, throw my jeans jacket on, and walk up to the house.

It smells stale—like old ashes and empty wine bottles, dirty pots and pans soaking in cold, greasy water. My stomach lurches.

Paul is curled up on the couch, asleep, without any blanket or pillow, and the house is freezing. The lights on the Christmas tree are still twinkling with determined cheer. When I bend down to switch them off, he stirs, then sits up abruptly, like he's wide awake. We look at each other.

Somehow, "Good morning" doesn't seem appropriate. "Merry Christmas" doesn't sound right either. So I just say, "I'll make some coffee."

"Thank you."

While I scrape the slimy remains of dinner out of the pans, then wash, dry, and put them away, he goes upstairs to shower and change. By the time he limps into the kitchen, wearing jeans and a red sweater, the coffee is brewed and the milk is hot. I fill his cup.

"How's your ankle?"

He takes a sip of his café au lait. "Not so bad."

"You should RICE it today." When he looks puzzled, I add, "Rest, Ice, Compression, Elevation. I thought all you jocks knew that term."

He tries to smile. "Did you sleep well?"

"Amazingly well, all things considered. I'm not even going to ask you."

"I'm surprised I could sleep at all," he says.

I fix his usual breakfast—*tartine,* three-minute egg, orange juice—and pour myself a bowl of cereal. We sit on the stools, side by side, eating in silence. He watches me clean up, sipping moodily at his coffee.

"What would you like for dinner?" I'm hoping to nudge the day toward a semblance of normalcy.

"I don't know. I may go out."

I look for some expression, some emotion, but there's nothing. "Okay. Whatever." I dry my hands and take off the white apron, hang it on the hook by the pantry, and start for the back door.

"Avery."

I turn around.

"I'd like to talk to you. If you don't mind. There are some things I should—"

I follow him into the living room, where he goes through the motions of building a fire.

"I think I'm having déjà vu." My attempt at levity falls flat in the silence.

When he's satisfied with the fire, he dusts his hands off and comes over to sit next to me. He picks up his coffee cup.

"I've always wondered what happened to it. The dress."

"When I went to The Good Earth that Saturday after Thanksgiving, Cookie gave me a—some of Isabel's things."

"It's lovely on you," he says. "Quite lovely." But he's not looking at me, just staring into the fire. "You know what I thought, of course."

"About what?"

"About you." Now he turns his face just enough to see me. "It was idiotic. Thinking that you and I—that if I had another chance, I could make up for—"

A hard little knot is forming in my throat. "Paul—"

"It doesn't work that way, of course." The cup goes to his mouth, but he doesn't drink.

"She was moving out, wasn't she?"

He nods, turning back to the fire.

"Is that what you were arguing about that night?"

He moves to the edge of the couch, like he's going to get up, but instead, he rests his elbows on his knees and looks over at me. Firelight glints on the plain silver band on his left ring finger.

"When I was working at Christie's in Paris, we used Tom a lot to repair and restore paintings and artifacts that needed a little touch-up before they were sold. His work was quite remarkable. *Is* quite remarkable," he corrects himself.

"He could fix water damage or fading from too much light or heat. A rip in canvas or a gouge . . . whatever. He could not only repair things, but he could blend his work so seamlessly in with the original that even our appraisers could barely see it."

"Which is where you got the idea."

"What idea?"

I fold my arms. "The idea of having him copy things—"

He runs his index finger along the side of his neck just inside the collar of his shirt. "You know?"

"I've heard rumors. And when I was up at his studio I saw things that didn't look like his stuff. A *retablo*—"

"The whole thing started almost as a joke."

"A joke?"

"I had an Indian ceremonial mask that Tom admired. He asked me if I'd lend it to him. To use in a still life. When he brought it back to me, he brought me two. They were virtually identical. I was angry at first—not so much at him, but at myself, because I honestly couldn't tell which was mine. He gave me back the original, and I hung it in the hallway just by the front door.

"Then one day, I think it was when the new refrigerator came, they had to bring it in the front because it was too wide to go through the kitchen door. When they were bringing it in, they bumped the mask off the wall and it fell on the floor and knocked a chunk of paint off, and I saw that the wood underneath was brand-new. When I called Tom on it, he laughed and said he'd been wondering how long it would take me to figure it out. He brought me the real original and fixed the copy and I put it in the Buena Vista. Two weeks later a doctor from Boston bought it."

"Did he know it was a copy?"

"Not till I told him. But even after I told him, he wanted it anyway, because he said it was such an incredible copy, nobody would know the difference. And it was true. Unless they thought to cut into it. Which is, of course, about the last thing anyone does with a piece of art."

"What about the rest of it?"

"The rest of it simply happened. I don't recall exactly how it got started. An acquaintance of mine in Mexico City made certain works available to us—most of it was religious art, some of it from churches, shrines. Unusual things. Works that the general public in this country rarely sees. Tom made copies of them, and I sold them." His voice fades like he's turned the volume down. "It was unbelievably easy."

"But the *retablo* I saw was so obviously new. How did he make them look old?"

"It's not difficult. There are chemicals, heat. Rollers. Tools of the restorer's art." His tone is mocking.

"What about the originals?"

"I sent them back to my contact. He was supposed to repatriate them." He looks away. "Or perhaps that's what I wanted to think."

"Paul . . ."

He rushes on. "Remember, this was years ago. When Tom was unknown and I'd just opened Pinnacle. We were both strapped for cash. The money enabled Tom to paint. If you're not an artist, you can't know what it means. To be able to live while you do the work you want to do. Not to worry about how you're going to eat, to pay your bills. Eventually, his work gained acceptance and we began to be able to sell it for what it was worth. More than enough for both of us to make a good living."

I raise my eyebrows. "So, of course you stopped selling the fakes—"

"No. We didn't." He rubs his hands together in a pantomime of washing them. "But the people who bought them—in a way, they were stealing—or they thought they were. Not one person asked for documentation, no one questioned the provenance. They didn't want to know. They didn't care where the work came from, whether it was legal or not. All they cared about was getting what they wanted."

"So you're saying they deserved to be cheated."

A sharp gust of wind bangs a shutter against the wall outside. I tuck my hands under my arms.

"Are you cold?" He gets up as if he's going to stir the sputtering fire but he just stands there with his back to me.

"The day of the party, Isabel had gone off for the afternoon. She said she was going shopping. I . . . didn't believe her. I thought she was going to Tom's studio, and I was right. But it wasn't him she went to see. In fact she knew he wasn't there. She went to retrieve something— a nude study he'd done of her that she wanted back.

"Apparently when she was looking for it she discovered his other workroom. She saw the equipment he had and some of the copies and she realized what was going on. She was very much involved with charities in Central America. Of course, she was furious. After the party, after everyone else was gone, she said she wanted to talk to me. I should have known what was coming.

"As soon as we were alone, she started screaming at me for destroying peoples' churches when that was all they had, calling me every name she could think of in English and Spanish. It was—"

"How did she know you were involved?"

"I suppose it was obvious that Tom didn't have the contacts either to obtain the originals or to sell the copies. I tried to explain how things happened. I told her I was sending the works back as soon as Tom copied them, but she wouldn't listen. She told me she was moving out in the morning. And then she said she was going to sleep out in the guesthouse . . .

"Avery." He turns his back on the fire and looks directly into my eyes. "I've had nothing to do with . . . all of that. Ever since the day she died. The pieces that were in my possession, I repatriated. I personally did, so I know they went where they belonged.

"It's just so . . . very difficult sometimes. When I saw you last night in that dress. It was just one more reminder that she's gone. That I, for all intents and purposes, killed her."

"You did *not*." My own vehemence surprises me.

His shoulders lift, then slump. "My greed and stupidity did. It's the same thing."

"Paul." I pull my feet up and sit cross-legged on the couch. "You guys kept breaking up and getting back together—did it ever occur to you that maybe it wasn't going to work out? That maybe you two weren't meant—"

"Never. I loved her—even that sounds so insipid, compared to the reality of it. And I know she felt the same way. We were just very different temperamentally. That's why we argued."

"But she was leaving you," I point out. "Maybe she was tired of all the high drama."

He gives me an indulgent smile. "Back to Liza's. It was almost a game. She'd go over there for a few weeks and then I'd go over there and get her or she'd come back here . . . Once we ran into each other in a restaurant and got back together. We both knew we'd always be—" He shakes his head in exasperation.

"I know you don't understand. I know it defies logic." He looks at me, his dark eyes round with a certain innocence. "But I still love her. I always will."

Part of me wants to throw cold water in his face and shout *Guess what, you're a fool. She wasn't just going back to Liza's. She was running off to*

Spain either alone or with somebody else. You were out of the picture. I could march over to the guesthouse, drag out the suitcase, wave her passport and ticket under his nose.

So why don't I? Isn't the truth supposed to set you free? Wouldn't he then have to accept it and get on with his life?

Maybe. But she's been dead for eight years. For all that time he's been able to rationalize everything that happened between them. Who's to say he couldn't just incorporate this new bit of information into his personal version of reality.

And if he couldn't, then what? I don't think I want to watch some-one's world collapse under the weight of something I said. There's a huge difference between having love snatched away from you by fate or luck or even by your own stupidity, and having it turn its back and walk away from you.

I can't do it. And I suppose that in some bizarre twist of role rever-sal, I'm protecting Paul DeGraf. Saving him from being abandoned by Isabel.

He picks up his coffee cup. "I have a lot of paperwork to catch up on before year-end," he says. "I'll be in my office."

"What about Tom?"

He looks blank, as if he's forgotten what we were talking about.

"Is he still making copies?"

An ironic smile hovers around his mouth. "Of course. Only now he signs his own name, and they're worth nearly as much as the originals."

On New Year's Eve Day, I decide to take some things down to the cabin—all things that I can just lock in the storeroom. Isabel's green box, which now holds not just her work materials, but her pass-port and airline ticket. The *Querencia* plaque. Two new kerosene lamps that I bought at the hardware store. I looked at a battery-operated camping lantern, but its strange blue-tinged light and some sort of low-level hum that the salesman swore he couldn't hear put me off.

Besides, the kerosene lamps with their soft golden glow remind me of Cassie.

On my way out of town, I stop by The Good Earth. Cookie called last night while I was eating dinner and left a message on the answering machine that she had something for me. Probably the herbs for the tea that I finally agreed to make for her.

When I get there, three people are standing in line at the register, so I wander around, holding crystals up to the lights, thumbing through herb books and free broadsides on somatic body work and vision quest.

When the customers are gone, she comes over to hug me. I ask how her Christmas was.

"Oh, a bit lonely. An old friend from St. Kitts came in for a few days, so I wasn't allowed to wallow in self-pity for too long. What about yours? How was the dinner? Did everyone like the dress?"

"Great." I smile. "Five-star chef and belle of the ball—who could ask for anything more?"

"So what does the new year hold for you?"

"I guess I'll have to wait and see."

She folds her arms, looking annoyed. "You're being awfully vague this morning. Where are you off to?"

"Bluebird Canyon."

"Oh, the cabin. How's it coming?"

"It's almost finished. I'm taking a few things down there today."

"When are you going to take yourself down there?"

"I don't know." I put the book on wild herbs back in the rack. "Maybe I'm waiting for a sign."

"Well. In the meanwhile, I have your herbs. I'll give you some small plastic bags for the tea. And . . ."

She's rummaging around under the counter, pulling out a stack of bags, securing them with a rubber band, putting them in a brown shopping bag along with the large Ziploc bags of fenugreek and black cohosh, lemon balm, ginger, and anise.

"And," she continues, still looking for something on the bottom shelf, "I took the liberty of ordering these." She pulls out a stack of what looks like thick brown cards. She takes one off the top, squeezes it, and it pops open into a box. "For the tea. They're made from recycled paper."

She hands me one, and I look at it for several seconds before my brain registers the image on the packaging. It's brown flecked and organic looking, except on one flat side there's a picture—a circle of green vines with delicate tendrils and tiny white flowers. Inside is the head-and-shoulders profile of a woman. She's wearing a red dress. Long black hair falls down her back. Arching over the top of the circle is the word *Isabel's* and cupped under the circle is the word, *Daughter*.

When I look up, Cookie's watching me anxiously. "I do hope I haven't overstepped my bounds here."

"I don't know what to say."

"Do you like them? I really hope you do, because I had to order two hundred and fifty to get a decent—"

The laugh comes up from deep in my throat, forcing my head back and closing my eyes. "Two hundred and fifty? Oh my God, Cookie." I try to catch my breath. "They're beautiful. They're just beautiful. But two hundred and fifty?"

Her grin blossoms into a huge smile. "Actually, I ordered five hundred, but I thought I'd just say two hundred and fifty, in case you didn't like them."

After I wash the lamps and dry them, fill them, and trim the wicks, I put them in the storeroom with the extra kerosene and the green box and walk down to Isabel's grave. The canyon is winter quiet, but surprisingly warm. We still haven't had much snow and only an inch or so of rain.

I sit down and pull a few plugs of grass off the grave, toss them aside. The summer's wildflowers—golden yarrow and the Queen

Anne's lace—sway listlessly in the breeze, their dried flower heads stiffly upright but lifeless.

A sudden cold ache settles in my chest. I close my eyes and let the tears seep out. This has been happening more often lately and I've learned that I sort of have to go with it. If I let it out, it's over in a few minutes. If I fight it down, I'm depressed all day.

I could drive myself crazy in a hurry wondering who Isabel really was—the talented, intense, driven artist. Or selfish, beautiful seductress. Or generous, tireless philanthropist. Faithless lover. Devoted friend. Did she love Paul? Or was she, as Cate Mosley said, a user—taking advantage of him to further her career? Was the trip to Spain a last-ditch attempt to get free of his suffocating brand of devotion? Or was it just a fling she'd have and then get tired of and come back to the house on San Tomás?

Paul lived with her and he obviously doesn't know. So there's no guarantee that I could know her any better if she was still alive. And maybe not even if she'd raised me.

The only thing I can know for sure is, she was my mother. I'm Isabel's daughter. It'll have to do.

I get to my feet, dust off my jeans, and walk back to the cabin.

There are still things to be done if I'm going to live in this place full-time. Alonzo said he would come in early spring and burn off the grass and weeds surrounding the cabin. This not only makes room for my garden, but it also makes a close personal encounter with a rattlesnake less likely. He said he and Maria would come help me turn over the ground after the burn and prepare it for planting. He's already got another of his *primos* lined up to supply me with chicken shit.

It'll be interesting living without a refrigerator. Even Cassie had one. I don't have any desire for a generator—too smelly and noisy. I suppose I could get a propane tank, which is what most people do out here, but they're so damned ugly. Like some big tubular UFO plopped down in your yard. Then there's the water thing. The good news is I have a decent well. In the warmer months, I can get one of those solar showers rigged up outside, but how am I going to bathe in the winter? I might end up being like a couple of old ladies in Florales that I'd run into at Begay's grocery now and then. Nobody wanted to get downwind of them, and when you did talk to them, you had to breathe through your mouth.

I put my new padlock on the storage room, take a last look inside the cabin, lock it up, and head out for Santa Fe. As I drive past the Rio Bravo, it registers that the brown Chevy parked off to the side is Bettina's. I jerk the wheel to the left without signaling, earning myself a honk and a hand gesture from the guy behind me, and roll into the half-full parking lot.

The place is just getting cranked up for lunch, and Felicia waves at me. "She's in the kitchen."

Bettina's back is to the swinging door and she and Miguel seem to be having a family argument. I start back out, but she turns and sees me.

"*Chica!* How are you?" She hugs me, laughing.

"I'm fine. How are you? When did you get back? Are you staying? What's going on?"

Miguel gives us a disgusted look and turns away to the stove. She holds up her left hand in front of my face to show me the gold ring.

"I am a married woman now."

"Oh my God. Congratulations! Ed Farrell?"

She nods, and my eyes stray over to the stove where Miguel stands, his rigid back a perfect expression of disapproval. She follows my gaze and makes a face at him, then links her arm through mine, pulling me toward the back door. We go outside, past Raoul who's sitting on a beer keg, having a smoke, over to a small table and bench in a patch of weeds. She sits on the table, feet on the bench, wrapping her full skirts around her legs.

"Miguel, as you see, does not approve."

"He'll get over it. Eventually." I settle down next to her. "But tell me what happened."

She smiles contentedly. "I simply did what I should have done long ago. I refused to see him when he came. I sent Felicia out with a note. I said that I was getting too old to play his games. That I wanted love, not a roll in the hay whenever he happened to come down this road."

"So what did he do, fall down on his knees and beg you to marry him?"

"Not at once. He went away that night. Then about two weeks later, I was cleaning up the café after lunch, getting ready for dinner, and he just came walking in, looking pitiful. He said he had something he needed to ask me . . ." She blushes. "And then he did."

"Where is he now?"

"He got a new job. A real job as a foreman on a ranch near Cimarron."

I let this information percolate for a minute, then say, "So, are you going to stay there?"

She nods. "I just came back to get the rest of my things. I thought I had better before Miguel burned them."

"Why is he so upset?"

She shrugs. "One, because I married an Anglo. Two, because I married a cowboy. Three, because I married. And I will no longer be here to work at the café." Her eyes slide over to me. "You aren't by some chance looking for job, are you?"

I smile. "Well . . . a little money coming in would be nice. But I really want to cook, not just wait tables."

She gets up off the bench. "*Venga.* We'll talk to Miguel. We'll work it out."

twenty-seven

My eyes open wide in the dark, and I lie motionless except for my galloping heart, trying to remember where I am and what woke me. A dream? A noise? I turn over to see the digital clock. Five-twenty-one A.M. The contours of the room, the furniture slip into their familiar places. I'm in the guesthouse on San Tomás, but something is wrong. Sweat mats my hair to my forehead.

Oh God. I left the stove on. I sit bolt upright, throw back the comforter, grab my keys, and run down the hall, still trying to jam my feet into my sandals.

I let myself in the back door quietly. The kitchen is dark and silent. And cold. I check the six burners on the range top. I lay my hand on the doors of both ovens. Stone cold. I sniff the air for gas. I bend to touch the radiant heated tile floor. Barely warm.

I shiver in the frosty air, rub my arms. Everything seems fine. But it's not. I know with a certainty that tugs at me like a little kid pulling my sleeve. I tiptoe into the dining room, the living room. Nothing's out of place in Paul's office. Back to the kitchen, my unease growing steadily. I let myself out, lock the door behind me.

Starting back to the guesthouse, taking my first step in the gravel, it amplifies from discomfort to dread. A flicker of light. Of heat.

One more step and then I'm running. Into the guesthouse, jamming my legs into jeans, zipping up as I shove my bare feet into jogging shoes, lifting the flannel shirt from the doorknob, pulling it on as I'm grabbing my purse and my keys and running for the door and trying not to trip on my untied laces, out the door, out the gate, into my truck and three blocks down Canyon Road before I remember to turn on my lights.

When I get to the Highway 14 exit off Interstate 25, the sun is shouldering its way above the horizon and a warm wind is gusting across the road. I drive fast, as fast as my little truck can manage, praying I don't see any cops. I remember the old joke about getting pulled over by the cop who says, "Okay, where's the fire?" It doesn't seem funny at all, because I know where the fire is.

It's in Bluebird Canyon.

I drive without questioning how I know this or whether I'm too late or even if I get there early whether there's anything I can do. All I know is that everything I own, and everything that I am, is in that cabin. And I hear Amalia's voice as clearly as if she was sitting in the cab next to me.

You have the gift, niña. *And someday when you need—it will come to you.*

Cresting the hill just above the Rio Bravo, my eyes find a thin plume of dark smoke rising in the hills, close to the spot where I think the cabin should be, and my heart sinks, but I push my foot down harder.

Before I get much beyond the café, I have to slam on the brakes. A New Mexico Highway Patrol car is parked sideways across the road. A husky guy with silver glinting in his crewcut ambles up to my side of the cab. I half expect him to ask me if I know how fast I was going, but he just says, "Going to have to ask you to turn back, Miss. We got a little brushfire workin' up in the hills."

"Brushfire? In February?"

"I know," he says. "Crazy, ain't it? Just been so dang dry, and then that pipeline explosion this morning up near Perdido." He raises his eyebrows into the shade of his hat brim. "This wind ain't helpin' matters either."

"But I've got to get in there. My house—"

"Where d' you live?"

"Bluebird Canyon, it's just up the road about a mile."

He gives me a level look. "Yep, I know where it is. Bad area for fire."

"Please, I've got to—everything I own, money, everything—it's all—" I don't even care that a couple tears have spilled out, dribbling down my face. I'll plead. I'll cry. Whatever it takes.

"Wait here a second." He ambles back to the cruiser, like there was all the time in the world, leans in, and picks up his radio. I sit bunching my hands into fists, my right leg bouncing up and down like the needle on a sewing machine. Please. Please. I start coming up with desperate options, like flooring it past him—he can't very well leave his roadblock. Except I'm not sure there's enough room to blast around him. I could leave my truck and run. He looks a little overstuffed; I could probably outrun him, but then it's a mile to the turnoff and just under two more miles to—

He suddenly reappears at my window. "Fire's moving slow right now," he says. "They're landing some crews up there somewhere, but they have to follow the main fire, so you can't count on them to get to your place. I can let you go get your stuff—"

"Thank you. So much," I blurt. I want to kiss him.

"Just get in and get out," he says. "Wind could change any time. When you get there, wet a kerchief and tie it over your face. And keep your eyes and ears open. You see the fire, you hear the fire, you haul yourself outta that canyon. You understand?"

"What does fire sound like?"

"You'll know it if you hear it," he says. "I'm gonna move the cruiser. Remember, don't dawdle." He looks at me sternly. "Ten minutes."

He barely backs his car across the line when I whip by him.

The gate is open, so I drive right in, going way too fast. The truck bounces and bucks in the ruts till I think my teeth will shake loose. I slide to a halt about fifty yards from the base of the ridge, jump out, and start running. The smell of smoke is on the breeze, although I can't see anything. What I saw driving down must be farther away than I thought.

I'm here, it's going to be okay. I'll get everything and then I'm gone. I'm focused so intently on the cabin that I don't see anything else, and then my brain pulls back for a long shot and I stop. I stand in the road and stare. The land all around the cabin is level and charred. My brain stumbles. Am I too late? Did I miss something? How could the house be standing if the canyon burned?

When I notice how straight the blackened edges are, it dawns on me. Alonzo. He said he was going to clear the grass for my garden. The cabin is sitting in the middle of a little square placemat of charred ground. I jog the rest of the way to the *portal*, unlock the door and go in. The air is still.

I don't have a kerchief with me, so I pull a square of plain blue cotton out of Isabel's box, wet it at the kitchen pump, and tie it around my face, bandit style. I put the green box on the bed, then my cigar box of treasures. I take the *Querencia* plaque off the wall, lay it on the pile. A couple of books I'd brought down with me. Rita's Missing-you-on-St. Valentine's-Day card and latest letter.

It looks like those funeral pyres in India where all the dead person's belongings get burned up with them. It seems odd that in twenty-six years, this is the sum total of my accumulation. This and the cabin that's probably going up in smoke here shortly. I wish I could take the furniture. The rocking chair and the hat rack I could probably get down to the truck by myself, but not the bed or the chest or the table.

All I have to do is fold up the four corners of the bedspread, tie it in a knot, and I'm on my way. I guess the question is, on my way to what? Back to Santa Fe, living in Paul's guesthouse? Driving down to work at the Rio Bravo three days a week?

I sit down on the bed, knowing I should leave, but reluctant. This is mine. The first place I've been that didn't belong to someone else. Where

I haven't felt like I was just passing through, drifting on to the next stop. Maybe because it belonged to Isabel. Because she felt safe here. Or maybe not. Who the hell knows? It tears at my heart to walk away.

I get up with a long sigh, pull the bedspread up around my things and open the door. And nearly break my neck tripping over something sitting just outside on the *portal*. A compact brown-gray bundle that squeals as my jogging shoe catches his scrawny ribs. Coyote Dog.

"What the hell are you doing here? You want to be Rover on Rice?"

He doesn't answer, just looks at me accusingly.

"Well, I'm getting out of here before this canyon turns into a giant weenie roast." I give him a meaningful look. "And it's your weenie."

I step around him and head for the truck. Smoke's a lot more noticeable now. Tiny flakes drift down like snow, dancing on gusts of hot wind. Except it's ash. That stupid dog is going to be a crispy critter if I leave him here.

He's half coyote, they have survival instincts. They know what to do in case of fire. Like what? Break the glass, pull the alarm? No, they just run away. Except in a canyon fire, he could get confused about where to run. He could be trapped in here. I look back. He's sprawled out on the *portal* like a dogskin rug, chin on paws, watching me. Oh for Chrissakes.

I whistle. "Come on, let's go." I slap my thigh. He sits up tall, his ears twitching. But he stays on the porch.

"Come on, boy. Let's go!" I make little kissing noises. He raises his back end like he's going to come, then changes his mind and lies back down. Head back on his paws.

"You stupid twit. Stay here then. Be a chicken-fried dog. I don't care." I stomp toward the truck.

When I've gone about ten yards, I decide I'll give him one last chance to listen to reason. But when I turn back, what I see kills the words in my throat. Black smoke is rising over the top of the ridge, and through it I glimpse tongues of yellow flame like a crown, all along the ridgeline.

I begin to run. Back to the cabin.

The decision is made in a split second, faster than the human brain can process information. It's not a conscious choice of the mind, it's a gut reaction. Or maybe a resolution of the heart. However I view it, it's done.

As I'm reaching the door, two thoughts collide in my head. One—the roof is metal, and that's good. Two—I've got kerosene in the store-room, and that's not good.

I literally kick Coyote's butt in the door ahead of me, dump my stuff on the bed, race back out, hands shaking as I fumble with the padlock, grab the can of kerosene, take it back inside, and empty the reservoirs of the two lamps back into it. The dog is starting to whine.

"Shut up!" I tell him, and he does. I screw the top on the can, slip out the door, and run for the truck as fast as my legs will move.

I read in a history book once about the great prairie wildfires the pioneers sometimes faced, how they survived by starting small fires that would burn the area all around them, forming a safe zone, where there was no combustible fuel left. So that when the huge grassfire came sweeping at them, they would huddle in their burned-out patch while the fire parted around them like the Red Sea parting for Moses, simply for lack of fuel.

Remembering this cheers me. I want to believe that *Querencia* truly is a safe haven, although, as I race back to the cabin, I see plainly what a pitifully small burnout I'm sitting on.

By the time I reach the cabin, flaming embers are beginning to fall nearby, smoldering in clumps of drought-dead grass. I watch transfixed as one explodes in flame, as if a small bomb had dropped there. I run inside and slam the door behind me.

Dog is whimpering softly. "You had your chance. Now just lie down." Amazingly, he does. I hastily undo my bundle, throw the bed-spread in the sink, and start pumping water on it, sloshing it around, section by section till it's all wet. I pile all my treasures in the middle of the floor and lay the wet bedspread over them. I pull the two pillow-cases off my pillows and wet them in the sink.

When I open the door again, it's like I've stepped into a war zone. Yellow-orange fires bloom all around like weird blossoms and the wind is gusting, pushing flames out horizontally, jumping them from bush to cactus to patch of grass. An ember lands crackling on the wooden floor of the *portal*. It hisses when I slap it with the sopping pillowcase.

I don't know what to do next. I feel helpless and incredibly stupid. I'm going to die and they'll all say, "Why the hell didn't she just drive out?" A cloud of black smoke catches a downdraft, engulfing the whole *portal*. I try to take shallow breaths through my wet scarf, but I choke anyway, and my eyes burn and tear.

Through my slitted eyes, through the gray air, I see with a leaden sickness that Alonzo only burned off the area in front and on the sides. Behind the cabin is a narrow strip of ground dotted with dry weeds and grass. Wet pillowcases aren't going to be much help back there. I drape them over my shoulders and run around to the storeroom.

The furnacelike blast of air blowing off the ridge almost knocks me over. Up the slope not fifty yards from me bright orange flames hop-scotch playfully from one brittle bush to the next.

When I touch the door handle on the storage room, it's like grab-bing a branding iron and I scream in pain. I kick the door open and hunt frantically in the dim light till I find my big shovel. I pull the door behind me and wedge it shut with my little trowel, then run behind the cabin where a patch of dry bunch grass is burning merrily. With the first thrust of the shovel, I understand how badly I burned my hand. I can feel the skin slip against muscle. Or at least that's how it feels. I wrap one of the pillowcases around it and resume shoveling dirt on the grass. The flames vanish abruptly in a belch of smoke, hearten-ing me.

Now a shriveled sagebrush ignites, seemingly by spontaneous com-bustion, and the flames leap at me, searing my cheek. I catch a whiff of singed hair. I keep shoveling. Hacking at the smaller brush, chopping it and batting away from the house with the shovel. My arms ache to the point of numbness, and my wet bandana mask is bone dry.

It's so hot now that I can't tell when I'm too close to a fire, and I nearly back into one. Embers and ash are falling like rain, tiny hot needles burning my skin. I slap at them and keep shoveling.

I break away to go back inside, stamping out some embers on the *portal,* and remembering to grab the door handle with the damp pillowcase. I rip off my mask to wet it again, stunned by the amount of black ash trapped on it. Just thinking about what I must be breathing in, my chest tightens reflexively. I wet the pillowcases again, tie one on my head, like an Arab sheik, the other around my shoulders. I strip the sheets off the bed, wetting them. Is it my paranoid imagination, or is the flow of water slowing down? One sheet I throw over the dog. He looks silly, like he's wearing a huge bridal train. I fold the other sheet in quarters to slap down flames and rush back outside, forgetting my face mask.

One of the posts on the *portal* is burning. Trotting out every swear word in my vocabulary, I attack the flames with my futile fury and little wet sheet. My eyes are burning now, tearing so that everything blurs. Hot grit fills my mouth and throat, each breath scorching my nose and searing into my lungs. I stumble back inside to get my wet mask. Dog looks ready to make a break for the door and I kick viciously at him. He slinks behind the rocker.

Time jells, becoming even thicker than the air. I know I'm slowing down. What I don't know is how much longer I can keep moving at all. I feel like an elephant. My legs burn from fatigue. My mind drifts into neutral as I stagger back and forth from the sink—it's not my imagination, the water is down to a trickle—to the back of the cabin, bending, digging, chopping, flinging dirt with the shovel that I can barely hold, slapping embers on the porch with my sheet. Brush flames up, cracking loudly like breaking bones. I'm moving through a dreamscape of orange flame and oily black smoke, stumbling, down on my knees, feeling nothing in my hands when I push myself up.

I feel my lips cracking, and my fogged brain can only think that Will Cameron won't want to kiss me.

At some point I stagger inside and shadows stare out at me from the dark corners of the room—I peer back, searching for a familiar face, but they're only eyes and silently moving mouths. I sink down on my knees, pressing my face into the wet bedspread, breathing the dampness into my parched throat, and I suddenly know I can't get up. I roll over on my side, pull the cool bedspread over me. I don't know if I'm going to die and I don't care.

I close my eyes, moaning a little.

Suddenly I'm hearing things—a train whistle, marching feet, rain falling on the tin roof, a man singing opera. An explosion reverberates in my head. The truck blowing up? I roll over and open one eye. Jesus God, there's a space alien in a green suit standing in my doorway.

"Christ Almighty," it says. Then "Ray! Quick! We got a couple of live ones!"

I shut my eyes and sleep.

epilogue

A full year has passed since the night I saw Isabel's portrait in Paul's guesthouse. *Querencia,* while it's still my safe haven, looks kind of forlorn, sitting in the middle of the patch of char that saved it, but already, little sprigs of green are poking up through the ash, and next week Alonzo is coming to help me get the ground ready for a garden.

Almost becoming a French fry has been a fairly humbling experience.

I spent a few days in the hospital—three? four?—being treated for burns on my arms and hands, smoke inhalation, and various cuts and scrapes. I also wrenched the hell out of my back.

I have only the haziest recollections of the first day—partly because of the trauma and partly all the drugs. They said I kept calling for Cassie, asking her if I was going to die. That makes sense, considering the only other time I've been anywhere near a hospital was the night I got bit by the rattler.

I don't remember when everybody started showing up, only that they always seemed to be there when I woke up. At first, it was only supposed to be family. So Paul showed up and told them he was my stepfather. Then Cookie came in, saying she was my auntie. The next night there were my cousins, Miguel and Bettina. He smuggled in dinner—turkey mole, Spanish rice and refried beans, sweet corn tamales with raisins and *piñones* and cinnamon. It was like a party. Too bad my throat was so raw I could barely swallow. But, God, the beer tasted good.

Later that evening after they'd gone I heard a commotion outside the door to my room—high heels and the nurses' soft-soled shoes, voices stretched taut like people arguing but trying to be quiet about it. Then I heard a familiar voice say, "I *am* family. She's my half sister, and I drove up here all the way from Albuquerque as soon as I got off work, and I *am* going to see her."

When Rita dashed into the room with the night nurse hot on her tail, tears massed in my eyes and spilled down my cheeks.

"Oh, Ave, look at you. You look like death eatin' a cracker." She came over and pulled a tissue out of the box on the table and started blotting my eyes and putting her cool little hand on my forehead.

"Ten minutes," the nurse said to me. "And no more talking."

Rita turned her sweetest smile on the empty doorway. "Don't worry, I'll do all the talking."

She scooted the only chair up close to the bed and focused her worried frown on me. I could tell she'd stopped using Miss Clairol Summer Gold. Her hair was more of a honey color than true blond, and curlier than I remembered.

"Girlfriend, you're crazy as popcorn. What the hell were you trying to prove?"

"Just taking care of the cabin," I rasped. "Who told you?"

"Don't forget, honey, I'm sleepin' with the top investigative reporter in the state. Jesus God, when he told me what happened, I was afraid you—" She looked away for a minute, swallowed, then said, "Oh, you know."

"Rita, thanks."

She brushed it off. "I had to come see with my own baby blues that you were okay. I just wish I could've got away earlier, but the office was a zoo today."

I close my eyes. "Not just for coming. For everything." I was starting to drift again, and then the nurse stepped in and told Rita time was up.

"I'll come back," she called over her shoulder. "Soon as you're up and around, I'm going to haul your butt down to Albuquerque for a long visit."

After she escorted Rita to the door, the nurse came back to wake me up for my sleeping pill. When I swallowed it, she gave me kind of an odd look. "Interesting family you have."

I smiled weakly, let my eyes fall shut again.

"My mother," I whispered. "She got around."

Once I was out of the hospital, I got better fast. Paul kept talking about postponing his trip to New Zealand, so I lied and told him I was going to stay with Cookie. As soon as he left, I moved back into the guesthouse. But Cookie came every day to put aloe on my burns and bring me loaves of home-baked bread or muffins or shortbread. Bettina drove over from Cimarron with a week's worth of dinners.

Lindsey came one afternoon with two bottles of wine, and we drank it all in a couple hours. She had this great idea that I should be a caterer in Santa Fe and she would be my silent partner. I explained as gently as I could that it was a really nice idea, and very generous on her part, but that just wasn't the direction I was headed.

The bandages are off my hands and arms now. My palms are funny, scarred in a strange wavy pattern of pink and white and red that reminds me of the Great Sand Dunes, but soft as baby skin.

I still have a lingering cough from all the smoke I sucked in, but it only bothers me once in a while, usually if I sleep on my back. The cabin pretty much smells like a cold campfire, but it'll air out eventually. I moved in last week for good.

And I've got some company, although you never know how long that's going to last. Yeah, Coyote Dog. They said that morning when the paramedics came to get me, they could hear him howling for miles.

I just call him Dog. If I name him and start treating him like a friend, he'll be down the road in a hurry, so we're being pretty casual about the relationship right now. But he knows I'm not going to throw rocks at him anymore. I talk to him, which is pretty much like talking to myself. He just hangs out and stares at me a lot, and sometimes he wanders over and puts his head in my lap and lets me scratch his ears.

Friday night there's a waxing moon, and when I first see it rising up over the hills to hang like a silver apostrophe in the pale blue twilight, I know right away what I have to do. I called him twice; once I even left a voice mail that he could leave a message for me at The Good Earth, but so far, he hasn't. I guess I can understand that.

I open Isabel's green box, digging through it till I find the straight pins in a plastic container. Sure enough there's a blue-headed one. I take it and a silver one, a candle, and a saucer outside to the *portal*. I push the blue-headed pin into the candle from left to right, and then the silver one from right to left, making sure they cross in the middle.

I light the candle and drip some wax in the saucer, enough to snuggle the candle into and hold it straight. Then I sit there cross-legged, eyes on the wavering flame till it's burning strong and steady, and I begin to think of him, first trying just to picture his sweet solemn face, his blue-gray eyes. The light brown hair growing down over the collar of his denim jacket, the little ridge above his ears from his hat.

In a few minutes I swear the breeze against my skin smells like him, like wind blowing through the high desert after a rain. Gradually an image forms. Kind of like an old TV set that takes awhile to warm up. He's driving somewhere, hands strong but relaxed on the steering wheel of his truck, shadows of clouds flickering across his face.

In my mind I start talking. *Will Cameron, it's me.* He shakes his head a little, as if he's about to doze off. *Will, it's Avery.* His eyes move first to the left, then to the right. He leans forward a little, looks up at the sky through the windshield.

I know it's way past Christmas, but there were just some things I had to do.

He frowns. Looks in the rearview mirror, then out the side mirror, moving his eyes to catch something in his blind spot.

I need to talk to you. Please come.

He shakes his head again, so hard this time that I lose him.

But a snapshot flares open in my mind, a memory from the future. *Sunday morning. Will and me. The two of us in bed, spooned up together, skin against skin. Sunlight on white sheets. Warm breeze fluttering a curtain. His hand resting gently on my slightly swollen belly.*

Jesus God, as Rita would say.

My eyes flood with startled gratitude—not the kind of gratitude that crushes you under the weight of obligation, but more a free-floating thankfulness that's practically a state of grace.

Saturday morning the sky is a pale, washed-out blue with a few streaky clouds, and the wind has stopped. I'm driving up to Santa Fe with a carton stacked full of packages of tea for Cookie. She sold out of the first batch in about a month, and she says women have been phoning and dropping by to see if she had any more. One guy even came by wanting some for his wife. He said his life was more pleasant when she had it.

The fruit trees are in bloom now, the apricots much further along, because they bloom first, and the cherry and peach and pear trees all coming on, slowly dispensing their pollen and perfume into the day. As the sun climbs higher, I roll down my window to let the air break over me in sweet-scented waves.

Red paintbrush blossoms along the road, and filigree, the tiny magenta geraniums, although the flowers aren't as plentiful as in previous, rainier years. Puffy white cottonwood seed rides the breeze and settles in drifts that look like snow.

I get to the store right at ten A.M. and Cookie's just put the teakettle on, and is slipping the change drawer into the register. She takes the box from me and gives me a big hug.

"Why didn't you come and get me? I could have carried it."

"I'm fine." I show her my hands. "Good as new."

"You are a crazy woman," she scolds me. "I trust now that you're healed and have your ducks in a row you won't be putting yourself in danger again any time soon."

I give her a mysterious smile. "Living is being in danger, yes?"

"And I do hope you won't begin talking like a wise woman or she who runs with wolves or—"

"Shaman. I can't help it. It's in my blood. You're the one who told me to listen."

She laughs. "I've created a monster."

The bell on the door jingles, and a middle-aged woman in a jogging suit with fake leather fringe comes in, glancing around. "Do you have any of that women's tea? My friend Janice Hayden was raving about it."

Cookie smiles at her. "We just got a whole new shipment. It probably won't last long; would you like two boxes? Perhaps you should get Janice another as well."

I have to walk away so I don't laugh. The woman is examining the box, reading the list of herbs. "It's all pretty straightforward, isn't it? No secret ingredients or anything."

"All natural, all organic," Cookie says.

"Well, I guess you'd better give me three boxes. It's a pretty package, too. Is there really such a person, or is it just a nice bit of marketing?"

Cookie laughs. "Not only is there such a person, but she's standing right over there." She calls out, "Avery, come say hello to one of your customers."

The woman turns to me, offering her hand. "Betsy Crane. How nice to meet you."

Disconcerted, I glance at Cookie. Her eyes are making little darting movements like she's saying *Yes, you. Get yourself over here and meet her.*

My first step feels like I'm stepping off a cliff, but then the creaky wood floor rises up to meet my boots, supporting me.

"Avery James." I smile and reach for her hand. "I'm Isabel's daughter."

**LITTLE FREE LIBRARY:
ALWAYS A GIFT,
NEVER FOR SALE!**

LITTLE FREE LIBRARY.
ALWAYS A GIFT,
NEVER FOR SALE!

ACKNOWLEDGMENTS

Isabel's Daughter is a work of fiction. Characters, events, and even some of the locations exist only in my imagination. I've taken certain chronological and geographic liberties with the state of New Mexico and the city of Santa Fe, and since this was done in the service of storytelling, I trust that no one will be unduly offended.

A thousand thanks to Donna Meador Mifflin, who opened the city of Santa Fe to me, introduced me to people and places, corrected my pronunciation, fed me information as well as food, and put me up at her beautiful home more times than she would probably care to remember.

Thanks also to:

My irreplaceable agent, Deborah Schneider, for her wisdom, candor, and friendship. My editor, Claire Wachtel, for continuing to demonstrate why God created editors. Jen Pooley, book wrangler without peer, for the thousand things you do. Honi Werner for so beautifully capturing all my words in a single picture.

Sally Boyd, Amy Terrell, and Grace Marcus, dear friends and trusted manuscript readers. Ron Greenspun for his insights and for listening. Kate Berry for the great reading list. Jill, Barbara, Barbara[2], and Alice of the Santa Fe Weaving Gallery for their enthusiasm, support, and friendship. James Avery Craftsman, for inspiration. And Janet Mitchell for her wonderul book *Summer in Santa Fe*.

Jo-Ann Mapson, best Bad Girl and dearest friend.

Geoff, for always being there.

And to the people of New Mexico for holding the line against twenty-first-century blandness and homogenized culture.

BOOKS BY JUDITH RYAN HENDRICKS

THE LAWS OF HARMONY
A Novel

ISBN 978-0-06-168736-5 (paperback)

An emotionally gripping tale of one woman's struggle to remake herself in the wake of loss and deception, told in the wise, empowering, and heart-renewing prose of an accomplished writer.

BREAD ALONE
A Novel

ISBN 978-0-06-008440-0 (paperback)

"Hendricks creates a compelling character whose wry, bemused, and ultimately wise voice hooks the reader. . . . A well-written, imaginative debut."
—*Publishers Weekly*

ISABEL'S DAUGHTER
A Novel

ISBN 978-0-06-050347-5 (paperback)

After a childhood spent in an institution and a series of foster homes, Avery James has trained herself not to wonder about the mother who gave her up. But her safe, predictable life changes one night when she stumbles upon the portrait of a woman who is the mirror image of herself.

THE BAKER'S APPRENTICE
A Novel

ISBN 978-0-06-072618-8 (paperback)

"Hendricks rolls out a delicious sequel in *Baker's Apprentice*. . . . Prepare to have your appetite teased and stimulated, often."
—*Seattle Post-Intelligencer*

Visit www.AuthorTracker.com
for exclusive information on your favorite HarperCollins authors.

Available wherever books are sold, or call 1-800-331-3761 to order.